Barker

A NOVEL

by Wayne Tefs

TURNSTONE PRESS

Turnstone Press
Artspace Building
206-100 Arthur Street
Winnipeg, MB
R3B 1H3 Canada
www.TurnstonePress.com

Turnstone Press gratefully acknowledges the assistance of the Canada
Council for the Arts, the Manitoba Arts Council, the Government of
Canada through the Canada Book Fund, and the Province of Manitoba
through the Book Publishing Tax Credit and the Book Publisher
Marketing Assistance Program.

Epigraph on page vii is from:
BLACKBIRD
Written by: John Lennon & Paul McCartney
©1968 Sony/ATV Music Publishing LLC. All rights administered by Sony/
ATV Music Publishing LLC, 424 Church Street, Suite 1200, Nashville, TN
37219. All rights reserved. Used by permission.

Printed and bound in Canada by Friesens for Turnstone Press.

Library and Archives Canada Cataloguing in Publication

Tefs, Wayne, 1947–, author

    Barker / Wayne Tefs.

ISBN 978-0-88801-493-1 (pbk.)

    I. Title.

PS8589.E37B37 2014   C813'.54   C2014-906359-8

for Kristen

Blackbird singing in the dead of night
Take these sunken eyes and learn to see
All your life, you were only waiting for this moment to be free
You were only waiting for this moment to be free
You were only waiting for this moment to be free

Barker

Part I

AS A KID I was a sideshow freak. Those who claim to know about such things say your chances of being the Lady with the Lion's Face or the Man with Three Legs are approximately one in fifteen million, about the same as winning the Irish Sweeps. I fell into that category. But I was doubly remarkable in that there was only one remarkable thing about me. Otherwise I was, and am, soup ordinary. Though I've always been in a hurry to get to places and do things, and that leads to rash decisions and plunging into situations where the only way out is do something low, like sneak away in the night or tell lie after desperate lie. I blush to confess. I'm also a storyteller, something I picked up in the carney, and storytellers stretch the truth, adding a colour-ful detail here, injecting a clever quip there, transforming, over time, eight hot dogs eaten in one sitting to eighteen. Half-truths and white lies are common fare among storytellers. So are big whoppers. I leave it to others to decide which category I fall into.

I grew up on a farm in southern Saskatchewan, one of five children. Three others died in infancy. Peace to their bones. There's a photo of the family in an album. We kids are wearing typical clothing for rural folk of the time: loose-fitting but durable cottons. We are not, it should be noted, wearing shoes. I'm the baby, on my mother's arm, looking away from the camera, as if an explosion has just distracted me. Or more likely, squirming to get away from her grasp. That's me, desperate to be on the move.

We lived near the town of Estevan and were dirt farmers. Making a living was a struggle. Money was scarce. We were dirt farmers who had little to eat but potatoes and onions and carrots, and sometimes just the dirt they grew in. We kept pigs and butchered them in the fall so there was the occasional plate with meat, but the old man sold off the best of it to buy gas for his Model T truck so he could go gallivanting. The family had been living on the prairies since the last century, scratching out the lives of impoverished immigrants. It was a typical existence: brutal and dull. Mother cooked and sewed and cleaned and gardened and between times had babies. We kids worked too. Hard. And attended school sporadically. We got to grade eight, the smart ones like me. We learned to read and write. Though I was left-handed and was forced to use my right when transcribing, which produced an angular scrawl that appeared more like chicken scratchings than English script. They were not happy times. My left hand was tied up in bandages for some weeks, and after that I was treated to the sharp crack of the teacher's yardstick over my head whenever I lapsed into using the hand that came natural to me. That seems to be the way of life: whatever comes natural to a man is beaten out of him by people with power who say it's for his own good.

Mother was a God-fearing Christian. Some would say Bible-thumper. All her kids were baptized and christened, and she made the old man drive us over to the church every Sunday morning, though he never crossed the threshold of St. Paul's Lutheran himself. Every night after the little kids were in bed, she sat with her Bible in the parlour and contemplated. Sometimes she read from it, pausing occasionally, but often it just sat in her lap with her small hands folded over while she gazed into space, turning over thoughts, a humble plough turning over soil. It was the only time her hands were still. She taught us the Commandments, most of which were straightforward enough, if not so easy to follow; but others were downright puzzling: *covet thy neighbour's ass*? She was a small woman with a sharp nose and an even sharper tongue. She kept a belt hanging from the towel rack in order to bring into line anyone who strayed off, but I never saw her use it. We kids knew intuitively that her life with the old man was difficult enough; she didn't need grief from us.

One of my earliest memories is of walking home from the schoolhouse and seeing the old man at work on the fence around our farmyard. I spotted him from a long way off, perhaps as much as a mile: the metal head of the hammer glinting sunlight, the flash of orange on the handle where it had been smeared with paint, a bright mini-sun. He was chewing tobacco, his jaw going up and down, like a cow at a trough. Every now and then he paused and spat.

Yes, a full mile. There it is, then. My freakishness lay in my eyesight. I could pick out small objects from an enormous distance: red-winged blackbirds roosting in the rushes of the slough behind the barn; a banana on the window ledge of a neighbour's house we walked past on the way home from school. In my innocence I thought everyone saw these things with the clarity I did: the orange splotch on the old man's hammer; the way he tipped his head down to spit; how his small ears stuck out from his skull, piggy style.

He was pounding away ferociously, driving staples into a

wood post that the barbed wire fence hung from. He never did any job slow; every action, every movement radiated ferocious intensity. His dark hair was being teased up by the breeze; a tuft stuck up from the crown of his skull. His jaw was set so hard that the veins in his temples bulged out. I was not fond of him. He was always in a froth and had a bonfire temper, sure to scorch anything within range when he became angry, which was about thirty out of twenty-four hours every day.

He spotted me when I was fifty metres away and shot me a wave that was singular in meaning: nothing of a greeting in it: impatience, rather, and fury. He shouted, "Where you been, you little bastard, you, you've been malingering again!" Inside his head there were snakes coiled about each other, tails in their own mouths, writhing and slimy.

It's true, I had been malingering. There was a red-haired girl at school named Peggy who had caught my eye and I'd loitered about the schoolyard flirting with her while my older, responsible brothers, Art and Phil, had made tracks home as soon as school ended to do their chores rather than get yelled at—or beaten. Peggy was a far better option in my opinion: a slight slip of a thing with creamy white skin and wavy red hair that fell to her shoulders and shimmered sunlight; I'm a fool for red hair, always have been.

When I came closer, the old man looked up from the hammering he'd resumed and shouted, "Get down the barn, pronto, slop them pigs, then help with the hay." His face was flushed red with rage. Half a cup of spittle ran past his bottom lip, brown, stringy. I kept my distance. "Git," he repeated, and he waved the hammer in my face, its head a hunk of metal as dull as his brain. I studied the hammer and wondered what it would take to wrest it off him and bash in his skull. He was not a tall man but he had muscular arms and his washed-out blue eyes were the eyes of a killer. It's a notable fact: animals with transparent blue-grey eyes are not to be trusted: they'll turn on you in a flash; and they're vicious.

I hustled away toward the house, scuffing up dust so it looked as if I was making a mighty pace, a trick I'd learned from my older brother, Phil. When I got near the house I slowed and then dawdled around the corner of the house, peering in a window to see who was about. Neither of my sisters, Vanora and Margy, was in the kitchen. My heart skipped. Before I'd left for school that morning I'd noted that Mother was mixing up batter for a batch of oatmeal cookies and I'd been thinking about them all day. I'd once eaten a couple dozen of Mother's cookies at a setting. Aces, I thought. I may have said it aloud.

Ten minutes later I was lugging the slop bucket around the corner of the barn to the pig sty, a cookie I'd snitched from the kitchen in my mouth, when I heard scuffling in the dirt behind me. I thought it was Skipper, my favourite among the dogs, coming for a scratch behind the ear, but the sound was more urgent, so I glanced quickly behind. It was the old man, sprinting, holding a chunk of two-by-four in one upraised hand, the way you see highland warriors with their claymores. He was bow-legged and when he ran he looked with every step as if he was about to go over flat on his fat face and I nearly burst out laughing, but this was no laughing matter. He bore down on me. I dropped the slop bucket and took a couple of quick steps. Just in time. He swung the two-by-four and it smashed into the siding of the barn. *Whack!* In my peripheral vision I noted how handfuls of blondish wood chips danced in the air past my ear. "Little bastard," he roared at me, "I'll have your hide." Hitting the barn with the two-by-four had slowed him a moment; I had the feeling he'd done something to his wrist when the two-by-four hit the siding because his voice had become shrill right then and hideous, an axe blade scraped along an iron bar: "Bass-tarrd!"

I ran. He pursued. The two-by-four made another contact

with siding behind me. I felt the *whoosh* of its draft tickle hair on the back of my skull. I flinched and leapt over the pigsty fencing, landing ankle-deep in pig shit, which splashed up my school trousers, and I remember thinking, There will be hell to pay for this. The old man roared again. Louder, shriller. A death cry. The two-by-four whizzed over my head; I felt its draft as it helicoptered past and landed in the pigsty muck. An eight-hundred-pound sow that had been dozing against the barn roused up and started coming at me.

Pigs. Nasty creatures. Wild pigs will charge at you and if they get you down, stomp you to death and then eat you up, bones, clothes, and all. They run in packs, too, and gang up on deer and whatnot in the woods. Penned in a corral, domesticated sows know exactly how to corner you against the side of the barn, and they'll grind away until they get you down, and then have you as mashed potatoes. They're solid and bulky, and slippery, too; you can't push them off and their bristles are sharp as barbed wire. They're killers, pigs, and I was thinking about that, heart in mouth, as I cleared the top bar of the corral, happy to be out of that sow's range.

The old man had come to a halt when he got to the fence and was roaring at me. I was listening but my real focus was on keeping my feet moving. Head down, in case he found another piece of discarded lumber to throw, I dodged and zigged away from the sty and shimmied over the ground as fast as a greyhound at the fair grounds and did not look back until well clear of the barnyard, where I stood trembling until I calmed down.

There'd been a night when I was just starting out at school—eight years old, six possibly—when he leaned across the supper table and belted me so hard in the side of the head that a tuft of my hair flew off. Mother gasped. One of the girls cried out. I'd taken one egg more than he'd decided was my portion. I scrabbled to get up from the floor, knees rubbery and ears ringing, hoping to register a protest. Mother had started to stand up and opened her mouth to speak but he pointed his thick index finger at her across the table and shouted, "Sit, woman!" And when she did, he added, "Not a word out of your mouth. Any of youse."

One fist grabbed me by the shirt collar and dragged me behind him across the floor and over the threshold. "Bastard," he muttered. "Defy me." The tops of my toes scraped along the ground as he pulled me across the yard. The dogs looked up from their feeding dishes. It was dusk and there were deep shadows from the buildings and trees in the yard. When we came to the outhouse we'd abandoned a year or so earlier, he wrenched the door open and shoved me in and I stumbled forward. My knees struck the bench where you sat to do the business. The door slammed shut behind me. I heard a stick shoved through the hasps where the handle had been and I knew I'd been locked in. Through it all he'd muttered things I didn't quite get because of the ringing in my ears; some was in German, *schweinhund*; and the occasional English word slipped through: *bastard, ingrate, strangle.*

He banged on the door once, so hard the wood splintered. "Have a think in there for a while," he shouted. "Think over that honour thy father bit your mother is so ready to spout all the time." I heard his boots go clomping over the hard-packed earth of the yard.

What had I done?

It was dark inside, black as a coal sack. I sat to one side of the toilet hole and stared straight ahead, trying to make things out. The black was just that impenetrable. After a while I closed my eyes. My ears were still ringing from the blow he'd struck, and there was crusty salt built up in the corners of both eyes, which, when I rubbed them, stung. The yard was quiet. Every now and then there was scuffling in the grass near the outhouse door; it sounded loud as a badger but was probably nothing more than a mouse. Sound is amplified in the silence of night. Doves cooed from nearby trees. Well past sunset, then. I moved my hands in little circles around the bench, which was cobwebby, and I pictured spiders and big black bugs being stirred up and readying themselves to pounce and sting and drew my hands away fast and placed them on my knees.

A lot of minutes ticked by. My eyelids felt heavy and my head nodded forward. I jerked up straight. I would not fall asleep; he would not come back and find me sleeping. I went over sums we'd been doing in school. I was good at that. Eleven times eleven equals one hundred and twenty-one; twelve times twelve equals one hundred and forty-four. That's as high as we'd got. What was thirteen times thirteen? I set to work puzzling it out. No, he would not find me asleep.

I wiped away tears that had formed in the corners of my eyes. What had I done wrong? Why did he always pick on me? I would ask Mother; maybe she would know. Cold and miserable, I struggled to keep from breaking down and wailing.

The scuffling of paws outside startled me from my deliberations. I cocked one ear to the door. I called out softy, "Skipper? Here boy." Skipper had been my best pal for a couple of years, a mongrel with the long legs and pointy face of a greyhound but the black and brown markings of a *daschund*. A nose snuffled at the door; I heard soft, wet panting and the scratching of claws on wood. "Skipper," I whispered, happy for his company, my spirits lifted, "just stay there and guard the door, pal, and warn me if the old man is coming. We'll make it a game between us, who hears him first. Skipper? There's a good boy." A voice from outside said something like *cansas loopy* and for a moment I tightened up in terror, but in the silence that followed the only sound was Skipper's wet snuffling. I wished I could ruffle behind his ears or feel his hot breath on my hand. My eyes were glazing over, I felt a rivulet of tears coursing down one cheek. I kept talking to Skipper but after a short while the sniffing at the door ceased and I heard the sound of paws receding across the yard. They say a dog is a man's best friend but my best friend went off pursuing his own ragged desires that night.

It was growing colder by the minute. I shivered for a while and then laid my arms across my knees and bent over and let my forehead fall on my arms, forming a little ball against the chill. Uncontrollably, I started to shake, then, and that led into crying for a while, crying and shaking, shaking and crying. I blubbed "Mother, Mother," over and over but I knew she couldn't save me, no one could. I was at his mercy. He was a bully worse than any at school and the bigger ones you just can't do anything about. I cried and snuffled onto the backs of my hands, wet stuff like snot. It felt good when it was all done, the crying and blubbing, as if a knot tight as a fist had loosened in my guts and I could breathe easy again. I sat up again and stared straight ahead into blackness. I'd been hurt by the injustice of it when he first locked me in and that had passed into anger and wicked thoughts about how I'd get back at him, a knife to the heart; then I'd been frightened before the crying began but afterwards I felt clean inside and empty. I wasn't angry anymore and I wasn't frightened either. I'd reached a sort of peace. Nothing I understood as peace, I was too young for that, just the feeling of being empty and okay, able to go on. I stared at the wall of blackness in front of me and then I stared at it some more. I didn't care anymore if I fell asleep and he found me that way. It no longer mattered what he thought.

There was a loud bang at the door and I jerked upright. "You," he shouted, "out, you!" The sound of the stick sliding back was followed by a shaft of moonlight splashing in on the outhouse floor, but before I could register it fully his huge hand emerged from the darkness and grabbed me by the collar and hauled me out. It hurled me forward on the hard-packed earth.

One moment I was standing, the next face down on the ground, eyeballs in muck. My ears were ringing again. "Defy me," he shouted, "defy *me*, will you, you little bastard!" A boot went into my ribs. He kicked me in the head right at the ear-hole. Blood came from somewhere into the back of my mouth. He leaned over so I could smell his breath, cabbage mixed with tobacco. "I could kill you," he whispered harshly, "and no one would give a shit." I was in a fetal position, expecting another blow to the head. He stomped away. Then he stopped and called back: "You learn, you little bastard, you learn a lesson from this. Next time I *will* kill you." The sound of his boots clumping on hard earth was a relief.

I closed my eyes and began to tremble again and cry some and mutter little sounds: weep, weep. I must have passed out. After a while I felt hands seize me under the arms and stand me up. I was dizzy, my knees were rubber, I started to fall forward but Phil and Art kept me upright and helped me stagger across the yard and into the house. The silence of the dead pervaded the hallway and kitchen. Our bedroom was in back and they made sure I was under a blanket so I'd sleep warm. I woke what seemed to be almost right away. There was a window in that room and I could just make out the moon shining its pale light onto the floor. It looked cold and hard and far away, not the romantic moon of songs but a remote and unfeeling chunk of rock floating in the sky that had no interest in what happened on earth. I felt that way myself. Empty inside. Yes, empty, and I knew he could not reach me anymore, the way he once had when he ruffled my hair to make me chuckle and had me go ticklish by rubbing his bushy moustache against the nape of my neck. I was too young to fully understand what had happened, and I knew it, but I also knew it was the thing that had saved me that night and would save me in the future. I closed my eyes and slept.

All that came back to me as I stood in the shadow of the barn watching the moon rise over the slough and the bluff to the south, high as a ship. It was up that night too, and I was able to examine the bottoms of my school trousers in its bright gleam.

Did I go in for supper that night? I probably fed the pigs and kept well clear of the house. Phil probably brought out something. I had done it for him. These outbursts were not uncommon. Once he actually got me in the back of the skull with a stray piece of two-by-two: it bled for days, even with the plaster Mother applied. I'd asked her that time, *What is it about me that makes him so angry; what's wrong with me?* She had smiled her suffering Mary smile and patted my shoulder; cinnamon. I'd eaten a bun at the fall fair with this scent: raisins, brown sugar, cinnamon, a dark and thrilling tingle on the tongue. Mother said, *You'll understand some day, son of mine—and his.* She said things like that, Mother, things I could not puzzle out.

The old man. He terrorized our days. The whole household cringed under his moods. His mouth was a garbage pit of curses and oaths, and he hit out at whoever happened to be within arm's reach, unpredictably and violently. It was a relief when he took off and went gallivanting around the countryside in the Model T truck he was so proud of.

He was a gadfly and a bully and a womanizer and a cad. He ran after women in other towns and left Mother at home for weeks at a time tending to her brood and the household chores, and when he came back, *not* chastened, he smacked her around for nothing more than looking askance. I swore to kill him and was devising a plot that involved sneaking up on him with an iron bar, which I'd hidden away in the barn, and bashing at his skull until it was a pulpy mass of flesh. I blush to admit I imagined bright red blood spurting out of his skull and the way his eyes gazed up at me in entreaty in his last moments of life while I stared back with a haughty curl on my lip. I knew there was a flaw in the plan and was holding back until I figured out what it was. I did not want to miss my chance, but equally I did not want to muff it. If I tried and muffed, he was sure to kill me. He was vengeful—and vicious as a rabid pig. He was also a warlock.

It was red-headed Peggy who set my heart a-flutter that first made me aware I was a freak. We were standing on the school-yard at lunchtime, gazing out on the town as we munched sand-wiches. Our hands were deliciously close. I was trying not to stare at the creamy white skin of her arm. I knew it would be as soft as kitten's fur. I wanted to enfold her fingers in mine and feel the throb of her pulse. A light scent was coming off her. I was used to the odour of Lifebuoy soap that Vanora and Margy used and this was something different: something silkier. She was the daughter of the grocery man, Finch, one of the town bigwigs, and her folks were going to send her off to school in Regina, it was rumoured, after grade eight. She was pretty and a bit flighty and she scared me. There was something risky about going after her. But then there was that headstrong thing I was just coming to acknowledge in myself, and its inevitable consequences. Red hair. A mass of curls warning me away. Hazard!

I finagled to have my fingers touch hers and felt a thrill from their tips to the roots of my hair. The heady odour of funeral flowers: cloying and sweet, a not entirely pleasant smell, I asso-ciated it with older women. I had heard the phrase *in love* but had no idea it involved such reckless feelings: I was prepared to abandon everything I thought and was to caress Peggy's little hand for one moment. To hold her warm little limbs against mine seemed the height of all anyone could desire. Instead I took another bite of sandwich.

The schoolhouse stood on a little rise on one edge of town, not much; anything on the prairie thicker than a phone book counts as a *hill*. "Look at that hat the preacher man's wearing," I said, trying for an easy conversation opener. The preacher was the butt of mild humour around town, as preachers are. The church stood on the far side of town, about half a mile distant; it had a spire with a cross on top, some kind of sheet metal that reflected the sun.

"Preacher," Peggy said, following my gaze, "what preacher, what hat?"

"Sombrero or something," I said. "Brown with a black band. See?" My index finger pointed the way for her.

She gave me a quizzical look, then squinted toward the church. "Don't see anything of that sort. What are you talking about, Harlan?"

"Huh," I went on. "He's putting a new coat of yellow paint on the border of the flower bed."

"Harlan," Peggy said firmly, "I can just make out the church. I cannot see the preacher at all, never mind sombreros and yellow paint." Her voice had taken on a peculiar strain of annoyance. I wasn't sure I liked it. Up to that point Peggy had been entirely enchanting, but it occurred to me that she might be among the worst of the other girls at school: limited and temperamental. "You're weird," she added.

It was my turn to be quizzical. "How about the wheelbarrow over by Nell's hardware?"

"I can make out the store, the building."

"But not the wheelbarrow."

"Nor the sign on the window that we know to be there: NELL'S."

"The Model T in front of the bank?"

"Nope."

"An ant taking a leak against the fence?"

"Harlan."

"Two women coming out of the post office? One may be your mother."

"Nope."

"Crikey." I swept my field of vision: a tractor in a distant field, chuffing black smoke; a white dog sitting on the stoop of the town hall, scratching behind one ear with a ragged paw. Apparently Peggy could see none of this, the way everything was a dancing blur to me out past the grain elevator, far in the distance. She didn't say anything and I was thankful for it. There was something here to chew over a special thing that had been granted me. I knew that if the old man found out about it I'd be the unhappier for it.

Somehow he did.

The carnival was coming to town in August, the highlight of the summer, and every waking moment he was gnawing over how to make money out of me and my special ability. "Take that little bastard out behind the barn," he told Art and Phil one night at the supper table. "Get him to shoot the rifle at something. Make sure it's at a distance, for Christ's sake. And don't waste bullets."

The next day they hung a paint can from a tree branch and we paced out fifty strides before stopping. It was a hot afternoon on the prairie and all three of us were sweating and would rather not have been there. But you didn't go behind the old man. Phil took a shot; the paint can jumped in the air and swung about for a bit. "Hah," Phil said, "got ya." Art took a shot. The paint can leapt up. He passed me the rifle. "There, Dick, have a go yourself, hot shot." I sighted down the barrel: BENJAMIN MOORE the lettering on the label read. I pulled the trigger. "Huh," Art snorted. "Nothing." The paint can had not moved. "Try again," Phil said, "maybe it was just nerves." He was closer to me in age and enjoyed skating on the pond in winter, same as me. We were both admirers of the local ball team and harboured dreams of playing for it one day. The inside of his skull was an endless prairie landscape: sere fields under a serene blue sky. I shot. Nothing. Art laughed. "Missed by a mile. So much for that," he snorted. "The boy who can see a mile." I shrugged, refusing to grant him the satisfaction of knowing what I knew. He had the same washed-out blue eyes as the old man. The inside of his head was a jangle of bare coiled wires, blue sparks leaping between them, the whole thing looking about set to explode.

We walked back to the tree branch to retrieve the paint can. Phil studied it: two bullet holes were near the edges; those bullets would have made the can leap when they struck it. But there were also two bullet holes dead centre, one overlapping the other. So perfectly centred, the can would not have moved on impact. I said nothing though the temptation to gloat was tempting. But they both understood what had happened. We moved farther away for the next shot. And the next. Soon our backs were against the wall of the barn. About a hundred metres away, the can leapt on impact when I shot. "Nice work, Dick," Phil said, punching my shoulder.

"Bullshit," Art said.

Phil was intrigued. He went into the barn and came back with a rusty tin from a pile waiting to be used to house nails or whatever; he trotted out to the paint can, took it off the branch and flipped it over and placed the tin on its surface. He dodged behind a nearby tree and signalled me to shoot. *Ping.* He pulled a peach stone out of his pocket and put it on the paint can. *Fupp.*

"How about that," he wheezed as he trotted back to us. "A peach stone at a hundred yards."

"Bullshit," Art said, but I could tell he was impressed.

After supper that night the old man scratched his chin and then tapped his fingers on the tabletop. He gazed at me and narrowed his eyes as if trying to get something clear in his head.

When the carnival came to town, he was waiting on the sand lot for the carneys to put up their tents. I was beside him, swatting flies and cradling the rifle. The old man spoke to the carney boss, who looked me over and gave a skeptical shrug. "Guns," he muttered, "hmmm, no, not good." He walked away and when he'd taken twenty paces he turned and held up a bill that he produced from the wallet in his back pocket. "Which is it," he called to us, "five or ten?"

I waited a good moment, enjoying how the old man fidgeted as he waited too. It was another hot prairie afternoon. It hadn't rained for weeks; the sight of a dark cloud above was remarkable: everyone watched its progress across the sky and silently prayed, Rain. But it didn't. The wind whipped up dust devils around our feet. The sun beat down on our heads. Everyone was talking drought those days; even worse times coming, that was the word. First the war, then them general strikes, now drought and starvation. Maybe another war in Europe. We'd be eating the pigs' slops. I focused on the carney boss. "It's a one, a one-dollar bill" I shouted back. I paused. We'd been doing dramatic reading a few weeks earlier in school. After I had him and the old man both dangling, I shouted the serial number of the bill he'd held up.

The carney boss studied it a moment.

"Shit," the old man muttered, "you're wrong, I'll tan your hide, boy."

"But I'm not wrong."

"You. You don't give me the lip, boy."

It took a while for the carney boss to saunter back to us. He had an odd look on his mug. He waggled his finger at me.

When the carnival opened to the public I was "The Boy Who Can See a Mile." The barker called out: "Turn your nickel into a quarter if he can't say precisely the serial number on any bill anyone can hold up. Pre-cise-ly." The carney boss had me wear a military-style jacket to do my bit, khaki, patches on the shoulders, his notion of a sharpshooter. I was surrounded by the dull and the even duller. He had me stand *to atten-tion,* shoulders back, chest out, and insisted I put my flat hand across my forehead, resembling a salute. And I was to peer for a moment before reading out the serial numbers. All adding to the drama, those actions were supposed to be, elevating the performance.

The nickels added up. The old man and the carney boss split the profits, fifty-fifty. It was revolting to see them grubbing over stained and worn coins and chuckling and thinking each of them was a sharp operator. But after the second or third night it was only out-of-town rubes who hadn't heard my story that lost their five cents.

"Hell and damnation," the old man said. I could see he wanted to blame me for turning off the tap of his riches, to hit me; but I was too valuable right then to risk it. Instead he begged the carney boss to give the rifle a go. But no dice. The gig was up. The old man stamped about on the hard-packed mud at the flap of the carney boss's tent and muttered and looked ready to take a swing at whoever. I kept clear. But I was relieved. Being a freak was not much fun. Some of my schoolmates had come to see my performance and point and laugh at me, Peggy among them. Later, my eyes had kind of filmed over when I thought about it. Freak. It's an ugly word.

I wasn't the Lady with the Lion's Face or the Man with Three Legs. But still. The old man counted his nickels and came to terms with his loss, as people do, and then started dreaming of gallivanting down the road after a married woman he'd spotted at the roll-a-bowl-a-ball stand, a woman with peroxide blonde hair and a high, witchy laugh: *look at me!* He thought we were done with the freak show. We were.

But chances and risks had got into my blood. Carney life had sunk its teeth into me.

I'd noticed that the carney did not have a barker as such. Sometimes Boss Man himself put on the red coat and stood near the big tent flap shouting out to the crowd: Lay-dees and

Genle-men; at other times Cookie was there; or Royster took a turn, stained, crooked teeth and all. A croak for a voice.

"You want to be the barker?" Boss man snorted at me. "You, at the age of what—fifteen?" Boulders took up the space on the inside of his head, round grey-blue boulders speckled with black dots, like certain bird eggs.

"Seventeen," I lied.

"You ain't even been laid yet," he sneered. "But you want a job enticing grown men to come into the can-can tent."

He grunted and made me do a pitch for the Folies Bergère: five aging tarts in a wobbly can-can line, painted-on makeup, baggy tits, varicose veins. Their success was a testament to the desperation of the times. Broken-down war vets, emaciated farm hands, over-anxious schoolboys. "All right," he said when I was done with the pitch, "you got a strong and clear voice, I'll grant you that, five cents a night."

"Fifteen."

We settled on ten. I had to pay for my own food, sleep rough, and hitch a ride to the next town on the carney's itinerary, however.

Dick, yes. I was christened Harlan Alexander Bauch, but as a toddler I was roly-poly, so Art and Phil dubbed me "Dick," which in German means *fat*. By the time I was in school, I no longer was roly-poly; and as the barker at the carney I stood almost a head taller than Art and was leaner than Phil, who was always beefy. But the nickname stuck, as names will.

Folks at the carnival called me that too. It was society in small, the carney. Cookie, who ran the mess tent and had a gambling problem; Early Big, the Indian who put together the carousel and operated the rig that drove it; the Folies, two of whom were *that way*; the Fabulous Phelans who did the riding show, standing on ponies' backs, pirouetting, leaping from mount to mount: foul-mouthed cheats, man, wife, and daughter; Boss Man, who it was said had strangled his wife in the bed he'd found her in with a knife-thrower, who understandably got off scot-free; the Stan Brothers who ran the arcade games and spoke broken English, refugees from the Great War; Baskin, the sword swallower, who stuttered; Laskey, the tightrope walker, always moaning about arthritis; Skinny Bobby, the gopher, rumoured to be Boss Man's son; Jimbo James, second in command to Royster regarding anything horsey; Doris, the Lady with the Lion's Face; Alvin, the Man with Three Legs; Celie who repaired the costumes and fixed hair and lived in the tiniest imaginable trailer with Jimbo the dumbo and had fine reddish hair that bounced when she walked and shimmered in sunlight and made me think I could watch Celie's little tits bouncing inside her blouse well into eternity.

There's lots of downtime in the carney, which is a peculiar life: dashing and fetching and performing in a flurry from six in the evening until past midnight. Then sitting around drinking over cards and unwinding from the day's labours until two or Boss Man broke up the game. Sleeping until noon, or in the case of the Folies, well past.

You can find work to do every waking minute of the day, of course. But there's also time to do nothing, loiter about, smoke, chew the fat. Malinger, the old man would say. It suited me fine. I liked sitting on the back apron of the carousel, where you could hear the sounds of the carney coming to life behind you as the sun rose, while you looked out onto the plains: wind in the grass; hawks riding air currents high above; the sun climbing into the big prairie blue. There didn't seem to be that many crows around town through the rest of the year, but come carnival time, they were everywhere: a mass of black, screeching from treetops and pecking about in the dust for scraps. I enjoyed watching them; so black they were almost blue, their beady eyes always on the move, their nasty, yellow beaks just waiting to peck out your eyes. They seemed to take a special interest in me; they hopped over near my feet and eyed me, twisting their heads this way and that and eyeing me closely; one of them squawked out what sounded like *carbus* and gave me a kind of miffed glower. I laughed.

That's where Celie found me. We'd moved on to another town by then, twenty miles down the road. Bienfait? She came up on me from the side shadows and startled me with her voice. "Watcha lookin' at?"

I was following the sweep of a hawk over the river valley, a golden eagle, actually, but I wasn't sure Celie would be able to see it, so I said, "Oh, just watching the world go by, thinking of the fate of my fellow man unrolling like a big wheel in the sky."

"You're a strange one," she said, smirking and moving closer. "With your celebrated eyesight and peculiar way of saying things. But you're in luck. I go for strange." She was on the grass below me and leaning forward, the top buttons of her blouse open, so from my vantage point above her I could see her breasts, round and creamy, which she knew I could, and the knowledge of that excited me as much as the beautiful round breasts themselves. "I need help from a big strong man," she went on, smirking coyly, running one hand back through her auburn ringlets, "I need strong arms to shift a box down to the trailer." She dipped her head in that direction, her breasts jiggling slightly, and smirked again.

"Ah," I began. "You see—"

"Don't worry. Dumbo has gone into town with a pony to see the farrier. He won't be back for some while. Some little while, if you catch my drift."

I gawked around. I was as both thrilled and anxious about going with her to the trailer. Go on, I told myself, no harm, the lie we always tell ourselves in such circumstances. I jumped off the apron and trailed behind her, intrigued by the sway of her ass in front of me as we made our way around the mess tent to the trailer. Shameless. The floor was covered in blouses and tights and bits of coloured cloth; wet balled-up towels and open jars of stuff on shelves, all helter-skelter. It about took my breath away. Mother was not one of them that screamed if you left something on the floor but her house was neat and tidy, everything with a place and everything in its place; daily we folded and put the clothes we weren't wearing on the end of the bed, and we swept the floor of the bedroom once a week. Celie's looked as if brooms hadn't yet been invented. She pushed a pile of coloured cloth half the size of the sofa under the table with one delicate toe.

"That box up there," she said, pointing above a cupboard to one side. I pulled it down. Light as dandelion fluff. She could have easily taken it down herself.

"Well, now," she said, grinning, "you deserve a drink now, Harlan, the Boy Who Can Make any Girl Smile." She laughed at her own joke, and then added: "Or do you prefer *Dick*?" She pointed at the couch. "Sit." I did. My mouth was some dry. I ran my tongue around my lips.

She produced a Coke and asked, "You like a glass?" I nodded. "I like to have a Coke in a glass," she said. "Coke in a glass has got class." She poured the Coke into one tumbler and then opened the cupboard and pulled out a mickey bottle. "And a shot," she said, laughing, "yes, just a teeny shot."

I let out a deep breath.

"You think that's dangerous?" She had a small mouth and a crooked nose and a pointy chin, each in itself not very attractive but somehow it all added up to a kind of beauty. And that hair. She smiled and went on: "I warned you, now, did I not, Dick, Celie likes dangerous."

"You said *strange*."

"Strange, dangerous, what's the diff?" Her laugh was a bird-like cackle. "Anyways, Jimbo will never notice."

I was prepared to bet against that. But I said nothing, though both my ears were tuned to the world outside the trailer, listening for the thump of boots. I imagined Jimbo's knife in my back. I should have just hightailed it out of there. *Shouldn't be here, should not be here,* a voice was saying inside my head. It was those breasts, I admit it. I was a fool. Am. But then aren't we all? Fools of lust; sometimes, even, of love.

She sat beside me on the couch, which was spongy and tiny and leaned us into each other. My thigh rubbed against hers and produced wicked thoughts and some notable disturbances below the equator. Her flesh against mine was electric; raspberry: you crushed them between your fingers and the juice was tart and sweet on the tip of the tongue, both at the same time. I sipped the Coke when she offered it but my mouth was still parched. "We're being bad," she said in a sing-song voice, "very bad, Dick and me." The scent she wore was making me dizzy. I wanted to grab her and I wanted to kiss those breasts and do whatever it is that men do with women, and at the same time I wanted to leap off the couch and dash out the door. She ran her hand along my thigh. I took another swig of Coke.

"You like that, don't you," she said. Her eyes were green; dancing flecks of light were set off by her reddish hair in a way that made a man swallow hard and push back the voice saying, *Should not be here.*

"Yes," I croaked, looking into the glass. I was having trouble putting two words together.

"I meant the other," she said, laughing. "Being bad."

"I knew what you meant," I said, though it was a lie.

"Well, then," she said dandling her fingertips up toward my crotch, "well then, Dickie-boy. Let's just be bad, shall we now?"

What we did after that didn't require much talking.

As I made my way towards the mess tent half an hour later I knew eyes were following my hurried stride. They would be laughing at us soon enough. Carney folk enjoy a good laugh at someone else's expense. They also don't mind seeing a knife stuck into a man having it off with another man's gal.

It wasn't once and it wasn't twice. It was a habit. Opium in my blood; I started to ache when I didn't have it and trembled with anticipation when I knew it was coming. It was wrong and it was stupid and it was dangerous, and it had its claws sunk into me so I couldn't think straight.

Celie. I remarked the name myself. She'd made it up. There were times after we were done on the bed when we went outside and took up a position in the moonlight where we could watch the flap of Boss Man's tent so as to scuttle our separate ways if Jimbo appeared. We talked, all casual-like. She'd come into the world a Doris in a small town outside of Regina where being a pig farmer was a big deal and the local women dressed in gingham and hadn't heard of silk crepe and whatnot. How she did is another story: a teacher from out East who took a fondness to her and then took her into her house and showed her books with pictures of Paris and fine ladies in hats and eventually took her into her bed. It must have been that creamy skin and red hair. Nigh impossible to resist. I was what could be called a victim of peaches and creamy skin my own self.

There's a photograph of me from this period, fresh-faced and open to whatever experience life was about to send my way. Do I look like a rube? I leave it to others to decide. The shirt is plain worsted-wool and the buttons are done up to the collar. There may be a cigarette package in the chest pocket. The hat is not remarkable for its time, either, everyone wore hats much the same, but hats have gone out of style, so it gives me a jaunty aspect, as if I wasn't just prepared for what fate would throw my way, but welcoming it. Which brings me back to Celie, soft and yielding Celie, intent and selfish Celie. Her lips were soft and her ass was round and when I laid my head between her lovely breasts, it was as if I was floating on a cloud of lilac perfume. She was headstrong and used to getting what she wanted, and she didn't hesitate to put herself—or others—at risk to get it. People of that kind are dangerous. She was right about that.

We were going at it like ferrets, once we got started, both of us crazy with desire and oblivious to consequences in the way of children. Only we weren't children and there were consequences. I suppose we knew the shit would come down one day; we were just pretending it wouldn't, wishing and hoping, blinding ourselves to the inevitable.

If she came and stood beside the carousel in the morning, I knew Jimbo was off doing something horsey and the coast was clear, we were *on*. On top of each other. Sometimes at night. Jimbo was a drinker who fancied his luck with cards. She'd poke her nose in at Boss Man's tent and ask when he was coming home, she was cold in the bed. He waved her away. He was playing cards. She was playing him. "C'mon, Jimbo, c'mon," she whined. She knew the more she begged the more he'd dig in and stay longer, just to prove to the other men who was wearing the pants. I'd think to myself, You wear the pants, Jimbo, you just go right on wearing them pants. As for my own.

They all knew, of course, except for Jimbo, which was surprising because he was a sneaky little bugger and had himself stolen Celie away from a butcher in Yorkton, they said, so he should have been the first to be suspicious, but that's how things work sometimes: the man who steals a gal away from another thinks he's exempt to the same happening to him a bit farther down the road. The human animal is a study.

The others were wise. Early Big would say, "That's been the ruin of many a good man." They called it *tail*. A piece of tail. It was a crude term with the stink of the barnyard about it. They could be crude company, carney folk. The words *niggers* and *sluts* were bandied around and even *jigaboos*, with Early

Big present. After he'd said that about women being the ruin of many men he'd stare at me hard until I dropped my gaze from his, black eyes and a scar that ran from the corner of his lip right to his ear. Maybe he'd been called *jigaboo* once too often. "The death of a few," Boss Man added one night, after Early Big said that, his voice dropping as if he was recalling a specific incident. Silence lowered over the table. Someone slapped down a card. Someone else went for the mickey in the centre of the table. Boss Man coughed; Early Big stared at me hard. Jimbo sniffed and muttered, "Women."

I got up a minute or so after, straightened my shoulders, yawned and patted the arm of Boss Man on the way out. He always grunted and said, "You take care, now, *Dick*," which brought a chorus of *hah*s from the other men.

I skinnied over to the trailer, heart thumping, knees trembling, already bulging in my pants. There might have been the brightest, most beautiful moon in the history of all astrology but I never noticed. There might have been wind. It might have been one of those long, warm, prairie summer nights when stars are bright overhead and the temperature never seems to drop. It probably was. I wouldn't have noticed. It was my own fevered temperature I was aware of, the tinkling of something not stars in my shorts.

She was waiting and she was eager. She always asked, "You got away, okay, Jimbo didn't notice?" She wanted to know that. She had a way of licking her top lip with her red tongue, a schoolgirl affectation. She wanted to know how close we were treading to the line. At first I thought she was afraid of getting caught and felt sorry for her; I could take care of myself, I reckoned, as long as I wasn't snuck up on by Jimbo wielding a knife, but I did not fancy the idea of her being hit; I imagined she was frightened of him and it bothered me some. But that changed. It was the danger, I came to see, the danger was as much the attraction for her

as the sex, which was not to be scanted. There was the ecstasy of
lust and added on to that the thrill of just about getting caught;
I admit it was a heady brew.

"Kiss my tits, kiss my tits," she cooed. They jiggled as she
squirmed under my tongue. She flipped over. "Run your nose up
my back," she called out, face in the pillows. I positioned myself,
straddling her from behind. "The centre, the spine. Yeah, yeah."
I fit myself between the peach halves of her bum. Her giggling
filled the tiny trailer. I ran my nose from the top of her bum to
the nape of her neck and into that glorious hair. Scent of cinnamon, skin like silk. I flipped her over again and held her breasts
tight against my chest and when I went into her, she gasped.
Through the entire time my ears twitched to every sound coming from outside. *I should not be here,* I was saying to myself, *Not
be here.* But she was a drug. And I had to have her.

"Horses do that," she said after, "run their noses down each
other's spines." She was laughing with a blanket pulled around
her body as I tugged my clothes on. I didn't know if she was
right about that and didn't care. I had to get out of there. I had
to jump on her again. The way her nipples, the feel of her soft,
round ass. It was that crazy. Lust piled on lust so a man couldn't
remember what his name was sometimes.

I was the Barker. "Lay-dees and genle-men, boys and girls."
There was a lilt to my voice, the promise of secrets and mysteries just past the tent flap, a world of delights so far removed
from chickens and harrowing fields and pigsties it was impossible to do more than hint at it. Dark mysteries, all available
for a nickel a head. Folies Bergère, dancing women in can-can
skirts and legs that ran all the way up to their asses. Something
almost dirty and certainly bound to set the loins aflame. Something only to be seen in Paris. One of the Folies had actually
been there and brought back the name, a long time past, it must
have been. I stoked the fires of desire in dirt farmers and their

lustful sons. As I laid out the pitch, so fevered at my work sweat built up under my arms sometimes, my shirt stuck to my back; sometimes I became so worked up about the Folies or the Lion-Faced Lady that I tossed the red jacket aside and went in my shirt sleeves, half believing the lies issuing from my mouth like a snake's tongue. It was a con. It was low. If I hadn't been so enamoured of my own voice, my success as a barker, I'd have cringed with embarrassment. But then I was already having it off with another man's woman, wasn't I? Low and lower. My soul had already been consigned to the fire-pits of Hell, so what was the diff, as Celie put it?

There were nights when Jimbo didn't come to Boss Man's tent for cards because he and Celie were going into town for pie and ice cream, or to a picture show. It was a relief in a way, but it also hurt, knowing she'd be with him that night. My girl. I'd come to think of her that way, and it was perilous thinking.

In the tent one night there was another man sitting in the corner against a pile of pillows and cushions. He was Terry Big, Early's brother; he lived in the town next over and had come visiting. He was strumming a guitar and singing softly sometimes, sad tunes mostly, about lost love and lives gone bad. "As I walked out in the streets of Laredo … " I wasn't much of a card player, not a gambler, not that way anyway, over money. No. Over my breathing flesh and blood with Celie, yes. I was usually to be found sitting to one side of the card table, kibitzing with the other men. That night I was watching Terry Big as he strummed his guitar, eyes closed, his lips barely moving. He looked up at one point and grinned at me. A while after he signalled me to come over where he was half-sitting, half-lying on the cushions. "You like the guitar?" I said I did. He grunted. "It's easy to play, you know. Here, I'll show you." He positioned my fingers on the neck of the guitar and told me not to press too hard on the strings and to strum lightly down at the sound box.

I was a natural; he taught me five chords that night and by two o'clock I could almost stumble through "Red River Valley."

"Jesu, you catch on fast, boy," Terry said. "What you say your name is?"

"Dick. Dick Bauch."

He reached out his big hand and shook mine. "Terry Big." His shiny dark hair was pulled back and hung from his neck in a long, knotted ponytail. Inside his skull was a wide blue lake, a bison in the foreground gazing over its placid surface, an eagle floating on air currents.

"I know," I stammered. "I heard your name."

"What you don't know is that it's actually Bigfoot. But Early said we should shorten it so as not to unsettle you white folks."

"My name isn't actually Dick," I said. "It's Harlan."

"Is that a fact?" he said. "Is that a fact? Hmm. Seems nobody is who you think they are around the carney." He laughed. He had a big wide mouth with thick lips and broken and stained teeth inside. "Boss Man," he went on, "you know that man's actual name?"

"No," I admitted.

"No matter." He chuckled and said, "You got talent with the guitar, Dick. I got an old one kicking round the house. It needs a couple strings maybe. I'll bring it around tomorrow."

He did. "There it is," he said, shoving it at me. "I put in a new G and C."

"Thanks," I said, "how much do I owe you?"

He placed his hand on my forearm, a big hand that rested there, heavy as an anvil. "That's not our way," he said. "Take it. A gift."

It was light to the touch and made of wood more blond than his own. It was scratched up around the sound box, but when I strummed it, it made, to my ear, perfectly fine music. "Thanks," I said again. I reached into my pocket and brought out a dollar.

"No, Dick," he said, "no. That's not our way." His voice was soft but his black eyes went hard right then and I knew there was no more debating it.

He squeezed my arm then. "I want to tell you something," he added, and I thought he was going to tell me about the origins of the guitar. But he was onto something else entirely. "There's a blue sea," he said, "or a lake, maybe, with a long shallow beach, and we walk into the water: toes, ankles, knees, thighs, all the way, until we begin to float on our backs under a blue sky and soon we *are* the water, there is no self, and we float and float and float."

"Nothing to fear, then. No pain, no crying out, no tearing and rending."

"Floating. Floating beyond floating."

The next morning found me on the apron of the carousel, strumming the guitar. I picked up tunes by ear. Play something and I'd listen close and could play it back, if not right away, in an hour or so. Celie came by. "Well," she said, "I didn't know you was musical."

"I didn't either," I said. I strummed up "Red River Valley" and she sang the words softly as I played.

"You're good," she said. "You got talent." She winked and added, "In your fingers." After a pause she said, nodding at my crotch, "And in other places."

A few days after that she showed up with something in her hand wrapped in brown paper. "Guess," she said.

I had no idea. I shrugged my shoulders.

"One guess—for little Celie."

"Bar of chocolate." It was about that size.

"Nope." She unwrapped the paper slowly.

"A mouth organ," I said.

"Harmonica," she said. "Mouth organs is played by Jews."

"All right," I said. "Harmonica it is."

I blew into it a few times tentatively. Lovely sounds issued forth, right up and down the scales. "Where'd you get this?"

"A friend," she said, going coy, rolling her eyes and tossing her hair back. "A friend who was in the carney for a bit and then—"

"And then was in a hurry to leave the carney."

"Don't be vulgar, now Dick. Be nice. Celie has brought you a nice gift."

"You're right. That was out of line."

I thanked her and went back to the guitar. Before I put my mouth to the harmonica again, I took it to the wash basin and scrubbed at it with soap until lather was thick on my wrists. No knowing, I said to myself, whose mouth has been at it. I boiled water and plunged it in for a minute. It was only while I was holding the thing in the steaming pot that it occurred to me that treating it that way might ruin its musical properties. I shook it hard and left it to dry overnight and when I blew at it in the morning, it was fine, in fact the sounds it made seemed sweeter. I reckoned the wood might have dried out over time without being played and the water had improved that.

Folks enjoyed the harmonica. You could play softly in the background or be the centre of attention, doing jigs they could dance to. Most of all, it was easy to carry around: into the jacket pocket, or if necessity required, back pocket of a pair of pants. I felt bad about the guitar, sitting unused, but then one day a kid of about fourteen was hanging around in the morning while I practised up a few tunes and I asked him if he'd like a guitar and his eyes went wide at the prospect, so I fetched it and gave it to him. "A gift," I said, remembering the words of Terry Big. It felt real good to do that, I admit, do it *their way*: the kid was delighted to receive the guitar and I felt warm all over in making the gift. The Indians have got a few things figured out, I reckon.

I played for Celie sometimes, too, just the two of us sitting on the apron of the carousel. We were hot all over for each other and the music calmed us a bit when throwing off our clothes and getting down to business was out of the question. Most of the time, though we were onto each other like minks.

One night when we were finished and standing in the moonlight, keeping an eye on Boss Man's tent, she asked, "Whatcha gonna do with your life?"

I hadn't thought much about it. There was farming but after the carney, dull dull dull. Men with suits and smart fedoras were making a lot of money buying and selling land in big cities, the newspapers reported. *Speculating*, Phil called it. A farmer, he was dead against that. The price of land should be fixed, whether it was farmland or in the city. "Land speculation," he said to me one night when we'd strolled behind the barn to sneak a smoke. He spat between his feet. "Man should be hung for that there." The idea of turning over a fast dollar on a sharp deal revolted him, but was much to my liking. I'd been giving car salesman a lot of thought. Even in what the papers were now calling "The Great Depression" lots of motor cars were rolling out of Detroit and gents with the money to buy them—lawyers, bankers, land speculators—were lining up for test drives.

The motor car appealed to me. Bright shiny paint, the huff of an engine, tires kicking up a trail of dust. Leather gloves to grip the steering wheel and goggles to keep dust out of your eyes. You just about looked like them fly boys all the girls went ga-ga over in the war. Motor cars zoomed across the land, as airplanes zoomed through the air. I'd always had itchy feet, witness that family photo, and speed held me in its grip much the same as sex. On the rare occasion when he deigned to acknowledge our existence, the old man would give the lucky one among us a ride in his truck. Lordy. Trees flashed past, cows jumped in the field; when you rode into town, everyone's eyes followed you. Okay. I was a sucker for that, the attention of others. It's been the thing behind my dreaming and scheming; and it's been my undoing. But what a ride. The motor car, then. If you became a salesman you didn't have to buy one. Not at first. You could motor around in the company car, it was a form of advertising. Oh, yes, everything about the motor car appealed to me. And they were perfect for quick getaways, something I'd been devoting more than a little thought to while bouncing on top of squidgy little Celie.

I said nothing to her about motor cars. It had the stink of escape to it, and if I've come to understand only one thing about women it's that they don't care much for the thought a man might be harbouring that idea.

She was waiting my answer about my plans. "Hang around the carney for a while," I murmured.

"We go down south, you know, for winter. Texas, Oklahoma."

"I know."

"Anyways, I actually meant do with your life—after the carney."

"I knew that too." I was smoking a cigarette, a filthy habit, I had to give it up. But somehow it never seemed to happen. Following a silence, I added, "I might go in for the city life."

"Office job? You?"

"Lawyering sounds interesting. I'm smart enough, to judge by some they turn out onto the unsuspecting public. And I got the gift of the gab."

"You do that."

"But there's a lot of schooling, a lot of years taken up studying the law in them thick tomes, and passing examinations and whatnot."

It was a dream, I realized, would never come to fruition: me in a pin-striped suit, with a tie and a fedora and a briefcase of legal papers in hand, walking into an office building with plate-glass doors and an elevator, the secretaries saying,

"Good morning," and me giving the wink to the red-headed one with the lovely breasts and asking her to bring in the coffee. The respect of businessmen, the envy of neighbours, a counsellor to whoever came in the doors with a problem. Pillar of the community. It would never happen; I had the brains but not the background, and that's how the world works; it was clear to everyone, including a simple rube like me. But it was nice to dream.

After I'd finished talking, Celie studied me for a while. "You're looking for something, Harlan," she said. "Something, well, not ordinary, something on the edge, is my guess."

"I'm just an ordinary guy," I protested.

"Your face," she said, "is a picture: with mountains in the distance, a sun that can't stop shining."

"You're a pretty girl," I said weakly.

"Pah," she said, waving me away. "It's in your eyes. You're a seeker. But you're afraid to admit to it. It scares you. A little bit."

I said, "You don't know what you're talking about, girl."

"Quite possibly."

I waggled one finger at her. "You're keen on dredging in my life. What about you?"

"I was thinking of the city too," Celie said with a sigh. "Going in for a secretary, maybe. As a way of getting my foot in the door. What I'd be really looking for would be a nice banker, or a dentist."

She whispered it wistfully and I realized that though the world of doctors and lawyers and such was closed to the likes of me, there were still plenty of opportunities if a man had brains and applied himself. But not for Celie. There was secretary and schoolteacher and raising babies, a narrow avenue growing narrower every day that young women had not fixed themselves up with a successful man. It was unfair but it seemed there was nothing could be done about it.

"I'm young and still pretty," she was going on. "You think I'm pretty, don't you, Harlan?" When she called me that she was being serious.

"You are," I said. "Very. No banker out there could resist you: that smile, that hair, the way your little tits bounce when you run a few steps."

"I'm being serious."

"So am I. You're a catch, Celie. Any man would be happy to have you."

"But not you."

"I'm not any man."

We laughed and she threw her arms around my neck and gave me a hug. Over her shoulder I was watching the flap of Boss Man's tent. Into the nape of my neck she sighed, "I knew you'd understand, Harlan." She stepped back and then put both hands on my shoulders. She was a little slip of a thing. Moonlight reflected in her eyes. "You're a good man," she said. I doubted it, I'd been screwing her behind Jimbo's back, and if that don't make you a bad man, what does? But I nodded and lifted her hands off my shoulders and kissed both palms and we let it go at that.

Boss Man came round soon enough and said, "We'll be hitting three or four more towns out near Regina, and maybe one or two more, if the weather holds, but then we begin the long trek south for winter." He wanted to know if I'd be hitching along. He told me I was a good barker, among the best he'd ever seen. He held back on saying *the best*. He'd given me instructions the first time out on how to do the pitches but he'd noticed that I had a flair for the dramatic, raising and lowering my voice as well as varying pitch. And I could read a crowd: on one night going strong on the Folies but on another talking up the Fabulous Phelans. He liked that. There was room for me in the carney permanent. I hemmed and hawed and made excuses about Mother. He read them for what they were; he knew it had to do with Celie. He nodded and said, "Make up your mind in your own good time, Dick, feel good about what you decide."

Whenever I was with Celie in the next while, I was saying to myself even as she gripped her ankles against the backs of my knees to pull me into her, *This is the last time, definitely the last*. She may have been thinking the same. Our lust for each other had not run its course but we'd been walking our own little tightrope for too long and were due for a fall. Time was closing in. That's how it is, though, when lust has you in its grip: *one last time*. You knew the shit was bound to come down. And it did.

It was a night of high winds. The tin roofs of the sheds where the horses were sheltered had rattled all day. Scraps of paper blew across the ground in front of the big tent and then swirled about on the edge of the carney grounds and blew back again. It was not a happy night to be a barker. Dust flew into my eyes and gawping mouth, spoiling some of the best parts of the pitch. It was necessary to time things to fit between gusts. Folks packed it in early, the crowd thinned fast past nine and Boss Man cancelled the eleven o'clock performance. Stragglers scuffled away shortly after. I hung up the red coat and helped Boss Man do the last bits of close-up, then we walked together to his tent. "You're getting mighty good on that thing," he said out of nowhere, referring to the harmonica.

"Practice makes perfect."

"Hmm. And not only at that."

The wind blew into our silence. "Which ones you like?"

"Say what?"

"Which tunes that I play are your favourites?"

"Oh, different ones on different nights, depends on my mood. One sad one you do reminds me of a girl I knew once, long time ago. And those jig numbers. You wouldn't know it but I was something of a dancer once, light on my feet." He laughed. "A bit like you. Maybe more cagey."

"You don't have to look out for me."

"Ah. But I do." He drew a deep breath. "Someday you'll understand."

I thought maybe he meant that all older men had be fathers of a kind to young men they came across. "Look at that," I said, pointing at the way the cook tent was being bashed by the wind, its sides caving in and then billowing back out.

"It's gonna be a rough night."

"Batten the hatches," I said. "Pack it in early."

A big gust brought us nearly to a stop and we grabbed at our hats and then stepped into the shelter of a tent for a moment. Boss Man was smoking and he took a long drag at his cigarette. "I don't blame you," he said, tipping his head in the direction of Celie's trailer. "She's a fine looking gal and you've got something she needs." He chuckled, glancing down below my belt and said, "No, not that. You're going somewhere, Harlan, and right now she isn't and she needs someone to look up to, show her the way, show her that dreams can be realized." The wind whipped between the tents and they rattled and flapped and we stood in silence and watched paper and grass blow around. "The thing about women," Boss Man went on, "is they think different than us. We get the wrong idea, you see, because they enjoy doing the same things we do, you know on the bed and so on, bouncing around. But while we're thinking, Hey, this is great, let's do this some more, their minds are chewing over little details, placing this stick here and putting that bit of grass there, and a pat of mud to hold them together, and before we know what's going on, there's a nest built and we hadn't even guessed sticks and building nests was the game. It's not a bad thing, it's just that we had no idea; we men thought it was just, you know, *that*, but all along it was the other. You see?" He blew smoke in the air and we watched it snatched away by the wind. "That's how I got it figured," he added with a wry smile. "But there's a lot more to it than that. And like I say, I'm just a man. What do I know?"

A rabbit darted from beneath the tent we stood beside and bounded across an opening that led down a slope toward a thicket just off the carney grounds. We watched its white tail disappear under the bushes. Safe.

"You now, Harlan," Boss Man said, "you're a good kid with lots going for you, but you're heading down the wrong road, you're chasing after this when you should be heading toward that. You see?" I'd been following every word out of his mouth and reached out toward him, eager to hear more. "Naw, naw," he said, holding up the hand with the smouldering cigarette. "I can't help you more because I do not myself know what *this* and *that* are, only that—" A square of tin sheeting about the size of a barn roof whirled through the air right over our heads. "Sheep shit," Boss Man shouted into the wind, "that could have sliced off our heads!" He chucked his cigarette away. He grabbed my arm and we sprinted across to his tent.

We came to the tent door. The sounds of the men setting up card tables and opening bottles of beer greeted us. "Anyways," he concluded, "you got talent in that direction, Dick, you could follow it up and be on radio and the like." People were always telling me that. I had talent. But I never could quite find the break to bring my talent to light. Maybe it's that way with many others: them that gets the breaks, lands in the right place on the right day, they make it. It's down to luck, much of life. Everyone says it's working hard and the right attitude but they're giving the lie to experience, mine anyway. A lot comes down to luck: what family you get born into, which connections are made for you; whether you're physically attractive and likeable. Very few who are ugly and born low make it anywhere, is my experience. The luck of the draw. And a lot comes down to whether Fortune smiles your way, if you come from my background, anyway. But

Peggy the grocer's girl sort of has a free and easy pass into the swanky house and the bright-eyed kids and all that.

There was a loud bang behind us and we both wheeled and peered into the gloom of the empty prairie stretching away to the west. Papers blowing like tumbleweeds, wind, dust. I shrugged. "How 'bout that," Boss Man said. We went inside the tent.

Early Big was in a foul mood. When I said, "Hey," he grunted but that was it. He and Terry had been talking to a farmer down the road about buying his truck. Terry had a plan to go into the trucking business, hauling things from Regina to the small towns in the area, commercial goods such as soap powder and sacks of refined flour from the mill. They thought they had a deal with the farmer: set price, delivery date. And they'd both been excited about the acquisition, toasting each other and making big plans the night before. But then the farmer balked. He wanted more money. "Jitters," Boss Man said, "it's called seller's jitters."

Early Big snorted. "Don't care what it's called, it's lying and cheating is what it is, backing down on a deal that's been agreed between men and sealed by a handshake. Man can't give his word and then go back on it."

"Business," Boss Man said. "It's the way of business."

"White man's business," Early Big shot back.

There was silence in the tent. Carney folk didn't much go for that kind of talk, white men versus Indians. Every now and then there'd be something in the papers, an Indian representation in Ottawa talking about land claims. Then I'd overhear things among the men. Royster was outspoken on the subject. "Their land was stolen, they claim," he said. "Everyone's land was stolen. You don't think my ancestors in Ireland back when in history just handed the land over to them English bastards when they came ashore, do you now? That land too was stolen, by the Jesus." He scratched his nose; there was a pimple there about half the size of a tractor tire.

Cookie said, "They got a treaty."

"Sure they have. You ever notice that the Indian has no time for things written on white man's paper, government documents and such, unless it's a piece of paper that favours them."

I stayed out of it. Most folks did. There was good folks in every group—Germans, Irish, Indians—and there was bad. That was my take. There was rabble-rousers and agitators way over on one side, and people who didn't give a shit way over on the other, and in the middle most folks, who went along with leaders who made sensible arguments, voting, if that was the way they saw their responsibility, but mostly leaving such matters to those who knew better. There's those, though, who have difficulty accepting that anyone does know better than their own selves.

Outside, the wind was whipping around. You could hear the leaves in the oak near Boss Man's tent rattling and the branches creaking.

I took out the harmonica and began to play a slow tune. It often had the effect of calming the mood in the tent when tensions rose over the card game or some slight had been taken. I closed my eyes and searched around inside my chest for the quiet space I liked to go to when I myself was agitated.

The card game started but there was tension around the table. Early Big was glowering over his cards and breathing heavy. Jimbo Jones rapped the table hard and said to the dealer, "Hit me!" I caught him giving me the glare and looked away, continuing to play but with trembling hands. I missed a note or two, unusual. Boss Man looked over and grunted. On another night he might have shot off a jibe at my expense but he held his tongue. Peace in the tent was more important. Maintaining it that night was a feat akin to walking the tightrope.

Outside, the wind continued whipping dust about and something bashed into the side of the tent, a rectangular object, a chunk of cardboard, maybe; it shook the overhead light bulb and sent shadows dancing this way and that. Everyone stopped what they were doing. "Rough night," Boss Man repeated.

Royster threw down his cards. "I'm out," he said. He was a chain smoker and was already digging in his shirt pocket for tobacco and paper. Royster was a friend of Art's; he had pulled me aside only a day earlier to say he'd heard Art had had a falling out with the old man and gone off to Regina or Winnipeg, or so he heard.

"You're out?" Jimbo snorted. "After one draw?"

"It's a man's right," Royster stated flatly. "Know when to hold 'em—"

"Bullshit," Jimbo said.

"Know when to hold 'em, know when to fold 'em."

Jimbo laughed. "You got no guts is how I see it." He must have been holding a good hand. It was rare. He was as bad at cards as at keeping his gal, going in for the big bluff when he had no hand the way only a fool does, and expecting others to do the same when he had a good hand.

Royster screwed up his face. "I got money in my pocket, though. I don't have to take money from a gal to buy cigarettes and beer." To make the point, he was striking a match on the bottom of his shoe and preparing to light up.

"No guts," Jimbo repeated. "It's sneaky and it's low." His voice had the ring of struck iron. I looked up from the harmonica. His back was to me but I could see the big vein in his neck throbbing.

"Cash money." Royster's voice had risen too.

It was getting as tempestuous inside the tent as out. Faces were red, fists were opening and closing.

"Enough," Boss Man said.

Early Big glared at me. "Shut that thing down," he growled. I stopped playing.

"'Bout time we packed it in for the night," Boss Man said.

"We just got started," Cookie said. He was the only one whose voice was normal and it brought a hush into the tent. He blew smoke into the air.

"We got it sorted," Royster said. "Just a little disagreement over cards."

Boss Man breathed in and out heavy. "That so?"

"That's so."

"Jimbo?"

"Yeah. You still in, Cookie? Or you weasling out too?"

"In," Cookie said. "So's Boss Man, so's Early. The kid would be too if a man could get him shut of that harmon-er-cunt."

Jimbo snorted.

Cookie said, "How's about a beer?"

"Sounds good." Boss man heaved a sigh. "And I could use another card."

"The kid will open us a couple beers, then," Cookie said, nodding toward where they were stashed in a little wood box on ice and sawdust.

I was happy to oblige. When I'd set a beer in front of each man, I passed the opener to Boss Man. "If you don't want me to play, then," I said, "I think I'll pack it in for the night." I looked at Early to see if he'd changed his mind.

"Sounds good to me," he growled.

"Right," Boss Man said. "On your horse, then."

I stood outside for a while, looking up at the sky. There was a moon and clouds were flying across it, west to east; there'd be a pool of moonlight near my feet for a few seconds, then nothing but shadows, then moonlight again. I had a smoke. Where did all them crows go at night, I wondered. Most nights this time you could hear crickets going at it in the grass and other sounds, too, night birds twittering, high-pitched whistles and chirping, cicadas, maybe. Not on that night. Only the wind, only the thumping of my heart in my throat.

My feet began to walk away from Boss Man's tent towards Celie's trailer. *Should not be doing this*, a voice in my head said. Another one answered: *One last time*. Such lovely tits; such a beautiful ass.

We were well into it. Celie liked to be taken from behind first and then have me roll onto her to finish. We were at about that point, our own wind up, matching the one outside when we heard voices approaching. "Quick," Celie whispered harshly, pulling away, "up, get out of here." The couch folded out into a bed, barely wide enough for two. She rolled away from me, smooth legs scrambling and lovely little tits bouncing this way and that, nipples erect.

I was still on my knees, my white hairy ass looking straight back at the doorway through which Jimbo was about to come. My member was as startled as my brain but continued standing-to. The big throbbing vein was blue with blood. All the wonder of the moment was gone, and what we had been doing seemed little more romantic than having a good crap, sordid and ridiculous. "Get," Celie whispered, "get out the window."

I hadn't known there was one. Above the couch and to one side behind a drape was a tiny window. She got up on her knees and found the metal tabs that slid it up and gave a heave and it was open. Wind whipped in, scarving her face in her hair. I'd jumped back from the bed and had pulled on my pants over my engorged self and was fumbling with my shoes. "No time for that," Celie insisted. "Just get." The voices were outside the door, close enough for words to be clear. "Ten dollars," Jimbo was saying.

"A lot of cash," the other voice said more loudly. I could not tell who it was. Maybe Boss Man. Maybe he was trying to warn me. There was something about the way he'd said *ah, but I do* that was nagging at the back of my brain.

I looked at Celie. I wanted to kiss her lips, hold her tight one last time. She was making shooing motions with her hands. *Get, get.* It was a shame to leave her so. She was a sweet girl, all things considered, and it hurt inside to go. But needs must.

I went headfirst through the window, knees and shins scraping along its bottom edge. There was nothing elegant about it. My hips stuck in its narrow width and needed a wrench. I felt Celie's palms on my butt, pushing. With a heave they were free. I went straight down the side of the trailer, nose banging wood, one handing grasping my shoes, the other groping for the ground. That hand hit a nail head, which snagged flesh and sent a flash of nausea through my guts. One shoulder struck hard earth. The breath was knocked out of me. I lay on my back for a moment. The wind was still whipping this way and that, a dry wind, there would be no rain from the look of the clouds scudding across the sky. Farm folk would be in despair and those in towns, whose livelihoods depended on crops and the money they brought into the communities, would be looking forward to another year of making do and belt tightening. They were bizarre thoughts to be indulging at the time. I got up on my knees and secured my own belt. The ride down the side of the trailer had not done my member any good; it was burning and sore and quite likely scratched. *What you get,* the one voice in my head was saying, *what you get for carrying on.* Celie's small head appeared at the window, hair dishevelled, eyes wild. She called down to me: "You have to trust yourself. You hear? Harlan?" Her head disappeared as suddenly as it had appeared. I listened for voices coming from the trailer. The wind snatched sounds away. Jimbo yelled something I didn't quite get: it might have been *bitch*; it made my blood run cold. Celie's high-pitched voice screeched back. I strained to hear more. Should I go back, defend her honour? I heard the window slide down. Celie had told me earlier that Jimbo was starting to get suspicious of her and me and he'd warned her that if he caught us together he'd kill us both, cut us at the very least. What if he was on his way out of the trailer at that very moment, coming around the corner, knife in hand? I pulled on my shoes but I did not do up the laces. I scuttled away from the trailer, sharpish. About halfway across the compound I passed on the other side of a tent where two men were standing outside the entrance flap, smoking: red tips of cigarettes glowing in the dark. One of them called out, "Go, boy!" His words were snatched up by the wind but I heard him laugh and the other man, too. I cringed but I kept my feet moving.

I scurried back to the low shed where the horses were stabled and where I bunked down at night in the straw with a blanket I'd scrounged. The irony did not escape me. Bedding down with the horses Jimbo fed and watered after bedding his woman. My bag of stuff was there: some underwear, a second shirt, socks. All the way across the compound I'd been picturing Jimbo going through my gear and stealing my cash. I'd left a ten in one sock, and as soon as I arrived back, breathless, I fumbled open the duffel and felt around for it. It crunched under my fingers and I felt greatly relieved. A more nasty man than Jimbo would have stolen that ten dollars. Or a smarter one. Perhaps he hadn't thought to go through my stuff. Perhaps he suspected someone else. No, you can lie barefaced to others and get away with it, but you should not lie to yourself and expect to: I was the low bastard and everyone knew it, Jimbo included, me included. I brought the ten out to assure myself it wasn't just a piece of paper stashed there to decoy me. That was the kind of thinking I was doing then: calculating and devious. I suspected every other man because I myself was guilty of low behaviour and deviousness. Maybe Mother was right when she quoted that old saw: *what a tangled web we weave.*

I sat on a straw bale until my heart stopped thumping. I had a second ten in my pants pocket. I'd split the two of them up in case the duffel was stolen or I was robbed. Suspicion piled on suspicion. Twenty dollars, my share of the king's gold.

The wind was not banging around quite so much then. The storm had blown itself out. I felt my shoulder then and I rotated it slowly to gauge how badly it had been hurt. I twisted my neck this way and that and a sharp pain shot along my spine, settling in the shoulder blade. One hand was bleeding from a cut on the fat of the thumb. The flesh was jagged, and a purplish red in colour. I licked it and thought, Not much, not much at all, considering.

Stabled in the shed there was a horse I was fond of, named Double, a quarter horse, same as the others, and when I said his name he nickered and I went over to the oats bucket and scooped up a handful. Royster had let me ride him a few times when he was saddled up and needed a bit of a run. We went along together well, as you can with some animals. I patted him on the neck and held the oats under his nose. He licked them up with his big, wet tongue and nickered again. I scratched behind his ears and then along the length of his back, knowing how much he liked it. Horses can't reach that area, and fly bites there drive them crazy. I scratched extra long, feeling his hot breath on my face.

"Tell me your problems," I whispered, into his ear, finally, "and I'll tell you mine."

He nickered as if he understood. "No kidding," I went on, "the paint? I wouldn't have guessed she was your type." It was a desperate effort to lighten the mood. After a while I stroked his silky neck again; I caressed the short brown hairs and ran my fingers backwards through the ridge of black mane that Royster kept trimmed to about an inch. Under the skin, sheets of muscles rippled in a brief dance. I pressed my cheek to his ear. I closed my eyes and breathed for some minutes while he stood quietly, blowing out of his nostrils from time to time. My arms circled his neck and I rested my cheek against his fine short hair and tears came to my eyes and after a while I trembled a bit and then the tears came faster and I blubbed into his skin and felt muscle moving beneath my cheek; and after a while I was calm and I stood back and brushed tears away and breathed deeply and stroked his long neck, as if in a trance for many minutes. I had gone away and come back emptied and calm. And then I went and sat on the straw bale. There was no one about. I studied the grey blanket, folded on the loose straw to one side. I could have bedded down and stayed the night but I was real low then and knew that if I crawled under the blanket I'd lie for hours with my ears twitching and heart thumping, expecting to hear footsteps come to deal with me, and fearing if I did nod off that the next thing I'd be aware of would be a chiv in my ribs. I got off the straw bale and picked up the blanket in one hand and slung the duffel over my shoulder. "Bye, Double," I whispered. I was leaving things behind: a girl, a job, a horse. A reputation. Abandoning them, some might say, same as the old man had abandoned us, same as Art, according to rumour. I pushed that thought away. I was not proud of myself as I walked out into the night.

I found the road going south and set my feet to the job ahead. The moon showed me the way. Gravel crunched underfoot. After a mile or so I saw the gleam of two eyes in the ditch. I slowed. There were wild cats around. And wolves. Every creature on the face of the earth was hungry, some desperately so. Wolves tended to hunt in packs, sheltering in the bluffs between fields and coming out at night to run something down. But things were bad with them, too. Food was scarce. Lone wolves had been spotted killing deer, and a boy coming in from his father's field had been attacked by one within sight of the barn. His pants had been torn, his arm gashed where he tried to fend off the fangs. Two dogs he'd whistled for had run the wolf off but it was that close.

I slowed almost to a stop. The eyes had not moved, bright as phosphorus in the black night. I peered into the ditch, hoping there might be a branch or stick handy. If it came to that, I'd need a weapon. I felt about my person. I had a pocket knife, better than nothing. In my back pocket the harmonica. Not much of a weapon. I wondered if playing it might have some effect. I took it out and blew into the alto end hard as my lungs were capable of. A piercing sound came out. The eyes remained focused my way, greeny yellow, but the head dropped a little and moved backwards. I blew a second time and a third, in rapid succession. My shoes crunched over gravel. The eyes shifted sideways and then were gone. Were they coming toward me? I stopped, ears straining. Only the wind in the ditch grasses. Only my thudding heart. I stood quiet for some minutes. "Go away," I shouted finally, growing more bold. "Get the eff out of here!" From the darkness I heard a short bark that sounded like *candid loupy.* I stood waiting to hear if there was more. Then I inched forward, fingers gripped on the handle of the open knife in one hand. Throw the blanket at it, I said to myself, if the attack comes, then the knife at the ready. I passed the spot where I gauged the eyes had been watching from. I walked backwards away from it for a number of paces, then turned and hurried on.

An hour passed, maybe two. The moon was directly overhead. It might have been four in the morning. My eyes were heavy and I crossed the ditch at a likely looking place where there was high grass on the edge of a field and settled myself into it, duffel under my neck, blanket up to the chin. The open pocket knife was in one hand. The wind was still blowing, the leaves of trees nearby rattling and branches creaking. I fell asleep almost right away.

I woke with the sun in my face, with the words of Celie tracking across my mind. Trust yourself? What did she mean? I had never heard anything of the kind spoken before. Certainly

I didn't trust anyone else. Life had taught me that: schoolteachers who beat me; the old man. Did I trust anyone? Margy, maybe, my wonderful sister who seemed to know intuitively what I needed. But trust yourself? It was a puzzler. I turned it over as I turned the tongue over in my mouth. It was very dry. I hadn't brought water. I'd need to get to a town soon. I stood up and got my stuff together and crossed back to the road and trudged along.

From time to time my shoulder ached. I tucked the blanket under the other armpit, where the duffel was slung, and rotated the shoulder slowly. A flash of pain, then another. But nothing was broken. In a couple of days it would be all right. I pictured Celie as I had last seen her: staring down into the darkness at me, hair dishevelled, voice high and insistent, concerned about my future. That would be my last memory, her intense little face haloed by hair, her red lips trying to tell me something, urgent. And then something else came back: the sound of Jimbo's voice as he'd entered the trailer. He was angry, cursing. He knew, and he was shouting at Celie, threatening her. In my haste to get out I hadn't heard that at the time. Or I'd blocked it out. But that was why I'd felt guilty crossing the compound and why I still did. I'd betrayed her by running out that way. Betrayed Jimbo out of lust and Celie out of fear. It was no wonder I tasted greenish bile rising at the back of my throat. I swore I'd never do something so low again.

I'd passed into an area where the land undulated, little rises followed by long descents. The grass in the ditches was green, a treeline hovered off to the west. There must have been a river or creek there but it was blocked from view by a low bluff. Meadowlarks were singing, crows flapped back and forth from one side of the gravel road to the other, a hawk rode wind currents in the distance where I suspected the creek ran. The sun had crested the treetops and was beginning to beat down on my head.

I'd never been so thirsty.

To divert myself I thought about the business of car sales, how much money could be made at it, the car I'd myself drive one day, something sporty with a bright paint job. My thoughts jumped to what Boss Man had said to me: about making the right choices in life. Did he mean chasing after flashy things like cars was a bad choice, that there were better choices to be made: more homely choices, a quiet life on a farm with a wife and kids and dogs in the yard? Or did he mean that I'd set my sights too low, that I should be dreaming bigger dreams? Whenever I'd given the future any thought, I'd assumed things would fall into place kind of by themselves, but I realized you could have a hand in your own fate, give it a shape and bring it about to a certain extent, and maybe that is what was meant by growing up: making choices and living with them. Like choosing a person to marry or a line of work to pursue. All I really knew was that I was restless for more than I had; I wanted more; I was sure there were bigger things for me than farming—or even selling Chevrolets.

A car came down the road towards me, trailing a cloud of dust. It slowed to pass and the driver and I exchanged waves. My throat was very dry. I began to wonder if I should hive off toward the bluff in search of the river and the cool drink it promised, but going off course that way seemed a waste of time and energy. Flailing about in the scrub and bush would only make me more thirsty. And I had no idea how far it might be to the river. I rested in the shade of a big oak on the roadside and listened to the crickets and studied the blue sky overhead. I picked up the blanket and the duffel and walked on. Then I heard a vehicle approaching from behind and I almost did a jig in the road as it slowed to my naked thumb. It was a truck, and a man and woman were seated on the bench in front, farmers, but I was happy to hop into the box where there were bags of barley and the strong odour of horse manure. We came to a town at the bottom of a valley where the grass was green and the trees tall. I hopped out in front of the café when the farmer stopped at my signal.

Inside, there were two booths and stools at a counter, and I took one of them and ordered water first and bacon and eggs and coffee to follow. The men on the other stools nodded and went back to their conversation. In the washroom out back I studied myself in the cracked mirror: my clothes were rumpled and my face dusty, and my hair, when I removed my hat, stuck up every which way. The hat band had left a red mark across my forehead. No wonder the gal behind the counter had taken a deep breath when I came into the café. I did my best to make myself presentable.

When I returned the woman smiled. I had a second glass of water, and when the food came tried to chew slowly so it would not be obvious how hungry I was. They were probably used to seeing men such as me, coming in off the road dirty and desperate, with just enough nickels in pockets to pay for soup and bread.

The guy beside me asked, "You on the road, then?" He nodded at the duffel and blanket. I told him I was. Alone, he wanted to know. I told him I was. "You want to be careful out there," he said. "Man was beaten and robbed just south of here a piece. Lost everything he owned, including his hat." The guy beside him nodded. "Came in here all shook up," he said. "We bought him a meal but he looked as if he was about to cry when he left, heading in the direction of Weyburn, where his older brother has a place." The waitress came up with a refill and another glass of water. "He was young," the first man was saying. "About your age, I reckon." The waitress stood back as I dug in my pocket for nickels. The look on her crinkled lips was not encouraging.

I swallowed back the glass of water. I was not going to make the mistake of going dry again.

When I got up to leave I asked them where I was. Camduff, they said. I calculated I had less than a hundred miles to go to get home. Two days, maybe one, if I got lucky with rides. Outside, the air was thin and hot. Tramping across the prairie was easier going with food in my stomach. The waitress had given me a jar of cool water and that was in the duffel as I swung along the road, watching the sun climb to its zenith, feeling its rays finger my face. There were cows in the meadows in the valley immediately outside town and the smell of cow dung hung in the air, a sweet, dense odour I found not unpleasant. All in all, not a bad day to be alive, not bad at all. Crows roosted in the trees, and farther along two sat on a phone line and when I passed below them I called out, "Caww, caww!" One barked back: "Caw, caw, *corvo*," angry it appeared to be. "Hey," I shouted, "that's my job, the barker." But no longer, I reminded myself. After I was past, one flapped up and flew along the road ahead of me and perched on a fence post. From a hundred yards away I could see a tuft of black feathers sticking up from the back of its head, kind of the way the old man's did—and mine, too, on occasion. I approached. "Ca-raw, ca-raw," I called out at a distance. The crow hopped up and then settled back down on the same post. Its beady eyes followed me until I had passed; then it flapped up, flew a distance into the air and came at me in a dive-bomb: "Caa-raww, caa-raw, *corr-vo*." I ducked as it passed within a foot of my hat. "All right," I muttered, "all right. You win."

No. I was no longer the barker. I'd left that behind and was a man on the lam. Celie would have woken up in the morning and I would have been out of her life. Permanent. It was maybe not such a bad thing. We'd been running close to the cliff edge for some time and it was a relief, in one way, to be done with that: the knot in the gut, the sweaty nights, skulking around in the dark and whatnot. So. Let it be. Boss Man would be without a barker. He'd get on; he was half-expecting it, I could hear it in his voice when he asked whether I'd be hitching on for the trip down south. No one would miss me, not really; but I felt bad, all the same. I'd let people down. They had relied on me and I had not come through. Worse, they'd be snickering if anyone mentioned my name, Dickie the Ding-Dong, Dickie the Dong. A man has only a few things that are worth anything in this life and one of them is his reputation. It can take a long time to gain people's trust and it can been thrown away in a minute. You had to work at it, and part of working at it was sticking to the straight and narrow sometimes, even if your desires pulled you in the opposite direction. Did I really believe that? I was in a sober cast of mind as I tramped down the road but what would happen when the next gal with lovely breasts and an easy smile crossed my path? I half knew and it hurt to admit it. Something of the old man lurked deep inside. Cut and run. Snatch and grab. It was in Art, too, that had come out when he up and scarpered off. But I thought I was above such behaviour. I wasn't. We were bad seed. Bauch. It could have been the German word for *bad*.

The road I was on came to an intersection with another. I'd been lost in thought and hadn't noticed it coming up. The other road ran off to the south and my object was to stay steady to the west. Far in the distance to the south, though, I saw something peculiar. At first it appeared to be a horse trotting on its own down the road. But no, this was smaller, it was a man on a bicycle. I'd heard about them and seen pictures in the papers but I had only ever seen kids riding them. I could see the man's feet going round and round, pedaling. A little spiral of dust was thrown up behind the rear wheel. He was climbing a little rise but moving at a good pace. What did that feel like? Riding a horse you could move fast, too, but you were always dependent on the animal beneath you, and you had to put energy into controlling it. And at the end of the day you had to feed and water it, and brush it down. On a bicycle you were freed from that; you were your own engine, was my take, pedaling at the pace you wished to move at, steering wherever you wished. I wanted to try it out and resolved that if one came my way, I'd give it a go. I walked on, stirring up dust and feeling my throat go more and more dry. A mosquito about the size of a dragonfly landed on my forearm and I brushed it away with a start.

I'd been hoping for a car to come along and give me a ride but none had materialized. The sun had moved past its high point. There were no clouds in the sky. Far away on the horizon, a few white wisps. Otherwise, just the golden ball beating down on my head and occasionally a hawk high up in the prairie blue, riding wind currents. I stopped under the shade of a tree and ate the sandwich the waitress at the café had wrapped in wax paper for me. I drank half the water in the jar and screwed the lid back on, and held it up for inspection, happy with myself for not glugging down the whole works. To lift my spirits, I sat with my back against the tree and played a few tunes on the harmonica. I had quite a repertoire; I fancied I could play in a band. I felt my eyes getting heavy and I stood up; I had to keep moving. My shoes kicked at the gravel for a while and I was lost in thought: Celie, Mother. They had both tried to tell me something but I didn't understand what: they were speaking in a foreign language, kind of. What did it mean, *seeker*? I was puzzling away at it when behind me I heard the sound of a car approaching and turned and stuck out my thumb. The car was painted bright yellow and was traveling at high speed, a plume of dust swirling up from its rear wheels. It came up to me fast and the driver braked sharply; the wheels skidded and kicked up gravel, which flew into my face. It was a young woman driving. She was wearing blue leather gloves and goggles, which she pushed up on her forehead. "Hop in," she called out. She shoved a pile of papers off the seat onto the floor. When I was seated with my duffel in the rumble seat, she said, "My name is Aritha but everyone calls me Ruthie. Hah."

"I'm Dick."

"Dick. Hah." The car was a Stutz Bearcat, canary yellow with a tiny windscreen and padded brown leather seats with buttons. The running boards along the sides were moulded to be part of the front and rear wheel-wells, in the shape of a gull's wing. There was a trunk; a spare tire was attached to it. The hood was in the doghouse shape and had two giant headlights attached. Henry Ford had set out to make a car that was affordable to every American. This was not it. Its brazen colour alone set it off from the uniform black of the Model T and that by itself marked Ruthie as exotic. I'd heard of flappers; a couple of girls had shown up at the carney imitating the look: hobble skirts and rouged knees. But Ruthie was the real thing: short cropped hair, bright lips, an utter disdain for looking *feminine*. An arrogant curl to her lower lip. I half expected a cigarette holder to materialize and for her to light up using both hands while the Stutz was left to steer itself.

She pulled the goggles down over her eyes and slammed the transmission into first gear. The car leapt forward when she gave it gas and I grabbed at the dashboard to keep from flying back. Wind whipped around in the cab. Ruthie, I couldn't help noticing, had on a man's blue shirt, the top three buttons unfastened, her breasts on display. She noticed me noticing and laughed. "You're a looker," she said. "Hah. You're a looker and you enjoy looking." She drove too fast with one hand on the wheel, so the car veered wildly toward one ditch, and then when she yanked on the wheel, toward the other. I thought, Well, you gotta go one way or another; may as well be in a car with a smashing girl.

"You got lover's lips, Dick," she said, "and there's something about your eyes. You a ladies' man?"

I put up one hand in protest. I could feel my ears turning red.

"Now don't give me that false modesty bullshit." She banged

one gloved hand on the steering wheel. It was wrapped in bright red leather that matched her lipstick. "My thinking is this," she was saying: "You got something going for you, why hide it under a bushel. Fifty years and you're dead." The car hit a pothole and veered off toward the ditch. She braked, the front wheels skidded violently, the car ran off the road and into the ditch, I don't know how she got it back on the gravel. "Jesus, Joseph, and Mary" she shouted over the rattling of metal, "we nearly bought it there, Dickie-boy."

I was coughing from dust and rubbing at my eyes. Grass had flown up from the ditch into my face. Ruthie laughed. She shifted into third gear and stomped on the gas pedal. The rear wheels fishtailed in gravel. She pointed at the floor near my feet. "There's a jar down there, Dickie-boy, lemonade. I've come all over thirsty. Grab that, will you?"

I dug it out from the newspapers around my feet and screwed off the lid and passed it over. She took a swig and smacked her lips. "Now that," she said, "hits the spot." She waved the jar between us as she talked. "Have a pull," she ordered me. I took a swig. Lemonade mixed with moonshine. "Now me," she was going on, "I got a great set of tits. Wouldn't you say?"

I nodded. I began to screw the lid back onto the jar. "Hold on," she shouted. "Let me have another pull of that." She drank rapidly, a little of the drink spilling down her chin. When she passed it back, I screwed on the lid and put it between my feet. "Now where was I?" She turned to me. Her eyes were bright green; they suited her peaches-and-cream complexion. "Oh, yeah. Tits. Hah. You got 'em, you may as well enjoy 'em. That's my motto." We came to the intersection of two mile roads; she blasted through it without so much as glancing in either direction. "You'd probably like to kiss my tits," she was saying. "And I'd like you to. I would. You're a looker, Dickie boy. We'd have some fun. But the thing is, I'm heading to Weyburn and am already late. My brother lives there, my twin brother. He's been kissing my tits since we were twelve. Very nice. Hah. He has big lips and a full mouth. I get tingly all the way from my toes to my eyeballs with his lips at me. Hah. Now don't you be scandalized, Dickie-boy; you don't want to come off *bourgeois*, a young fella with your promise." She blatted the horn. Two crows were on the road, I hadn't noticed them. My hands were in my lap, trembling. The crows flapped off. Ruthie reached over and patted my thigh. Coconut: a sweet delicious cream, if you sucked those tits coconut milk would flow into your mouth. "Now don't be taking offence," she said. "Ease up, Dick, take life as she comes. Hah." We came to a junction. Weyburn was to the west, Estevan to the south. I signalled her to pull over. When I was standing on the gravel with the duffel over one shoulder, she shouted, lifting the goggles for a moment, "You take care now, Dickie-boy. I'll be watching for you out here on the road. I got my eye on you. Hah." The Stutz roared off; a little blue-gloved hand emerged from a cloud of dust swirling up behind it, waving back at me.

I walked for a while as if stunned. The sun was still beating down, my ears were ringing. The empty prairie opened up ahead, grasses waving in the ditches, shimmering light coming off the land. Had that really happened? Had I been dreaming? Not even in the carney had I seen anything so strange. I ran my tongue around inside my mouth: the taste of lemonade and moonshine. If it had been a dream, it had been a powerful one. Ruthie. I walked for a while. My eyelids were drooping again. I hadn't slept much the previous night. The food and the heat and the lemonade were having their way with me. I crossed the ditch and rested my back against a tree and fantasized about Celie for a good while. I nodded off.

I woke to the sound of a car going by and cursed myself for not having had a chance to hitch a ride. The moon was visible above the treetops. I stood up and got moving. I wasn't sure I was on the right road. I'd missed the setting of the sun in the west. I wasn't sure where I was going in the other sense, either. My life had reached a crossroads, I reckoned. I was a man now: I'd held a job, I'd been with a woman, I had money in my pocket. I was going home because that had been my first instinct when I fled the carney, retreat to the safety of the family, give Mother a hand around the place. That was okay, there was even some honour in it. But soon enough I'd have to make my own way in life, find something to put my hand to. It wasn't the carney, it wasn't being the carney barker, that life was too scattered—and there was no future in it. But it wasn't farming either. The carney had given me a taste for excitement, for being the centre of attention. I was a slave to desire, I realized, and probably a fool for it. I had the salty taste of life lived on the edge on my lips.

An hour passed. Darkness fell. The sounds of frogs in the ditches and crickets in the grasses. The road curved sharply and I saw in the close distance a red smudge; it was a fire, and as I drew closer I made out a truck parked on a tongue of gravel and two figures sitting at the fire. I smelled something, food being cooked, not meat but a heady odour that made my stomach gurgle with desire. The larger of the two men spotted me. He waved me over. I should have hesitated and thought the situation through but the smell of the food and the invitation of the wave drew me in. They were a man and his son, Al and Joe, and they were roasting potatoes, it turned out. "Sit," Al said. He had a bent nose and his teeth were yellow and broken. Tumbleweeds tangled together in his cranium, sticks, a rolling ball of filth. The son had a bandage on one hand, and the pork pie hat he was wearing did not fit him well, it was perched on top of his skull, looking as if it might topple off at any moment. They were both beefy and had small, beady eyes that peered out of fat faces.

They were both bigger than me, too, and had the stink of desperation about them. I'd made a very bad mistake. I swallowed hard. "I'm bothering you," I shouted as I approached nearer the fire, "I should just be moving on."

The son stood at that. The hat tipped forward on his brow and he had to steady it with one hand. It did not fit him at all; it was someone else's hat.

"Sit down," Al told him sharply. To me he said, "Joe's a bit touchy about some things, he takes offence easy."

Joe had both fists clenched at his sides. It might have just been the firelight but his faced seemed aflame.

"No offence," I offered, "none intended. It's just—"

"Nonsense," Al said. "Take a load off. There's an extra potato."

"No, really."

"C'mon now," Al said, "we won't bite." He tipped his head toward Joe, who was still standing, within arm's reach. "And we don't want Joe here to … to …." I saw now that there was a scar running from Al's lower lip down to his chin, jagged and roughly healed, the kind you get in a knife fight.

I drew a breath. Lord be with me, I thought. I'd done some foolish things in my life but I'd never sat down to eat a baked potato with killers.

I dropped to my haunches and stared into the fire.

We all three gazed at the embers and the ash. The fire sizzled, smoke blew up in little clouds around our faces. Al broke the silence. "You going far?"

"Alameda," I said, hoping that was the name of the next town to the south. "My brother's got a spread."

"Is that so?"

"He's expecting me. Tonight."

"That so?"

"I shoulda been there by now." I looked up at the moon, as if its ashen face was some kind of clock. "He's a nervous Nelly about things. Being on time and such." I tried to make it sound as if he'd already be on the road searching for me because I hadn't shown up. I was dead certain that wasn't the message the sweat on my face was conveying.

Al had a knife in his hand. The blade glinted in the moonlight. I wondered how quickly I could get my own out of my pocket. Al watched me watching him. He reached the knife into the embers and rolled out three potatoes. He picked one up and then quickly tossed it from hand to hand. "Hot," he said, "damn hot." He tossed it at Joe, who flipped it from one hand to the other and cursed. Al laughed; Joe grunted. Underneath the ill-fitting hat, cats' claws occupied his head, a twitching tail, yellow-green flashing eyes.

My potato was hot too. I brought out my knife and opened it deliberately and not too quickly. Joe's beady eyes followed the movements of my hands. Al had salt in a small bag and passed it around when we were all seated with our potatoes cut open and steaming. We ate in silence. "Could use a drink," Al finally said. "Moonshine. You don't happen to have a bit of moonshine in that there duffel?"

"No. Socks and underwear is all."

Joe grunted.

"Too bad," Al said. "Man gets thirsty after a long day in the sun." He laughed. The white flesh of the potato was set off by his stained teeth. A piece fell out of his red mouth and rested on his chin. I felt the urge to brush it off.

"Working the land?"

"No. Me and Joe been hauling a load of flour sacks out Weyburn way."

Joe grunted.

I counted slowly to ten. I swallowed back the last of the potato. Maybe the last thing I ever eat, I thought. I ran my tongue around my lips, savouring the salt. Would they ever find my body in the little stand of scrub on the far side of the truck? I pictured a mouldering skeleton lying among brown leaves.

"You know" I said, "I gotta go for a piss." I stood fast, but not too fast, and turned my back on them as I made my way past the tailgate of the truck. I unfastened the buttons of my trousers. I peeked into the box of the truck. It should have been covered in flour dust. It wasn't. I thought of bolting, then, lighting out across the ditch and down the road as far as my legs would take me before I sensed headlights behind, and then into whatever bush was handy. The duffel and blanket would have to be left behind. Ten dollars in the sock. But my life was worth ten dollars, wasn't it? I still had the other ten—and the knife and the harmonica. I heard a sound behind me, like feet crunching gravel, and I whirled about, still pulling on the zipper of my pants. But there was nothing there. Only the moon, only the thumping of my own heart in my throat. *Now*, I said to myself; *should bolt now*. Al's voice startled me. "You gonna be there all night?" He laughed and I guffawed loudly, echoing him.

When I came back into the fire's circle of light, I saw that the duffel and blanket had not been touched. "You know," I said, "I should be moving on. I don't mean to be rude. It's just that I—"

"We understand, don't we Joe," Al said, "your brother's waiting and all."

I picked up the duffel and slung it over my shoulder. The muscles of my arms and back were so tense then I felt them in my teeth. I reached down for the blanket. Joe's beady eyes followed my every move. "Well, then," I said, when the duffel was settled on my shoulder, "thanks for the potato. It was kind of you."

"Nothing to it," Al said. "We men on the road gotta stick together."

I swallowed hard. "I appreciate it."

"Nothing to it," Al repeated. "And you be careful out there on the road. No telling what a man on his own is likely to run into."

Joe spit into the fire. There was a sudden sharp sizzle of fluid hitting embers. "Yeah," he added, "no telling at all."

I crossed the gap to the road, quickening my pace with every step. As I hurried away I could not hear the crunch of gravel underfoot over the thudding of my heart in my throat. I moved along at a clip. Then I broke into a run. My heart was beating so hard my eyes hurt. I ran and ran, crazed with fear, fear accumulating on top of fear, my shoes scuffing gravel, the duffel joggling on my shoulder, heart racing until my chest hurt. When I judged I'd gone half a mile I looked back. No headlights on the road. Only moonlight turning the gravel white. I trotted for what I gauged to be another half mile before looking back again. Nothing. Then my legs gave out and I sank to my knees. Saliva dribbled out of the corner of my mouth. I spit into the gravel. I was on the verge of throwing up. I took several deep breaths and closed my eyes. My ears were ringing. I slid the duffel off my shoulder and fumbled out the jar of water and finished it off. When my breathing had steadied out, I stood on my quavering legs and walked for some time. I wanted to be well clear of Joe and Al before I lay down to sleep.

My sleep was troubled by dreams. A giant crow flew down out of a tree, screeching at me: *corvus!* Its enormous yellow beak was coming for my eyes. I threw up both hands. I woke sweating. Then I was climbing a sheer rock face and thinking, I've never climbed a rock face in my life, and I slipped and fell backward and woke just before hitting the ground, blood surging in my ears.

I lay quivering, studying the moon and listening to night sounds in the bushes. After a while my breathing slowed and I felt my eyelids drooping.

When the farmer who picked me up in his car the next morning dropped me off in Estevan it was approaching noon. I bought a sandwich at the café and chewed it down slowly and then ordered coffee and raisin pie, my favourite, and savoured every bite. I was feeling flush after the night previous, when I'd been sure I was going to be left a corpse in a copse. There were a few men at the counter, locals, guys I half-recognized, and one asked me, "Done with the carney, then?"

"It's called the *circus*," one of his buddies spat.

"Circus takes place in a big circular tent," the first man insisted, "and is fixed in one town. We been through this before."

"So you say."

"It don't go on the road. Like the carney. That's the difference: if they go on the road." There was a long silence and considerable throat-clearing, then the first man repeated to me, "Word is you done with the carney."

"I liked it. But they were off to Texas."

"Hoo, the Deep South. Don't know if I'd go for that. Every man in Texas carries a sidearm and isn't reluctant to use it. Man's as likely to get himself shot there as get rained on." There wasn't much laughter around but this guy brayed like a donkey taking a piss out in a field: *gronkkkk.*

"Warm, though, Texas," another guy said. "Come winter."

"We got hot," the first man muttered. "What I'd like is rain."

"Yeah, of course, so would we all. I'm just pointing out." A certain tension hung in the air for a moment. I could not help thinking, These are not happy times.

I got up to leave. I placed three pennies beside the nickels for the food.

A third voice behind me said, "You heard, then, that your brother Art has took off?"

"Yeah," I said. "I heard."

"Bright lights of the big city," the first man said.

"No work there, either."

All three of them grunted. The tension of a moment earlier dissipated.

It was hot and dry outside. I'd had the waitress refill the jar with water before I left. I walked along at a good pace but not fast. I was wondering what kind of welcome I'd get at home. Part of me was excited to see Mother and the girls and little Ernie. And Phil. Part of me wondered if word of how I'd behaved at the carney had got back to them. Should I lie? Should I laugh it off? Mother would not be forgiving if she knew I'd been with another man's girl and then abandoned her. A sick feeling worked its way from my gut into the back of my throat. It was hot on the road. I took off my hat and fanned my face with it. I had a sip of water. She'd be happy with the money I was going to give her, though, Mother. And they'd all be pleased by the tunes on the harmonica. My spirits lightened at the thought of sitting down at the table at night and bringing on their smiles with music. When you have nothing else, there's always music.

As I crested the final rise before our place, I saw the old man was out near the barn with two strangers, a man and a woman, wife and husband, I guessed from the way they stood beside each other. I did not want the old man to be the first of the family to see me, so I cut into the scrub at the edge of the farm and made my way through the bushes. High grasses grew there, singing their usual ditty: *flow gently sweet Afton*; I hummed along quietly as I brushed through them. When I reached the yard I skulked along the side of the barn, intending to skirt it and make my way to the house without being seen. The old man's voice arrested me. "Now," he was saying, "you take a little walk down the road, Glen, about fifteen minutes, and then Alice and I will be done here."

Warlock. He claimed to have magical powers. People came to him with various ailments: constant headaches, sores on their skin, inability to sleep, vomit attacks, not being able to have children, many others. I'd never seen him do whatever it was he did, but I'd seen people leave, smiling and waving. They gave him money. A dollar, maybe. That was what got to Mother. Not that he was a healer of sorts—you could say John the Baptist was a healer, even Jesus his own self. She was dead against the idea of an ordinary mortal usurping the role of God, it was a heresy of some kind, but she could have let that go if he hadn't taken money. That made it the devil's work. *Satan*, she'd whisper harshly to us when people came to have him work his magic. "I want none of you kids to have anything to do with that." It would never be me, I swore. "Sends a shiver down my spine," Vanora had confided, "going on that way, touching people and then taking their money."

I stood stock-still at the side of the barn, straining to hear what would happen. "Alice," he said to the woman. His voice was soft, a tone we never heard around the house. I took a quick peek and saw that she was massaging her hip and wincing. "Now just relax, Alice," the old man went on, "I want you to take deep breaths until you feel relaxed, all your troubles behind you, going into a deep peace." There was silence for a while. I heard the moving of feet but mostly deep breathing, two sets of lungs. After a bit, he went on: "Now," he said, "I will place my hand on the leg. It's the left, correct?" There was a murmur of assent. "All right," he said. "You'll need to shift your skirt down a little so I can … so I can touch you. Just a bit, don't be alarmed." A bit of shuffling followed. A brief gasp. "There," he said. Another long silence. In the trees above me a bird was twittering. On the far side of the yard one of the dogs was barking. I glanced up at the sky. The sun was high overhead. I had the sudden desire to scratch my nose but I controlled it. "All right," his voice went on. "Now I want you to do two things. Close your eyes. That's right. Now try to match your breathing to mine. That's it, in and out, deep breaths, let your mind go blank, try not to let any thoughts distract you. I'm closing my eyes too now, so we're totally matching, in and out." I took a peek around the edge of the barn. They stood facing each other; he had his right hand on her left hip, not on it, exactly, sort of just above the skin, just barely touching, maybe not even making contact. She was facing me, eyes closed, the breeze teasing her dark hair. She was an attractive woman: a round face, full lips, slender but not skinny. They stood that way for some time; maybe five minutes. I wasn't watching all the time. I'd drawn back to the shelter of the barn. I heard him saying something quietly: "Let your pain go now, Alice, let your pain flow out of your hip and into my hand, breathe it out, let it just flow out and leave you in peace. Keep your breathing exactly in rhythm with mine." I took another peek; Alice had let her head fall forward but he was standing quite straight, his hand motionless. It must have been a feat, I reckoned, holding your hand that steady that long without having a spasm or shaking. After a few more minutes, he said quietly, "There, then." Their feet shuffled; there was the sound of clothes being resettled. I felt the urge to cough and wanted desperately to be out of there but stood steady. Then the husband could be heard crossing the ground and Alice greeted him. She thanked the old man and so did the husband, and the old man muttered something. Feet moved on the earth. I assumed they were all walking away, backs to me. I took one quick peek. The woman was walking free and easy at her husband's side, holding his hand.

I ducked backward but instead of going to the house I sat on the grass, leaning against the barn. It was magic of some kind, the laying on of hands; I did not understand and was inclined to think it was a scam, but they had paid him, I'd heard the man say, *one dollar was it?* And the woman had walked away, moving as easy as her husband and the old man. Magic. In the carney I'd come to distrust the mere hint of it. Trickery, same as fooling people with cards or the shell game. I'd assumed what he did was of the same order. But I needed a think about this. It defied reason. But there it was: the woman had walked away, the pain in her hip apparently vanished. Maybe she'd wake up the next morning and the pain would be back; it would have been a scam. But something told me that was not what was going to occur. I didn't understand it. It was beyond my experience and logic. It occurred to me then that though my reasoning had always been sound on most things, my experience was limited. There were more things on earth than I could account for.

I remembered that he'd told us one time how he came to have his special powers. Maybe it wasn't us, Mother would not have wanted to hear. Maybe it was a visitor; maybe he'd told Art and Art told me and Phil. Irregardless, he claimed it started one day when he was out putting up the fence. Years ago. He'd been setting posts in holes he'd dug, then pounding them home with a sledgehammer. It was a stormy afternoon, dark clouds overhead and rain threatening. Thunder rolling in the sky. At the top of one of his strokes, there was a sharp crack of lightning and the next he knew he was twenty feet away from where he'd been standing, face down. The sledgehammer was nowhere in sight. He was wearing rubber boots; it had been a rainy and mucky season. His hat was gone too. There was ringing in his ears but after a while he stood up. His eyes felt odd, he said, as if there was pressure on them from behind; they were bulging, he felt, and about to pop out of his skull; and they throbbed with pain severe as headache. It was electricity, he said, a surge of power going through him that made the crown of his skull tingle. He hadn't known what had happened and didn't realize that it had given him a special power. He was lucky to have escaped with his life; the boots had saved him. He only figured out one evening weeks later that he had acquired a special power when he was sitting beside Art in his little bed; Art had fallen and skinned his arm badly. He was crying. The cut refused to heal; blood kept oozing out of his skin. The old man held his hand near the wound, an act of comforting. When he lifted it away, the bleeding had stopped and the wound had scabbed over and the pain was gone.

Did I believe it? I'd always thought it was so much horseshit, the old man trying to win us over, show us he really was a good man. He was a bastard, in my view. And being a liar fit right in with that, devious and low, the behaviour of the con artist. I'd never thought about it any different. But after what I'd witnessed my own self, I thought I might be wavering on that, so I closed my mind to it.

In the tree above me I heard rustling. It was a crow, preening its feathers. It stared down at me with its beady eyes. *Corvus*, it said, sticking out its thin tongue. I shook my head. Had it really spoken? *Soonlater*, it said, *soonlater*. I was spooked. I'd had a restless sleep, broken by nightmares; but still: hearing a crow speak? Maybe the old man's blarney had addled my thinking.

A few minutes later I heard his truck start up and then glimpsed it going down the road, plumes of dust behind. He was off gallivanting, it seemed, it was not uncommon. He'd take money and light out, maybe to Estevan to eat a meal at the café or sit at the beer parlour. Maybe to chase after that woman in Alameda whom he couldn't stop pestering. In any event, I was relieved to see the truck disappear down the road. I whistled back at the crow. My step was light as I approached the house.

Mother threw her arms around me and wept tears into my shoulder and then stood back with her hands on my shoulders. Dark and sweet cinnamon floated around our heads. Her eyes fixed on my face, seeking my eyes and she held me in a gaze. "Oh, Harlan," she said quietly, "will you ever find what you want?" I took that to mean she knew about me and Celie, as mothers do. Vanora came in and she took on some too. She wanted to know if I was going back to the carney, and Margy, when she came in, wanted to know how far I'd gone down the road. Ernie, who was twelve, stood back and appraised the goings-on. Then I gave

Mother one of the tens and she started crying all over again and blubbing that I was a good boy, her best son and whatnot. Soon we were all teary with red noses. To lighten the mood I took out the harmonica and started to play. Their eyes lit up. I lowered myself into a chair and they all sat around with rapt looks on their faces. Mother bobbed her head to "Blue Moon," a popular tune on the radio, and Margy and Vanora got up and did a little dance, bumping into the kitchen table and setting the kerosene lamp to teetering, which made us all laugh. Phil came in from chores and he stuck out his meaty hand and gave mine a long squeeze and said, "Dick, I'm glad you're back, Dick, we missed you, by gum." We were all misty then while the girls made a pot of tea and put cookies out on the table. I told them about the carney, leaving out the parts that reflected badly on me. As I said, I was a liar. They were curious about Early Big and thought Boss Man was taking advantage of men like me. And girls like Celie. But most they just wanted to hear about other towns, how women in them dressed and what the Folies said and did in their off time, and so on.

After a while I was tired of talking. Phil said, "C'mon outside then, Dick." He tipped his head toward the door. I followed him out. He had a mickey of whisky stashed in the barn and he offered it to me. Mother didn't approve of drink. She thought it was the first step down the road to damnation. "What she don't know, won't hurt her," Phil said. "Anyways, we're grown men, Dick, we deserve our little pleasures." We took sips and muttered stuff about the weather and how the animals were getting on. Phil was not much of a thinker or a talker. He'd taken to chewing tobacco. He offered the tin to me but I said it kept me awake and I wanted a good sleep that night. It was something of a lie: it reminded me of the old man chewing tobacco; I wanted no truck with his habits.

"Art's taken off," he said.

"I heard."

"Yeah, no secrets around here."

I hoped there were a few. "Is it Regina, then?"

"No. Winnipeg. Aunt Helen and Uncle Ralph. Remember?"

"Yeah. Mother misses her sister."

"He thought maybe they could put him up until he found something."

We stood in silence, watching the moon rise above the tree-tops. We took more sips from the mickey. I was getting woozy. I was not much for drink.

"Well," Phil said, "six o'clock comes round pretty early on a farm."

He stumbled to bed but I sat up for a while, heart thumping from all the excitement of the night. I took out the harmonica and played softly to settle my nerves. "Climbing Jacob's Ladder," maybe. Margy came in in bare feet. She was wearing a white housecoat with a raspberry pattern. She smiled and stood in front of me. I looked up at her. "You want something a little more peppy?" She nodded. Her hair, raven black, was done in a bob that made her look quite modern and swish. The little light in the room shone on it in such a way that made it gloss. "Stand up," she said. When I did she put her hands on my shoulders. Cornflowers, overlaid with sweet honey. She unfastened the top buttons of her housecoat. Her breasts fell out. "Hush, now," she said, "do not be frightened. Nothing's going to happen." She undid the buttons of my shirt and pushed its wings back and pressed her breasts against my chest. Her arms were around my shoulders. "Hold me," she instructed. I felt the coolness of her flesh, the points of her nipples. "Harlan," she whispered, "I want you to remember this. It is not sex. Forget about what's happening down there." She chortled. We both glanced down and chortled together. Not very elevating. "Just remember this moment. This is what you yearn for. You yearn for this—not all the girls you will chase and find. Can you remember?" My hands were on her hips and we were both swaying slightly. I croaked out: "Yes." Though I had no idea what she was talking about.

The next day I lollygagged about the house, telling more carney tales as the girls peeled potatoes and Mother fussed with a pot roast. She wondered if I knew "Church in the Valley," and I played it for her and she stood with her hands palm down at the table and hummed along with closed eyes. "Oh, that's good for the soul, Harlan," she said. Vanora and Margy wanted "Blue Moon" again and then "Red Sails in the Sunset," and they both claimed I had talent and was wasting it not being in a band. Toward evening I helped Phil with the chores: feeding the horses their oats, slopping the pigs, throwing hay and straw bales in the barn. "You've grown some, Dick," Phil said. "You got a man's muscles now—and a strong back."

"I learned a few things in the carney," I admitted.

He chuckled. "I heard."

Over supper the girls said Friday night was barn dance night. I had to go, they insisted. Phil went every week. "That's right, by gum, Dick," he said, "and it's a good time, too." Lots of girls, the girls said. Everyone has a good time, forgets their troubles. And bring the harmonica, too, they insisted. I promised—the one but not the other.

It was true. The place was filled with laughter and music and dancing when we arrived. The girls plunged right in, polkas, waltzes, square dances. I stood on the sidelines for a while with Phil. He raised his hand and waved at four guys seated on straw bales on the far side of the dirt floor. "I'm going over, Dick," he said. "Join us if you want." I said maybe in a minute. There was a girl with bobbed, orangy hair that was giving me the eye whenever she danced by. At a break I strolled over and introduced myself. "Harlan," I said. "Fay," she said. "But I know who you are. The carney guy." She laughed. It was kind of a horsey laugh, which suited her; she was tall and had noticeable shoulders. And good breasts. We did a polka or two and then a waltz. I had my hand on her back as we finished, and as the music died, I turned her toward me and put both hands a little above her waist. Nutmeg: you put your nose in the open tin and your eyes watered at its tantalizing, acid bite. "Aren't you the bold one," she said. "You learn that in the carney?" She was a cousin of a girl I'd gone to school with and was from Regina, getting a taste of the country life. Which she enjoyed, she told me: hoeing in the garden and slopping the pigs. She loved the sun and being in the open air. We were both warm from the dancing and I felt sweat on my lip. I took her hand and led her outside, around one side of the barn where it was private. We kissed. She had thick lips and a wide mouth and she liked kissing. I put my hands under her blouse at the back. She did not resist. We went on kissing. We rubbed our crotches together and she moaned. I moved my hands up her spine to the bottom of her brassiere. Just as I was fingering its little hooks, a voice came out of the darkness. "Here you are." Her cousin, Louise, appeared out of the shadows. "Stop canoodling, you two, and come inside for lemonade." I felt my member shrink. Caught in the act.

Inside I stood at the table with a glass of lemonade. It was good stuff, lots of lemon and sugar. I needed it. My throat was dry. Kay and Louise sat on a straw bale a little distance off, sipping their drinks and leaning in towards each other and laughing. Phil spotted me and waved me over. He passed me his glass as I came up and introduced the other men. "Dick here has just come back from the carney," he said. "All growed up, he is." They were Phil's age and older, two or three years my senior. They nodded and tipped their glasses at me. The lemonade was spiked with moonshine. I took a sip and was passing the glass back, but Phil said, "Go on now, Dick. You're a grown man. Take a drink like a man." I took one sip and then two. I felt woozy and teetered a bit as I passed the glass back to Phil; he and his buddies chuckled. "That's the good stuff," one of them said. I was just about to say I needed some air when Margy came up to me and told me Vanora was outside being sick. "I don't think she can walk home," she said. We found her on her hands and knees under a tree. In the moonlight she looked pretty green. She had her forehead pressed close to the ground and at one point vomited on my pant cuff and shoe. I rubbed her neck and Margy fetched water and after a while she started to come around. "I can do it," she said. "I can. Just don't let Mother see me this way." I wondered who had given her alcohol; I would have fancied a chat with him, man to man, fist to chin, but that seemed beside the point right then. The three of us walked slowly home in the moonlight. Margy whispered to me, "She means it, about Mother."

"Mum's the word then."

Margy poked me in the ribs. "Bad pun," she said. "But, yes, *non a vox ad madre.*" She was bookish, Margy, and she smirked after saying it but I was busy wiping vomit off my shoe and did not ask her what it meant.

It was the next evening around supper that the old man returned. He was hardly through the door when he spotted me. "You," he said, glowering, "I was glad to seen the backside of you."

I'd been playing the harmonica and I stood up, sliding it into my back pocket. "You want me to leave?"

"That's exactly what I want. Right out. March down the road. This here house ain't big enough for the two of us."

He was bloody-minded, the old man. There was no budge to him.

Mother had stood up, and Phil too, who'd been sitting by my side tapping his size fourteens as I played. Mother began: "Now..."

That's all she got to say. He glowered her way and raised his hand.

"You don't dare," I said.

He snorted. "I know this one, I know what he's up to."

He was a little shorter than me but wiry and mean; we would have made a good match. But Phil was standing beside me and he was trembling in a way that said he would not stay out of it. If he'd grabbed the old man in a bear hug, he could have squeezed the life right out of him. The old man clenched and unclenched his fists. I stared at that tuft of hair on the crown of his skull and the image of a crow crossed my mind briefly—and my own little rooster tail. I pushed the images away. The old man tugged at his handlebar moustache and then wheeled away, and in a moment we heard him preparing for bed in the bedroom. Mother was standing with her hands folded together, as if in prayer. The girls were silent. There was a vicious curl on Vanora's lip. Mother muttered something like *that's the end, the final straw*. In a few moments Phil tilted his head towards the door and gave me a knowing look.

We walked out to the barn in moonlight. "She's getting quit now," he said quietly. "Taking the girls and young Ernie and heading east."

"Don't blame her. She's taken enough of him. We all have."

Phil chuckled. "He'll be cooking his own food now."

I snorted. "Maybe he'll conjure meals out the air."

"Idiot can't even fry an egg."

"The bastard. He was going to hit her."

"Winnipeg." Phil looked out across the open prairie. The way he said it made it sound exotic as London or Paris. Far away and full of romance.

"It's the right thing."

"I reckon so, Dick. She wants to be close to her family. Aunt Helen and Uncle Ralph."

"The Beuchlers. Yeah, I know."

"I'm going too," Phil blurted.

"What? Winnipeg?"

"Naw. You know me. I'm a farmer, born and bred. I can hardly put a sentence on paper, and doing sums makes my head hurt."

"It's not that hard."

"For you, Dick, no. Me, I'm just a simple farmer. Plant the seeds in spring, harvest the grain in fall. There's good land out that way; Red River bottom land. That's for me."

"They got the drought too."

"That'll end. And people gotta eat. They got families to feed."

He claimed he was a dumb farmer, Phil, but he was canny. He wasn't missing a trick. Land was cheap; it was a good time to get in. In five years he'd have his own place and a house full of kids, maybe. Kids he wouldn't beat. He was slow-moving but in the way of a glacier. Nothing would deter him from his course. He'd get what he wanted; he'd get there. He brought out his tobacco tin, pinched off a chunk and slid it under his lip. He offered it to me. This time, I took a tiny pinch to be sociable. As kids we'd never been that close, Phil and me. He'd hung around with Art when we were in school. It didn't bother me; I was a bit of a lone wolf. And I distrusted Art. But that night, gazing at the moon rising over the barn, I felt as close to Phil as I'd ever felt to anyone. I knew I'd be able to count on him if push came to shove; and he probably felt the same.

He spat between his boots and grunted and I knew he was done talking for that night. We left it at that and went inside. Vanora was helping Mother fold clothes and was making little piles that she placed on the couch. She gave me a look. This wasn't just doing the weekly laundry and ironing. I nodded and let them get on with it.

In the morning I helped Phil with chores and then he started up the truck and honked the horn. The old man came out. He was driving Mother and the girls to the church for Sunday service. Phil and I walked. Thistles grew along the roadside and goldenrod, larkspur, and wolf willow struggled to hold ground among them. When we were seated in church Phil put both his big hands on his knees and breathed heavily. I enjoyed going to church. There's a quiet inside the walls of a church that occurs nowhere else and a hush inside a hymn that heals a troubled heart. I breathed in time with Phil and breathed in the holy silence of the homely little building erected by local men over decades, men who gave up Saturday afternoons to raise timbers and fit lintels. Church was one of the few places where I did not bounce my knees or glance around for escape routes and I wondered how preaching would fit as a way of life. A quiet life, you helped folks through their troubles. But too quiet, I decided, too low-key. Still, I felt the pull of it. There was something of the barker in preaching.

Mother prayed hard that day, her forehead crinkled, and when we came out, she stood and talked to the preacher a long time. The old man arrived and Mother and Ernie climbed into the truck. The girls were staying in town to eat at the café. On the way back, Phil and I were alone. The meadowlarks were singing and as we passed little sloughs, frogs that had been chirring away went silent. Milkweed and geraniums grew along the roadside. They were singing a tune as we passed by and I hummed along with them: *dona nobis pacem.* "I like that one," Phil said, "we sang it in school. Peaceful. Though I don't remember what the words mean."

"I like it too. *Give us peace*?"

"Yup. The peace that passeth all understanding." We walked in silence for some time. "We go into a long tunnel," Phil said. "At the end of the tunnel is a yellowish light, not bright, the hue of yellow. We kind of float toward the light through the tunnel, and when we come to the light, it folds us in, enfolds us, you might say, cool, comforting, clean water in a pool. Death."

"It's peaceful, then, not frightening."

"Nothing scary about it. The peace that passeth all understanding."

"Nice."

"A sort of immersion."

"Baptism, a second baptism."

"Baptism in reverse, you might say."

We left it at that. Dust drifted up from our boots. After a while I cleared my throat and said, "I'm going to head out east, too."

"You are? What about the carnival?"

"It's fun and there's money there, but it's a dead end."

"Fun," he said wistfully. "That would be a nice change. Fun don't seem to be happening much in this life."

"Anyway, I think the carney and me had better part company. Before I end up with a knife in my back."

"I heard about that." Phil chuckled and kicked some stones into the ditch. We walked for a while. "Anyways," he went on, "you're made for better things, Dick. You got—well I don't know rightly what it is you got. There's just something about you. You feel that?"

"Maybe." It was a lie. I'd been certain of it for some time. But unwilling to admit it and afraid to speak it aloud.

Flies buzzed around. The sun was warm and birds were twittering in the bushes along the roadside. Phil stooped and picked a little bouquet of daisies and black-eyed Susans. They were for Mother but he did not say so and neither did I.

"And she needs some help," I said. "Ernie is just a kid."

"There's no work there either, Dick. Winnipeg."

"I'll find something. There's always something."

Men were still riding boxcars up and down the country,

looking for work, but there was no work. The government was starting projects, like building stone walls along highways, and the lucky ones caught on there. *Relief*, it was called, relief work. Every now and then a factory placed an ad and three hundred men lined up for three jobs. Soup kitchens in Regina and so on were overrun with hungry men who were growing more and more desperate. There were riots and mounted policemen enforcing law and order with night sticks and clubs. The whole country was kind of holding its breath, anticipating a riot that would end with burning factories and shootings and deaths. "Class war," some were calling it in the newspapers, ordinary folks rising up against the powers that be. The working man taking back what was rightfully his. That was not my take. There were no politics involved as far as I could see: just a whole generation of men who wanted to make a decent day's wages and weren't being given the opportunity. They were just asking, Why did we fight to preserve democracy and capitalism if all that we sacrificed came to, in the upshot, poverty and humiliation?

Phil didn't say anything. He was not a deep thinker and what he did think he kept to himself. Maybe he was pondering over Mother's situation. I had no way of knowing what he was thinking. I hoped it was something positive.

"Anyway," I added, "she says Uncle Ralph will find me a place at the hospital."

"The laundry?"

"Yeah, he's a kinda foreman there, it's a big operation, sheets, blankets, all that."

"Huh. And you'd do that?"

"It's work. They don't pay much. But something else will turn up."

"Sweating all day in steam and heat, Dick? Stuck inside breathing stale air?"

"A man can get used to about anything. Art's on the killing

floor at the packers. That does not sound very enriching. No, laundry would be okay."

"You're an optimist, Dick."

"You make it sound like a character defect."

Phil snorted and kicked at the gravel. "You got a funny way of saying things. You should be on the radio."

I'd thought about that. I had a strong and appealing voice, people were always telling me that, and words just came natural to me, which is not always a blessing. Being quick with a quip can get you a punched mouth among men who have no other way of responding. The barker can end up a victim of his own glib lip. Being sharp of tongue was good on the radio, though, and if I'd known how to get a toehold, I'd have fancied trying it. I'd considered going into the station at Yorkton and checking out the lay of the land but something else came up all the time and I'd never got around to it. That was for another life. Art had run off to make his own way and Phil was a simple guy who didn't see his responsibility to Mother the way I did. So this life required me to put aside my own desires and take up the job the old man had abandoned. I was leaving that very afternoon, I told Phil. I'd hop a bus to Weyburn and once I'd made my way to a highway, try my luck at hitching. My duffel was packed. I'd hook up with Mother and him when they got to Winnipeg.

Part II

WINNIPEG WAS a much larger city than what I'd imagined. People seemed to sprout right out of the ground in front of you. Cars were thick on the streets, horns blatting. Horses too. Gutters filled with horse droppings and clouds of flies circling above. I'd seen pictures of trolley buses in newspapers, but up close they were noisy as they banged along on their iron tracks and made turns and stops: *clang clang clang*. Buildings five and ten stories high belched smoke from chimneys. Everything seemed to be pounding out a tattoo: *we're busy, get out of the way*. I did. I found my way to Aunt Helen and Uncle Ralph's, a narrow three-story house in the city's west end, postage-stamp front yard, sidewalk along one side and chicken-wire fence on the other. Wooden stairs leading up to a veranda. About three feet separated the house from those on each side: you couldn't fit a broomstick in the space.

It was just past noon on Thursday. I was exhausted from

walking and hitching rides. Aunt Helen welcomed me with a big hug and made me stand back so she could look me over. Lavender: sweet; I thought of it as purple and could handle it only in small doses. "My," she said, "you boys do grow up fast." She and Uncle Ralph did not have children of their own. It was obvious she was Mother's sister: same brown eyes, same bump on her nose, same lanky hair. She fed me and showed me the cot in the attic, where I was to sleep. I had a bath and flopped onto the cot and slept until a voice woke me calling: *Harlan, supper!* It was Uncle Ralph on the first floor landing. I came down, stopping at the bathroom to straighten my tousled hair. We had a stew with potatoes and carrots. When I filled my plate the second time and took another piece of bread, I noticed Uncle Ralph and Aunt Helen were grinning at each other. We'd said grace before eating but Aunt Helen said another one when we finished with the stew, then got up and fixed tea, which we had with cookies. She left then and Uncle Ralph and I sat across from each other.

He was chewing his lower lip. A short man, he had a brush moustache and it quavered when he spoke. "I'm so sorry, son," he began. A trembling finger touched one of his temples: a prairie sunset occupied the inside of his skull: a round, orange globe in a background of purple and pink and blue hues.

I'd been feeling pretty good with the stew in me, but the cookie I had in my mouth turned to sawdust.

"It was all set up for you, but then." He paused and wiped sweat from his brow. He was a man with a gentle voice.

I felt myself choking. I felt tears welling in my eyes.

"It was the mayor, see. The mayor from Brandon knew the big boss and he had a son who couldn't find any work, so our mayor, he tells the plant boss to make a job for this man's son—this man from Brandon."

I took some deep breaths. No one has died, I said to myself, no one has died. But I felt the tears welling up in my eyes.

"I tried," Uncle Ralph was saying, "but this mayor's kid, this Chuck—"

"It's okay," I said, "something will turn up." Though I didn't believe it.

"We can give you some pocket money," he said. "If you're—"

"I got pocket money. And you're putting me up, you've already done a lot for me, you and Aunt—"

"I'm so sorry, son."

He'd gone all teary-eyed and I got up and went over and patted him on the shoulder. "Don't fret yourself," I said. The climb up the stairs to the cot was long but I did not remember it when I lay down and stared at the ceiling. I'd never felt so low. I stared out the little window in the attic and there it was again, the cold and unforgiving moon. You could write a song about that, I thought, a song so sad no one could bear it. After a while, I drifted off.

The next day I was up early. Aunt Helen pursed her lips and shook her head from side to side. She was teary-eyed too. After eating toast and coffee, I headed out into the city. Men were lined up outside the factories, smoking and talking and pulling on their caps and cinching up the notches on their belts one more time. I went and sat on my haunches among them and played some tunes on the harmonica. They nodded their heads and some tapped their toes to the rhythm. There was work, I heard someone say, at farms down south, if you knew about slopping pigs and milking cows and taking care of horses. No wages. But room and board. Seven days a week on the job.

I left and walked to a park and sat for a while and studied the sky and felt low. When I took out the harmonica I could play only sad tunes: lost love, the end of things, cowboy ballads about betrayal and separation and death. A man came up to me after a while and sat on the bench too. "That's nice music," he said. "A nice mouth organ." He was older than me and had greasy hair and one walleye. I shifted about on the bench. He asked, "Mind if I have a look?" I passed the harmonica over and he studied it, turning it around in one dirty hand. "Hobner," he muttered, "the best. Worth a few bucks." He gave it back to me and got up and walked away. I patted it and lay it on the bench beside me, where its metal flanges twinkled the midday sun.

My eyelids were droopy. It was the heat of the day and I was still tired from four days on the road. And I was exhausted from the troubled sleep I'd had. I stretched out on the bench and closed my eyes and felt myself drifting off. But before I actually did so, I sat upright with a start and made certain the harmonica was securely in a pocket. The mouth organ. Why would a guy who smelled like a bum be interested in my harmonica? Two bucks, is why. What a rube I was. I had nearly fallen asleep and lost the one good thing I had going in my life. I was furious at myself and enraged at the bum. I got up and walked briskly around the park. Yes, there he was, sitting with his back against a tree, with the bench I'd been lying on in plain view. He'd been waiting for me to drift off so he could skulk over and swipe the harmonica. Welcome to the big city. I stood with my hands on my hips, glaring at him. I should have gone over and punched him in the mouth. Instead I took it as a lesson well learned.

I stopped for a sandwich and coffee at a café. When I'd paid, I was down to the ten-dollar bill. Almost certainly I'd be hitching south to find one of those situations on a farm. I didn't even know how to go about doing that and cursed myself for not having got the name of a farmer or a town. I was a rube.

Back at Aunt Helen's it was nearly supper time and I put back another big meal, sausages and cooked cabbage with potatoes, real down-home German fare. Aunt Helen insisted on seconds. After, I sat in the living room with Uncle Ralph and read the paper: war in Europe now seemed inevitable. British men my age were signing up in droves to be Tommies: stop the Hun. Was

I a Hun? Feelings were running high about what was happening east of the Rhine. Best to keep a low profile on my ancestors' origins, I thought.

There was a clumping on the veranda steps and in came Art with a smile on his face and a big hug for Aunt Helen. My heart skipped a few beats. I'd been feeling low but he'd lifted my spirits. When he offered it, I took his hand in mine and we held the shake a bit longer than usual. I hadn't thought I cared about him, but he was my brother; we'd grown up side by side and he'd never really done me any harm, only neglected me, probably because I was five years younger. "Dick," he said, "you're a grown man now." He appraised me, and I him. He'd developed the habit of twiddling his thumb and index finger. Quite a strong odour of aftershave came off him. Aunt Helen said, "Look at these two, will you Ralph, two big strong boys; your mother must be very proud." Art had stayed with Aunt Helen, too, when he first came to the city, and she treated him as if he were one of her own. We sat down. We shook our heads over the drought and tsk-tsked about what was happening in Europe. "War," Art said with disgust, "didn't we just go through one of them?" When we'd talked for a while with Uncle Ralph, Art said, "Come on down to the beer parlour with me, Dick. I'll treat you to a glass or two." My hesitation was palpable. Uncle Ralph smiled and nodded: *go on.* "C'mon," Art repeated, "forget your troubles for an hour or two. I'm meeting up with a guy who's a real card. You'll like the stories he tells." I agreed to go in a little while. Art got up and clumped to the entrance; he gave Aunt Helen another hug.

I went upstairs and lay on the cot with my ankles crossed and listened to the lug-dub of my heart. I was low. I'd come to the city with prospects and they had turned to ash. I was going to join the swelling ranks of the hungry and desperate. I was going to become a no-account bum. Soon enough I'd be taking a room-and-board job on a farm. That was okay for Phil, but

I had ideas and dreams and it would kill me. I'd be of no help to Mother, either. I lay and stared out of the little window and sighed. There were tall trees across the street, a breeze was teasing its leaves. C'mon, I said to myself after a while, shake off the self-pity. You're down now but you'll be up again soon enough. What harm will a beer or two do? I said that but I had a difficult time getting off the cot and making my way to the front entrance.

At the beer parlour I spotted Art sitting with another man, a guy with a squarish head and ears that seemed small and red. Art waved me over. "Dick," he said, "this here is Andy Finnick. He was just telling me a story. Go on."

"Aw, it don't matter," Andy said. "I'll tell it another time."

"No," I said, sitting. "Go on. I like a good story."

"All right," he said, leaning in. Art pushed a glass of beer toward me and gave me a wink. The story was about a man and his wife. Finnick had worked, it seemed, at a fishing resort up north the year previous, helping the owner at close-up time in the fall to cut wood: some of which was for fuel for the winter upcoming and part for logs to construct a third cabin on the site. The man and his wife were there; and Finnick and another man. The fishing and such were done for the season and they were the only human creatures in the area for miles and miles. Sometimes all three men climbed onto a wagon pulled by a horse and went out into the woods for the day to cut timber. Sometimes it was only two. On a particular day, Anderson, the owner, went out by himself. It was a Sunday, time off for the hired hands. "Well," says Finnick, "you'll never believe what I saw." He had a peculiar way of chuckling: *heh heh heh*. Art laughed. "I have an idea," he said, looking at me with a sly grin. Finnick said, "Yeah, you would, Art, you got the dirty mind." They both laughed. "It was the wife," Finnick said, directing his commentary at me, "the wife and this other guy, Roberts, is what I saw, together under this tree which I'd climbed and was watching from." Art took a sip from his beer and said, "And they were....?" Finnick gave us a grin and a chuckle that was more cackle than laugh: "What you guessing?" Art snorted. "You tell *me*." Finnick took a swallow of beer. "They were, you know, getting pretty hot together, kissing, which led to ... which led to even greater involvement, heh heh heh." Art snorted again: "*Involvement*." Finnick stared at me. "But that ain't the half of it." He sat back and took a swallow of beer and looked from me to Art and then back at me again. He had another sip of beer. "Dick," he said, "you ain't drinking no beer." I lifted my glass and took a swallow. I was enjoying the story; I enjoyed the way Finnick strung it out and made a point of holding information back for dramatic effect. "Well," he said, leaning in close again. "This here part is the kicker, now. A couple weeks later this Roberts goes out into the woods along with Anderson and you know what transpired while they're out there?"

Art said, "You went after the wife."

"Hah," Finnick said, "that would have been a totally different tale, heh heh."

"Tail," Art said, "that's a good one."

Finnick looked at me: "What did I say, Dick, your brother's got his mind in the gutter." He cackled again and ran one hand back through his black hair. "No," he went on, "I did not go after the wife, though she was a looker, big jugs, you know, it would have been an inviting prospect. But no." He cleared his throat and glanced over one shoulder, then the other and leaned in secretively. "We carried a gun on that wagon, see, there was bear around and wolves, and the gun was there for protection. A .303. Well, about two o'clock, hardly gone lunchtime, here's Roberts driving the horse at a clip into the clearing in front of the cabins. The gun has gone off, he says, Anderson is in the back, hurt bad. Only he wasn't hurt," Finnick said, "he was dead, he'd been shot dead. Now what do you think about that, Dick?" I was wondering what he'd been doing up in that tree in the first place. I'd been wondering what sort of a man climbs into a tree and then spies on people. A few words came to mind but I did not share them. Nor did I ask the question. Finnick had been so animated while telling the story, and he'd taken so much pleasure in gauging our reactions to it that it seemed wrong to cast a shadow over the proceedings with a question.

"That's something," Art said. "By gum but that is something."

Finnick cackled again. "He got away with it," he said, "accident, the coroner concluded, gun went off by its own self."

"There you go," Art said. "The way to kill a man is somewhere remote where the cops can't gather evidence." He took another swallow of beer. "We need another round of these," he said.

Finnick nodded and smacked his lips. "Next thing we'll hear," he concluded, "next thing is that they're getting hitched, Roberts and the wife, heh heh." He scratched at his skull with one index finger. Inside his head a monkey was hanging from a tree branch by one arm and grinning crazily as it swung back and forth, white teeth gleaming behind blue-black gums.

We drank beer and talked about what was happening in Europe. Finnick had heard they were opening recruitment offices down east. There was a rumour that Winnipeg would be next. Boys would be signing up and going off to Europe again to help out the English. Andy turned to me. "You're not much of a drinker," he said.

"No. It addles my brains. And I got few enough of them."

"I like that," he said, "I'm going to remember that."

Art got up to go to the bathroom. Finnick chuckled and repeated, *few enough brains.* Then he said, "Art tells me you got yourself some bad news."

"Bad news seems the only kind I get any more."

"Huh."

"Job fell through."

"Ain't it the way. You willing to work six to six?"

"I'm willing to work six to ten."

"Whoa. Let's not be giving no boss-man ideas." He took a swallow of beer and put the glass down carefully. *Plink.* "Well," he went on, "a guy down the coal yard where I work gave up today. City Supply, you won't have heard of it. Man name of Johnson. His lungs couldn't take it. Coal dust, you know? Some men's lungs can't take it."

"I heard," I said. Though it was actually news to me.

"You show up six o'clock tomorrow morning, you could have that job."

"That's Saturday."

"We work Saturdays too. Supposed to be until noon only, but a lot of the time—"

"I'll be there."

"Don't be in too big a rush." He signalled to the waiter for six more beer and then started in on the one in front of him. "It's a long day," he went on, "and it's dirty work, shovelling coal. Hard to breathe sometimes, and the dust gets all over you, in your ears, down your back. I've found it in my arsehole from time to time, heh, heh."

"I'll get on."

Art had returned and he settled into his seat.

"Dollar a day," Andy was saying. "It ain't much."

I drank off the beer in front of me and looked at Art, who shrugged his shoulders. I shifted my gaze to Andy. "Where you say this coal yard was?"

"I'll come by your aunt's tomorrow at five-thirty. I don't live but a few blocks away. We'll walk together."

"That would be swell."

"Swell is them beers coming on that there tray."

"I'll pay," I said, patting the ten in my pocket. My heart was feeling light; so was my head.

"No," said Art. "My treat. It'll be yours when you get that first pay packet."

Andy took a long swallow of beer. "You got an old pair of dunagrees you don't mind gets filthy?" He glanced under the table at my feet. "We're about the same size, Dick," he said, "same size feet. I got boots you can wear until you find something better."

We sat and drank beer. I'd been down in the afternoon but now I felt as if a fifty-pound weight had been taken off my shoulders. There was a lesson there, I reckoned: don't get down too low; don't get up too high. Easy to say but not so easy to do. I was feeling light in my heart and light-headed from beer and needed fresh air and wanted to get a good night's rest. I was not one of those who could show up at work on four hours' sleep. I got up to leave.

Andy said, "Bring a hat, too, you got one. And gloves, but that ain't important. A little coal on your skin. It washes out." He held his own hands up: black cuticles, grey wrinkles on the knuckles, coal under the fingernails. "Well, not entirely, heh, heh." He shrugged.

"It ain't blood," Art said, "it ain't the stench of death in your nostrils, it ain't the squealing of animals being stuck with the death prod."

Andy grunted. "And bring a sandwich," he called out as I walked toward the door. "Five-thirty, mind."

Outside, the wind was whipping the branches of trees, and leaves were falling in bunches. Autumn was coming on. On farms the harvest would be in full swing, threshing gangs moving from one spread to another, men living in bunkhouses and eating at a long table outside the house or in the barn. Long days on the fields under the sun and pleasant evenings sitting around on cots and chewing the fat. Someone always had a guitar to strum. The harmonica would have gone over swell. There would be cigarettes, their tips glowing in the semi-gloom as the moon rose over the land. Prairie sunsets: purple and orange and pink, swathes of colour that could take your breath away. A man would have a mickey and it would go around the circle sitting outside a granary that had become a makeshift bunkhouse. Someone would tell a yarn and it would be matched by another yarn, truths getting stretched—the twelve boiled eggs a guy had eaten becoming eighteen, the times somebody's girl hit her climax rising from six to sixty. Everyone smiling and nodding; no one fool enough to believe what was said but happy to enjoy the telling of the tale and have a laugh and forget their troubles. My thoughts wandered back home. I wondered about the dogs. Skipper had been replaced by Skeeter. I thought about Mother. Aunt Helen had heard from her. Any day now, it seemed, she and the girls and young Ernie would be leaving the farm. She would be well shut of the old man.

All that was miles away. All that was behind me. And I had a job lined up, after all my fretting. I was nearly back at Aunt Helen's. I did a little jig on the sidewalk. My heart was light and full of song. I thought: the great wheel turns. We never know what's going to come round next.

The sharp call of an owl interrupted my thoughts. I looked up into the trees. It was on the roof of a nearby house, ears pricked up. At the distance it was away, another man would not have seen it but I remarked the dark circlets around its eyes. It ruffled its feathers a few times and called again. Then out of the trees I heard: *acadicus*. I let out a long breath. Animals who spoke? To me? Three smaller owls fluttered down from a tree and sat on the roof. A family. Eight eyes swivelled my way when I whistled. Then they flew off as one. I stood for a while, wondering about what had just occurred. Why were animals talking to me? I shook my head to clear it. It was beyond me.

I wondered about Andy Finnick. He was a card but he was also devious and crafty. A man who climbed into a tree to watch a couple of lovers. A man who did not go to the police with what he knew. A man to be watchful of. He could get you into trouble, if you weren't careful. Still, he'd gone out of his way to help a country boy he hardly knew to get a job, when there must have been thousands he could have asked first: friends and family. Sometimes guys who knew about a job coming up charged five or ten bucks to help you get your foot in the door. It was just another aspect of free enterprise; not a very likeable one. In fact, the free enterprise system was proving to have a few cracks in it, and not only in Canada and the U.S. Germany was a shambles; that's why Hitler and his crowd had been able to come to power so easily it seemed; and Britain was a mess too. Wartime sacrifice to fight the Kaiser had turned quickly into peacetime belt-tightening once he had been defeated. And now instead of the Kaiser we were going to get Hitler. Soon enough people who couldn't afford a loaf of bread would be asked to buy bonds to back yet another war.

I thought again, too, about how important luck is in the way a man's life unfolds. I had been lucky to have an uncle in the position to find me a job in the first place; but then bad luck had undone that prospect when the mayor's son had got the job at the laundry; first I'd been up and then I'd been down. I had spent some black hours bemoaning my fate. Life had given me a kick in the teeth. But then I'd met Andy at the hotel and now my prospects were good again. Up and down; down and up. That's how life seemed to work. And most of what occurred had nothing to do with how hard you worked or how good you were as a person. So much came down to blind luck; it was not an encouraging outlook on life.

At twenty past five the next morning I was on the front steps with a sandwich in my pocket. Aunt Helen had fixed me toast and coffee at five and then gone back to bed. The sun was just creeping over the eastern horizon and sending a glow over the city. Birds were twittering in the trees. Squirrels were chasing each other down trunks and then digging furiously in the soil of the tiny flowerbeds bordering the front of the house, throwing up earth every which way. Squirrels go crazy in the autumn, burying things and digging up others with equal fervour and no logic I'd ever been able to puzzle out. Andy came down the street, swinging a pair of boots in one hand. He rubbed his eyes as I pulled them on. "Hangover," he muttered. "That beer was green."

The streets were coming to life: people hustling and bustling, cars stirring up dust, everyone in a hurry. Trolley cars were rattling along tracks, voices called out, horses whinnied and nickered. In the pale dawn light the city looked fresh and clean, radiating energy. I strolled along beside Andy with a bounce to my step and felt good to be there, taking my place in the mighty organ that was the metropolis.

At the coal yard, we walked up stairs to an office on the second floor. A little man with wispy red hair and thick glasses was seated behind a desk. He looked up from a ledger when we came in, watery blue eyes that peered out of cheeks that might have witnessed thirty or fifty years, it was impossible to tell which. "Dick here is looking for work," Andy said.

"That right," the man said. He looked me over quickly and then dropped his eyes to the ledger again. He'd marked the spot where he'd left off with one index finger. The inside of his skull was a tight criss-cross of green and red lines, a graph, a chart.

Andy coughed. "That's right, Mister Mitchell. You'll recall that Johnson packed it in yesterday."

The watery blue eyes swum up. "So he did, Finnick, so he did."

"So I need a new partner."

Mitchell looked me over more carefully than before. "You a farm boy?"

"Yessir."

"Farm boys got strong backs," he said. He seemed to be addressing the wall behind me. Or talking to himself. "Farm boys are good workers."

"I hope so. Sir."

"How's that?"

"I'm used to hard work."

"Is that a fact? Is that a fact, now?" He looked down at the ledger and moved his finger along a column of numbers. "All right, Finnick," he said, without looking up, "let's give him a try. Dick, you say?"

"That's right. Dick. Though my name is Harlan."

"All right, then. Dick Harlan."

Andy took a set of keys off a hook and we clumped down the stairs. At one end of the yard five trucks were parked at bays and men with shovels were filling their boxes with coal. It was usual, Andy told me, for new men to be put on yard work and for men who had put in their time working the yard to get the delivery jobs when they came open; they were more desirable. But Johnson's departure on Friday necessitated an alteration from routine. So I was doubly lucky in landing the job and getting to be on a delivery route. I knew what he was getting at.

When the box was loaded, Andy started the truck and drove it out of the yard. It was clear within a few blocks that he was a bad driver. He liked to talk, was the problem, and he waved one arm to make his points. The truck weaved around on the road as if the steering was out of whack; it crossed into the far lane capriciously for twenty frightening seconds with vehicles bearing down from the opposite direction and their drivers leaning down on their horns; then came swerving back with a

thump and a bump and crossed onto the grass strip that bordered the road, cutting up the sod before returning to the gravel
lane it never should have left. I found my hands fisted into white
knuckles. Andy muttered and cursed: idiots, watch where *you're*
going, pal. He was better in the back lanes. We were making
deliveries to houses in River Heights, a posh neighbourhood
located near the Assiniboine River. Three-storey brick places:
gabled front entrances, lead-jointed windows, two-car garages.
The homes of doctors and lawyers, businessmen, bankers, Winnipeg's well-heeled families.

Andy was better in the back lanes because the truck was
moving slower: he hit a garbage rack and scraped along the side
of a garage and brought it to a sudden stop behind a tall cream-
coloured house. We jumped down. There was a long chute on
top of the load of coal and we fit the hooks fastened to one of its
ends over the truck box and manoeuvred the chute to a square
wooden door inset on the outside wall of the house. Andy went
to the entrance of the house and rung the bell; a woman came
to the door and he went inside with her and moments later the
wooden square opened on hinges. I could just see his eyes peering out. "Drop the chute in," he called out, and I did. And then
I hopped into the back of the truck and began shovelling. The
coal rolled down the cute and into the house. "All right," Andy
called out after a bit, and I stopped shovelling. He pushed the
chute out of the square mouth and closed its little door, hinges
squeaking. In a few seconds we were back on the seat of the
truck, heading to the next address.

"How about that Mitchell," he said. "He's a study, what?"

"He struck me as a book man. Mind somewhere else."

"Mitchell," he said. "Odd name for a Jew."

"You think he's a Jew?"

"What else? The coal yards is all owned by Jews."

"He the owner?"

"The owner's son-in-law. The wife is ... well, you'll see. They say this Mitchell only married her to get a foothold at the yard. They keep it in the family, Jews. They're close to their money."

"So are your Scotsmen. So's your Mennonite."

"You know about them, Mennonites?"

"Fellow gave me a ride from Brandon into the city. He was pointing out colonies along the way. Your Mennonite, he tells me, is not just close to his cash; he comes at you, this fella says, with the Bible in one hand and a knife in the other."

Andy laughed. "I'm gonna remember that one, Dick. Heh heh."

It didn't matter to me where a person's ancestors came from. We were all Canadians, was my take, we were all immigrants of one sort or another and there was good and bad in every lot: Irish, Polish, English, Jew. The only thing that bothered me was when an Italian or English started going on about how wonderful it had been in the old country, how beautiful the hills or the winding rivers, and so on. If it was so great over there, I'd said to more than one, why did you come to this country in the first place? I had a mind to add: and why don't you go back if it's so damn wonderful over there? But I'd never said that second part.

The sun was up by the time we'd emptied out the first load. Andy had a pocket watch and he gave it a look. "Good time," he said, "we're making good time, Dick." He knocked over a trash can on the way out of the lane and drove the tires onto the trimmed grass of a corner lot as we came out on Sherbrook Street. I held my breath and studied the buildings going by. The sign on a café caught my eye. Coffee and a piece of pie would have gone down nicely. Andy was busy dodging cars swerving away from us in the opposite lane and honking and cursing other drivers.

At our first stop on the second load I was just pulling the chute out of the house's little coal door after the delivery when I

heard Andy say in a harsh whisper, "Dick, grab this now, Dick."
A brown paper bag came flying out of the basement and landed
at my feet: *thunk*. A moment later I could just make out Andy's
eyes peering out at me. "Into the truck," he went on, "under the
seat. Quick now." It felt like a bottle was inside the paper bag. I
stepped lively over to the truck and slid the package under the
seat. My heart was thumping, there was sweat on my lip. Andy
emerged from the house, calling goodbye to the missus, all
cheery, and proceeded to bash into the neighbours' picket fence
as we made our getaway. "Bring it out," he said when we were on
the side street, "let's have a better look." It was a bottle of wine
with French words on the label. "Crap," Andy said, "I meant to
grab whisky." He swerved past a parked car and lost control for
a moment getting back in the lane, and narrowly missed a giant
oak growing on the corner.

"It's our bonus," he said when we pulled into the next back
lane. I was thinking dark thoughts about policemen and jail.
Andy reached over and with a fist punched me lightly in the
arm. "It's our tip, heh heh, a way for the rich folks to thank us
for doing a good job." I stared out the window. "You don't like
it, do you, Dick? You see, the thing is, they'll never miss it. You
shoulda seen all them bottles they got in racks in the basement.
A man couldn't drink them all in a lifetime." We drove on in
silence. "Don't worry," Andy added, "there's no chance of getting
caught."

I snorted. "That's what everyone says just before they do get
caught."

"Well, lighten up. I'm careful, see, I only take where it won't
be missed."

The truck scraped along the side of a garage. Andy brought
it to an abrupt stop behind a bungalow made of large yellowish stones. He noticed me looking at the walls. "Them's called
Tyndall stone," he said. "They're nice. They got a quarry east of

the city. Pretty stones. Expensive." We off-loaded the coal and went on to the next address. "Now, Dick," Andy said, "this here burg is owned by our very own Mister Mitchell." It was a squarish, red-brick place with a chimney that ran up one wall. The fireplace on the main floor was gigantic, to judge by the space it took up on the outside.

"Quite the fireplace," I said.

"The real fire's not the fireplace," Andy said, "heh heh. I told you now, Dick, at this place it's the wife who's hot."

We set up the chute and Andy went inside. When he opened the coal door a few moments later he called up, "Red dress today, oo-la-lah."

I was doing the outside shovelling and didn't think I'd get to see it. But when the coal was in, Andy came out on the stoop and waved me in. "She's got lemonade," he said, "heh heh." I knocked the coal dust off my trousers and took my boots off at the entrance. She was short with raven black hair and skin so white it was almost translucent; red lips, an ample mouth. Breasts that made me swallow and look at the floor. The red dress fit tight everywhere. She was curvy and well-proportioned. She gave Andy a glass of lemonade and then put one in my hand. My throat was dry; I took a sip. Looking straight at me, she said, "And this is?"

"Dick," I said. "I'm new."

"You are. Freshly minted."

Andy laughed. She turned to him. "Andy," she said, "Can you do Mister Mitchell a favour and lay a couple shovels of coal on the furnace hopper?"

When he was gone into the basement, she came and stood right in front of me, her breasts touching my chest. The smell of vanilla came off her hair: I thought of it as white, fresh cream, sweet, but not over-sweet. Breath of mint. She had round black eyes that looked up into mine. "Kiss me," she said. My knees had turned to rubber. *Bad idea, bad idea,* was going through my head. But I put my hands on her waist and she looped hers behind my head. I cannot describe her tongue; I cannot find words for the way her crotch writhed against mine. Our bodies squirmed together, our mouths were hungry. We only stopped when the sound of Andy's feet clomping up the stairs left us no choice. I wiped my mouth in case there were traces of lipstick. Sweat had formed on my lip. She stepped away. "Tomorrow afternoon," she whispered quickly. "Mister Mitchell won't be here. Aaron. Every Sunday he visits his mother."

I lay trembling in my bed that night. I was a sinner and a cheat and so low a person that sweat broke out on my brow at the thought of Mother finding out. Surely, that must be the acid test: what would your mother say if she got wind of what you were up to? Bad idea. Should not go. Should go to church with Aunt Helen and Uncle Ralph and cleanse my mortal soul.

Her nipples were brown, I should have guessed from the raven hair. The insides of her thighs were soft and smooth as kitten down. She made squeaking sounds at first and then whispered: *more, give Sheeny more.* She closed her eyes with the effort and screwed up her lips at climax, her breath hot in my ears. "That was good," she said after, "so fast, so hard." Once again I was listening for sounds outside the room. Shameless. Low. The bed was big, the pillows soft, the mattress firm. *Should not be here, bad idea.* The knot had returned to my gut; my heart was racing. "Ari," she said "it's so terrible with Ari." She was running one finger up and down my breastbone and as she stroked me, she started to hum, "Truckin," a popular song. I would have enjoyed playing it for her on the harmonica. Her nails were painted a dark red that matched the lipstick she wore. For a short woman, her fingers were long and slender. "I hate him," she said finally. "Sheeny hates Ari. And always has." I was pulling on socks and pants, eager to make an exit. "Why marry him, then?" She sat up and pulled the blanket over her breasts. "How young are you, Dick?" I shrugged. I felt my ears burning. Why were people always asking me that? She told me they only married their own, Jews; she said something about wombs, a quotation from the scriptures, I gathered. Jewish women were only allowed to marry Jewish men; Jewish men could marry non-Jewish, but that was frowned on too. The womb quotation came up again. "It's awful," she said. "A kind of slavery and bondage." And sometimes, she said, the pickings were very thin; a girl had a difficult time finding a Jewish man who was good and kind and not outright homely. Like Ari. She shivered when she said his name. "He wants kids," she said, "of course. Sons. A son. He wants to jump on me. It's a wife's duty, he claims."

Bathsheba. That was her name, though everyone called her Sheena. It was a name from the scriptures, she said, the story of a woman who was made to suffer at the hands of her husband. Which she found appropriate. Bondage has been around since forever, she said with disgust. Biblical bondage is not the only kind going.

We stood at the entrance and kissed. I felt stirrings down under and she patted me there and laughed. "You're a feisty one," she said; "you, Dick, are something of a stallion." I was anxious to go and she knew it, and she gave me a glass of water before I left. And said, "On Saturday afternoons he goes to synagogue. Ari. On Sundays to his mother's. The patterns never varies. Up at six-thirty on weekdays, home at six for supper. Regular as clockwork. You can set your watch by him."

I walked a few blocks to a park and sat on a bench and rolled a cigarette. Filthy habit, I thought, it's going to be the death of me. I may have said it aloud. I puffed smoke into the air above my head and studied the sky and felt good about myself. On the stroll home there was a bounce to my step. I was not in love;

but I was in lust. Breasts, creamy thighs. It felt wonderful. It felt dangerous. Once again I was dancing on the cliff edge.

One day bled into another. We developed routines: we shovelled coal; Andy bashed the truck against things; at lunchtime we stopped at a café and I went in and bought coffee; and then we sat in the truck or on a park bench and ate our sandwiches. Andy brought out his tin of chewing tobacco; I rolled up a cigarette and we yakked about this and that. He was the son of a fisherman who had come over from Finland and his name was Andreas-Pekka but his mother had decided *Andy* was more suitable for a Canadian schoolyard. He had a sister and a brother, both married and living in the Interlake. He had thought to go into selling pharmaceuticals but as with most people our age he had been knocked off course by the Depression and settled for what was on offer, work in the coal yard. Maybe someday, he said wistfully. There was a lot of that going around. Defeated dreams; ambitions put off, long sighs and regrets. "Maybe Someday" would have made a popular song on the radio.

On the coal route he always went inside the house and I did the shovelling from the truck. It was hard work while you were at it, but then came the little breaks driving between addresses. Once a day something came flying up out of a basement and landed with a *thunk* at my feet: bottles of whisky were the favourite; every now and then an entire roll of cheese. "What are you going to do with that?" I asked the first time. Andy grinned. "I know a guy will take it off my hands for a couple bucks. Italian, heh heh, runs a restaurant." Worse and worse, I thought. Stealing a bottle or whatever now and then was one thing; involving a third party was another thing entirely. Tentacles reaching out into the world at large; connections that would suck you down. I told Andy. He raised his eyebrows but said nothing. So, yes, checkmate. It was difficult for the man screwing the boss's wife to take the moral high ground, even if he was right.

I thought about her all the time. Shameless. On Mondays I was relieved to be out of the vortex of lust which was spinning me further and further to damnation, but by Thursday began to get edgy from desire and by Saturday was tense and irritable with desire. Andy laughed and poked me in the arm but said nothing. One Friday at the end of work Andy told me we were taking the truck home for the night. Mister Mitchell had asked him to make a special delivery in the evening outside the city limits—a friend, Andy had the address. He dropped me off at Aunt Helen's; he had a goofy grin on his face as he waved good-bye. The next morning he drove up to Aunt Helen's at five-thirty, everything as usual, another Saturday of coal dust and bad driving. Except.

There was a dog on the seat, a wiry white mutt with irregular black spots, one covering an eye. Andy said, chuckling, "This here's Pitch." That was the big secret, apparently: he'd driven somewhere out in the country to make some sort of delivery— and had ended up bringing back the dog. I was banging shut the door of the truck as he told me about it.

"Howdy, Patch," I said, reaching out a hand to his muzzle.

"No," Andy insisted, "not Patch. Pitch." I gave him a quizzical look and said, "I reckoned with that eye patch and all—"

Andy shook his head. "Never thought of that. No, this here is Pitch, like coal, black as pitch."

The dog was all over the seat, his entire body wriggling. At one moment he had his front paws on my legs with his nose out the window on my side, his wiry tail in my face, *whap whap whap*. Then he was down on the floor, sniffing around my feet and jamming his nose into my crotch. I pushed him away. I tried shoving him down but all that did was make him jump back on the seat, and leap into Andy's lap, his tail hitting my arm, *whap whap whap*. The full force of his weight landed on Andy's crotch. He yowled and shoved the dog away. He was back at me then, wet tongue slobbering on my cheeks, drool dripping on my arm, breath like rotten fish. Andy chuckled: "Heh, heh, heh, you're a rambunctious one, ain't you, Pitch?" He was unruly, is what he was, the unruliest creature I'd ever come across. He should have been smacked, not indulged, he should have been brought in line. Dogs need to be brought into line. Pitch needed a little disciplining and I could have done that, but Andy was a city boy who did not understand that animals need a firm hand, not coddling and spoiling, and he was so taken with the mutt it didn't seem right to interfere. But I was happy enough to get out of the truck when we got to our first delivery and get shut of his whipping tail and drool and fish breath.

Dogs. Every second person in the city, it seemed, owned a mutt. They crapped in the street; they barked from behind fences; they came charging at you in parks and you didn't know if they were going to bite you or jump on you and slobber on your clothes. People who own dogs think they're the greatest: cute, smart, wonderful companions. They're a nuisance. They should not be allowed in the city. They're country creatures that need wide open spaces to run in, not fenced-in backyards and leashes. May as well have a kangaroo for a pet—or a wolverine.

I hoped Pitch was not going to be a regular thing. He wasn't. Just that one day, it seemed, that Saturday morning. On Monday we were back to the usual routine: walk to work as the sun rose; fetch the truck keys at the office; drive; shovel; return to the yard for another load; lunch; shovel; and so on. After we parked the truck for the night, Andy scooted up to the office to return the keys. There was a newspaper lying on the loading dock and I picked it up and glanced at the headlines. *Conscription Threatened. Innocent Victims Feel Force of War in Warsaw.* There were blurry pictures from the Polish city. I was so absorbed in reading that Andy came up and startled me. "It's all they print these days, the war," he said. "It's their way of getting us used to the idea."

"Men are signing up across the country. The recruitment office they set up downtown is doing a roaring business."

"Not this cowboy, Dick."

I looked up from the paper. Andy had a faraway look on his face. "There was a guy here at the yard a year ago or so," he began. "He'd fought in that last war, the war to end all wars. I want to tell you his story." I folded the paper and clasped it in one hand and we headed out of the yard. The guy, Andy said, had been in the trenches. Horrible: rats, soaked clothes, dysentery, bombs exploding in the face of the guy standing next to you. That's when the men weren't *going over the top*, straight into barbed wire and machine-gun fire. Stupid; the stockyards where Art worked were not as gruesome. Half the soldiers died before even seeing action. In one action more than twenty thousand lives were lost. This guy, Andy said, had not one good word to say about that war; not one. It was the lords of England against the barons of Germany. Only the actual fighting was done by farm boys from the prairies and fishermen's sons from the Maritimes. The lords and barons themselves were to the rear of the battle lines, studying up maps and sending carrier pigeons with instructions and eating off china with silverware while the ordinary stiff got bully beef, if he was lucky, and a shot of Dutch courage before being sent over the top. The kicker was this: the guy was one of a pair of twins; he survived but was subject to headaches and wooziness; but his brother was picked off by a sniper on the morning of the armistice. Crapola piled on more crapola, Andy said. "No, Dick," he concluded, "I ain't having nothing to do with no wars. I'll shoot myself in the foot first and spend the war in jail, if that's what it comes to. I'll go hide out on a farm."

On Friday night I was sitting with Uncle Ralph in the living room; he said, "Hitler won't stop now. He thinks Europe is his for the taking. He thinks the English are weak and the United States will stay out of it. He's puffed up like a little bantam rooster and he's strutting about the barnyard of Europe saying *I'll do whatever I damn well please, just watch me.* There's only one way to stop him now. The talking, the negotiating is over. The only way to negotiate with Hitler is with a gun."

"He claims it's justified. *Lebensraum.*"

"Ach, *Lebensraum.* There's always a fancy term for naked snatch and grab. Hitler has his *Lebensraum*; the bankers have their *aggregate demand.* All so much hot air." He glanced toward the kitchen to make sure Aunt Helen was out of earshot. "All so much pissing in the wind."

Phil was sitting with us. He'd come in from the farm he was working at as the hired hand to have supper with us and look around the city; and to hear the latest news about Mother and the girls and Ernie, who were on their way to the city by train, finally, according to Aunt Helen. Phil sat with his giant hands on his knees and nodded at what Uncle Ralph said but he himself offered nothing. His conversation skills were not great, but his appetite was, in a farm-boy kind of way. I doubt he knew what he'd eaten an hour afterwards; he shovelled the food in whether it was roast beef and dumplings or chicken stew with potatoes or whatever: *chomp chomp chomp*, the fork never stopping except when the knife was applying butter to a thick slice of bread. It was all as one to him: fodder; and it was to be put down as quickly as possible, burp.

Later we went out onto the stoop, just the two of us, for a smoke and a chat. "That war's getting closer," he said, "by gum. It'll soon be on top of us."

"I know. Uncle Ralph's right."

"Satan says he's been good for Germany. Hitler has."

"He would."

"Satan says they've got full employment over there. Not like here."

"Huh." We'd taken to calling the old man *Satan*, and not just because of Mother's disgust over the warlock business.

"You gonna sign up?"

"Me? You know me, Dick, dumb as a goat. I'll go on farming. Those boys gotta be fed. At least that's what the government tells us."

Zombies, men who chose to do that were called: avoid putting on khaki for one reason or another. There were other terms, too. Worse. Maybe Phil didn't know. I didn't say anything about that. I blew smoke into the autumn air and Phil let fly a giant gob of tobacco juice. "Me," I said, "I'm gonna sign up."

"Yeah. I guessed."

"King and country, all that."

"They all are. Jimmy Milko, the Zarestsky brothers. Signing up."

Pictures of men standing outside recruitment centres had been on the front pages of newspapers. The Germans had subdued Poland and were casting covetous glances toward France. Maybe England itself—Canada's home country, teachers had always told us—would be threatened, too. Above the blackboard at school hung a big map of the world, countries of the British Empire in pink. We'd sung "Rule Britannia" as well as "God Save the King," and "The Maple Leaf Forever." A long time ago. Peggy. I never had kissed her. I had heard from the girls that she was married to a dentist and living in Regina with two kids. Celie's fantasy was actually being lived by Peggy.

"I'm going to," I repeated. "Sign up."

"You do what you think best, Dick, but listen to this, and listen good now. Do not let on about your weird eyesight. Understand? You do, they'll turn you into a sniper. You know what's a sniper?"

"Yeah, 'course. Sharpshooter, kind of thing."

"Them snipers is the worst thing to be. You're on your own, up in a tree, picking off enemies with a rifle. It's cold-blooded, Dick, and lonely too. And God help you if the enemy catches you. They don't just kill you when they drag you out of that tree or church steeple, no. Chop you up alive, arms, legs, private parts, while you're still breathing and wallowing in your own blood and guts."

"All right."

"You seen a butchered pig?"

"I get it, Phil, I understand."

"Worst thing to be, sniper."

On Monday I said to myself, One more week and then I sign up. Mother and the family arrived on Wednesday. On Saturday I said, One last time. It was October, the nights were getting colder; most mornings when we walked to the coal yard our breath made ghosts coming out of our mouths and the shallow puddles on the streets had a thin skim of ice on them before the sun was high in the sky. There was more and more demand for coal. Aaron Mitchell put two more trucks on the routes. Coal was piled higher onto truck beds; the sun set earlier by the day; we worked later into the evenings. My shoulder ached some days and I'd be stopped short when one of them electric stabs of pain hit me and think of Celie: what was she doing, where had she gone? Had she stayed with Jimbo? Had she gone in for a secretary and begun her campaign to marry a banker? Sometimes Andy had to shout up from the basement of a house to break my reverie.

One day Andy wheeled the truck out of a lane blindly and bashed into the back of a car parked on the street. I was thrown forward and my head struck the dashboard. Andy cracked his skull on the steering wheel. We were both bleeding a little, but fortunately the truck was not going fast, so neither we nor it were damaged badly. The owner of the car came out of a house. There were scratches on both bumpers but otherwise the vehicles were okay. The owner looked at how the truck was angled coming out of the lane; he shook his head and said, "How did you manage to hit me?" Andy shrugged. I said, "A dog came flying out of nowhere into the street and Andy here swerved to miss it." It was a bald-faced lie. The owner pursed his lips.

When we were back in the truck, Andy said, "Thanks." I waved one hand in the air. He said, "I hate driving the thing, you know. You want to give it a try?"

"I don't got a licence."

"Licence? No one's got a licence, Dick." We changed seats. Phil and I had puttered around the farmyard in the old man's Model T when we were sure he was long from home. This was a different thing altogether. It was a Mack and it had a clutch for shifting gears. You still had to get a feel to get it into first, but after that, the transmission went smoothly. And the steering was firm and true; even in the back lanes I managed to manoeuvre well, and it was only backing up that gave me the sweats, and that only for the first few days. "You got a touch for this baby," Andy remarked as I backed up in the coal yard for a load. "Same as you got a touch for the ladies, heh heh."

I grew itchy as weekends approached, knowing I'd be spending time with Sheena. I'd taken to dropping by for a couple hours on Saturdays and spending Sunday afternoons with her. Sheena came to the door in wool knit sweaters that accentuated her breasts. She threw her arms around my neck and held me tight, and as we immersed in vanilla, we kissed. She dug her nails into the hair on the back of my head and I thought I would explode in my pants right then and there. In bed she grew more and more bold. "I ride you like bool," she crooned as she straddled me, nipples calling out to my lips. "Toro! Toro!" She wanted to be taken from behind and when we were at it she gasped and cried out, and I thought of the last time I'd been with Celie, and despite the hunger of lust driving me onwards, my guts shrivelled up and I wanted to do nothing so much as crawl under the bouncing bed and weep. I disgusted myself but I could not stop. *One last time.*

Vanora had landed a job at a pickle factory near the stockyards: a dollar a day on a factory line, stuffing gherkins into small jars, and sliced cucumbers and onions into bigger ones; Margy was waitressing at a café. Ernie went to school. Mother stayed at home with Aunt Helen and did cooking, washing, cleaning. The four of them inhabited the three rooms on the second floor and I bunked down on the cot in the attic. In the evenings we sat with Uncle Ralph and Aunt Helen and played cards or listened to the radio: it was all Poland and Hitler and Mussolini and the stock market bracing for what war would bring; threats of rationing on the way and conscription if necessary. People were beginning to hoard things: rubber tires and auto parts.

It snowed in early November. I bought a heavy jacket to work in. The last of the birds gathered in parks and swooped around in mighty flocks, preparing for the flight south. When I walked in River Heights on the weekends the heels of my shoes clicked sharply on concrete. One Saturday evening Vanora said over supper, "I'm going to the pictures tonight with a girl I work with at Dyson's. Della. You'd go for her, Harlan."

She was a brunette, not tall, but thin, so she seemed tall. Bouncy and wavy hair that fell to her shoulders; and bright green eyes that looked directly at you without wavering. When Vanora introduced us, she offered her hand and gave mine a manly squeeze, though her fingers were long and slender. Cheese: a musty tingle of milks and sweet acids. "Harlan," she said, "that's unusual; it's all Joe and Stan and Walt where I come from." She laughed and added: "But I go for the unusual. And Nora says you're nothing if not that." She smirked.

She told me everyone called her Del. It had started with her brother calling her Deltoid in school and had transformed. In the theatre Vanora sat between us and I got up before the feature and bought popcorn and sodas, making sure to pass them to Del first. The movie was a comedy and we were still laughing on the street as we made our way to a café for coffee and pie. She seemed always to be laughing or just about to laugh, which I found made me want to smile and laugh too. "You remind me of someone," she told me.

An actor? I offered.

"Hah," she said, "don't you think a lot of yourself."

I gave her my biggest smile. She placed an index finger on her upper lip and shook her head in mock disapproval. Like my goofy smile, it was teasing and flirting, we were testing each other out. I was intrigued by the way she'd gripped my fingers in hers when we'd first met, and by the fact that she'd called me out for having a swollen head. She must have found something in me attractive, too.

"No," she went on. "You remind me of a boy from where I grew up. He went in for a pilot not long ago, the Air Force. Came home on leave in a smashing uniform. You would not believe, Nora, what that uniform did for that scrawny prairie boy." She'd addressed her remark to Vanora, but she was looking at me. I felt I had to say something but I was without words.

Vanora said, "Harlan's thinking of the army."

"Not so much any more," I said, chuckling.

"And what," Del asked, "has changed your busy little mind?"

"You have."

"Hah. Me?"

"Oh-ho," Vanora said. "I have to hear more of this."

"Me too," Del said. She took a forkful of pie and pinioned me with those green eyes. It was a dare.

"Well," I said, laughing, "If I sign up, they'll send me to basic training and I won't get to look into those gorgeous green peepers anymore."

"Oh," she said, "you're such a fibber." She turned to Vanora. "You didn't tell me your brother was a shameless fibber."

"Well, not entirely," I offered weakly. I took a sip of coffee and looked at the pie on my plate.

Vanora said, "Do you two find it getting a bit steamy in here?"

Two guys in uniform came in. Vanora said, "That's all you see now, boys in uniform."

"And girls in tears," Del added. "They go together. War. Horrible. Men die but women are left as widows and mothers raising kids alone. They may as well be orphans. It's no way to live a life." It was a pronouncement; there was no room for argument.

I looked at Vanora and raised my eyebrows, and she raised hers at me.

We dropped Del off at her boarding house, which was only a few blocks away from Aunt Helen's.

Vanora waited until we came to an intersection. "Well?"

"I'm debating whether to ask her out."

"Debating?"

I couldn't look her in the eye. My sister, after all, what do you say to your sister about the attractions of another woman? Del had stirred something in me and the something was mostly above the waist, which was not the normal for me. That was intriguing. But it occurred to me this girl with the defiant eyes was offering a future, and I was not a future kind of guy. I was—what?—I was the barker, a carney freak and a fool. I wanted and then I wanted more, and that was no good for women like Del. She needed to meet Phil.

On Sunday afternoon I set out for River Heights with a spring in my stride and a woody in my shorts. I slowed as I crossed the bridge along Academy Road, thinking of Del's tinkling laugh and serious eyes, and my gut tightened slightly as I approached Sheena's house. I was the definition of the word *cad*. But I tripped up the steps to the back door and thought, *not this cowboy.* I clutched Sheena to my chest and opened her red mouth to kiss her; oh yes. Vanilla, sweet vanilla. I let her unbutton my shirt; and even though I had images of Del's lively eyes in my mind, and that gave me momentary pause, still I crushed Sheena's luscious breasts to my chest and threw her onto the bed and spread her trembling white thighs.

Shameless and low. *Should not be here. One last time.*

We went to the movies almost every Saturday night, Del and me. At first Vanora came too, but when we sat and talked only to each other, she took the hint and stopped accompanying us. Anyway, she'd started seeing a guy named Mac—MacDonald—and over Christmas things between them heated up, so Del and I went to the movies by ourselves. It was something to do. But it was not hot and heavy. There was some kissing on the stoop at Del's boarding house after the pictures, and once I put my hand up the back of her blouse, but she was wearing a heavy coat against the cold, so getting anywhere amongst the folds was awkward, and in any case, she pushed my arm away, gently but firmly. "You're in a rush," she said laughing. "But, we'll just wait on that, mister." I said all right and withdrew. "Though," she went on, giving me a knowing look and a grin, "you're probably used to getting what you want in that department." Was she fishing for information? Had Vanora been telling stories? Did Vanora know where I went Sunday afternoons? Maybe I came back flushed and rumpled. I hadn't thought about it, about how I might appear to others, and I thought then of Mother, and shivered. I did not want her to think me a low-life, the old man all over again. I decided Del had made a lucky guess about me and other women. But a tremor went through me.

At the beginning of March, Vanora came home from the pickle factory and said, "You'll never guess what happened."

"Hitler showed up at Dyson's and offered you a job in a munitions plant."

"Shush, Harlan," Mother said sharply. "Can't you see Vanora's upset?"

She'd been crying. There were red lines in her yes. "Sorry," I muttered. I was a dolt as well as a cad.

She threw her coat over the banister going upstairs. "Del's father died." Mother sat down abruptly, one hand to her chest. We were all standing at the steps that led upstairs. I put a hand on Mother's shoulder and she placed hers over it. He was driving home from the city, Vanora told us, behind the wheel of his truck. He and Del's mother were market gardeners who lived outside the city, in an area called Birds Hill. Del had said she'd take me out to visit sometime. She was a country girl; she loved the space and the quiet. He'd had a heart attack and the truck had gone off the road and into the ditch. He had died almost immediately.

"Forty-seven," Vanora said.

Mother put her face in her hands. "There are children at home," she murmured. "Tell me there aren't."

"There are," Vanora said. "Two boys of sixteen and fifteen and a girl of twelve."

"Oh, Lord," Mother moaned. "Why do these things happen? The poor woman."

"Mister Dyson came onto the floor himself," Vanora was saying. He had taken Del by the arm and walked with her back to his office on the mezzanine. He'd given her a glass of water and had her sit on the couch in the office. That was very kind of him, Vanora said. All the girls agreed. And he'd given Del the remainder of the day off with pay, very thoughtful for a Jew. And said to take as many days as needed to sort things out, there would be a job when she returned.

"He's a Jew? Dyson?"

"That was very good of him," Mother said. "Whatever his faith."

I wondered aloud how Del was handling the whole business. Vanora said she'd gone to the country to be with the family. I pictured her getting on a bus and sitting by herself as it made its slow journey into the country, wringing her hands and weeping silently while other passengers looked on and shifted about on their seats uneasily. She was a strong girl but losing a parent that way was about as much as anyone could handle. She needed people at her side.

It was a Thursday. On Saturday I took a bus out past the city limits and got off in the country, where I asked directions. It was cold and I walked fast, huffing ghosts into the chill air, shoes clicking on frozen ground. I thought, This is where Del walked only days ago, her little feet tripped over this very road. Lost in thought, I stumbled over a pothole in the road and hit an ice patch; my legs were out from under me in a second, and as I went down I caught in the periphery of my vision the sight of a rut that my head was going straight down onto. No, I thought, but there was no time to shift my shoulder so as to make it take the blow instead of my head. No.

I came to a few minutes later, or so I judged by the look of the sky above me. My head was ringing and a kind of pulsation was spreading from the back of my skull to my temples. I wondered if I dare try to stand; maybe I'd go down again and further injure myself. I was flat on my back and rolled onto one side and then slowly tried to get my legs under me. I stood. Jolts of hot electricity shot from one temple to the other, straight through my eyeballs: it felt as if they were going to explode out of my skull. I put my hands up to my temples; my head was hot, searing to my fingertips, the electricity shooting back and forth, forth and back; I expected I'd collapse and perish in the road. As

I stood in a daze, my body rocked back and forth for a few minutes, but then my balance came true. I took several deep breaths and squared my shoulders. The searing in my skull was subsiding but my ears were ringing. That's when I noticed the animal on the side of the road. Its back feet were in the ditch, but its front paws were on the gravel. It was a wolf, a big black-and-grey male. I supposed it had been watching me for some time, waiting to see if I would expire—or for the right moment to pounce. Neither of us moved. I studied its silvery eyes and long pointed snout. I was not carrying my pocket knife; I was not carrying the harmonica. If it came to that, it was going to be my bare hands against the wolf's bared white teeth. I swallowed. The wolf opened its mouth; yes, it had a full mouth of glittering teeth to sink into my legs, my arms, my throat. Its eyes were transparent blue. I looked at its glistening, deadly canines. It twitched its tail like a dog about to attack: slow, deliberate flicks. This is it, then, I thought. I stepped backward carefully on the icy road and found my most solid footing. I had no idea what I was going to do. Strike a blow to its chest, if I could manage, knock it out. I crouched a bit to protect my throat area. *Canis lupus.* The words seemed to come from the wolf's mouth. *Watching,* I heard. I dared not shake my head, but I blinked and thought, This is not happening. I felt a surge of blood move from the back of my skull to my forehead, and that made me blink again. The wolf stepped backward, but its eyes never left mine. And they did not blink. *Watching, not waiting.* The wolf wheeled, its tentativeness gone, leapt across the ditch, ducked under a sagging barbed wire fence, and loped away, into a stand of bush some distance off. I put one hand to my eyes. What, I thought, was that? I stood without moving for some time and then I stooped and picked up my hat, which had fallen off, and continued down the road.

I stopped after a while again and thought, *what was that?* The ringing in my ears had ceased and I felt steady on my legs but my mind was a-whirr: had I really heard a voice? *What was happening to me?* Befuddled, I walked on.

From the description I'd been given I recognized the house at half a mile's distance. A modest bungalow but recently painted white, with red trim around the door and windows, the first house I'd passed that wasn't shabby. Del met me at the door. How had she known I was coming? "Harlan," she said, "you shouldn't have," but I could tell from her eyes that she was glad I had. She gave me a hasty hug and then introduced me to her sister, May, and brothers, Mike and Pete. None of them remarked on anything odd in my appearance. I was beginning to wonder if the moments with the wolf had actually occurred.

Del's mother was at the kitchen table with a group of women, all wearing black. The casket was in the living room, pushed against one wall. "You needn't bother," Del said, reading my mind, "it's all family in there." Women in black were sitting with heads bent over beads.

"You're Catholic?"

"*They* are, those women with their crosses and beads and prayers. But my parents ... my parents had a falling out with the priest."

"I'm not much for church myself."

Del snorted. She said, smiling bravely past a red nose and swollen eyes, "Do you want a cup of tea?"

It was a miserable two hours. My neck and skull still hurt and I couldn't shake the feeling that my thoughts were running on two tracks at the same time: Del and the wolf. I met Del's mother and blubbed something and she nodded distractedly and I left with the sun going down fast and clouds moving in from the north. I turned my coat collar against the wind; I slowed at the spot where I'd fallen and cocked my ears to the ditch, but all I heard was the wind. A quick scan of the bushes produced nothing. *Watching, not waiting.* What could that possibly mean?

I came to the bus stop. An older man wearing a cloth cap was waiting and we nodded at each other. After a few minutes I saw a young man approaching in the distance. Tall and beefy. He was wearing pink slippers and pyjamas and had on a jacket much too large for him, and he was swinging his arms in a wild manner as his slippers flip-flopped over the ground. He was shouting, too, a kind of chant: *meerily-keerlie Mary blue barn, horily-borily corn underground.* Nonsense words. He strode past us, elbows flying this way and that, so we had to duck out of the way, and after a few dozen strides, he wheeled around and came back at us again: *gorbily-shnorbily inches not green, itsy and witsy cows margarine.* There was a rhythm to it but no sense at all. His black hair stood straight up off his skull. He did not seem to notice we were there. When the bus arrived, he pushed on first and strode down the aisle to the back, where he sat in the middle of the bench seat and thumped his hands up and down to his loud chanting. An older woman was sitting back there. She got up and came and sat in the seat across from me. She looked over and raised her eyebrows. Inside the close space of the bus, the chant was unbearable: *noggily-foggily beans underwear, stitchy and itchy lords over where.* We sat in silence as he thumped the bench seat and shouted his monotonous nonsense. The old man took off his cap, looked into it, put it back on. I shifted my feet. Do something, Harlan. I wanted to go back there and punch him in the face. The bus driver's hands trembled on the wheel. I thought, Stand up now, walk there, straighten this out; you're going in for a soldier, Harlan, take charge. But I did not. I stared out the windows; I stared at the floor. *Orggy banana Macdonald and whore.* The old man took off his cap again and then put it back on and took a lot of time adjusting it into place. The woman gave out a huge sigh, then stood up and strode down the aisle and stood directly in front of him. He seemed oblivious to her. She struck him hard on the cheek with her open palm.

She shouted, "Stop that!" He did. She wheeled and strode back to us and flounced into her seat. She gave me a long glare. The man had started up the rhythmic chant again, much quieter, his fingers thrumming the bench seat.

We drove on in silence to the city. As the fields gave way to scattered houses and then densely packed neighbourhoods, my head cleared somewhat. What had happened on that road? Had a wolf nearly killed me? Had I actually heard it speak? I was befuddled. *Watching, not waiting.* Had it meant it was watching over me? Keeping me safe? I was befuddled and I sensed something in me had changed. And maybe for the worse. The world had shifted in the slightest way and yet in a crucial way, too. I was no longer who I had been just days earlier. The seismic shift occurring inside me needed studying over.

That would come. So would I.

On Sunday I walked into River Heights, thinking, This one last time, and knowing it was not and feeling low about it but also whistling a tune from time to time. Oh, Harlan, I thought to myself, you big Dick. Slave of desire. Sheena knew something was amiss right away. "You've met a girl," she said, "you've got a girl." She was wearing a tight wool knit sweater and I put my hands out and caressed her breasts; they felt full and round in my fingers and I wanted them. Clouds of vanilla wafted over us.

"No," I said.

"Don't bother explaining," she went on. "It was bound to happen. I was expecting it." She led me by the hand to the bedroom. While we were taking off our clothes, she said, "She'll break your heart; you know that, don't you?"

I shrugged. "You got hold of the wrong end of the stick."

"All right," she said, "we won't fight about it; we won't fight."

What we did that afternoon was desperate and hungry and could only be called love by stretching the concept, but we were both in need of it, and after we lay side by side and I felt her trembling, and when I looked over toward her, the tears in her eyes matched mine. At the door she said, "Is this goodbye?"

"No," I said.

"But something has happened."

I shrugged again. "But not a girl. I need some time to think."

"You're a liar," she said. "But it's okay; I'm a cheating wife. We deserve each other. But watch yourself on that, Harlan. It may be a fatal weakness."

"I'll explain," I said, "sometime."

"Sometime," she said. "Sure. You won't be back."

"I can't live without those tits. I can't live without that ass."

"Go on," she said, snorting and shoving me toward the door. "If you come next week, good; if you don't, also good."

"I'll come."

"Hah, hah. We've had enough of that joke. No?"

"No."

"In any case," she added, "you did nothing wrong. You're good, Dick, you deserve a good girl. Forget what I said earlier. I didn't mean it."

"You did," I said laughing. "But it's okay. And I'll be back."

"Yeah, I guess."

From the look in her eyes, though, she was convinced that I would not be. What was it women saw in me that led them to think that way? To feel that I was always one step away from flight? It's your eyes, I told myself, the eyes of a dreamer. But it was not that. It was something else, something on the dark side of human nature. Something I'd got from the old man, I feared, an itchiness to keep moving.

Out of the blue, she said, "You should sing more, Dick."

"I got the harmonica."

"Not quite the same thing." She tapped my chest. "Singing comes directly from here. It eases the heart."

"So you say."

"So I know."

"I always liked 'Jack Was Every Inch a Sailor.'"

"A sea shanty, yes. Very good for the ailing heart. You should belt out a couple of verses every day."

"I'll keep it in mind."

"You'd be surprised."

Monday was the funeral of Del's father. She'd told me not to come and had said it in such a way that it was best to heed her. I moped through the week. I went out for a beer on Friday with Andy but was too miserable to enjoy it. I was terrible company and went home before eleven. I moped about in the house on Saturday, and in the afternoon sat on my cot and played sad songs on the harmonica. I liked the tune of "Can the Circle be Unbroken," but was puzzled by the title. Wouldn't the singer of the song want the circle of family and loved ones to be reunited in heaven? The circle was the symbol of unity and wholeness according to the Bible passages Mother quoted at us; why would a religious person want it broken? It didn't make sense. If you write a song or poem, shouldn't it make sense?

I sat up, tapping the harmonica on my knee. It was a spring-like day, and though the air outside was chilly, the sun shone in through the window and warmed me. The angle at which the glass deflected it into the room threw a splotch of golden light about the size of a silver dollar onto the wall. I stared at it for a while, having one of those blank moments. I felt my breathing slow and my heart with it. I might have sat that way for fifteen minutes or it might have been an hour, in a kind of trance, with my breath going deeper and longer and not a thought crossing my brain. Empty; I was empty. I became one with that pool of light, I felt as if I had entered it somehow and was beyond the cares and troubles of the world. I heard a voice behind me: *Harlan*. It was Mother's voice, the voice I'd heard as a child when I lay sick in bed and she had come to the curtain at our bedroom and whispered my name: *Harlan*. I jerked around abruptly, but the room was empty. I was sure I'd heard it. And it had not just uttered my name, the voice. It had said: *Time to go now.* I had known instantly what it meant without reflecting for even a second. I lay back down on the cot and folded my hands over my chest and stared at the ceiling. Time to go now.

The recruitment office was crowded: men and boys crammed into a tiny space filling out forms and talking in hushed voices, sweating over the decision they were about to make, and trying to laugh it off with jokes. We looked at each other and thought, That's the man who will be standing beside me with a rifle one day soon, that's the man I'll be counting on to cover my back. It sent a shiver down the spine. You gave that man a thorough study. The next day we were lined up at a makeshift doctor's office where men in white coats with stethoscopes around their necks prodded ribs and tapped knees and shone light in our eyes and checked our feet and looked into our arseholes before giving us the all-clear. Our vision was certified, our hearts cleared, our arches okayed. Nothing about our characters. We could have been murderers or adulterers or both. The army took us: heartbeat regular; feet adequate; vision normal. Also: cheat, cad, psychopath. Off you go to fight Hitler.

Report to an address on Dominion Street in exactly one month.

Shovelling coal was easier then. My heart was light, my arms whipped the shovel in and out of the load and tossed it down the chute. Twenty-eight days turned into twenty-four. I no longer winced when Andy threw a brown paper bag up from the coal door. I whistled as I worked. Less than four weeks and I'd be a soldier in uniform. I tried not to think about what Andy had said about that previous war, the war to end all wars: the pointlessness and brutality . This was going to be different. Hitler and his crowd had broken all the rules of civilized conduct and we were going to make that right. On Saturday night I went to the pictures with Del and afterwards took her hand over the table at the coffee shop and told her what I'd done. She was not as pleased as I'd anticipated. I squeezed her fingers. Ripe, soft cheese, butter and apples. "It's the right thing," I said. "Sometimes you have to do the right thing even when it's not the easiest thing." It was a rehearsed speech, which I had tried on Mother, who looked at me long and hard before pursing her lips and saying, "That's just so you, my boy, that's just so much my Harlan, looking for what he needs in all the wrong places." Del had a similar look on her face. She didn't trust me. She was the kind of girl a man settled down with, and I was the kind of man who got all edgy just thinking about settling down: we were heading in two different directions.

Her eyes blinked and I thought she might be angry. "It is the right thing," she whispered.

"But—?"

She looked away.

We both knew what it was. Though she admired men in uniform, it was a fashion thing, I'd come to understand; she hated the war, and she could see that I was dodging, ducking and running, like the coward I was, signing up to avoid making a commitment to her, which, as she guessed, scared the bejesus out of me. Things were moving too fast for me: responsibility, marriage; it felt as if walls were closing in on me. And not only that: there were lots of girls like Del and I was soon going to be wearing the King's cloth, for them to admire. We soldier boys could have our pick. It was an awful way to think, but I thought it. I was a low-life who wanted to live the carefree life of the soldier on the move. A girl in every town. Playing it free and easy. There were fantasies of orgies on the road somewhere at the back of my lust-addled mind. Girls in hotel rooms, girls in ditches, girls behind barns. It was rumoured that girls were happy to go with soldiers, and good girls, too, not just the trampy ones. Women prepared to make their own contribution to the great sacrifice the boys in khaki were about to make.

I couldn't say that to Del, so I said nothing. She took the initiative. "I won't be a war widow. And that's final." She'd withdrawn her hand from mine and was wringing it with her other.

Those were the words I'd been secretly hoping to hear.

"But," I offered in a voice with greater passion than I felt. "What about … what about love?"

She snorted. "Oh, Harlan. You're not interested in love. Look at you. Love? That is not why you rushed out to sign up without even asking me. You are such a liar you've begun to believe your own lies." It came out so sharply I tipped over the cup in my hands and coffee ran across the table and we both grabbed napkins to wipe it up. Hot coffee dripped from the edges of the table onto the floor. Del was wiping furiously at her fingers. I was reaching down and smearing coffee on the floor and the tops of my shoes. She started to laugh. I wadded up the napkin and dried my hands and reached across the table for hers.

"Go away," she said, pushing at my hand. "Go off to your war, go do the basic training. Live in tents and whatever. Destroy the German war machine. When you're done, if we feel the same way—"

"I'll feel the same way," I insisted, a shameless lie, and we both knew it, but I did not know what else to offer. I did sense, though, that I was wriggling off the hook, and my chest expanded with relief.

"We'll see." She studied me for a moment. "But don't lie to yourself, Harlan. You have something special. It's not just that people take a shine to you; they trust you; they sense the goodness in you and are drawn to you. But half the time you're so busy ducking and dodging you have no idea who you really are or how much good you might—"

I disliked this kind of talk. "We'll see." A note of irritation had come into my voice. She heard it, but the way she stared into my eyes told me she wasn't giving in to it. There was an element of toughness to her, despite the smile—and I found I was drawn to it, the way I'd been drawn to Celie's vigour.

"About us," she went on. "I'm not saying *yes*; if anything I'm saying *no*."

At the door of her boarding house she went rigid when I tried to crush her in my arms. We kissed quickly and I walked away into the night. It seemed to me that Sheena was right when she said that Del would break my heart. But I squared my shoulders and strode along the sidewalks with my head held high and thought, *We'll see* is right, I'll show you, young lady, but I had no idea what I would show her, other than my backside in flight.

We arrived in dawn light. There were few preliminaries. Our heads were shaved; dog tags issued; weight recorded; arseholes checked again—why, no one knew; kit distributed. The quarter-master had three sizes of everything; the uniform fits, he told us, emphatically, though arms were sometimes too long and legs short and caps tight to the skull. We were taken to the parade ground and instructed in standing to attention, at ease, stand down. How to hold the Lee-Enfield for parade, march, attack. Marched around the square. Yelled at, cursed.

From time to time announcements came over the public address system: Loose Lips Sink Ships. Hitler, Mussolini, Hiro-hito, "Axis of Evil." Tonight's movie: "Sergeant York." Stalin and Satan: Communism Corrupts.

The pack weighed twenty-seven-and-a-half pounds and the first time you pulled it on you felt the shoulder straps dig into your armpits. The material it was made of was heavy canvas; it was not designed for comfort. A blanket was fitted over the pack with straps and a mess kit attached to the main unit; there was a loop for a folding shovel to hang from, hooks for grenades, another loop for canteen, yet another for a bayonet. The helmet hung from the top of the pack, and a loop at the bottom of the pack was provided for *supplementals*, a gas mask if called for, wire shears. A thick leather belt was equipped with six ammunition pouches. The cap folded in half to be tucked under the shoulder epaulette. Loaded down with equipment as we were, we did not look like the actors in war movies.

We were ordered into the back of a covered truck and driven out into the country where we stepped down onto a gravel road. The sergeant barked; we moved out on the trot. It was a warm spring morning, the prairie sun climbing into the high blue sky; meadowlarks in the fields; frogs in the ditches. For the first fifteen minutes it was easy going; we were young, our muscles strong, our hearts eager; it was a lark, a sort of school outing. Then the twenty-seven-point-five began to dig into the shoulders; sweat started on brows; feet and calves cramped. Two sergeants were on the road, one to the rear, the other up front. They shouted and cursed us. These sergeants were another kind of barker altogether.

We crossed mile road after mile road. The sweat was running now. Men were beginning to cough; a guy up ahead stumbled and the sergeant barked the "c" word at him. We slowed. The trot turned into a shuffle. The sergeants barked and for a hundred yards the pace went up; but then it sagged again. A man to the rear fell to his knees; there were curses from the other men, who had to dodge past; the sergeant cursed and shouted that no one was to stop or they'd get a kick in the ass. The twenty-seven-point-five felt like fifty, its straps chaffing underarms, the blanket hot on the neck, the butt of the shovel banging the backbone. The man beside me was wheezing; the guy beside him was gasping over and over *bastards bastards bastards*. The gravel underfoot turned to loose stones; ankles were twisting, men staggered this way and that; one man bumped into another and the line became a string of dominos; two or three rows ahead a man barged into another, who stumbled into the ditch and fell face first into the grass. Guffaws. Laughter. "Get up, soldier," the voice of the sergeant blared; he leapt into the ditch and kicked the fallen man in the side. I was saying to myself, Push through, don't be the one to falter, one foot down and then the other. Finish this mile; finish this mile. We came to a bluff, oaks and poplars to the side of the road, shade, green grass. "Stand down," the sergeant up front barked and men stopped right where they were and fell to their knees. Huddled in the shade of the trees, we slipped the packs off our backs and unsnapped canteens and drank. Tepid water. Prairie grasses grew in the ditches; they swayed in a breeze, singing their familiar song: *swing low, sweet char-i-ott, comin' for to carry me home.* We sat with our knees akimbo and our elbows propped on them and our heads down until the sergeant yelled: "Move out!" My back ached, my ears rang. Don't be the one to falter; one more mile. Every joint in my body was aflame: ankles, knees, hips, ribs, elbows, wrists, neck. One more mile. The shuffle slowed further; we were barely moving. A man up front called out, "No, Loretta," and laughter rippled down the line. The road dipped and we saw in the distance the tarp-covered truck. Someone yelled *huzzah.* The sergeant barked, "Silence!" I staggered to the narrow band of shade at the side of the truck. We climbed in. On the ride out of the city there had been animated talk and suppressed laughter over cigarettes. On the way back, nothing. Heavy breathing. Fingers wiping sweat from brows. A couple soldiers collapsed and lay in fetal balls on the floor of the truck, feet twitching.

Back at the camp the sergeants had us line up for inspection. It was an effort to stand steady. Muscles twitched. Limbs turned to rubber. The sergeants walked up and down the line. Poked a soldier in the gut; told another to straighten shoulders. Eyes front, head erect, thumbs down, heels together. A captain was coming out to review. One minute crept into another. The man beside me began to shake. A chorus of coughs ran along the line. A soldier dropped to his knees. His cap fell off, his forehead slowly slumped forward until it banged into concrete. The soldier to his side flinched, as if he might be reaching to help. "*Eee-zee!*" the sergeant called out. I could feel my head beginning to swim; my vision was blurring.

The captain walked along the line. With his baton he poked at one man, then another. "Pathetic, sergeant," he said with emphasis. "This is the worst assembly of reprobates that this man's army has ever seen." The sergeant said *yessir*. The captain wheeled at the end of the line and stomped back into the Nissen hut he'd come out of.

The sergeant barked, "You hear that?" No one responded. "No," he said with satisfaction, "there's not a goddamn thing more to say." We stood staring straight ahead for some minutes, the twenty-seven-point-fives becoming heavy as cannonballs. When he barked, "Dismissed," there were men with tears in their eyes.

The man in the bunk beside me was short and round with fat red cheeks and a ready grin. "Larry," he said, extending his hand. He was from a small French town in the country west of the city. Laurent Coulombe. But *Laurent* was too difficult for limeys to get their tongues around, he told me, so it's Larry. He giggled; he was something you do not expect: a soldier who giggles. After we'd stored the twenty-seven-point-fives, we went outside for a smoke. Larry's stubby hands rolled out paper and tobacco with remarkable speed and he sucked in the smoke as if getting it into his lungs was the last thing he'd do on earth. "Filthy habit," he said, grinning, "and evidence of personal weakness as well. I really should quit."

"Me too," I said. "Tomorrow."

"Tomorrow sounds perfect." He slapped one knee and

chuckled as if we'd come up with the wittiest remarks ever uttered and blew smoke out both his nostrils. It was a pleasant spring evening. Crickets were busy in the grass. High in the sky geese were honking as they wheeled about, as if lost, first heading to the west, then north.

"Lucky bastards," I said, studying them.

"You'd like to be a fly boy?"

"They get all the girls."

Larry chuckled. "We'll get our share."

Images of the women I'd been with crossed and recrossed my brain: Celie in the final moment I'd seen her, blanket gripped across her breasts, her small worried face looking up at me as I grabbed the sill of the trailer window and began to hoist myself out; Sheena straddled over me calling Toro Toro! One filled me with horror, but both filled me with delight. Ruthie's breasts swaying above the buttons of her man's shirt. I was the fisherman and she was the one that got away. Oh, my lovely girls. I missed them already: their scents, their smiles, their little wriggles and jiggles. All out of reach. War was not just killing and getting killed, I was discovering: it was an exercise in self-denial that I was not finding easy to accommodate.

Larry grunted and inhaled and I felt nicotine run in my blood.

The crackly voice of the PA system said: Tonight's movie: "The Road to Zanzibar"; Remember Soldiers—The Walls Have Ears. We blew smoke in the air and watched the sun dip down the horizon. The sergeant came out. Mess time, he announced. We chucked our butts on the ground and stubbed them out with the toes of our boots. As we crossed to the mess tent, Larry said, "*Tabernac*, but every bone in my body hurts."

"*Tabernac?*"

"It's like *suffering Jesus*; there's no direct translation."

I grunted. "Did you go down? Out there?"

"No, but I might have. One of guys who did was right beside me. Dixon, who's two bunks over. Bastard sergeant kicked him in the ribs."

"They're bastards all right."

We had crossed into a world where there were bastards who forked out shit, and we were the ones who ate it. There was no point complaining about it; there was no point in even thinking about it. Go about business and shut up, that was the rule best followed. Larry knew it, and I did too. There were soldiers on the line who did not and it was going to be painful to see them learn the lesson.

Six o'clock reveille startled us awake. The piercing blat of a bugle. The guy in the bunk to one side groaned, "The fuck is that?"

Somebody farther down called out: "Shoot that bastard."

"Stick that bloody horn up his arsehole."

We stuffed in hard-boiled eggs, greasy bacon, and toast and coffee. The sergeants marched us around the parade ground. Blisters had formed on the tips of my toes. Calf muscles screamed in pain. The twenty-seven-point-five dug into the shoulders; the straps chaffed the armpits. When the sun was clearing the tree-tops, the covered trucks arrived and we climbed aboard. Smokes went around as the truck rattled over the streets and into the country. We lined up at attention on the same gravel road, rifles at port arms. Right face. Move out. After the initial screams from the muscles, it wasn't so bad; we thought we knew what was coming. Leg down, leg up. Think past blisters; don't think at all. Foot down, foot up. Breathe in deep; exhale slow. It was the blank-the-mind business all over: go down into whatever pain there was and keep descending through that pain into a zone where there was nothing but emptiness and the simple animal instinct to go on. Don't be the one, don't falter. Foot up, foot down.

The spot with the trees shading the road came up. Fall out. A few men did just that. I slipped the twenty-seven-point-five off and sat in grass. *Swing low, sweet chariot.* Larry came over and we shared a smoke. My heart was racing and sweat continued to run down my cheeks. Larry's were flame red. We drank from our canteens. Fall in. We stood in a hastily formed line at attention. The sun beat down as the sergeants walked in front of us. Port arms. Thumbs down, heels together. A soldier three along went down to his knees, then face-first into the gravel. A sergeant walked over. "Get up, you bastard!" He kicked the man in the ribs. A meadowlark called from the ditch. The frogs had resumed their chirping. Otherwise, not a sound from the line. Move out.

Down the gravel road. It was a test, it was a way of hardening us up; it was brutal, stupid, and inhuman, and there was nothing to be done about it except grind it out. As with so much of life, I was coming to see, it was a matter of getting through it and coming out on the far. Slog, plod. Empty yourself and pretend it was not happening and live to fight another day.

As I lay on the bunk after lights-out the muscles in my calves jerked and in the night I woke with a start and had to rub cramps out of my feet. Beside me, Larry snored on. Everyone snored. Soldiers ground their teeth; some whistled through their noses; others groaned and grunted. It was a symphony of torment and suffering. I lay and listened and began to laugh quietly and then had to hold my ribs to keep from bursting into a roar. Was man really made in the image of the Almighty Himself? I thought of Mother: had she been witness to the racket in that bunkhouse, to the smell of farts emanating from every second cot, her faith would have been put to the test. What a sad and sorry lot is mankind: driven by desire, betrayed by bodily functions but ever ready to theorize and pontificate on the meaning of life. Ever ready to brutalize fellow human beings. Kill and be killed. Turn into a Nazi.

Nazis everyone called them, but there were a lot of ordinary German men in their army, I reckoned, as there were ordinary men doing their duty in ours; and we had our share of bastards, too, but no one wanted to admit that: it was them against us, and they were bad and we were good. That didn't make sense to me: Uncle Ralph was Ralph Beuchler and for years he had written letters to his uncle, somewhere in Germany, a baker who'd had three children, one of whom had gone to the nearby polytechnic to study dentistry. Were either of them Nazis? Or were they ordinary folks getting on with life, no more a Nazi than I was? Propaganda, was what it came down to. People had be riled up to make the sacrifices necessary for war—to die by the thousands on battlefields, to live by ration books back home. That was understandable, as far as it went. And Hitler's dream of controlling all of Europe was monstrous; he had to be stopped. But that did not make every soldier in the German army a monster. I thought these things but I dared not say them.

After mess in the morning we were marched around the parade ground and stood to attention and then ordered into the trucks again. This time they drove us outside the city to a firing range. A quartermaster issued ammunition and the sergeant lined us up in front of targets some fifty yards off. "You're firing," the sergeant barked, "the ten-shot Lee-Enfield .303 field rifle, the best rifle in any army anywhere." He explained how the bolt action worked and how to aim through the rear sight to the front. There's a photo of me at the range, sighting down the barrel: butt fast to the shoulder to absorb the impact of the recoil; left arm extended down the barrel for stability; cheek on the stock for steady. The twenty-seven-point-five has been replaced by a lighter pack and the blanket is not there. Remark the belt; the stance of the feet, the puttees.

"This is your best friend," the sergeant barked, brandishing the .303 over his head, pointed to the sky for all to see, "more important to your life than the man beside you, more reliable than your girl. Take it to bed with you, coddle it, cherish it." He grunted. "It's been called the *smelly*, and you can call it that, if you're a fool. I recommend you give it your girl's name; I suggest you make love to it as you would your girl back home."

We went from *ready* to *aim* and stood in the *fire* position. Feel the blood in your temple, the sergeant told us. Listen to your heart; breathe in, and then breathe out. In and out. "Are you with me? In and out. Stop tittering. You're grown men, your life depends on this." He was a rifle-training instructor and his voice told you he had a sense of humour behind the barking; he was not an outright bastard like the drill sergeants. At his command we flicked safeties off. We were keyed up to fire. I felt my arms begin to tremble. Was everyone as nerved up as I was? We all seemed to be shaking and vibrating. Port arms, the sergeant barked. Stand easy. "And remember," he barked, "you fire as you release your breath; and you squeeze the trigger, not jerk it." When we'd regained control of muscles, we returned to *fire* position. At fifty yards I could see creases in the paper target and a flaw in the way one of the circles was printed. This time he called out Fire! I thought of my last conversation with Phil and placed two bullets at the bottom of the twelve-inch target, then two into the largest circle, one off the target entirely, and so on. Not one near the bull's eye; no fancy results. A nice scattering of ten shots, but not a grouping, nothing to give me away as a marksman. I saw the sergeants studying Larry. We stood down while the targets were being collected by a soldier operating some kind of contraption. We were marched fifty yards to the rear. While we were firing again, the sergeants studied the targets, which the soldier had brought down for examination. I made sure not to place shots near the bull's eye, but my thoughts were occupied by Larry, two positions down from me. His hands moved through the bolt movements as if he were playing the piano.

Click click click click. The same dexterity I'd seen when he rolled cigarettes. He got his ten shots off before I had fired five. *Crack crack crack crack.* He couldn't possibly be firing each time on the release of breath. To one side of us, the sergeants held the targets up for closer examination; one of them muttered something; the shooting instructor glanced at Larry over the top of the papers. They moved us back one hundred yards; a few men muttered they could hardly see the target; then we fired again. Though at that distance I could see every detail of the target clearly, I made sure two shots missed altogether. It hurt my pride a bit when I knew I could have achieved a perfect score, but recalling what Phil had said about how snipers were knifed and gutted on battlefields cured any pride I might have been inclined to indulge. Larry seemed to be oblivious to the attention directed at him by the sergeants. He seemed to be having fun. At three hundred yards some men did not hit the target once; I missed twice in a scattered performance that I was proud of. Pleased at my cunning. I studied Larry's target; there was nothing unusual in it; nine out of ten hits on target, scattered. It was the speed of his firing that was remarkable: he seemed to regularly get off ten shots to my five, whatever distance we shot from.

We stood down. We climbed back into the truck and drank from canteens as the truck rumbled back into the city. Cigarette smoke curled up to the roof of the canvas tarp and floated out the back end. I said to Larry, "You shoot fast, my friend."

He looked at me quizzically. "And here I was feeling proud of how many times I hit the target." He giggled.

"We did okay."

"We did. But my effin' shoulder is starting to hurt."

"Bruised probably."

Larry snorted. "Does nothing in the army come without bruises?"

"The food?"

"That bruises my stomach," Larry said, giggling.

I blew smoke to the roof. "That bruises my sensibility as a diner."

Larry giggled again. "You got a funny way of putting things, 'arlan."

Dixon said, "He's got the gift of the gab, that one. Shoulda been one of your shysters."

He was dark-haired with a thin black moustache. I recalled he'd come close to falling on the jog-trot the first day and had flopped straight onto his bunk when we had been dismissed, the twenty-seven-point-five still strapped to his back. He had a ready smile, a barrel chest, and a bit of a smoker's cough.

"I hope that's a compliment," I said.

He grinned and went into a coughing fit.

"Filthy habit," Larry said.

"Tomorrow, we quit."

It was still early in the afternoon when we finished lunch in the mess tent and walked back to the bunkhouse. Mighty flocks of birds were flying around the parade ground; one of the oaks closest to the street was dark with crows, there must have been almost a hundred roosting in its branches. Spring sun was beating down. We had an hour to kill and inside the bunkhouse some soldiers had set up a dice game, but Larry and I went out onto the stoop for a smoke.

I studied the end of my cigarette and said, "*Smelly*?"

Larry giggled. "It's the serial numbers, a guy said, on the Lee-Enfield."

"Huh." I had noticed when we were reloading: SMLE something.

"They jam, you know."

"I'm not, as the man says, surprised to hear it."

"Metal overheats in the magazine mechanism; a kind of smoke drifts up."

"No doubt it smells. No surprise it's called *smelly*."

I didn't mind shooting drills but firing the rifle had made me aware what the whole purpose of our going through basic actually was: we were training to efficiently kill other men. Shoot fast, shoot accurate, kill often and without thought. There was a bayonet attachment at the end of the rifle barrel and using it would come one day soon. You stuck the blade in the enemy's gut, I gathered. That did not sound pleasant. The recruitment posters had made signing up seem glamorous, but war, no matter how you cut it, was basically authorized murder and a pile of horseshit.

The sergeant came toward the bunkhouse, tramped up the steps, threw open the door, and blew a whistle. When he was gone I stood and chucked my cigarette butt onto the grass. "McDorn," I muttered to Larry, "I don't care for this guy."

"McDork," he said, giggling. "*Le batard*."

"The bastard of all bastards."

We lined up on the parade square for inspection.

When we were at attention he stamped up the line. "What's this?" The soldier he addressed looked down his tunic. "Button undone. Give me ten." The next guy's boots had a scuff. Ten push-ups. One soldier's cap sat askew. Another had not checked a strap on the twenty-seven-point-five. McDorn had thick fingers and he poked each man in turn in the chest. He waited while each soldier did the push-ups. Some did not meet his approval; repeat. The sun was beating down. Sweat ran down my cheeks. My vision began to blur. A soldier raised a finger to flick sweat off his face. McDorn barked out *twenty*. Button not polished; thumb not pointed straight down. Beside me Larry was breathing hard. I shifted my eyes but kept my head pointed forward: sweat was coursing down his inflamed cheeks. Two men down from me someone coughed: Dixon? McDorn glared down the line. When he came up to Larry he barked, "You hot, soldier?"

Through gritted teeth Larry said, *Yessir*. McDorn snorted. "Not the right answer; in this man's army you're never hot; never cold either; got that soldier? You're always just fine." Larry said, *Yessir*. "Give me ten." He stood directly in front of me. My eyes were fixed on the tree with the crows in it: a particularly big one had a tuft of feathers sticking straight out the back of its head; it was opening and closing its beak rapidly, not unlike the way that thin-lipped McDorn was opening and closing his ugly bastard mouth. I suppressed a smile. He jabbed his thick finger into my breastbone. "Ten," he said. No explanation. I dropped to the ground. I kept my spine level to the ground through each push-up, as he had instructed. I stood to attention. He glared at me. We were enemies; it was in his eyes and it must have been in mine: *fuck you; fuck you*. He moved along the line. When he came to Dixon he gave him an extra hard poke in the chest, a shove. For a moment Dixon lost his balance. McDorn snorted. "You the man coughed earlier?" *Nossir*. "Don't believe you, soldier. Gimme twenty." Dixon dropped to the ground. By fifteen his back swayed; he was gasping for air. On the final push-up he could barely lift his torso. He wobbled to his feet. McDorn laughed. He stepped back and barked down the line: "What we got here is a soldier who can't do push-ups; what we got here, grunts, is a soldier who needs to practise. Twenty more, soldier." Dixon dropped to his knees. It was clear what was going to happen. At five one arm gave way; Dixon's shoulder hit the ground. He did two more. Beside me Larry was making whimpering sounds. Soldiers up and down the line were breathing heavy. On ten Dixon fell flat on his face. McDorn waited for the count of three. He stepped close and kicked Dixon in the ribs. Beside me Larry flinched.

"Bastard," someone along the line muttered.

McDorn leaned over. "Soldier," he barked, "you're not half done. Soldier, these men you call your comrades are waiting on your sorry ass; hop to it!" He kicked Dixon again. A ripple of tiny movements ran up and down the line. Toes twitched. McDorn glared one way, then the other. He kicked Dixon one more time, then stepped back and continued the inspection. When he was done, he stood at the far end of the line for some minutes. My knees were rubbery; beside me Larry was breathing hard. The soldier beside me was clenching and unclenching his fist. Five minutes turned into ten. Sweat coursed down my cheeks; my back under the twenty-seven-point-five was wet with it. Ten minutes turned into twenty. McDorn glared along the line: would another man drop? Stand easy. Dismiss. Two men near to Dixon leaned over and put out hands to his body. "Leave him," McDorn barked out, "leave that piece of shit where he lies. Goldbrick."

"Does anyone ever shoot them?" Larry was sitting beside me on the stoop, smoking before the call to supper. Dixon had lain on the parade square for an hour and then come staggering into the bunkhouse. I had poured my canteen over his head and Larry had poured his down Dixon's mouth. He'd swallowed hard. His eyes had rolled around. He was out on his bunk, had not moved a muscle.

"They should be shot," Larry repeated. He glanced over his shoulder and added in a harsh whisper, "Kill the bastards."

"They get beat up if they show at the bar," I said. "A good shit-kicking."

"So I've heard."

"Three or four guys jump them. If the bulls don't interfere, they get theirs back." I was referring to the military police, called *bulls* by ordinary soldiers. They tried to protect the sergeants from being beaten up.

"But it makes no difference. Next set of recruits, same thing."

"Probably they enjoy it. Men who enjoy hurting others also enjoy being hurt themselves."

"Go figure."

I blew smoke into the air. "The human animal, there's no accounting."

That night we sat on the stoop and watched the sun set. I brought out the harmonica and played "Sunshine of Your Smile." Larry hummed along and soon Dixon came out and joined us. His face was pale but he seemed in good spirits, so we let things lie. I played "My Devotion." Dixon thumped out the beat with one foot and tapped his hand on one knee. "You're good on that," he said. He had an uncle who played trombone in a swing band, he told us. He stroked his thick moustache as he talked. He'd played the piano as a kid. "Can't carry the piano in your back pocket when you go off to war," he said with a chuckle. Larry giggled. Dixon blew smoke into the air and we looked at the moon as it came into view over the treetops. Dixon said, "You know 'Cow Cow Boogie'?" I told him I'd never heard it. "Upbeat," he said. "Peppy." I played a few numbers at quicker tempo and he smiled. After a while his head fell forward and his jaw rested on his chest. Larry said, "You all right, Dix?" He nodded but when he raised his head his cheeks had gone white and his gaze was off-centre. The inside of his skull was full of swirling waters, rapids, froth.

"Bastards," Larry said.

"He'll get his," Dixon muttered. He stood slowly and looked at the moon for a while, hands trembling at his sides; then he went into the bunkhouse.

Mail call was four in the afternoon and one day there was a letter for me from Margy. Mother was suffering some kind of stomach problem and had gone in to see a doctor and been sent for tests. Nora and Mac had married on the sly and were living together in a boarding house with a forgiving landlady; usually, Margy wrote, landladies rented only to singles—no visitors after ten o'clock, no couples. She had not heard from or about Del since Nora had moved out. I hoped she was well. It had been only two weeks since we'd separated but it seemed half a lifetime ago. How could that be? The demands of basic: they occupied most of a man's time and drained all of his energy; we were drilled from dawn to dusk and fell into beds exhausted. And we were isolated from everyone we'd ever known: families, girlfriends. That was the point of basic, it seemed: to isolate men from affection and drill energy out of them, while at the same time building loyalty to comrades-in-arms and filling every moment with army concerns. Del was in another country, the country not-army, and I was glad our romance had ended as it had. I was sad, too; but overall glad.

By the end of third week we trotted the gravel road at a good clip. Spring was turning to summer; wind and rain gave way to sun and breezes. In the fields, farmers were ploughing: the rich ones with tractors, the others with teams of horses. As we trotted beside the fields, I hummed along with the grasses: *comin' for to carry me home.* We continued shooting at the range. Larry had been pulled aside one day and made to fire from a special rifle equipped with a twenty-round magazine. Apparently there was a record for getting off rounds at three hundred yards in a minute; thirty-eight hits on the twelve-inch target, by a British instructor during the Great War. When he adjusted to the bigger magazine, Larry hit thirty-four during the *mad minute*, without missing the target. Everyone was disappointed he'd fallen short of the record by only a few rounds. But firing a rifle the way he did, he was bound for the infantry.

The quartermaster issued gas masks, which we practised taking on and off at speed, on our backs, while trotting. Bayonets came next: soldiers in other units, we were informed, used the "pig sticker," a spike bayonet, but we were issued the blade style, some with serrated edges. On the training ground we fixed them to the boss end of the .303 and ran at dummies, uniforms stuffed with straw. Thrust, rotate half turn, withdraw; thrust, rotate, withdraw. The .303 grew heavy in my arms. More practice with the gas masks; more running at straw-stuffed dummies. Two more excursions to the country to trot through the farmer's field. One more session shooting .303s at targets. Our leg muscles were taut and hard; our arms lean and muscular; we could trot five miles at a good pace carrying the twenty-seven-point-fives. Our shooting was adequate, if not brilliant. We approached the end of our training. We'd become soldiers in the service of His Majesty's realm. Everything from our earholes to our arseholes had passed muster.

"I hear they're moving us west," Larry said one night as we sat out on the stoop.

Dixon wrinkled his brow. "What, not Ontario?"

"It's the Japs they're worried about now. After Pearl Harbor."

I said, "So, no Hitler?"

"They're pushing Hitler back in France."

"They say they went down by the thousands in Normandy. The Krauts were waiting with machine guns."

Dix coughed. "Sitting in pillboxes, they were."

"It wasn't us. We can be thankful for that."

"Poor bastards."

"*Tabernac*," Larry said. "I joined up to fight Hitler, not no Japs."

"It's what I hear," Dixon said. "When we get our orders, it's west we go."

"First there's furlough."

"Jesus, yes," Dix said. "That gal of mine is getting a working over, let me tell you that right now." He went into a coughing fit.

Larry giggled. "A month's a long time without any."

Dix asked, "You got a girl, Larry?"

"I do."

"You don't want to get in the habit of saying them words," I muttered.

Larry asked, "Which is that?"

Dix laughed aloud and punched me in the arm. "*I do*. See what I tell you, Larry, this Dick guy and the quips."

Larry said, "He talks big but he's got a girl, too. He's headed to the altar."

"I'm headed to whoever's sweet loving arms will take me."

"That's the ticket," Dix said. "Love 'em and leave 'em." He stroked his moustache and grinned.

Talking racy made us all edgy. It had been a long time. We were soldiers now, ready to die for our country. Didn't we deserve a little something back?

We watched the moon turn brighter and brighter. It was a clear night: stars twinkled overhead. Birds were twittering in the bushes. On that farm down south Phil would be finishing evening chores and heading to bed; *six o'clock comes early around here*. It struck me I might never see him again. Or Art either. Cut down on some field somewhere far from home. I hummed a few bars of music that had popped into my head. A song seemed to be taking form in the recesses of my brain. It pleased me, but it also startled me; I wondered if maybe there were many things going on inside a man's skull that he couldn't account for in the usual way.

Over the PA system the gnarly voice said: War Bonds, Your Family's Future. This Sunday's Chapel Service: What Does Sacrifice Mean? Stalin's Soviet Union Is Your Enemy, Soldier: Better Dead Than Red.

Dix coughed and asked, "What did you do about the postings?" There had been sheets with lists on them on the bulletin board of the officers' hut. Each soldier was asked to indicate where he might like to be placed. All bullshit, of course, they'd assign us at their whim; but we had all dutifully penned in our names.

Larry snorted: "It's the infantry for me."

"Of course, you shoot too good," I said. "You're Machine Gun Kelly without the machine gun."

"That was a mistake," Larry said. "Infantry is *merde*. I always wanted to drive one of them there tanks."

"It's too bad about that record," Dix said. "A few more seconds and you woulda beat out that Brit bastard."

"*Mon dieu,*" Larry said. "Would have been nice to beat a British."

I felt the same way. All we ever heard was Sergeant Toffee-Nose of the King's own, private whoever from the something foot. Hadn't Canadians distinguished themselves throughout the Great War? Weren't the Aussies the fiercest fighters in the British forces? We were just colonies, and agents of the empire were constantly sticking it down our throats, so that after a while we believed their propaganda ourselves; they'd not only made a colony of the land itself, but of our minds, too. If Larry had beaten the record of that Brit rifle instructor, he'd have made a mark for the Canadian forces—and Canada itself.

Dix said, "I'm for the infantry too. Too dumb for anything else."

I said, "I put down for transport."

"Transport?"

"I enjoy driving trucks. And they got motorcycles, too: *vroom, vroom.* That looks to be some fun."

Larry giggled. "That looks to be certain death. On two wheels."

"I probably won't get in. If it's down to who you know, I'm buggered there for sure. And if it's down to luck, I don't got much in that area either."

"Transport," Dix said. "Now why didn't I think of that?"

I was surprised when my name was posted under TRANSPORT.

A captain lined us up for inspection on the parade ground. We were to be checked out again by medics, he told us: eyesight, heart rate, blood tests that told them about inner workings. They didn't want a man taking a fit behind the wheel; that kind of thing. Then there would be driver training; some would pass, some would not. After that there was learning the workings of internal combustion engines. It was a weeding-out process: the steadiest nerves, the quicker wits, the most reliable hands when it came repairing the engine.

Why they had to look up our arseholes again remained a painful mystery.

Driving, I was already good at; I had a knack for it. I'd had a peek under the hoods of trucks at the coal yard and picked up a few things: the quickest way to replace a fan belt; how to adjust two-barrel carburetors; where the thermostat was located. With a screwdriver in hand, I had a feel for air and fuel intake valves, I could transform a sputtering engine into one that purred like a kitten almost as fast as Larry could fire off fifty rounds.

On our last day of basic we were jittery on the parade square but McDorn took no notice and made the final inspection long and painful: gimme ten, gimme twenty. "I'll give him five," Larry muttered when McDorn's back was turned. His hand was clenched in a fist at his side. "Easy," I whispered, "no point in screwing up now." We pushed down the usual grub but drank beer in a special tent set up for us and at ten o'clock we were loaded onto trucks and driven to the city centre. We had our orders in our pockets. *Wainwright, Alberta,* mine read. For two weeks I was my own man, free to follow my own desires. Oh, my wonderful girls. How I missed you.

I'd decided not to see Del. Clean break. She'd made her position clear. Boys she'd known in her school days had gone down on the beaches and others were *missing in action* shortly after as the Allied armies pushed farther and farther east into France:

a Zaretsky, a Spelchak; their families had been sent telegrams that were supposed to soften the blow but actually made matters worse. What did *missing* mean? It created false hope, Del had told me. War was brutal for men in action, she acknowledged that, but for wives at home it was pain and suffering and she wanted none of it, so she would not be waiting for me outside the gates of the barracks on Dominion Street and she would not be waiting for me at the bottom of the steps at Aunt Helen's, either. I was released from her and commitments that came with her, and, consequently, relieved. My breathing came easier than it had in weeks.

Did rump roast swimming in a gravy Uncle Ralph called *Swiss* ever taste as good as it did that night? Roasted potatoes and carrots. Dumplings. Germans may not excel at a lot in the kitchen, but one thing cannot be cavilled with, even by the harshest critic: dumplings hot from the pot on the stove. Through supper Aunt Helen stared at the shortness of my hair. Ernie studied me with wonder in his young eyes. Mother touched the fabric of the uniform with her fingertips and said I'd lost weight, I needed to put on ten pounds. Uncle Ralph had the latest news. After supper he spread a map of Europe on the dining room table. Countries were in different colours. He'd drawn a line in blue ink to show the advance of Allied troops, from the west coast of France farther and farther inland. Paris, he asserted, would be reclaimed any day. In no time at all Hitler would be pushed back into Germany. You see, he said, sounding as if he were the man on the radio news, he made the mistake of fighting on two fronts—Hitler—an error of judgement that was costing thousands of German lives and victory in the war. Our boys, he explained, meaning Canadian troops, were mostly to the north in Europe—and in Italy. "And you'll be joining them," he said, placing his hand on my elbow, as we studied the map. I told him about rumours around boot camp. "Ah," he said, "yes, Japan and the Far East, now that Hitler is on the run."

"Better weather," I said, repeating the joke among the recruits.

He snorted.

"But more disease," I went on. "Jungle disease."

"In any case," Mother said, her voice tinged with anxiety and fear.

"Right. No point putting the cart before the horse."

Mother was standing to the side, chewing her lower lip, looking unhappy. She'd been against me joining up and she had not changed her mind. She was a mother. Let someone else do the fighting, was her position; let someone else's son die on a battlefield far away.

We dropped it at that. I went out onto the stoop and lit up a cigarette and looked at the stars and the moon. They calmed me. I'd been agitated from the time I left the barracks, excited to see my family and excited in ways, too, that I could do little about. A month without a woman's skin against mine had made me edgy; I needed to adjust folds and other things in my pants. Sheena's breasts inside her form-hugging sweaters crossed and recrossed my brain, my tongue could almost taste them. I was a man without a woman. My throat was dry. I blew smoke into the air and sighed. Nicotine. A pale substitute when a man needed what a man needed. I was charged up with a stallion's energy and nowhere for it to express itself. I whinnied and laughed at myself for doing it. Then I threw my head back and yowled. It did not help.

The next night Andy and Art were waiting for me at the beer parlour. I put a dollar on the table, enough to buy twenty glasses of draft beer. "My turn," I announced. Art nodded approval and Andy said, "The King's own coin right there, heh heh." We drank.

"Coin of the realm," I said, a soldier's saying.

Andy said, "You're looking very trim, young man."

"They ran it off us. And the food."

"You'd be a cinch on the coal shovel, Dick. The guy with me now, he swings the shovel like my grandmother. And she'd dead. Heh heh."

Art said, "It went okay?"

"It was pretty tough at first. But, yeah, it went okay." There was no point going into details. They didn't want to hear anyway. No one wanted to know. In fact, I myself didn't want to know about the battles in Europe: the enfilading of German foot soldiers; what actually happened when a grenade went off beside you. These things were better left in shadows while the war was in progress and returned to the darkest corners of mankind's awareness as quickly as possible when the fighting was over.

Andy tipped his glass at me. "You got—what, ten days?"

"Eight now. I'll blink and it will be down to one. Then we'll be eating shit again."

Art said, "Andy here heard quite the story about a soldier come home on leave."

Andy chuckled. "Maybe," he said, "Dick doesn't want to hear it, him being a soldier with a girl back home and all." He had a devilish look in his eye, part old-fashioned fun, part challenge.

"I don't have a girl," I insisted. "But I'd like to hear the story. Go on." I finished my second glass.

"So, okay," Andy said, leaning in. "This soldier right here in town doing the basic, same as you were, Dick, he hears a rumour about his wife. He hears that she's been screwing around with another guy while he's doing the soldier thing. It's not just from one source. A buddy. His sister. He's some riled up over a beer or two and about to go AWOL and do her in, stick a knife in her or whatever but his soldier pals calm him down and remind him that a man hangs for killing his wife, soldier or no. It's a sobering thought: kill your cheating wife but hang for it. One of those out-of-the-fat-and-into-the-fire alternatives, which is to say, no alternative at all, heh heh. So he gives the whole matter some deep thought. He ponders on it while waiting for his leave. He makes sure when he's leaving camp to tell a few men how he's looking forward to seeing his sweet wife, a sergeant included: just wants to love her all up, kind of thing. She's waiting for him when he arrives, and he doesn't yell at her or nothing of that kind, according to the neighbours, no shouting, not even a scowl. Instead he does what? You tell me, Dick? Instead he throws both arms around her in a crushing hug. Yes, he's a big man, did I mention that—barrel chest, thick arms kind of thing—and he throws both them big arms around her and just crushes the life out of her. He strangles her to death with love. Can you beat that? There's cops and an investigation, of course, but he hires a good lawyer, one of your shyster types who's always getting his name in the papers, and here's the kicker: the judge rules it's not murder—as the wife's family would have it—but manslaughter, one of the lower levels of manslaughter, at that; they let him go back to his unit after thirty days. Can you beat that now, Dick? Death from too much love."

I drank too much beer and stumbled back to Aunt Helen's knowing I'd have a hangover in the morning. I was feeling blue and wanting the warmth of a woman and irritated that I was stuck in a situation where nothing of that was on offer. I took the harmonica out of the pocket of my tunic and sat on the stoop and played a few melancholy tunes. It was late. A man walked down the street and tipped his hat at me. I gazed at the moon and stars for a while and smoked a cigarette and then played another sad tune. The sound of a woman's heels clicking along the sidewalk arrested me. She came to the bottom of the sidewalk and stopped. I saw the red glow of a cigarette in her hand; after she blew smoke into the air, she walked towards me. I noticed her high heels and the cut of her dress and the jaunty angle of the hat she wore. "Soldier boy," she said, as she came up to me, "you're blowing that as if you're lonely."

I tapped the harmonica on my knee. I'd been giving a go to "Blues in the Night," which was on the radio a lot that spring and summer. "Some of those chord changes are giving me a hard time."

"Hard time," she said, laughing.

The way she held her cigarette reminded me of someone. And that laugh. She was thin with hollow cheeks and I thought maybe she was hungry. I said, "There's a diner at Portage, I could treat you to a nip and chips."

She laughed again, high pitched. "That's really kind of you, soldier boy, but I actually had something else in mind. If you know what I mean."

I looked up into flashing dark eyes. Ruthie, that's who she reminded me of, Ruthie who'd swept up in her Stutz Bearcat and left me on the side of the road nursing an erection and befuddlement. "Is that so?"

"I was just heading to my place, up the block." She nodded to the three-storey building at the bottom of the street, apartments.

"The block down the block," I said, laughing.

She snorted. "I've got a bottle of gin there. Not the best, but passable. We could have some fun."

I was on my feet and sliding the harmonica into the pocket of my tunic.

She reached out her free hand and squeezed my arm. Mint: Mother grew it under a window on a south-facing wall of the house, a heady childhood-laden odour, my knees felt weak. It radiated off this girl. "I'm Tina."

"Dick."

"Oh, I should have guessed that. Dick. Yes."

We walked a few steps and she said, "You're good on that thing."

"It calms me," I said. "When my nerves are all jangly."

"You're probably good at other things, too. Dick."

Though it was mixed with ginger ale, the gin still tasted of gasoline, oily and skunky. The first sip gave me an instant headache. I put my glass down. "Well," Tina said, "we're not really here to drink, are we, Dick?"

I reached out to take her in my arms but she side-stepped and put one hand out to caress my face. With the other she reached down. I shook like a leaf when she put that hand on me and said, "What have we here?" There was not a lot of kissing but I held her close for a while under the sheets just for the pleasure of smelling a woman's hair and feeling a woman's skin. I was in too much of a hurry and it ended fast. She laughed and patted my leg. We lay back on the bed with a cigarette each in our mouths, and she put her crossed arms under her head and stared at the ceiling. "We'll do more later," she said, "you can have me again. Slower."

"I'm always in a rush. I've been accused of it."

"I can see that. I can see your toes tapping in your eyes, if you know what I mean."

"Life is short."

"Um. And you mean to cram in as much as possible while you can. It's a good philosophy. Especially in wartime. I subscribe to it my own self."

"Thing is, you never know what's just about to walk around the corner."

"You never know."

"Could be a girl in high heels with gin in her room."

"Could be a soldier boy playing sad tunes on the harmonica."

When I kissed the nape of her neck, she squirmed and moaned, and when I ran my tongue along the inside of her thigh she murmured *ah hah, that's so good, don't stop.* She wrapped her legs around my hips, delicate small feet digging into my sides, I could feel her ankle bones pinching my ribs. Though I had no intention to, she repeated *aha, don't stop, aha,* and I shifted around so I could kiss her breasts as we pumped away, and she made grunting noises, it was glorious, wicked abandonment, without thought or consequences, as sex should be but mostly is not. Beads of sweat ran down my cheek; there was perspiration on her upper lip.

.We lay side by side and I looked out the window. Stars were visible over the treetops. "I should go," I said.

She ran her fingertips along the tops of my shoulders. Her breath on my neck was warm and spicy. I pulled on my pants and was buttoning up my tunic. "Soldiers usually give me money," Tina said, "but I go for your sad tunes, Dick, so this one is on the house."

I blinked. My face betrayed what I was feeling.

"A girl needs a dollar, too, Dick. It's the way of the world."

I fumbled with my buttons taking it in. How I had I not suspected? Once again I'd been proven to be a rube. I swallowed hard. "I'm happy to give you a dollar," I choked out.

"That would ruin it. It was lovely and you are a fine soldier boy who plays lovely sad tunes, and money would ruin all that." She pulled the sheet up to her neck. I leaned down and kissed her on the forehead. Our heads in a cloud of drowsy mint.

"Good night, Dick," she murmured.

"Good night, Tina."

"You know," she whispered as I turned away, "where to find me."

The days did fly by. I went to the pictures on my own. It was a detective story, about a falcon, and when we came out I thought, I'm going to buy a hat same as Sam Spade's, a classy hat with a bent-down brim. The movie had been confusing but overall I fancied the tough way Sam Spade talked, and the way he looked at women. Love 'em and leave 'em.

On Saturday, Phil showed up for lunch. He and Uncle Ralph talked about wheat prices and how the government was going to oversee the production and distribution of things like milk and bread and hogs and maybe beef. Marketing boards, they were calling them. *Socialism,* Phil snorted, and I was tempted to remind him that he was the one who thought land specu-lation was evil and that the government should regulate real estate prices. *Creeping socialism,* Uncle Ralph said, chuckling. He thought it wouldn't do any harm for families to know what price they were going to pay for the basic necessities; he was against the kind of gouging that occurred in wars. In Germany, he reminded us, before the rise of Hitler, it took a wheelbarrow of marks to buy a loaf of bread. Phil told us about the new tractor the farmer he worked for had just bought; rubber wheels instead of steel rims. Uncle Ralph said the man had been lucky. Rubber was rationed now. When a man got a flat he had to spend half a day repairing the inner tube and the tire itself. We steered clear of the subject of army life. I could tell Phil was bothered by the fact I'd signed up and he had ducked out by working on a farm. Maybe he'd been called out on it. People said cruel things; they said them to soldiers, too: on the street I'd heard mutterings as I passed by in uniform, and I'd wished more than once that the army had let us wear civvies while on furlough, but that was not their way of doing things.

As the afternoon wore on, I walked Phil to the bus station. He told me it was lonely on the farm; he wished he had a girl, someone to talk to at the end of the day. The sex part would be nice, he said, but that was over in fifteen minutes, and what he really missed was companionship. One day, he said, one day. We're all making sacrifices because of this war, Dick, by gum. The spring weather, he said, promised good crops; now that summer was in full swing, things looked very good. The Dirty Thirties were over. At the bus station we stood and smoked until it was time for him to leave. "You take care, Dick," he said, "out there. Mother is worried about you." He held my fingers in his ham-like hand for a few seconds and I saw his eyes were glazed over a bit. But that was it: Mother is worried about you.

I strolled west along Portage back to Aunt Helen's place. It was not a long walk. I turned north at her street. Three blocks up something arrested my eye: fire and thick, black smoke were pouring out of a car. I quickened my pace. A man was running around the car with his hands on his head. His mouth was opening and closing rapidly; he was calling out or wailing, his thin blond hair standing up between his fingers. People had gathered around the car. I began to jog-trot. A burly man pushed the first man aside and grabbed the handle of the car, but immediately he let go; he seized the hand in the other, then began to shake it. I was almost up to the car when a man wearing a cap darted out between two houses with a crowbar and set to work jamming at the door in an effort to pry it open. People were shouting. The first man had dropped to his knees but his hands were still locked over his head. "Ella, Ella," he cried out, "don't let this happen, don't let Ella die." A woman standing at his side put her hand on his shoulder; he was sobbing, his neck and back in spasm. The guy with the crowbar was working frantically, but the smoke was blown in his face and he dropped the crowbar and began to cough in giant heaves. Another man grabbed the crowbar. The woman inside was slumped forward, head on the dashboard. I knew it was all over for her; she was dead; what surprised me was the depth of conviction with which it came to me: it was not just ordinary, the conviction, but a certainty that frightened me, so that I stopped everything I was doing; every thought left my head except that one, as if a gong was going off in my skull. *Dead dead dead.* That was not the worst of it. In a moment it was replaced by a second singular conviction that was as strong as the first and far more frightening: the man had killed his wife. He'd killed her by locking her into the car and then setting fire to it. He continued to wail and sob and tear at his hair but it was all a sham. I staggered up a sidewalk and sat on the steps going into a house. The police had arrived: sirens, flashing lights, one with a completely unnecessary bullhorn calling out: Stand back! I sat for a while trembling; the scene in front of me went in and out of focus. The back of my head hurt. A woman walked up the sidewalk and stood in front of me. "Soldier," she whispered, "you look like you seen a ghost." I waved her away, but she went inside the house and came out with a glass of water. I drank half and spilled the other half down the front of my tunic. After a while I could breathe normally again and I thanked her and stood and debated whether to tell the cops what I knew. They'd take me for some kind of nutcase, I decided; I had not seen the man or his wife at the critical moments—getting into the car and that sort of thing—so what I had to say would be taken as wild conjecture, the ravings of a drunk soldier, though I hadn't had anything to drink. But in the eyes of the cops, all soldiers were drunk soldiers. I walked up the street, more shaken by how I'd arrived at the knowledge I possessed than by the death of the woman itself, a mysterious awareness from some other dimension than the one I was used to living in. It made my chest hurt and my throat go dry.

On Sunday I could hardly hold myself together as we sat in church and then ate lunch at Aunt Helen's. I had no idea if Sheena would be waiting for me but I was dead certain that I was making my way over to River Heights on the chance she was. The doorbell rang and I shifted from one foot to the other, edgy as a stallion in a corral. She opened the door. What a smile! My beautiful black-haired, baby reached out to me with both arms, painted nails twiddling, and the feel of her body made my knees go weak. A pool of vanilla, I swam into it. I held her tight; I ran my hands up and down her back and brought them to rest on her wonderful round ass. "My darling," she crooned.

She was my darling, if by that is meant the dearest thing in my pathetic and wretched existence. We held each and enjoyed doing just that, a lengthy minute with the chest of the other pressed close, hearts beating together, her sweet breath on my neck and wonderful clasping fingers on my spine. Then we stood back, looked at each other and laughed. Sheena crooned, "Ohhhh," and I threw my head back and yowled until hoarse. If there is anything under God's heaven better than the sex that afternoon, I do not want to know about it. We spent and we were spent. Afterwards, lying in each other's arms, I said, "See, I came back." Sheena snuggled closer. "I was wrong," she whispered. "It was a mistake, and you will have to spank me for it. I've been a bad girl."

"Happy to oblige," I said, patting her naked bum.

It was early in the afternoon and there were hours before Ari returned, so Sheena insisted on making coffee. We sat at the kitchen table with steaming cups and date cakes Sheena had baked, her one domestic accomplishment, she claimed. I found I was bouncing one knee under the table.

Her eyes followed mine. "Anxious to be going?"

My ears went red. "I'm anxious for you. What if—"

"He won't be home for hours. It's yourself you're thinking of."

"No," I protested, "I am thinking of you."

"You're the same as every man. Dick. You think with that thing in your pants."

"Ouch. Really? That's your opinion of me?"

"I've witnessed your. … your urges."

I sipped at my coffee and did my best to look hurt. But she was right. Everything I'd done, everything I was since the carney was based on lusts and urges and needs. I could fake goodness and sincerity and often did—to good effect—but the truth about me had less to do with those things than grabbing and snatching at whatever was on offer.

"When," she asked, "are they shipping you off to wherever?"

"You mean Europe?"

"No, you lummox. For that next course of training here. In Canada. Down east or wherever."

What she knew about how the army worked always surprised me. "It's two days."

"And this girl?"

"There is no girl."

"No? No *wandering wife* in Harlan's life?"

The army moved soldiers from town to town where they received special training in the use of different kinds of weapons and in different terrain. It was supposed to harden recruits and make them adaptable at the same time. The whole business was supposed to be hush-hush, but it was widely known and talked about, down to the names of towns. Wandering wives were women who followed their soldier husbands from town to town until the soldier's unit was shipped overseas.

Sheena's dark eyes studied me but she held her peace and waited for me to respond. When I didn't say anything right away, she pushed the cake in my direction and winked.

I offered weakly, "It's not much of a life."

A smile played on her lips as she lifted her coffee cup to her teasing mouth. "You're slippery, soldier boy. I'm never sure what you're actually thinking. What's going on in that devious brain." Vanilla came to mind; Celie's raspberry lips; nutmeg; mint; ripe, soft cheese. All my succulent girls.

We both laughed. And we left it at that.

The train station was crowded with men in uniforms: some sat on duffel bags, smoking; others stood chewing the fat with soldiers they'd just met who were bound for the same destination: smiles; laughter; jokes; cutting up on the platform, where a civilian had produced an accordion and was playing tunes. A chaplain was strolling around, handing out pamphlets. A holiday atmosphere hung over the station, it reminded me of the carney: everyone letting their hair down, restless with expectation. On the train men bumped into each other and laughed and slapped each other on the back.

I passed by groups of four and five soldiers setting up card games and found a window seat at the end of a car and chucked my duffel overhead and settled in for the ride. I enjoyed trains. As a boy I would go down to the station in Estevan to hear the clickety-clack of iron wheels on iron rails, and at night when I was with the carney I sat out on the carousel to listen to their lonesome wails as they rolled into town. I closed my eyes and felt the train's speed pick up on the way out of the city, and I thought of the look in Del's eyes as she turned and gazed softly at me on the steps of her boarding house when I stepped away, an expression of anxiety mixed with relief. I'd felt it too. We were heading into something bigger than ourselves, events we could not control but which would determine everything for us, a future that did not include our being together. And for good reason. Soldiers had died by the thousands on the beaches in France, and others had come home maimed and wounded and completely messed up mentally: they'd never be the same again; they'd never be functioning human beings again. Basket cases, they were called. Finished at twenty years of age. It might be better to die on the field of battle than to face that prospect. It *was* better, most soldiers agreed , though saying that in the hearing of officers or chaplains or civilians was not something that you let yourself do. My thoughts tumbled into the rhythm of the train's wheels as they clicked on the tracks, one idea crossing over into another, my heavy head dropping forward. When I opened my eyes, there was a soldier sitting beside me with an open book on his lap. He glanced at me and smiled. He was smoking, with his free hand dangling into the aisle, the smoke spiralling up past his face, which was round and fleshy. One of his eyes twitched a bit. He said, "You want a cig?" I took one from a silver case he opened and saw there was an inscription on the inside of the lid. He noticed me noticing and said, "My gorl, a farewell gift from my gorl." I told him it was nice, and it was, and we lit up and inhaled and blew smoke into the air above our heads. I liked his easy manner, the way he didn't press talk between us; he could sit silent without being nervous with it. I nodded at the book. "You doing some heavy reading."

"This," he said, turning the book so I could see the cover. "This I would not cawl heavy reading."

I studied the cover. "I like Zane Grey. He's my favourite."

"Now why," he said, grinning, "did I already suspect that?"

"*Riders of the Purple Sage*. Read it twice." I was not much of a reader but I did go for stories about cowboys and wide open spaces. Zane Grey had a way of making his heroes seem part of the country they lived in—and the other way around. There was a straightforwardness about his writing, though I knew the tales were only tales, and that he stretched the truth of life on the plains a great deal, as writers were disposed to do.

"This is a new one," he said: "*Thundering Herd*." I gave the cover a more careful look.

"Maybe you could lend it to me, when you're done."

"Glad to oblige. If we're headed for the same place."

"We are," I said. He gave me a sideways look. "Wainwright," I added.

"How did you know that?"

"Lucky guess," I said laughing. I waved my hand with the burning smoke in the air. He shook his head and I laughed again. But it wasn't luck. It was something else entirely, an echo at the back of my skull, only without words: an electric surge of knowledge without language. The eyes of a wolf at the side of a road crossed through my brain. *Watching, not waiting.* These things troubled me.

Did he see that in my expression? After a few moments, he reached a hand over and said, "Jonathan Hoeschen, but everyone calls me Charlie."

I took the hand he offered: long dry fingers, which went with his wispy blond hair and moustache. Blood orange tiger lilies inside his skull, streaks and dots of black creasing the petals. "Dick," I said, chuckling. "But christened Harlan."

We both laughed and blew smoke in the air.

He said, "You going in for the bombardier corps?"

"Transport."

"Right. Trucks, driving, motorcycles, engines. Suits you, Dick. I'm doing the bombardier." And bombardier suited *you*, I might have said: a fancy word for firing an artillery gun.

We nodded and smiled at each other and inhaled and exhaled, and after a while he turned back to his book and I looked out the window. It had been a gray horizon at dawn but the sun was climbing the big blue sky. The prairies unfolded around us: mile after mile of mile after mile. Flat fields and small bluffs where deer and rabbits sheltered. Wheat and barley fields, farmers on tractors and behind teams of horses, gusts of wind that blew dust up where it swirled into little clouds and passed over the roof of the train compartment. Phil would be milking cows or harnessing up a team for ploughing or seeding.

As a boy I'd loved riding horses, being out in the early morning in fresh air cantering through grassy meadows and along dirt tracks that wound their way through the stands of bush around the old man's farm. I liked the smell of horses and the way sweat built up in their mouths and blew back sometimes onto the chaps I wore over my jeans. The smell of horse dung, too, and on some days when I was returning from a ride I could catch wafts of it coming from the barn and I'd inhale deeply and wonder if being a cowboy wasn't the best life possible. Art hated saddling up and brushing down horses, and Phil was a bit of a lunk and was never really comfortable in the saddle. He was a farmer, bred and born, as he put it. He'd dodged out of enlisting and one day there might be a price to pay for that. *Zombies.*

Zombies were shirkers; men who were afraid to die and found a way out of service. They should be put on trial; forced into service; be lined up against a wall and shot. It was desertion; running away from a man's duty. Sitting at the ends of the tables at mess, the sergeants nodded silent assent and let such talk run on. Women were Suzie rotten crotch; soldiers who curried the favour of officers were ass-kissers; deserters shitbags; men who ducked out of service sleazy cunts. Contempt was not limited to civilians. Flyboys were flea-brains; sailors were scuzz-holes. Only the guys in your unit, only the soldiers on either side of you were worth more than spit. Far from discouraging such talk, the sergeants threw in fresh terms; they encouraged exclusiveness and bile. It was a way of building loyalty and group identity. Camaraderie, they called it, a fancy term for what amounted to little more than bullies on a schoolyard. A lot of recruits were fooled, the same way they were conned by flag-waving and brigade songs and a lot of other nonsense that masked what soldiering was about: killing other men and getting killed. Maybe the COs had it right. I did not know about that; what I knew was I felt uneasy when I pictured Phil hiding on a farm and Art praying not to be conscripted while I had put on the uniform and was training to kill men much the same as myself—and be killed by them. I nursed a smouldering resentment in my gut that a man shouldn't harbour about his brothers.

I fell asleep and dreamt I was trying to climb up a rock formation above a raging river, only when I got near the top the rocks formed a sheer cliff and other men in uniform who had been climbing with me, but whom I hadn't noticed were falling off the cliff and into the river below. I woke in a sweat and fell asleep again and this time I was driving a coal truck that lurched forward and then lurched backward and I sensed there was something behind it that it was about to crash into, killing me, and when I woke with a start that's what the train was doing, lurching forth and back. Beside me Charlie was smoking and grinning at me. "You were twitching, soldier," he said. "Having bad dreams."

I took a cigarette he offered and lit up, fingers trembling. After a while he said, "You think much about dying?" He was easy with silences, this Charlie, and direct in his talk, both of which I was attracted to. No shilly-shallying, no dancing around things.

"No," I said, teetering on a lie. "You?"

"Just dreams."

"Nightmares. I always seem to be falling. The men beside me too."

"With me it's drowning. I'm in the water and then I'm under it and I know I'm going to suffocate. Funny thing is, I'm a good swimmer."

I grunted and he grunted. We smoked and looked out the window. The flat plains of the prairie had given way to rolling hills past Saskatoon but the train was still crossing Saskatchewan. How long before Alberta?

I tapped my fingers on the seat rest. "You think they mean anything, dreams?"

"No. Not the way people claim, anyway. Shrinks and so on."

"I wake up sweating. They must be telling us something."

"That we're shit scared. That life hangs by a thread, army or no. One minute you're strolling along, happy as a lark, whistling a popular tune, and then a piano falls on your head. It's all over. Well, that was fun. But we'd hardly got going." He looked at me and grinned and we both chuckled.

"They're like voices you hear," I ventured, going back to dreams, which I had been thinking about a lot, "voices that speak in garbled words you can't quite understand but know are important. Voices that echo in the back of your skull and leave you with a conviction you can no more shake off than a wildcat that's pounced and got its claws in your back."

Charlie laughed aloud. "You're quite the poet, Dick."

I guffawed. "Things trouble me sometimes."

"I know. It's this war. You have a feeling you may not come out of it, and you think maybe you should understand a little something about life before it's all over."

We weren't very equipped to; that was the problem. We were reasonably equipped to jog-trot a couple of miles with the twenty-seven-point-five pack strapped to our backs; we could shoot guns and run at dummies with bayonets; but we'd had no basic training in understanding the value or meaning of life. We knew about women—about sex anyway—but had little experience of how they thought and why they did the things they did—and none whatsoever about children. Did we trust politicians? No. Did we think we were going to heaven when we died, as the preachers said? No. Did we believe things in books or speeches given by men in suits? No. That war before the one we were suited up for had shown those things to be a sham—and the hundred-dollar words that went with them: honour, loyalty, camaraderie, faith; a great many more that were hollow at the centre when you looked at them with any scrutiny. We could pull a trigger and dig a foxhole and we were prepared to die; but we didn't even know how to do that, really. It was sad. It led a man to melancholy resignation on the one hand, and the conviction to snatch and grab at whatever you could, on the other.

These were thoughts a soldier best not entertain. I took out the harmonica and played a tune that reminded me of Celie. Another for Sheena. Oh, my girls, my lovely sweet girls. I sat back and let images of pink and brown nipples alternate with soft, white, round bums and open, eager, red mouths. These I did understand. Shameless, I admit it. I was a slave to desire and lust. I shifted on the seat to relieve my burgeoning member. I opened one eye and stared out the window at the landscape roll-ing by: the rolling hills had given way to terrain that resembled the Shield: rock faces, pine trees, small fresh-water lakes. Next was Alberta's oil country and then Wainwright, the north coun-try. It was uninhabited territory but its emptiness and starkness were appealing: inviting because not civilized; a place where a man could breathe and live his life the way he wished; a land where you could get in touch with nature and not feel tram-melled up with the rules and restrictions of the city. Looking out at it passing by, I could not help sitting upright and squaring my shoulders.

"Yup," Charlie sitting beside me said, "we're almost there."

"It's stunning country."

"I love the pines; but I hate the mosquitoes."

I laughed and he did too. "I'd forgot about them."

"Maybe they'll spray the campsite. I hear they got a chemical that keeps the buggers down."

"Huh. I hope so."

After some minutes Charlie said, "You think we'll see action?"

"You mean combat against the enemy?" He nodded. "I hope so. Shame to do all this training for nothing. All that shit we ate in basic."

"That ain't over. Not by a long shot. There's a lot more shit to be eaten in this Wainwright place, Dick. But the boys over there are pushing Hitler back every day it seems."

"My uncle has a map of Europe; he's keeping track of the Allied progress by drawing a line in blue ink every couple of weeks to show the front. There's been a lot of progress since they stormed them beaches. So what about the Japs?"

We traded rumours and opinions back and forth. No one

had signed on to fight Hirohito and his lot; that somehow seemed the Americans' problem; but there was as much likelihood we'd be shipped into the Pacific Islands as to Italy or wherever. Soldiers go where soldiers are told to go. I did not fancy the idea of dying in an Asian jungle. I'd always imagined going down in a field in France or Germany, the homeland my ancestors had come from. I don't know why it mattered to me, but it did. Bringing the family history full circle, maybe.

We were coming to the end of the train journey. Charlie leaned over to me. "About what we were talking about earlier," he began. "We lie down in cool grass under the shade of a big tree, and the sky above is blue, empty and blue. And we sink into the grass. Very slowly. We become a part of the grass, sinking deep, shutting down, sinking deep and shutting down. We find peace. At last." He looked into my face. "It's not the same for us," he murmured, "we men who march to the beat of a different drummer." He nodded at me knowingly. I nodded back. We both knew what he was talking about. "We become part of the grass," Charlie was continuing, "we become one with the grass. Peace." He drew in a deep breath. "Lovely, deep, and lasting peace."

It was late in the afternoon before the train pulled into Wainwright and we were mustered and transported in trucks to the barracks. For the next two days we were paraded around in full pack and sent out on a ten-mile march to make sure we were in condition. Next came assignments to units, and getting familiar with the trucks. The idea was that we drivers practise efficiency in hitching up the anti-aircraft guns to the trucks and driving them around on difficult terrain: backing them into firing positions, unhitching, standing by to aid in loading and unloading of ammunition, learning the rudiments of shooting the guns, should it come to that. I was to be a driver, and another private was to be assigned as my backup; he'd be in the passenger seat and prepared to take over behind the wheel, should it be necessary. All very military; all very organized on the surface; all teetering toward collapse and chaos in the event of a real disaster, but no one was allowed to say that; we were not to think it, even. But everyone knew. Military discipline hung by a thread. We were young, untested recruits: who knew what would happen once bullets started flying and shell fragments were raining down on our heads? Some were likely to run away screaming and pulling their hair.

The army was all hurry-up-and-wait, hurry-up-and-wait. We stood around at attention for an hour, then stood down for a while, then were on the run for an hour, when we were stood to attention again, for another hour, then dashed off somewhere else. Shoulder the pack; dash to the truck; stand at attention for inspection near the gun; over and over. Total foolishness; a waste of time. It made the officers feel good, maybe, to have us prancing around like trained bears in the circus. One of them was a captain, McAngus. Before the entire corps had even been marched out for his inspection, word had gone down the line: bastard. He was. Slight and thin, he was a wiry bundle of nerves with a pencil moustache and a squeaky voice that made him easy to hate right off the hop. He came down the line. "Shoddy," he said to the sergeant, "shoddy, the entire works." A ripple of irritation went up and down the corps. We were not raw recruits. We'd been through humiliation and put-downs. It was behind us. McAngus poked a soldier in the tunic with his white baton. "This soldier cannot stand up straight. Put this soldier on detail, sergeant." The sergeant nodded curtly but looked away. He did not want this either. He was an instructor, not a boot camp ass-kicker. McAngus tapped a soldier's head. "This man needs a haircut, sergeant. Put him on detail." Feet shifted up and down the lines. A soldier coughed. *Fuck you,* someone muttered. *McAnus,* someone else said. McAngus shot his gaze around. There was no obvious villain for him to pick on. "These men," he barked to the sergeant, "these poor excuses for men, need another ten-mile route march to bring them in line. See to it, sergeant." We stood in the sun. Mosquitoes buzzed about. "Meanwhile," he snapped, "mark time MARCH!" We stood in formation and lifted our feet, up-down, one minute turning into two, two into four. Marching on the spot, a schoolboy's gig.

Over the PA a sing-song woman's voice said: Keep Calm And Carry On; Tonight's Feature "The Yank in the RAF." United Against Hitler: Churchill, Roosevelt, Stalin.

There were tight jaws and blazing eyes on the return to the bunkhouse. Oaths muttered under breaths; packs thrown roughly on bunks. A soldier punched a wall and another kicked a tin bucket down the aisle between rows of cots. The bombardier from my unit bunked two over. He came and plunked himself on the edge of my bed. "Fuck that," he said.

"Fuck that," I agreed. We lit up smokes and sat tapping our toes on the wooden floor.

"I'm a gunner," he went on, "in a fighting unit that is proud to have me. So what the fuck's with the ass-kicking captain." It was not a question.

"Gunner," I said. "Not bombardier?"

He snorted. "I fire a gun. I try to hit planes in the air. You," he went on, "drive a truck, you're a truck driver, not a *camionneur*, or some such." We both laughed but I wasn't sure I understood him. "*Camion*," he said, "French for truck." We both laughed again. He was short and dark with a brush moustache and a twinkle in his eye. "Max," he said, putting out a big hand, "which to my mother is short for Walter." His laugh was infectious: a fast run along a musical chord.

In the morning we did the ten-mile route march at a pace the sergeant called *slow march*. In the afternoon the gunners were sent to a tent to study the appearance and insignia of planes, enemy and friendly. Drivers gathered at the trucks, tinkered with engines, tested tire inflation and practised backing with the Bofors rig attached. We were introduced to reading map coordinates and told that the next day there would be a test. It was not a paper test; we were given coordinates and a land survey map and told to drive the truck to where our calculations took us. Was there a trick? The army loved playing tricks— and then punishing soldiers for screwing up. I studied the map carefully; plotted the coordinates. Drove the truck; checked and double-checked the map. A captain and a sergeant drove up in a jeep. "Ten hut!" We stood by the truck. They walked over the area, hands on hips. A peg had been driven into the ground. The truck was parked ten feet from it. "Good work, private," the captain said. "Good work, Bauch," the sergeant added. Return to camp, we were told. They drove away. It turned out no other drivers had come within fifty feet of their peg.

The next day we hitched the guns to the trucks and repeated the drill. The gunners were still studying insignia. They were projected on a screen, Max told me, for two seconds and in another three seconds you had to tick off from a list what you'd seen; twelve images a minute, then a minute of rest, then the same thing over again. Max had a headache. He'd done about average: 70% correct on identifying airborne drones.

With my backup driver I pored over the coordinates. We, too, were on the clock: fifteen minutes to plot our course on the map; half an hour to have the gun in place. After we were parked, the jeep drove up. The captain and sergeant walked over the ground. They stood beside the jeep, consulting their own maps for a few minutes. I heard the sergeant say, "But I put the peg in myself, sir." They walked the ground again. Private Anders and I stood at ease beside the truck. We were sweating. I had a bad feeling. I saw myself being returned to the infantry: slogging through mud, digging foxholes, cut down by machine guns, falling in barbed wire. The sergeant had out an instrument, which he pointed first one way, then another—was the peg magnetized? Was the instrument for triangulation? Anders cleared his throat every few seconds; it was beginning to drive me crazy. The sergeant walked over to where we were standing; then he surprised us both by stooping and looking under the truck. Anders was beginning to tremble; my knees felt all rubbery. The sergeant dropped to one knee. "Sir," he called out. The captain was standing at the jeep, still studying the map. He was chewing his lower lip. He looked up, then crossed to us at quick march. He too stooped and gawked under the truck.

"By the Jesus," he said. "I never saw anything to beat this." The sergeant gazed up at me. "Take a look," he said, "the both of you." We peered under; the peg was directly under the truck; it could not have been more dead centre. When we were standing, the captain squared his shoulders, looked me in the eye and saluted. "Bauch, is it?" he said. "Private Bauch? I'm Wiley." He finished his salute in ceremonial military manner, turned on his heel, and quick-marched back to the jeep.

The sergeant whistled under his breath. "Someone," he said very quietly, "has just made an impression." His salute as he left was quick and sharp.

Weeks rolled by. Every day we gave the trucks the once-over: oil level, tire pressure, water level. Fiddle with carburetor; check the steering pinions. The aiming crew, three privates and Max, our bombardier, practised "laying" the sights: one on horizontal, one on vertical, one calculating the lead required for a round of ammunition to hit a moving target. Other corporals did recon on motorcycles on the mountain passes. Everyone was busy but not at drills and boot-camp foolishness; this was serious army business: the sharp end of killing and being killed. Exhilarating stuff. You could read it in the faces of soldiers at the end of the day: things were being learned; skills were being honed. Hitler and Hirohito would be made to pay.

One day a corporal on motorcycle recon came down a mountain pass in dawn light too fast. His machine skidded through a corner, bounced once at the edge of the road, flipped in the verge and plunged down the mountainside: rocks, bushes, stunted pines, more rocks. The two motorcyclists behind him pulled over, peered over the edge, radioed for assistance. The medics had to be lowered on ropes. The motorcycle was located fifty feet into the canyon; the corporal twenty feet farther down. Broken neck. Dead within seconds. His body was put into a rough casket and a ceremony was held the next morning on the makeshift parade ground; side of a mountain, soldiers standing awkwardly on its slope, one foot lower than the other. A Union Jack was draped over the casket; the chaplain said a few words; Captain Wiley said a few more.

"Nice ceremony," Anders said after. He was standing with Charlie, and I strolled over to them and we lit up cigarettes and looked at the mountains in front of us and thought our private thoughts.

"Yes," Charlie agreed, taking up what Anders had said about ceremony.

"Except," I said, "for the flag."

"You got problems with the Union Jack?" Charlie took the cigarette out of his mouth and studied its glowing tip rather than looking me in the eye.

"This country needs its own flag," I said. "We been a British colony for a long time, but now we're our own country, Canada, we proved it in that last war and we're proving it again in this one."

"You got a point there," Charlie said. "A sovereign nation among other sovereign nations."

I grunted. "About time."

Anders said, "They're shipping the body by train to his home town. Some tiny burg in Sask-a-bush."

"Easy now," I said. "I'm from God's country myself."

That night Captain Wiley's sergeant took me aside as we were leaving the mess tent. "Chief wants a word." We crossed to the officers' Nissen hut.

Captain Wiley stepped out from behind two card tables shoved together as a makeshift desk. "Bauch," he said. I was standing to attention. "Stand easy," he added. He eyed me up and down. "Bauch," he went on, "that was a terrible thing, what happened yesterday morning. We hate losing good soldiers like … like—"

"Shaw, sir," Sergeant Peters said.

"Shaw, yes." Captain Wiley had looked down but he raised his gaze to mine. He was short and slight but had steel-grey eyes that made me want to shift my feet or back away. "With Shaw gone," he went on, "this outfit needs another corporal. I was thinking, Bauch, that you might be the man." His voice rose on the last word. "Peters here tells me the men respect you, Bauch, and I've seen your deportment myself on the parade ground and in the field. You're officer material, is the point." He paused, cleared his throat, and then raised one hand slightly.

It was my cue to speak. "Thank you, sir. Kind of you."

"So what do you say?" He raised one hand up to the bill of his cap. There were snow-capped peaks in his head, a faint blue horizon, a hawk floating lazily.

I cleared my throat. "Begging your pardon, sir, but I'd rather not."

"You wouldn't?"

"No sir."

Captain Wiley he ran his fingers through his moustache for a moment. "May I ask why?"

"I'd rather not say, but if you insist, sir."

"I think I do, Private."

"Well, sir, begging your pardon. And Sergeant Peters' too. Well, the men take a view of officers. They—I don't know how to put it exactly."

"They don't trust them."

"It's not that. Actually. It's that they see the officers as separate from the men. When it comes to sitting around chewing the fat, say, or going to town for a beer, things of that kind. Getting together with the wives and playing music and dancing."

"And you'd prefer that."

"To giving orders, yes. I'd rather just be one of the men, if you get my drift. Just an ordinary soldier among other ordinary soldiers. Begging your pardon, sirs."

There was a long silence. Captain Wiley looked at Sergeant Peters, then at me, then at Sergeant Peters again. "All right. I understand you, Bauch. I see your point. I think you're making a mistake, mind. You got smarts and you got backbone. And you're nobody's fool. But have it your way."

"Thank you sir." I saluted. He saluted back.

"Bauch," the captain said. "One more thing. You strike me as a religious man."

I hesitated a moment, pondering what he might be getting at. "Mother had us to church every Sunday, if that's what you mean."

"So you know the rudiments?"

"Abraham and Isaac, the parting of the Red Sea, David and Bathsheba."

"That last one is an unusual choice."

"I looked it up, sir."

"So more than the rudiments, then." He cleared his throat and glanced at Peters. "You might," he went on, "want to join us at our regular Tuesday meeting. We talk about the divinity and nature, and man's place with them."

I shifted from one foot to the other. Peters' gaze was unblinking; did *our* include him, or was it some other group that the captain referred to? My lips were dry. I ran my tongue over them. "Sir," I managed to get out.

"Tuesday. I think you'd find it informative, Bauch. And uplifting. We follow the teachings of Guru Jani, who leads us in seeing the oneness of all life: nature, man, divinity."

Outside, the mountain air felt very cool on my face. I stepped across the clearing to the bunkhouse smart and stood outside and lit up a cigarette with trembling fingers. The stars above were bright and I looked for the Big Dipper and the Bear, and when I located them, felt my heart slow and my mind come to peace. I breathed deeply for a while. It was no surprise when an owl in a nearby tree hooted three times and in the silence that followed a whisper rose from somewhere in the darkness at my side: *Guru Jani.* I shivered. What was going on? I stood outside the bunkhouse and smoked for a while. A cool breeze made me turn the collar of my jacket up. In the pines trees nearby the needles were soughing their song: *there is a balm in Gilead.* I hummed, gladdened.

Mail call one day produced a letter from Margy. Young Ernie had left school and was working on a construction crew as the "gofer." One night Mac had hit Nora but that seemed the sum total of it. Mother's tests had led to the scheduling of more tests. Del, Nora reported, was going out with one of the guys she'd gone to school with, Walter something, who was taking the training for city cop. I was happy for Ernie but the other things upset me: life was going on *back there*, but it was going on without me, and I felt melancholy when I re-read the letter and knew it was over between me and Del, which was what I had wanted, but which still left my gut in a good-sized knot. I was a soldier; my unit and my brigade were now my family; my preoccupations were firing guns and driving trucks and learning the brutal arts of war.

The weeks rolled by. Soon all the drivers were getting their trucks to within twenty feet of the pegs; soon the Bofors were in place in under half an hour. The gunners could identify 97% of the drones dragged behind gliders in the field, even though the images they saw in the gun's sights were upside down. The unit could load for *fire* at a crisp and steady pace. It was time, we were told, for field manoeuvres.

They were scheduled for a Thursday. We looked smart in the days before: the engines of the trucks purred; we disassembled and reassembled our rifles at quick time; our uniforms were spit and polish. At parade we snapped to attention and saluted smartly and briskly. On the Wednesday afternoon I was crossing from the mess tent to the bunkhouse when I heard a voice behind me: "Private Bauch." It was Captain Wiley. He caught up to me. Before I could, he threw me a salute.

"We missed you," he said, "on Tuesday night."

I cleared my throat.

"No worry," he said. "We did a reading from Madame Blavatsky and had a round-table discussion. It was enlightening. On the subject that nature is not dead matter but a living entity, same as we humans—rocks and trees and so on, too, not just animate nature, horses and so on. The oneness of life, you see, Bauch. All of life."

"I see, sir."

"Yes, very enlightening."

We stood for a moment silent. "I talked with Sir Isaac Newton yesterday," he said. "Very interesting. Newton has the same deep grasp of the wholeness of being as Guru Jani. It was very enlightening."

Newton, I was thinking, didn't he live a hundred years ago?

"I know what you're thinking," Captain Wiley said. "It's unusual for a man of Newton's renown to speak to the likes of me, a simple soldier in this man's army. But that's not how it works. I've had a long confab with Charles Dickens, too, who had uplifting things to say about mesmerism."

I had no idea what mesmerism was. A plant species? A certain kind of rock formation?

"It was right here," Captain Wiley went on, looking around. "This exact spot. Where I spoke with Newton. Would you call that a coincidence, Bauch, that you and I are meeting at this exact spot—a coincidence, or an omen?"

I swallowed hard. "I wouldn't know, sir," I offered.

He studied the mountain in the distance for a while, his eyes fixed on a snow-capped peak far away. "Enjoy the manoeuvres," he stated flatly. Then he wheeled and strode away before I was able to salute him.

It was dark when we rose. Before we set out, a jeep with a sergeant and captain came around. It was McAngus. When he stopped at our unit, we stood smartly to attention and saluted. He did not deign to climb out of the jeep. Sitting, he gave the merest response. "Don't," he barked at us, "embarrass your officers in front of the other corps." They drove off.

We carried rifles with live ammunition and the anti-aircraft corps was issued rounds to fire at drones that would fly over the battlefield at certain points. Infantry units were brought in. It was a full-scale operation. The ground forces were to seize unarmed machine-gun emplacements located on the side of a mountain, but only on strict command, and exacting discipline and dispatch. The anti-aircraft units were to act as cover, firing at the drones overhead. In the backs of trucks there was high nervous energy as we double-checked hitches and tied down tarps. It was field day at school. Everyone was keyed up, smoking, laughing, joking.

We did our co-ordinations and drove the unit to the location. It was just after dawn, the army's favourite time for manoeuvres and attacks. The infantry was spread out over the bottom slope of the mountain, dug in behind mounds of earth and bushes, but not in foxholes. Gunner Max had the crew set up the Bofors. We stood at the ready, Private Anders and I, and then, .303s in hand, ducked behind the wheels of the truck, as we'd been trained. As drivers we were not actually part of the action; we stood in reserve, in case something went amiss in the artillery crew. A whistle blew and the infantry began to move forward. Targets had been set up on the slope, giant yellow and orange cardboard constructions that were standing in as enemy gun emplacements. The infantry moved forward and on command, blasted away at them. Hundreds of rounds of ammunition fired; the noise was impressive. When the targets had been blown to smithereens, the infantry ran forward and took their places and dug in again. It was organized, and it looked impressive: first one unit on the advance; then another. The infantry was taking the hill. Light was coming into the sky. A chill breeze blew down from the north, and brown leaves from the previous autumn swirled about. A biplane came into view, dragging a target drone behind it; an anti-aircraft unit dispatched it. The boys in our crew gave a brief cheer. Another drone; a second unit knocked it out. Our crew was next. Max was fondling his brush moustache. The infantry was on the move again; fifty yards forward. The racket of .303s being fired and reloaded filled the air. Another drone came into sight; Max called the crew to alert. Lock and load. But then Max called: Hold fire! The drone bore the marking of a British Spitfire. Radios crackled. It was a setup, an army feint to test the total preparedness of the corps. Max had passed the test. But now that his unit's fire had been aborted, was he to take the next drone or was the next unit down the line to take it? There was confusion; voices were raised; Max gesticulated as he talked on the radio; all the apparent army organization was crumbling. I looked at Private Anders and we both shook our heads. Just then a jeep came careening forward on a rough track from the bottom of the slope. A sergeant and Captain McAngus, who had binoculars dangling around his neck. The jeep bounced past, making its way up the slope, in pursuit of the infantry. We watched it climb. The infantry advanced in methodical passages, ever upward. Another drone came into view. Max called the crew to alert. Fire! The drone went down. Mutterings of satisfaction came from our crew. The radio crackled and Max spoke briefly into the receiver. Above us, at the farthest point of advance of the infantry, the jeep crept to a halt. McAngus stood up from his sitting position. He had the binoculars to his eyes; he swept the battlefield with them. I watched him lift the glasses from his eyes and say something to the sergeant. He looked such a cock of the walk the way he shifted the glasses from side to side and nodded his head. The sergeant had his hand out toward McAngus, fingertips tugging his coat. McAngus glanced down at him, a sneer of contempt on his lips, then he put the binoculars to his eyes again; then he crumpled: both knees went out from under him; he sagged onto the shoulder of the sergeant, who was trying with both hands to prop him up and push him into his seat. As he went down below my sightline, I saw a stream of blood running from beneath one ear into the collar of his coat.

He was dead before the medics could get up to him.

I thought of Larry saying that officers should be shot for humiliating men in basic; and of Dixon saying, They get theirs in the end. I wondered if they'd hear about this incident, if the army would report it as anything more than an accident during manoeuvres. When I saw McAngus go down a twitch ran through me and a silent cheer came to my lips. *Bastard*. I expected the feeling to pass. It didn't. My gut tightened and my jaw locked, but that was it as far as feeling grim was concerned. There were no feelings of sympathy, not even a tingle of pity. He was a bastard who deserved to die. And he had. End of story. In the cruel mathematics of war, he got the number that was coming to him.

"I didn't see a thing," Max told me later.

"It was some distance up the mountain," I told him. "I saw him slump down but that was it." A lie, of course: I'd seen the way he'd cocked his hat to fit the binoculars to his eye; how he'd swept the field with the glasses—even that was done with a hateful arrogance, as if he owned everything he laid eyes on; and the flapping of his lips as he addressed the sergeant; the sergeant's tug at his jacket, perhaps an indication that he feared the fatal bullet; the stream of blood in which McAngus's life leaked away. I'd seen it all. McAngus had been killed by one of his own men, one of my comrades.

"They are going to bring someone in," Anders said. "An investigator." He was sitting on the end of Max's bunk, opposite me, his blue eyes wide with wonder. "Some expert who might be able to figure out from the angle where the shot came from."

"Impossible," Max stated. "There were hundreds of soldiers on that slope, dozens at any given angle from the jeep. And who could possibly determine the angle the shot came from without knowing the exact location of his feet at the precise moment the bullet struck?"

"You're right, Max," I said, "It's all nonsense, this talk of experts. The kind of thing the army lets leak out to convince you they know what they're doing."

"Or," Max added, "to trap some fool into giving himself away."

"Which the man who did this," I said, "is not. A fool."

Max nodded. "The man who did this...." He looked from Anders to me and then studied the floor between his feet.

We said nothing more. You could tell by the look in men's eyes that they were glad McAngus had got his due, but no one was saying anything of that kind. It was treason. And despite the strong feeling against McAngus being widespread, there were always, in the army, sneaks and snitches who would report things to the officers to weasel favours, even though it meant getting another man in trouble. "The walls have ears" a popular slogan went, and it applied inside the army as well as out, which had its share of bastards and low-lifes.

In the morning there was reveille as usual, and breakfast in the mess tent, and parade. Captain Wiley and another captain addressed us on the manoeuvre, which was deemed a great success. Nothing was said of the incident. We broke up into our units to go over how things had gone for us in detail, and then the rest of the day we were left to our own devices. We smoked and a guy produced a softball and bat and we played a game of ball as best we could on the rocky, sloped terrain of Wainwright. I played the harmonica and a guy accompanied me on guitar. The "wandering wives" of our corps had found a house to live in on the townsite and a bunch of us went down there with their husbands and drank beer as the sun dipped below the mountains. The guitar and harmonica were a hit. The couples danced. It hurt to see bodies pressed against each other and sly, but not covert, smiles between men and women exchanged at the end of dances. One of the wives, tall with raven hair and flashing black eyes came up to me and asked for "If I Were a Blackbird." It was one of my favourites and I said so. I could see she was a handful, as they say, and was glad that I closed my eyes as I began to play, and though I thought some wicked things about Sheena that blended into the look in that woman's eyes, never mind her perky breasts and ass, I did not succumb to temptation, as I well might have, shameless beast that I was.

Two days later came word that we were being moved to Nanaimo, British Columbia. The island. Captain Wiley had gone ahead. I heaved a sigh of relief. Our meeting on the clearing had unnerved me. Newton, Dickens, Guru Jani, and Madame

Blavatsky? I hardly knew who any of these were. I was happy for
the mindless chatter of Anders and was looking forward to long
stretches of silence on the road to Nanaimo where I could study
up the words to a song that was taking shape in my head.

On the long drive across British Columbia, Anders and I
spelled each other off. The sun blazed down and created heat
mirages on the highway. At night, headlights came out of the
darkness towards us and I closed my eyes against the brightness.
We were part of a convoy of twelve trucks dragging Bofors guns.
Motorcycles in advance; motorcycles to the rear. When Anders
was driving, I napped and played the harmonica. Mile after mile
unrolled. We checked the engine oil, the tire inflation, the water
level. Going up mountain passes, the truck worked hard in low
gears; going down, the weight of the Bofors gun forced the truck
to accelerate and drivers had to brake and gear down carefully—
otherwise the trucks would have gathered momentum and
gone off the road. The convoy swayed through curves and tires
ran into the gravel shoulders, scattering stones, but we stayed
upright. On the flat stretches Anders and I talked: he told me
about his family, farmers from the Interlake. He had a brother in
the Navy. "Can't even swim," Anders said, laughing. "What's he
doing in the Navy?" He liked jokes: the one about the priest, the
pastor, and the rabbi parachuting out of a plane. The one about
the Irishman and the Aussie taking a leak in a public urinal.

The miles rolled by. On the flat lands crossing the interior, I
said, "So now Stalin is our friend?"

"He wasn't always?"

I was smoking and threw my butt out the open window.
"Were you not listening to the PA all those months?"

"Who listens to the PA? Something about church service."

"You didn't go to the movies?"

"I hate the movies. It's all made up. I go for real things, a history book or a baseball game. The movies? May as well read a novel; I can't never figure out what they're trying to say."

"I like them. The funny ones are funny; the detectives give you a puzzle to unravel; the serious ones try to say something about life."

"Not for me. Give me a hockey game: crash and bash. Manly stuff. Book reading, well, it's for women, isn't it?"

"In any case," I said. My voice had a tinge of annoyance. I lit up another cigarette and offered one to Anders. After a while I said, "Stalin was our sworn enemy. Remember? Better Dead Than Red."

"Commies. Shoot the lot."

"Exactly. That's what they were telling us when we signed up. Stalin was as bad as Hitler. Two years later and Stinky Stalin the low-down Commie has become our friend; Churchill and Roosevelt and him meet up somewhere and parley and now we're suddenly buddy-buddy. He's our pal."

"The old flip-flop."

"They're leading us on like trained bears, the officers, bears with rings in our noses. What's a man to believe? More important, who's a man to believe?"

"Believe your officers; believe the prime minister. Your betters."

"Bullshit, I say. It's all just propaganda, friend. It's all just them in power brainwashing us. First Stalin's our enemy; then our pal. It doesn't wash, I tell you."

"Easy now, there, Dick."

I took a couple deep drags and studied the Bofors gun attached to the truck in front of us as it bounced over cracks in the highway. I clammed up. What I'd said, what I'd nearly said was treasonous. I pondered over a couple of miles whether or not Anders was trustful. Would he turn me in to the MPs? He seemed to be a solid kid, a little simple, maybe, but straight, not the type to sneak behind a man's back with rumours. But you never knew: Loose Lips Sink Ships. And for a quite while I sat in silence and thought about how I'd have to practise keeping my mouth shut, not easy for the man to whom being barker came as natural as breathing itself.

There were things the carney had taught me that I was grateful for. It was an education in shamming and slippery dealings. Was the pea under this cup or that one? How could a guy give you back the card you'd picked out of a deck blind? Did the Man With Three Legs really have three legs, or were you being manipulated into thinking so by dim lighting and fast talking and the frailty of your own imagination? The carney taught you to be skeptical; taught you to look below the surface; to ask questions. And when you graduated from the University of Carney your first instinct was to listen carefully, to distrust by rote the patter of slick talkers, officers and politicians included. You learned to think for yourself—and that could be a dangerous thing. Especially in the army. I'd learned something else in the carney: keep your trap shut, if you don't want to get in trouble. That was difficult for me. I had opinions and was prone to speak them, come what may. *Dangerous,* Harlan, *dangerous.*

A ferry took us across to the island and the camp outside of Nanaimo. It was a sunny day with high white clouds. A cool breeze was blowing over the water and gulls swooped above the treetops. Anders and I stood down from the truck, looking back at the Rocky Mountains. "What a view," he said.

"It's a remarkable country. So open, so big and beautiful, so empty."

"Breathtaking."

"Why would anyone want to live anywhere else?"

We were taking it in: Canada. Two oceans, the Great Lakes, mountains, prairies, the Shield, thousands of freshwater lakes; true wildlife: bears, moose, elk, wolverines, bobcats, coyotes. I said as much to Anders. I was swinging one arm in the air, taking it all in. The view was spectacular. I was in love with our native land.

"Mosquitoes," he added.

"Everyone always adds: *mosquitoes*," I said petulantly. "What's with that?"

"They're everywhere."

"So are flies; so are grasshoppers; so are ants. Why pick out mosquitoes to bitch at?"

"You're an odd one," Anders said. "Anyone ever tell you that?"

I snorted. "This you can say about Canada—about Canadians. Show an unusual quality or idea, behave a little different from the crowd and they label you odd. In this country a man has to conform or he's strange. We don't even allow for a dash of eccentricity in a man."

"You take things too hard." Anders offered me a cigarette. We inhaled and blew smoke into the air.

"Filthy habit, this," I said studying the glowing end of my butt. "I gotta quit this."

The days in Nanaimo had much the same feel as they had in Wainwright: hurry up to get there, then sit around waiting for something to happen. Marches, inspections, bad grub in the mess tent, everyone keyed up, but no one going anywhere.

Days turned into weeks. The gunner crew practised sightings of drones, and then of real aircraft, which had decals pasted to their fuselage. Anders and I tinkered with the engine of our truck until we could take its components apart and put them back together, blind. The infantry joined us and we went on manoeuvres, honing skills, polishing attacks. We were given days off and we hung about playing cards or going down into the town. One day I went into a café and was served by a waitress who smiled at me when she brought out my eggs and coffee. Raven black hair, it might have been dyed, but expertly; green eyes that seemed to take in everything about me at once. I watched her walk away from the table and into the kitchen in back. Ample bum. How long had it been? She came out in a minute and served another table and when she passed, she glanced at me and we both smiled. She asked, "Anything else?"

"You look as if you might enjoy picnics?"

"I'm working today. Over lunch."

"A picnic can be at three o'clock. Or four."

She tilted her head and bit the inside of her cheek and said. "You move fast, soldier boy." Her mouth was large and her teeth bright white.

"There's a war on."

She laughed. "Good excuse. But I have the feeling—"

"It's a weakness. Wanting too much too fast. I have many."

"I don't doubt it." She cocked her head and added, "Four it is."

I watched her backside sway away from me again and felt dizzy. Such a full-bodied figure. I didn't even know her name.

Georgie, it turned out. Samantha George. At school she'd hated being called Sam, so when she left school, she'd gone with Georgie. We walked to a park five or six blocks away, *so the girls don't give me grief,* she said, and we found a quiet spot beneath a tree where birds were twittering and singing. I'd bought buns at a shop and cheese and a tomato, which I cut into slices with my pocket knife. Georgie made sandwiches. She'd brought two bottles of cold beer. I watched her take bites of sandwich and glug back swallows of beer. She noticed me watching her. "I know," she said with a giggle, "I'm a girl of appetites."

"You have appetites," I said. "I'm overeager."

She took another swallow of beer and smiled at me. "Over-eagerness. A fault I recognize. Because I have it too."

I rested my back against the tree trunk and chewed and took

sips of beer. A hawk circled overhead. I could see it open and close its beak as it flew. Was it getting ready to plunge? I said, "It's lovely here, on the island."

"Oh, please," she said. "Do we have to talk in clichés? I hate it here. I'm getting out as soon as I've saved enough to go to Vancouver."

I raised my eyebrows but before I could say anything, she went on: "You mean the—" she sighed. "The landscape: clouds and mountains and that crap, but you don't have to live here. It's a small-minded place. Everyone knows everyone's business. And it's dull. Everyone's a McCracken or a Roberts or Robinson. British and bland as bread."

"On the prairies it's Poles and Germans and Ukrainians and Icelanders."

"Ugh. Solid and stolid. Pass."

"And you?"

"I'm what they call a *free spirit.*"

"I'm prepared to guess what that means."

"It means girls want the same things—the same thing—as boys, but girls have to be careful they don't get a *reputation.*"

"You're a maverick."

"I'm just my own person. But this." She gestured around with one arm. "It's utterly boring. And utterly stupid."

I was watching her lips and taking in the fit of her sweater and pondering what might not be boring. Everything about her, I wagered.

Her landlady worked in a dress shop during the day and didn't come home until after six. Her room was small with a dresser and night table. The bed was narrow but we weren't interested in sleep. Our hands roved over each other: she was lemon mixed with honey, it tickled the nose and went straight to the sinuses. I didn't know how long it had been but I squirted myself all over the place with Georgie. I hadn't noticed that her breasts were as large as they were. Giant brown nipples. "My fun bags," she called them, laughing, when I kissed and sucked. "Ooh, more, more, more, do not, I repeat, do not stop. Harlan."

"Everyone calls me Dick."

"Hah. It fits."

We were without shame, I admit it. Whenever the landlady was working nights or out visiting or at church, I was quick-marching into town with a song in my heart and a bulge in my pants. Max and Anders would spot me leaving and sing out, "Roll me over in the clover, roll me over, lay me down, and do it again."

One Sunday morning as I was making my way through town on my way back to camp, I spotted a bicycle leaning against a fence. Bicycle. The ideal transportation for covering the couple of miles from camp to Georgie. It had a tag pinned to it: two dollars. I inquired inside. A gent with a full head of white hair dressed in a tweed jacket answered the door. "For you, a soldier," he said, "just a dollar. One soldier to another." I passed it over. He told me about how he'd ridden bicycles all his life. This one was just the latest of twenty-three he'd owned. Raleigh, he informed me, the best bicycle on the road. We stood at the fence for some time while he sang the bike's praises. I got on and tee-tered about for a few minutes before I got the hang of balancing it and then I was off down the road. "All oiled, tickety-boo," he called after me, "and the tires are inflated." As I pedalled away, I waved over my shoulder.

As I guessed, I loved riding a bicycle: the thrill of speeding on downhills, the freedom to go places you wouldn't otherwise have gone. It was a release; and for a soldier, subject to orders barked at him every hour of the day, and constrained to camp by curfews, a welcome liberty, like being able to fly. There's a photo of me arriving at the landlady's house and standing the bike against the picket fence. That's a pipe in my mouth. Georgie gave it to me for my birthday. "Better," she said, "than cigarettes, you don't have to inhale." We inhaled each other. We drank each other up. Lemon, I had not thought I fancied it; lemon and honey, dew of the gods.

She liked to straddle me. "Grab my ass," she insisted. "Roll me over now and hammer." The bed was narrow and we lay together after, a tangle of arms and legs. "Cunt," she said, "we have good cunt." She was lying in my arms but she drew back to study my reaction. "That's what Mister Lawrence calls having sex."

I raised one eyebrow. "I've heard the word."

"Yes, as a swear. But Mister Lawrence means it as something good. As in, we have good cunt together."

"Who," I asked, "is Mister Lawrence? An old boyfriend?"

"A writer," she said gaily. "He wrote a book about an upper-class British woman who has an affair with a gardener. Gardener? Gamekeeper, maybe. It doesn't matter. The book is *Lady Chatterly's Lover*. She's Lady Chatterly."

"Uh, huh. And what's the gardener's name?"

"I don't know. Gardiner?" She laughed and I laughed with her.

I gave her a look. "And if I wanted to read this book?"

"Can't. I haven't got it. It's banned here. My copy taken by a man I knew."

"Knew," I said knowingly, screwing up my lips.

"Slept with," she said, "yes. Had good cunt with." She tossed her head of hair and kissed me on the mouth. "Oh, Harlan," she said, "don't come all over bourgeois now."

I was toying with her curly locks. "You're the second person who's said that to me. I don't know what it means."

"It means all fussed about behaviour that isn't on the straight and narrow, the preacher's wife—or your bitchy aunt. It means afraid to say *sex* or *got laid*. Never mind do it. It means afraid to be yourself, afraid to do things that aren't conventional."

"Do what everyone else does, think what everyone else thinks?"

"Yeah. March to the beat of your own drummer."

"And this fellow, he was that way?"

"He was a lawyer, Terence Anderson, born and raised in Sweden, but went to school here. His ideas were unconventional for here, but not for in Europe." She paused and pulled a lock of hair loose and twisted it around in her fingers. "He didn't know, for example, that what we were doing, me a schoolgirl, was against the law here."

She twisted the lock of hair and sighed.

"And?"

"So Andy had to leave town. In a bit of a hurry."

I laughed. She let the lock of hair drop and poked me in the cheek. "It was not funny," she said. "Don't laugh."

"I was thinking of how I had to skip out one time. I was laughing at myself as much as your Andy." She lay back in my arms. "It was Andy," she said after a while, "who introduced me to Mister Lawrence."

"I'd guessed that." I loved the feel of her skin against mine, the scent that came off her hair—honey in the makings with the hint of lemon—her warm breath on my shoulder. "I will try," I said, "not to be bourgeois."

One afternoon we did it a second time and then dallied in each other's arms, murmuring things and drifting in and out of a doze. A door slammed below and we became alert. Georgie put a finger over my lips and shook her head. We strained our ears, listening: footsteps crossing the floor below. "Shit," Georgie whispered. I was pulling on clothes, heart in mouth. Georgie nodded towards a window at the foot of the bed. I peered out. It dropped to the roof of a garage about ten feet below. Georgie worked the mechanism that opened the window and pulled off the screen while I pulled on socks and shoes. I was just beginning

to lower myself over the sash when she said, "Hsst," and we both
froze and listened to feet clumping up the stairs. I inched over
the sash. Georgie had pulled a sweater over her head and the
last glimpse I had of her was her bum sticking up in the act of
pulling on a skirt. I wriggled downward, with my toes trying
for purchase against the wall, and when I was fully extended
I took a deep breath and let go of the sash and fell to the roof
of the garage. It was made of tin and clattered under my feet.
I stood for a moment getting my bearings and then tiptoed to
the edge of the roof. About six feet to the grass below; maybe
eight; I launched myself off and landed with knees bent, as
we'd been trained in boot camp. A stab of pain, sharp as a jolt
of electricity shot up my spine. Something cracked in one
knee. I was on hands and knees and remained that way for
a minute or so. When I righted myself, I saw an old woman
was studying me from across the street, a shopping bag in
one hand, the other resting on the top of a white picket fence.
I touched my hand to my temple in greeting, then strolled
around the corner to the place between a fence and a bush
where I'd stashed the bicycle. I tried to ride off in a dignified
manner. I don't think it worked.

It was a week before I returned to the café. I'd hurt my shoulder in the fall and had pain in one knee when I had to walk any
distance. Fortunately, we were not called out on parade or made
to do a route march. There was quite a bit of teasing about the
occasional wince I gave as I got up from my bunk in the mornings and after sitting on the end of Max's playing the harmonica.
"The old third leg acting up?" Max asked loudly. "Look at this
here, boys, look at Dick limping about now."

When I went back to the café it was in the late afternoon
near the end of Georgie's shift. She winked as she put pie and
coffee in front of me and later we walked to the park and sat on
a bench. The weather was changing. There was a wind and dark

clouds were scudding across the sky. "They say," Georgie stated, "the war is coming to an end. The Nazis got their back to the wall. The RAF is bombing the bejesus out of Germany."

"Don't believe everything you hear."

"You think you'll still get into action?"

"The Army tells us nothing. We're drilling as if we're getting on the boat to head to the Jap islands tomorrow."

"I don't believe it." Georgie had a way of stating things that seemed to bring conversation to an end. But oh, those green eyes; and pale, pale cheeks, remarkably white. Raven hair, green eyes, alabaster skin: it hurt sometimes to look at her, she was so beautiful.

"I'd be happy," I said quietly, "if we didn't see action."

"Grown sour on the war?"

"I signed up to fight Hitler. Hitler's on the run. But now they're sending us to fight the Japs. We didn't sign up for that. Jungle fighting."

"It makes a difference where you fight?"

"I don't want to die in a jungle from a bug bite or something. I signed up to set things right in Europe and now we're being sent to the stinking jungles to fight Japs. All because of the Americans."

We were holding hands and she lifted mine to her lips and kissed it. It was a small thing, tiny, but it made me feel better. I lifted her hand to mine and kissed her fingertips. My head swam in honey. "She wondered," Georgie said, laughing, and changing subjects, "about the noise she heard coming from the garage roof. I'd closed the window by then and played dumb and when she looked out, you were already gone."

"A bit of luck there." I squeezed her fingers. "But I did something to my knee and re-injured a shoulder I'd hurt once before."

"Jumping off a garage roof?" Georgie laughed.

"Actually," I said, "it was a not unlike circumstance." I

laughed and shook my head, and then she laughed too. I'd put my arm around her waist and had one hand on her rump.

She said, "You get a kick out of being bad, do you?"

"I thought you were the one who didn't want to behave *bourgeois*."

"Ouch," she said. "You got me there." She patted my knee. "What was your childhood like, Harlan? How did things go on with your father?"

"The old man? Hated him. Why do you ask?"

"Oh, it's just. You seem to have trouble with authority. You seem to enjoy putting yourself in situations where you can defy authority and get away with it. You get a kick out of being able to say: Ha, got the better of you there—teacher, dad, sergeant."

"And this has something to do with my old man?"

"Ah, who knows? I'm talking through my hat." She patted my leg again. "One thing for sure, Harlan, you are not, I repeat, not, bourgeois; my lovely Dick is not bourgeois."

"It was close," I said, "with your landlady. Maybe we should—"

"No. Not on your life, no. Don't even think it. Sundays morning's coming and there's something about doing it on Sunday morning that sends shivers up my spine. Did I tell you my father is a church minister?"

"You are a preacher's daughter." I patted her rump and gave her a long squeeze. "You have to be kidding!"

"I never kid about sex. Or about my father."

So there was Sunday, and there was the next day when I had leave, and there was another Sunday. But we were living at the caprice of the Army. After reveille one morning we were called on parade before mess. Captain Wiley and a sergeant walked up and down the line. When they were satisfied, the captain cleared his throat and stepped back; but it was the sergeant who spoke: "Staging for Courtenay at eleven hundred hours. Repeat:

that's eleven hundred hours. Pack up and be ready to ship out, soldiers."

No time for goodbyes. Hardly time to pack. One of the married soldiers whose wife was settled in with the *wandering wives* borrowed my bicycle and flew down the hill to share the news. I asked him to tell her to pass the word to Georgie. I had no great hopes she would. So I left without saying goodbye; another of my lovely girls to dream about as I drove the truck up the coast of Vancouver Island and smoked the pipe she had given me. I was not supposed to inhale, but was too much a slave to my needs: nicotine had its hold over me, as did breasts and bums and eager tongues.

Courtenay was smaller than Nanaimo, a staging site for ships that carried soldiers and their equipment into the Pacific theatre. It was raining throughout the drive north. Wind lashed the trees and giant leaves tumbled over the road and swirled into the ditch as the convoy passed. Anders said, "Ain't so lovely now, is it Dick, your celebrated Canada?"

"Fall," I muttered. The sudden move had upset me, and so, too had the prospect of engaging in jungle war. The weather was just one more straw on the camel's back: wind storms and rain and that let up for only two hours at a time and then started again. Miserable, I sucked on my pipe and tried not to think of Georgie and all my lost girls and to concentrate on the babble coming out of Anders' mouth. He was maybe less than a year younger than me but seemed little more than a schoolboy. Gee whizz, aw shucks. I laughed quietly to myself. He was a farmer's son, and like Phil, both simple and easy to get along with. Whereas I was subject to moods and grated on people sometimes, I was coming to realize. Did I think too much of myself? Did my opinions put people off? Maybe one, maybe the other; possibly both. Well, fuck them. If a man wanted to be his own person, not a bourgeois flunky, that's the risk he ran.

Courtenay was just another army base. Hurry up and wait, hurry up and wait. We were inching closer to the action but were not already in it. We had been hung up in a bureaucracy for what seemed like an unusually long time, but that happens in a big bureaucracy, where men, like machinery, can be lost for long periods and then suddenly rediscovered like misplaced ammunition.

Days of waiting to be shipped into action turned into weeks; weeks into months. The rain fell and the winds blew and storms blew inside and out of every man's heart. I took to playing the harmonica most nights, melancholy tunes, because that's the way we all felt. I had completed the song I'd been making up my own self. It was called, "Don't Forget Me, Little Darling," and it was a hit with the men when I played it and then sang the chorus for them: "Don't forget me, little darling, when I am far across the deep blue sea."

There was no leave at either Christmas or New Year. The cooks put up a turkey supper for the one and steaks for the other. We listened on the radio to the New Year come in at Times Square. And then a special program on the CBC for *our boys:* Guy Lombardo Orchestra; Juliette; Don Messer's Jubilee. In the years we'd been in the Army, we had been trained to kill and be killed, stiff upper lip in the face of death, but there were very few dry eyes that night.

There were letters from Margy every now and then. Mother was at home after a stint in hospital, but bedridden, it sounded. Ernie had gone into the recruitment office but been turned down: flat feet. Nora seemed to be happy with Mac, possibly pregnant. I paused over the words. *Seemed, possibly.* No word of Del, but I was thankful for it; that was in another country. I inhabited the country of kill-and-be-killed.

One afternoon when we were off duty and lazing about, I encountered Captain Wiley crossing from one side of camp to the other. We saluted. When we were past each other, he stopped and called back to me: "Bauch." I wheeled and returned to where he was standing. He stroked his thin black moustache, uncertain whether he should go on. "Angels," he said finally, "a host of angels with white wings; one of them takes us up in his arms and we float up into heaven, a place of light, we are the light and the light is all, soon we are only light, part of a great placid light."

"That does not sound like the way a soldier would go. Machine guns clattering, black smoke in the air."

"It all recedes. There is only the angel and the floating into pale light on white wings, and the hushed murmur of an unseen choir of seraphim in lullaby."

Water, grass, light. Something was beginning to take shape in my mind.

January passed. Did the sun come out once? The West Coast was lovely but its winter weather dreadful—for boys raised on the flatlands where the sun shone most days and the big prairie sky was almost always bright blue. So we became tetchy: anxiety about what would happen to us next, dismal weather, no women; they all played a part. Curses, arguments, fistfights. One night at the card table Plotnikov pointed a fat finger at Max and said, "You a cheating faggot, gun boy." I cleared my throat. Max was slow to anger but if he got into it, he was in it up to his ass. One of his hands had slid down to the knife he kept hidden in his puttees. There was silence as the two of them eyed each other up. The rest of us held steady. Max placed his cards on the table, face down. "You a kiss-ass bum-fucking faggot," Plotnikov went on.

I cleared my throat again. "No need for that kinda talk here," I said.

"You," Plotnikov said, turning his black eyes my way. He was missing an incisor and the rest of his teeth were stained and broken. His brain was a tangle of string filaments covered with dirt and bits of wool.

We'd crossed paths before. He spit on the floor near my feet. "Bauch," he said, "that's a German name."

"And Plotnikov is what—Polack?"

"Russian."

"Commie. Polack and commie."

He pushed his chair back. The card table tottered and Max steadied it with his hand. I was sitting on the end of a bunk. I stood up.

"Communists are our friends. So too Russians."

"The communists are dirty lying scum. Stalin. He's worse than Hitler."

"He's our ally."

"He's *your* ally. Because you don't got a brain to think with. A year ago he was our enemy, a low-down commie; resist Stalin, defeat communism, the PA blared at us day after day, but now suddenly he's our friend. Well, he ain't my friend."

Plotnikov stood up. He was short and stocky but he had big fists. The vein in his neck was bulging out. I felt my cheeks burning.

"You're a dumb Polack," I went on, my mouth a hurtling mountain stream plummeting out of control, a blur of words flying out of my head and into plain hearing; "you've been brainwashed by the army and are too dumb to even know it."

His first blow was a ridiculous haymaker, which I ducked. Phil had taught me how to fistfight. Throw a punch from the shoulder, a speedy stab at your man's belly. He'll throw his hands down for protection; that's why your next shot is straight at the nose. Throw from the shoulder; break it, if possible. You may take a punch or two, but you'll have him blinking teary eyes; then finish him. It didn't work out quite that way. We both went down. I'd grazed his cheek near his eye; my lip was busted. We were instantly a tangle of arms and legs, grunting, flailing, cursing. Our heads bounced on the wooden floor of the bunkhouse, our arms tore at each other's clothes. Plotnikov had my head trapped between his hip and a bed leg. There was a dying fly on the floor near my mouth, it was spinning in tight circles, toward my lips. I reached one hand down between Plotnikov's thighs and formed a fist over his balls. He howled out and shifted off of me. I was on my feet in a flash and he was on his knees. From his position below me, he had my hair twisted in a fist, tearing at it; I was striking him in the face, my left hand my main weapon, blow after blow; my knuckles snapped, I felt the bones of his face cracking but he would not go down; he tore at my hair as I smashed at his crumpling face. *Go down, go down.* I did not want to hurt him bad. We were at that for only a minute or so but it seemed hours. Two MPS broke in on us before anything else happened. Enough, they said. And it was. I was glad of it. My mouth hurt bad and my scalp was aflame. Someone helped me out into the fresh air. Someone helped Plotnikov to the end of his bunk.

The next day Sergeant Peters came into the bunkhouse after reveille. He stood at the end of my bunk. "Report to the Chief," he said curtly.

Captain Wiley was reading a report when I walked in and he kept me at attention until he flipped through two pages of typing. "Bauch," he said, no preliminaries, "they tell me you've been fighting." It wasn't a question, so I said nothing. "That's not good. Not good at all." He stood and looked me in the eye. I'd never noticed before but one of his eyes was two colours, half brown and half grey. "But it happens," he went on. "That's not really the problem here, is it Peters?" That wasn't a question, so Peters too kept mum. Captain Wiley took off his hat and ran one hand back through his black hair. "Here is the problem, Bauch. Bauch, that's German, isn't it? The problem, Bauch is you've been speaking out of turn, you've been saying things that are out of line, you been saying the army brainwashes soldiers."

"It was a mistake, sir."

"A mistake."

"Words uttered in the heat of the moment."

"Huh. The thing is, Bauch, you're a man who thinks too much. That can be a bad thing in this man's army. A soldier obeys orders; a soldier does not think. But you, now. I saw it when you refused my offer of an officer's stripes. It was out of line, that, but I let it go because of what we'd seen you do on the logistics drill. With the truck. I admired that. So I let your snub of the offer I made you go by the board. But what you've done here, Bauch, this comes close to treason. You understand?"

I nodded. At my side Peters nodded too.

"So here's the deal. I'm letting this pass. Let's say I got a soft spot for you. But you march out of here and we never hear a word out of you again. No more talk about politics. No more brawling. Clear, soldier?"

"Clear, sir."

"Dismiss."

Plotnikov was sitting outside the bunkhouse on a chair when I got back, one eye blackened, with a red rim, cheeks raw from where they'd been struck by my blows. He smiled a crooked smile as I approached and spat in the dirt as I walked by: his spit rolled into a little ball of dust and landed on my boot, then it rolled off. I walked through the bunkhouse, head high, though the crown of my skull throbbed with pain from where tufts of hair had been torn out. My knees trembled as I sat on my cot. "This effin' war," I said to Max, who was lying flat on his bunk, feet crossed at ankles, pillow under his head. "I don't know why I signed up in the first place."

Part III

WE NEVER DID ship out to Bonin Island, which had been the rumour. The Japs, like the Germans before them, surrendered. Parties, drunkenness, racy behaviour with girls on the streets and wherever else possible. Plotnikov fell out of the second-storey window of a hotel and broke both his legs. Max and I speculated whether he'd get an army pension. Wounded while in service. Maybe he'd be a cripple for the rest of his life. A part of me wanted it to be so. Correction: all of me.

The army kept us around for another month, then we were demobbed. I wondered if Georgie had made it to Vancouver. Sweet Georgie of the ready laugh and lovely lips. It had been a long time and the need in me was great. That was the past, though; even if I were to locate her, it would never work out. Still, going to Vancouver tempted me, it did; but then I thought, if the weather in Vancouver was similar to Courtenay, no thanks. Maybe Victoria, which was rumoured to be milder and less dismal. I was dithering over possibilities and wondering what direction my life might go in, the army no longer in charge of my every waking moment—what hour I got up, when and what I ate, when I took a crap. My mind was made up by a letter from Margy.

Things were not going as well between Nora and Mac as might be hoped, she hinted. But more important: Mother was seriously ill, a stomach problem, possibly the worst imaginable: another hint; nothing stated directly. I packed my few clothes and sundries into a bag; I took the twenty-seven-point-five, too, which I had become fond of, God knows why. Maybe if you suffer something over a long enough period of time you become attached to it, in a perverse way; it's part of who you are, willy-nilly.

The train chugged into the station in dawn light, and along with my fellow passengers, I rubbed sleep from my eyes and prepared to engage the so-called Chicago of the north. Winnipeg was much changed. The war had cost many lives but it had brought an odd kind of prosperity, too, and in its aftermath a feeling of buoyancy that bordered on euphoria: rationing had ended, and all sorts of things were becoming available by the day: washing machines, rubber tires, refrigerators, small appliances—toasters and irons and such. The streets were crowded with shop workers and businessmen and women wearing nylons on the march to Eaton's and The Bay, with dresses and dinnerware and God knows what all in mind. The newspapers were filled with uplifting articles: the Allies would not ask for retribution from the Axis countries, as they had after the Great War, but were actually going to help them rebuild their devastated lands with the Marshall Plan. The reconstruction everywhere was all good and it was all promising to be better.

I walked from the CN train station down Main Street and then along Portage Avenue. People were bustling about, many of them in that part of town newly arrived refugees from Europe: Hungarians and Czechs and dispossessed Jews, speaking a babble of languages. I went into a café Del and I had frequented after the movies. It was much changed: new red leatherette seats, bustling waitresses shouting *hot food* as they danced around tables with steaming bowls of borscht and plates of sandwiches and French fries. Suits and ties, the sparkle of good times in people's eyes. I took out my pipe and lit up and smoked for a while as I sipped coffee and thought: I have to get in on this. The coal yards crossed my mind but I dismissed the thought. I was made for better things, and I'd figure out what they were after visiting with Mother and the others.

The house was silent when I walked in, and I took it as a bad sign. I put my hat on a peg at the entrance and peeked into the living room and then the kitchen. No one was around, so I went upstairs. Mother was sitting up in bed, her Bible under her folded hands, eyes closed, her once shiny, dark hair lanky and falling in strings down to her shoulders. She'd aged twenty years since I'd last seen her. I put one hand out and steadied myself against the frame of the door. Each beat of my heart pulsed in my fingers. I don't know how long I stood there, but when she opened her eyes a wan smile crinkled her lips and she motioned me over to the bed. I sat on the very edge and took her hand as lightly as possible. A thin whiff of cinnamon, not much; residue. "I'm not china," she said, "I won't break if you lean over and give me the kiss I want." My lips touched her warm forehead. "There," she said, forcing brightness into her voice. She squeezed my fingers. "Don't fret, now, Harlan. You know I'm going to a better place." She smiled thinly again and added with a sigh, "Only a little sooner than I'd figured."

Margy came in then. She rushed over to me and I stood abruptly and she threw her arms around me; cornflowers on a warm afternoon, a day of light breezes; I breathed them in.

Her breath was shallow and raspy and her body trembled in my grasp. I'd been in the army, I realized, and free of the burden of this, and Margy had been suffering it alone. Ernie was too young and Nora had her own worries, so the burden had fallen on Margy. And what was I doing? Playing at soldier and chasing into town to spend time with Georgie and getting into fistfights with Plotnikov. What a low-life. While I was being a soldier, I'd felt that the five dollars the army had been sending by mail every week in my name to Mother was a generous thing, that it made me the good son, but as I held Margy against me I realized how paltry that gesture had been compared to the daily care she'd been giving to Mother. The fret, the worry, the sitting by helpless as Mother's life leaked away. Margy was a saint; and I whispered that to her as we stood clinging together at Mother's bedside, knowing that nothing I would ever do would make it up. "You did your part," Margy whispered in my ear, "without the money I don't know how we would have made it."

Mother came down to supper and picked away at the stew and bread Aunt Helen put before her on a small plate. I could hardly choke down the meal. We said the after-grace in a solemnity I did not know was possible. And then Aunt Helen said cheerily, "There's strudel and tea with sugar, oh thank the Lord this war is over." Mother went up to bed and Margy to her room. Ernie was doing a shift at the hospital laundry, a part-time job Uncle Ralph had arranged for him.

He took me into the living room while Aunt Helen cleared up the dishes, and he pointed to a chair near the fireplace. "Over, then," he said with a sigh. He was referring to the war.

"Finished, yes."

"And no worse for wear?"

"I wish sometimes I'd seen action."

"Yes, now. There will come a day when you'll be glad of it." He kept a bottle of schnapps under the kitchen sink and he'd brought it out with him and poured us a small glass each. "*Prosit*." I tipped my glass towards his. "We're proud of you, Helen and me; and your mother, well. You know that, yes?"

Nothing was said of Phil and Art, who'd ducked out of service, but their names hung in the air between us. "We're proud of you, son."

"I'm glad to hear it. Thank you, sir."

"Sir," he said, grinning. "I could get used to that."

We sipped our drinks. In the kitchen there was rattling of dishes and hot water ticked in the pipes. After a while he said, "There's a man I want you to meet, Harlan. A man with a good heart, who's trying to help soldiers like you get back on their feet. I've arranged for you two to meet tomorrow."

His office on Portage was small but everything was neat: doormat saying REMOVE SHOES PLEASE just inside the entrance; three leatherette chairs placed side-by-side along one wall; pencils lined up precisely on a desk; a perfectly coiffed and smiling secretary. One clock hung on the wall behind her, where pinned to its panelling was a large-scale map of the city and environs. Another clock hung on the wall across from the secretary: in the silence of the room a thin red hand ticked off seconds. It was 9:02. I was late.

Harvey Stevenson sat just out of sight behind a partition in the room, the very tips of his fingers the only part of him visible: tapping a paper lying on a desk: *tap tap tap*. When the secretary called out, "Mister Bauch is here," he came around the partition with his hand out in greeting. I could not help but notice the glittering blue stone in the ring on his finger and the precise part in his dark hair. "Everyone calls me Stevey," he said; "a holdover from school." An assortment of nuts littered his head, like in a Christmas bowl: macadamias, walnuts, almonds, filberts, cashews.

"Thank you for taking the time to see me, sir."

"Not *sir* to you," he said chuckling. "You're the hero back from service."

A silence fell in the room. "Come back with me," he said, but before we were seated he added, "There's something I have to tell you. I'll tell you and then we'll speak of it no more." I swallowed hard. It was the story of his son, who had died on the beaches of Normandy. They had received a telegram ten days after the landing: missing in action. His eyes misted over. "You have no idea," he said, his voice low and throaty. He put one hand out and rested it on my forearm. "We tell ourselves it was over quickly, that he didn't suffer, but I know what wars are all about, Bauch. Men—boys, Bauch, boys the same as you—half out of their minds, drowning in the seas, choking on their own blood...." He straightened his shoulders and gazed past my head for a minute, gathering himself. "Well," he concluded, "enough of that."

It was real estate he did, and when we were seated behind the partition, he discoursed on it, explaining how the city was due—"overdue, Bauch"—for a major expansion, especially in the south end where people wanted to reside, away from the rail-yards of the north and congestion of downtown. Houses—"no, I correct myself, developments, communities, Bauch"—were going to spring up everywhere, and people currently in houses in other neighbourhoods were going to upgrade to them, while people currently renting were going to purchase *their* places. He waved his arms in the air as he talked. Transaction after transaction. If you're a go-getter—"and you look to be one, Bauch"—there's no limit, no limit at all to where you can go. "I know what you're worried about," he said before I'd got in one word, "you're concerned about the licence; but we'll enrol you today"—he glanced at his wristwatch—"we'll enrol you in the course today, Bauch, and in a month you'll have the licence." A course of classes beginning at three in the afternoon and ending at eight; an examination in three weeks and presto, certified to sell houses. In the meantime, I was to accompany him when he gave appraisals and wrote up listing agreements, and showed houses, and closed sales.

We were in his Buick driving to an appointment with a couple on Dowker Avenue before I had spoken five words. He hadn't even asked if I wanted the job. He assumed there was nothing a demobbed soldier would want to do more with the remainder of his days than sell bungalows and two-car garages. And that is just what we did. He talked, he smiled, he joked, he manipulated and answered questions, he talked more, he closed deals.

We dropped by his home in Crescentwood frequently. "Just have to check on something," he told me. I'd loiter in the living room while he went in back for a few minutes. One day he came out with a weird smile crinkling his lips. "Look at this," he said. He reached one hand gingerly to the inside pocket of his sport jacket and drew his closed fist out carefully; he opened his hand and on the palm sat a white mouse. "Alvin," he whispered to it, "meet Harlan." He stroked its back with one finger. Its nose was pink, its tiny ears twitched, its pink eyes gazed up at me. "One of my little pals," he added, grinning. He turned and left the room, and in a moment I heard footsteps descending stairs. I went to the kitchen sink and poured a glass of cold water and drank it down quickly. I'd felt a twinge go up my spine when the mouse raised its eyes to mine, and I thought I'd heard a word coming from the palm of Harvey's hand—*mucus*, maybe, something on that order—and I did not want to think about it. I put Harvey and his mouse out of mind.

"Bauch," he told me one day, "when you answer questions about concrete or plumbing or roofs, never say more than you need to say." On another day he said over a cup of coffee: "In a market like this, houses sell themselves. It was not so during the war; then we sweated every sale. But now: put up a sign, walk through with buyers, get out the pen for the purchase agreement."

I went to the course in the basement of a church downtown: fluorescent lighting; stacking chairs; on the walls pictures of Jesus drawn by Sunday-school kids—Jesus as a baby, Jesus with the fishes and loaves; Jesus giving the Sermon on the Mount. The course was taught by an older man with thick spectacles who said "uuummm" after every second or third sentence. Above us, on the main floor of the building, a choir practised for Sunday service. We perused a three-ring binder filled with real estate jargon: amortization, encumbrance, fee simple, lean, loan, guarantor, contingency, carry-back, rate lock, default, trustee. I mouthed the concepts on the way home. I was becoming a real estate agent, a mover-and-shaker, maybe one day a pillar of the community. Is that what I wanted, the barker, the demobbed soldier? It was a step up, but was it a ladder I wanted to climb? I could always step off, I told myself, I could always change courses. On the weekend before the examination, I bought a car, which Harvey insisted I would need in the business. A 1943 Dodge Club Coupe: six cylinder, two-tone green, white-wall tires. A substantial vehicle, though not a flashy one, as befitted a real estate agent.

When I got my licence, he took me out to supper: Moore's on Portage, a steak and a baked potato. Salad. It was a warm fall evening and after our heavy meal, we strolled south on Memorial Boulevard toward the Legislative buildings. "We're all very proud of you boys," Harvey told me, "the sacrifices you made— were prepared to make."

"Thank you, sir. It was what a man did."

"Heroes. By George."

We parted at his car, parked on a side street. "Come by the house," he told me, "at eight o'clock sharp tomorrow. We're to meet a couple at the Cambridge listing at nine." I walked to my car, a few streets over. The moon was high in the sky: I leaned on the fender of the Dodge and looked up at it and took out my pipe and had a smoke as people strolled past, laughing and talking. He was a great guy, Harvey. He'd taken me into his business as if I were his son, he'd paid for my course and licence. Shown me his mouse: a trust, I gathered, rarely bestowed. He was setting me up for a lifetime: a home of my own, marriage, children. My eyes misted over; I brushed at them with the back of my hand. I realized that since I'd left home, no one had ever really cared about me. The only notice I'd received was to be barked at by this one or the other.

He met me at the door and pointed at the mat—REMOVE SHOES PLEASE—and made a gesture that indicated he was on the phone in a back room. I sat on a couch in the living room that looked back toward the kitchen and a breakfast nook. There were magazines on a table and I picked one up and flipped its pages: advertisements for next year's cars: a red Mercedes with doors that opened wing-style caught my eye. One day. One day. I'd brought along a handful of papers, too, relating to the house on Cambridge, and I reluctantly put down the magazine and took them up.

The shuffling of feet caught my attention. A girl of maybe nineteen, a young woman, had come into the room from the hallway leading to the back of the house and the sight of her stopped my breath. Hair like a burning bush, long legs running up to a black-on-blue tartan skirt, a pert ass peeking out from under its precisely pressed creases, full breasts blossoming beneath an off-white tennis sweater under which there was no blouse, so the tops of an ample set of creamy white breasts was just visible.

"Oh, good God," I thought." I may have said it aloud. She was in every sense of the word *luscious*. I had to look away, I had to feign interest in the papers trembling in my hands. Real property papers, an offer to purchase, one of the most mundane and tedious documents devised by lawyer-kind; this is what I had to concentrate on while the most beautiful young woman in the world was in my presence, almost at arm's length. Does life throw curve balls? Is life cruel? It does; it is. I swallowed hard and tried to focus on the words dancing in front of my eyes: a blur of characters spelling inanity.

The room was silent, the air dripping anticipation; I glanced up and she was looking at me, had been for some time apparently, because my looking up caused her to smile a certain way: aha, *I do have your attention!* Impertinent. That was the look in her green eyes. Her smile broadened and I thought at that moment, No, must not do this, must not. Think of Harvey, his expansive heart, think of the lost son and how much it must have cost him to take you into his confidence, think of how good he has been to you, do not. But it was already too late.

"Elinor," she said, anticipating my every thought. "El. Or, in the secret circle, Hellinor. But you have to earn your way into the secret circle."

"Harlan," I said.

"Oh, I know," she said, coyly tossing her glistening hair back over one shoulder to expose a long peaches-and-cream throat, throbbing downwards into the V-neck of the tennis sweater.

"And how," I asked, knowing the answer would likely be the death of me, "how do you get into the secret circle?"

"That," she said, laughing, "is the secret."

Don't, Harlan, don't, I was enjoining myself over and over, a mantra.

Just then Harvey came back into the room and I was able to glance down at the papers in my hand. They were crinkled slightly; there was a moist ring on the top sheet where my thumb had been. "My daughter," he said curtly, head tipping towards her, "my daughter, Elinor. Elinor, this is Harlan."

Hello," I said weakly.

"'Lo," she said. She was standing behind him and was looking over his shoulder and she made a face at me, tongue out, head wagging side to side. It was a come-on of the most ridiculous kind. I had to keep myself from laughing aloud. I bit hard at the inside of my cheek. I tasted blood.

Harvey was oblivious. He had a document in his hand and his attention was focused solely on black words typed on white paper.

"Are you a student, then?" I asked to quell the throbbing in my throat.

She gave me a quizzical look, then said, "SMA, you know. Down along the river? The girls' school. I graduate this year."

"That must be a relief," I said. "School can feel so...so—"

"Confining," she said. "Yes. I've enjoyed it, though. But I'm ready to ... to move on."

"I would think so."

"Confining," she repeated. "I'm looking for—for a little excitement. If you know what I mean."

I did. I nodded. I swallowed a mouthful of blood mixed with saliva.

Harvey was looking at his watch. "*We* should get moving," he said to me abruptly. "That couple is probably waiting on Cambridge."

I stood up. I was flattening the creases on the thighs of my trousers when I glanced up and saw she was looking directly at my crotch. She smiled without opening her mouth and then stuck her tongue out again and waggled it over her red lips.

I could have cried out. I could have pushed Harvey aside, grabbed her up in my arms and taken her right there beside the breakfast nook. Good God. Instead I drew a breath, and when Harvey looked down, I took the opportunity to return her mockery, sticking out my tongue, which was covered in blood from the biting my teeth had been giving my cheek. She screwed her face into a theatrical expression, *eewww*. But it was just that: theatre. I was used to it from the carney. It was a mask, covering up for the delight she was actually feeling. The pleasure she was taking in my discomfort. And what she knew was coming next. *A little excitement.*

There's a picture of her standing in a grove of trees. Remark the smile, the almost disdainful set of her mouth, the hair perfectly coiffed but looking as if it might come undone at any moment. Undone. Wild. Her attractiveness lay in the untamed, the possibility that like her hair Elinor could come undone in a most unruly, delicious way. *Hellinor.* Does she look like a hellion?

Harvey put his hand on my elbow and steered me to the front entrance.

"Bye, Daddy," she said; "bye, *Mister* Harlan."

I did not say anything more, I did not look back. To look back would have been my death, like Lot's wife or those other Biblical characters who were told not to look back, and did, and paid for it with their lives. It was a Biblical story that made sense to me, though I was sweating mightily.

The point was I could taste her in my mouth, though I had not touched her, had not been closer than ten feet: soft and juicy as a ripe peach, she was. Good God, Harlan. The words ran through my head: Do not, do not. But lust is a runaway train looking for a smash-up to get into.

When we were seated in his Buick, Harvey said, "Schoolgirls. Her mother and I have no idea what's going on in her head."

"It's a trying time," I croaked out. "Big changes."

"It was good of you to take an interest in her. She lives for that, attention; they all do." He shook his head and drummed the steering wheel with both hands before going on. "Schoolgirls," he repeated. "No idea what she's liable to do next." He sighed.

I thought, I have a very good idea. One which will be the end of me.

We closed the house on Cambridge, and when we returned to the office, there were three calls waiting for us. All about the house on Cambridge. But Harvey went into his smooth patter, steering away from it subtly but quickly, talking up a house on Somerset and another on Renfrew, and at the end of it, he was meeting one couple at the latter and I was on with a second at the former.

It was a matter of presentation, as Harvey had said. Putting the buyers at ease, listening to what they actually said or asked, rather than steamrollering over them with the pitch you'd decided on beforehand. He was good; but I was better. I had the carney behind me; I'd learned the knack of reading faces and interpreting looks, gestures, the tiniest of verbal clues. I could tell which of any couple called the shots behind closed doors— mostly the women—or if one of them didn't like the look of a place from the get-go, or even if things were a little rocky between them. I could tell if the two of them studying stucco walls was a way of plastering over cracks in the marriage vows.

At the Somerset house, a three-storey, twin-roofed, rambling burg with dark and broad woodwork I had the children of established money, looking to replicate mommy and daddy's mini-mansion on Kingsway, or one of the other fashionable avenues. Windows is what they were interested in, lots of light; and a library. We did not even get to the basement, which had several serious cracks in the walls, evidence of spring groundswell, and shifting, and costly concrete repairs looming. I had only to hint that there was another party interested and we were sitting at the oak dining table with the papers in front of us. Oh, what easy pickings the real estate game was. The carney with its reek of shabby deceptions and its two-bit returns was, well, two-bit. Of the five percent commission that would be charged on the Somerset closing, I would pocket two: numbers whirled through my head. Thoughts of silk ties and Italian shoes, the kinds of things that would impress the graduate of a girls' school. Thoughts that rushed ahead on that runaway train and arrived abruptly at the cliff that was Elinor and tipped me into disaster.

I could have stopped myself. I was not fool enough to think that amour between a demobbed soldier and a schoolgirl was foreordained, a coupling dictated by powers beyond our reach. No. That may occur: love at first sight, the perfect conjunction of this X with that Y, I've seen it, two people looking for something, desperate, you might say, for something: they walk into a room and there is the answer to their mutual need. It happens; it works out, even. But this between Elinor and me was not that: this was dalliance: wanton, pure and simple; or not so pure, and liable to be complicated. Lust.

One week Harvey and I listed three houses and sold two of them before the signs were put up on the front lawns. We engaged in a mini-competition: who could sell the most houses in a month. When I was to meet potential buyers, I made a point of brushing my teeth beforehand, and of giving my Italian loafers the spit and buff, army style. I straightened my shoulders getting out of the car and presented myself with a firm handshake: *call me Harlan.* My bank account swelled. A photo from the time has me in a three-piece suit, white shirt, sporty tie and pocket handkerchief. Note the fedora, the jaunty bend in the brim, the hat black, its ribbon grey. Hands deep in pockets. On first appearance I'm slouching slightly backward, but it's not out of indifference to the camera; it's swagger, as is evident in the buttoned-down waistcoat, the tilt of the hat and my chin, my downward-looking eyes, verging on arrogance. Do I think a lot of myself? I leave it to others to decide.

At first it was exciting to close sales, but I saw there would come a day when the whole business of real estate would become tedious. Maybe I would go into something else. Already I had my eye on empty building lots on streets out toward the university where waterworks were being installed, and soon would come paved streets and hydro poles. When selling houses became boring, I could try my hand at property development. The idea set my toes to tapping. I had to quell the urge to jingle the keys in my trouser pockets.

One afternoon I was showing a house and I'd left the interested couple in the kitchen to talk between themselves. I wandered into a bedroom. I enjoyed looking at photographs people put on their dressers: parents, children, friends, partying groups, the wedding. The bed was rumpled. The neatness of rooms was something I usually checked before meeting potential buyers, but I'd been in a hurry and it had slipped past me. No matter, I thought, no harm done. I reached out to give the bedspread a straightening tug and noticed on the floor a condom. I glanced over my shoulder and pushed at it with the toe of my shoe; it rolled but went under the bed. I chuckled quietly thinking about how the bed had got rumpled when a bubble burst in my head: empty house, key to the lock-box in my pocket, inviting bed. I had not seen the possibility before. I had to sit on the edge of the mattress to gather myself together. Another man might laugh at how slow I'd been on the uptake. I was usually a quick study, but the uprightness I'd inherited from Mother sometimes blinded me to certain possibilities, among them the carnal.

She was fading daily, Mother, and it hurt to enter her bedroom and sit with her hand in mine, her pulse weak, her breathing irregular. Sometimes I took the harmonica in with me and played her favourites: "Church in the Vale" and so on. I swallowed hard when she smiled wanly afterward. One day she whispered, "Play that at the funeral." My legs were rubber as I mounted the stairs to my bed and I lay on the cot for a long time before my heart stopped hammering in my chest. It was then I heard a voice say: *musculus.* I closed my eyes. "No," I said aloud, and I directed my thoughts to Elinor, which was a relief, but a guilty relief. I would have to face up to these voices some day. Their speaking to me was not random or arbitrary.

I thought of Elinor a lot. When I was showing a house I thought: where is she right at this moment? I pictured a change room, I blush to admit, naked girls coming out of showers after gym class, glistening bodies, wet hair. I lost the thread of conversations with buyers: Elinor with her elbows on a desk, eyes gazing at a teacher; Elinor walking across a quadrangle of grass on her way to lunch; Elinor on elbows and knees. I contrived to meet Harvey at his home and twice I encountered her, once as she was standing in the entrance, ready to leave for school. She reached into a pocket and passed me a small card on which was written a phone number and a date and time. I called. On the second ring, she picked up. I heard her call out, "I got it!" She said into the telephone, "Eight, Thursday." The line went dead.

Over the intervening days, I fussed and I fumed. Should I wear cologne? Should I arrive in casual dress, slacks, without tie? Should I bring something—flowers? On Wednesday I visited Eaton's and purchased cologne. I awoke in the middle of the night with these words on my lips: *it's a test.* By the Lord, Harry, I thought, I was being put to the test by a schoolgirl. I'd damn well show up as I pleased and she could take it or leave it. But I wore a freshly laundered white shirt, and pressed slacks, and dabbed on the smallest bit of cologne. Talk is cheap. Bluster and bombast cheaper. But I had a lady to win and I would do what was required. Truth be told, I would have stood on my head for one tiny sniff of her breasts.

She met me at the door. She asked, "Where did you park?"

I hadn't expected such practicality from a teenager in bare

feet, busting out of a tight angora sweater. "Two blocks down." I said. "In the shadow of a giant oak."

She waggled one finger at me. "Do you want a drink?"

I wanted to be on the far side of town; I wanted to be sitting on the edge of my cot playing the harmonica. I wanted to throw her on the floor and have my way with her. But that would have been unseemly, I reckoned, so I said, "A soda, if you have one."

She went and brought back a Pepsi in one hand and a glass of white wine in the other. She sat prettily on the chair across from mine, legs crossed at the ankles and took a sip of her wine. "The Germans say *prosit*," she said, smiling over the lip of the glass, "the French say *à votre santé*."

"Down the hatch," I offered. "That's what we said in the army."

"How cute." She reached across and *tinked* her glass against the Pepsi bottle. "We have plenty of time," she went on. "Mommy's at WA and daddy's at one of his mystery meetings. They never get home until after ten." She was studying my feet. I hadn't realized it but I had one leg crossed over the other and was bouncing it rapidly. She drank off her wine and came and sat in my lap. Some light scent: whiff of peaches, sweet juice, dribbling down the chin. We kissed; her lips were full and she was a good kisser, plenty of tongue but at the same time quite delicate and not at all forceful. I was immediately erect and had to shift about on the chair. She pretended not to notice and ran one slim finger along my cheek. "Your eyes," she said; "you have the oddest eyes." She pulled back. "No," she went on, "it's not the colour or the shape but something else entirely. Utterly. I don't know what." She led me to her room, a clutter of clothes on backs of chairs, shoes scattered about the floor and a single bed with a white bedspread featuring a cherry blossom design. Girlish. We lay side by side and kissed a long time. I had the feeling I was her first, so I did not want to rush. Her body was long and her breasts full; the hair on her mound was silky orange. I paused as I ran my fingers over it. Then she lay back and spread her legs and instructed me: "Come on then." She seemed to like it.

"Technically," she said as we lay side by side after, "I was a virgin."

"*Technically?*"

"Girls' school. We do three things—other than scheme to exasperate the sisters. Make drawings of nudes in art class; play field hockey; go to bed with other girls."

"Hmmm," I said. I raised myself up on one elbow. "So, orgasms, then."

"Sufficient to suffonsify."

It was cramped on the single bed and I sat on its edge and ran my fingers from her belly button to her clavicle, over and over. "That's very nice," she said, smiling. "You've been with a lot of women; you know how to be gentle."

I looked into her big eyes. "Not a lot of women."

"I'm glad of that. I really am." We smiled at each other and touched each other's bodies with fingers. "Well," she added, "you may not actually be tapping your toes, but you're doing it mentally, I see it in your eyes."

"It's guilt. He's been so damn good to me."

"Pooh. Parents."

When we stood in the foyer it was nine-fifteen. She kissed me on the cheek and I grabbed her one last time in a hug, crushing her to my chest. She said into my shoulder, "Next time?"

"I can call you again?"

"Same time, same day."

"I'll call."

"Oh," she added, as she closed the door behind me. "You can officially call me Hellinor." I heard her laughter as I descended the concrete steps.

I skulked away.

On Tuesdays I called; on Thursdays we met. She took to it like a duck to water. "Do it really, really hard," she said one night. I was happy to oblige. "Slow," she said another time, "pull all the way out and then go all the way in, then all the way out again. Oh, Mother of Mary!" I did whatever she wished. If she straddled me, I ran my tongue in circles around her nipples; when she wanted to do it standing, her legs crossed over my hips, I banged her against a wall; doggy-style; on the dining room table. It began as an education for her but soon we were both trying different classes at the University of Fornication.

Peaches it was, and pears: sweetness, tartness, juice that called out to be drunk in, flesh that could not be resisted.

At home Margy waggled her finger at me and said, "You've got a girl."

"I'll admit it if you admit you've got a guy."

"All right. He works in the same office. And before you ask, he is not, repeat, not, married." Margy had a job at the stockyards, secretary to one of the bigwigs. It suited her: she was smart, she was efficient; she knew how to keep her mouth shut, maybe the prime virtue in being a first-rate secretary.

"Let's keep it between just us two."

"Right. Our little secret."

Upstairs I sat on my cot and wondered what Harvey would do if he found out. When he found out. Harlan, Harlan, should not, should not.

On Sundays when we went to church with Mother I prayed earnestly for forgiveness, but we kept on committing the same sin, Elinor and I, so it was hard to see how praying could help. I would have to change more than my heart to be truly forgiven, and my heart was in thrall to my loins.

As Christmas approached real estate sales dropped off. "Happens every year," Harvey explained as we sat in the office, drinking coffee, waiting for the phone to ring. "A seasonal cycle, December into March, most years, sales drop away, but then the phone starts to ring off the hook." We tried to keep busy by putting posters up on the bulletin boards at grocery stores, and having flyers delivered by the post office.

Winter descended. There were houses for sale, but no one was buying. "People spend all their dough at Christmas," Harvey said. "They got nothing left for January and February."

"And the weather," I added. "Who wants to move when there's three feet of snow on the ground and it's twenty below zero?"

"That too," Harvey said. We both looked at the phone. I stood up and jingled the keys in my pocket. Harvey sighed. He pushed back the cuff of his jacket and looked at his watch. We left the office at four o'clock and came in at nine. We listened to the radio. We took long lunches. We ran out of things to say to each other. We played cribbage, game after game. Harvey, I noticed one day, cheated when counting. I gave him a look. He gave me a look. We let it pass. One cheat to another.

One day I came in and Harvey said, "There's a new listing for you to check out. Along Kildonan Drive, river side." He'd written the address and a name on a piece of paper. "Get on it," he added.

It was only as I made the turn off of Main Street that it crossed my mind: why had Harvey sent me and not taken the listing himself? I drove slowly on Kildonan Drive, checking addresses. "Nice houses," I said aloud, tapping the steering wheel with gloved hands, "nice homes." Harvey had insisted on that: calling properties *homes*. I didn't agree with it; a house is not necessarily a home; you have to make a home out of a house. But it was part of the sales pitch: making the place sound comfy and welcoming, even though it was only plasterboard walls and stucco; sinks and toilets; plumbing, electricity, and concrete floors in basements. Tubs. A house was four walls and a shitpile of potential headache; a home was a place where children grew up and could always return to. But an agent did not say those words. So I was back to being the barker: come-ons, pitches, manipulations—only massaged in a lot of soft soap and gussied up to appear to be neighbourly assistance.

I pulled up outside a two-storey with Cape Cod windows, grey siding, black trim. A scraggly-haired woman met me at the door as I was raising my finger to push the bell. A woman with a bent nose that had a mole on it and wrinkled cheeks that went with the scraggly grey hair. If you looked it up in the encyclopedia, you'd find her picture beside the word *witch*.

"You must get me out of this house," she said before I had pulled the door shut behind me.

"It's nice. Spacious, lots on light coming in the windows. And the view of the river."

"Not for me. Not any longer. It's … well, let's say it no longer suits."

I looked around. Shiny hardwood floors, wide doorways, lots of woodwork, an old gem. On the walls there were pictures. The one in front of me was of a cat sitting on a cushion. I glanced right: cat prone; to the left: two green cat's eyes staring out of a black background. All of the pictures on the walls were of cats. "You like cats."

"Cats," she said, "have been worshipped since ancient times. *Like* does not enter into it. It's my cats who do not want to live in this house anymore. They insist we leave."

I looked around. "Your cats? But I don't see any—"

"These right here," she said, sweeping her arm in an arc around the room.

"And they—"

"Tell me it's time to leave this house, yes. Yesterday, if possible." She ran her hands through her grey hair again and shook her head. "Pronto."

I took the pen out of my breast pocket. "Let's get some details. I'll just jot some details into my little black book and then—"

"Wait," she interjected. She indicated I should pass the notebook over and she held it against her breast and closed her eyes and seemed to hum a tune to herself for half a minute. When she reopened her eyes, she said, "Yes, we're okay." I took the notebook back. "Look me in the eye," she went on, abruptly. "No, the other one. Did you know that most people look people in one eye only? And that it's almost always the right eye? But it's the left eye that speaks truth. The Devil's eye." I shifted my gaze to her left eye and felt her staring into mine. "Exactly," she said. She nodded slowly. "You have a nickname," she said, "that you do not like, which you no longer use. It's part of an old self, a self you have shaken off."

I was thinking of the day when I'd seen the car on fire and knew that the woman inside had been murdered by her husband. Knew. The scraggly-headed, twitchy woman in front of me, she knew too. I was without words. Though I could feel my heart choking up my throat.

"I sense powerful vibrations," she went on. "Emanating from you. Do you see things? Do you hear things?" I drew in a breath. But she was running on: "Of course you do. Why do I even ask?" She motioned to a chair and sat opposite me on a couch drowning in cushions and throw rugs. "Tomorrow," she said, "you come here, eight o'clock. Don't be late."

I adjusted my tie. I nodded. It was as if I was in the power of a force I could not resist; as if we both were. A force that was unspoken but could not be denied any longer. At that moment I realized I'd been resisting something for most of my conscious life, denying it, and this was the time to acknowledge it and embrace it, or turn my back on it forever and be much the less for it.

We signed the papers. Neither of us were interested in collateral, escrow, or foreclosure. Something was in the air that was bigger than bridge financing. I did not even look at the rooms, or take the usual measurements, or check the foundation for cracks. None of that mattered. "You should get a cat," she stated as I was leaving. "Abyssinian, grey. Or, no, a wolf cub. Hmm." On the sidewalk I turned when she called out, "Eight sharp. Don't tell a soul where you're going."

Soul, I thought, a curious word for what we were about to engage in.

That was a Wednesday. On Thursday afternoon Elinor met me at a listing in the Wolseley area, not far from her school and we played on a double bed in an upstairs bedroom for a couple of hours. Go at it; drink a little white wine I had obligingly brought along; go at it again. She enjoyed prolonging matters, racking up orgasms, I imagined from the way she bit her lower lip in the throws of coming. I teased her about it: "What was the score that time: 6-2?"

She laughed. "I lose count. After three, they blur into each other."

"Mine do not blur."

I drove her to within a few blocks of her parents' place and she kissed me once quickly on the cheek before getting out. Aroma of ripe peach. I winced. I was terrified when we were together that someone would spot us. Winnipeg was not a big city; more a big town. Eventually everyone found out about everything.

That night I arrived before eight and Vera showed me into a large room in back that was dimly lit and had heavy curtains drawn over its windows. People were sitting around a very large wood table, ten or twelve, those toward the far end mere shadows in the darkened space. A cloying odour pervaded the room: incense. Vera pointed to an empty seat and sat next to me. She said, "Friends, this is Harlan."

The others said as one voice: "*Saluto*, Harlan, *pax*."

Vera took one deep breath, then two, then three. By the exhalation of the third breath everyone around the table was breathing in unison. I found myself joining in. Vera placed her elbows on the table, and her hands together to form a steeple. From their laps everyone produced a small figurine, similar to a token in a board game, and placed it before them. Most were animals, but the man two down from me had a three-crowned mountain. Vera's was a cat, sitting upright. Before me she placed a wolf. She was clearly the leader; the others waited on her. She said, "We seek the Way."

The others chanted in voices barely above a whisper: "The Way."

I calmed myself by breathing in and out slowly. There was another odour in the room besides incense: cat fur.

We joined hands. Vera's was small and dry, fingers delicate as bone china. The woman beside me had warm, sweaty palms. We breathed again, then: once, twice, three times, in and out; a memory returned to me of such breathing but I had no time to place it. After some minutes, Vera whispered very slowly, "The Wayyy."

There was silence around the table. The hair on the back of my head had begun to stand up—right at the collar first, and then farther up. The eyes of everyone around the table were closed; I closed mine too; it felt right to do so; and when they were closed, it was as if they had opened in another dimension, into a realm in behind my head. Vera was kind of moaning; what came out of her mouth sounded like *ohnnnnnn*, prolonged and at the end of her breath; the others were following her lead. At the top of a breath I joined in: *ohnnnnnnn*. Something in my chest released, a slow-motion explosion, and I found my eyes were tearing up, even though they were closed. It was the most peaceful moment I had felt in my entire life; it seemed as if I was no longer me but had merged with a greater thing, not just the people around the table, but all of us with something yet greater than that.

"Oneness," Vera whispered; and we all joined in: *oneness.*

A wind blew in, then, and the curtains fluttered, and the hair on my head went straight up and I found I was chanting with everyone else: *ohhnnn, ohnnnnn, ohnnnnnnn.* We continued for some time; I felt I was sinking farther and farther down, out of who I was, not into my self but out of my self.

Then Vera began to speak. "We seek the oneness of all," she said, "we seek the inner light in outward manifestations. *Speramus.* We wait. Only the exhalation of spirit enables us to cross the radiant bridge."

The others said as one: *speramus.* The curtains blew up again and a thrill resembling terror shot up my spine, but it was not terror; it was a loosening of all the muscles in my body—back, shoulders, neck. The tears I'd felt in my eyes before leaked down my cheeks and I began to tremble. I dared not open my eyes. But it was not because I feared I was making a spectacle of myself; it was because I wanted to prolong the feeling as long as possible. I surmised the others felt much similar because we sat that way, holding hands, breathing in unison, for some time.

Then the wind died and the curtains fell still and Vera said, "*Pax,* friends." And we opened our eyes and looked straight ahead past the shoulder of the person across, and after a while, when we were calm, at each other. Everyone was smiling and nodding and some were fondling their token. I picked mine up and caressed it with my fingers.

"*Lupus,*" the woman beside me said, "a most powerful icon." I looked into her eyes. I'd met her before. But that was not possible. Curly black hair, green, green eyes, pale white skin. I was staring at Georgie at the age of fifty. An electric jolt as jagged as dread ran up my spine.

People were standing up. Some were putting on coats and preparing to leave, saying goodbyes. Others stood and conversed in whispers. One of the men who had been seated at the far end of the table came forward with his hand extended to me: it was Harvey. My knees gave way. Fortunately he had reached me by then, and he held me up. "Easy," he said quietly, "easy now, son." We stood quietly for some time, hearing voices saying goodbye and the entrance door open and close. "We should go now," Harvey said. And we did.

On Friday I had difficulty concentrating on showing Vera's house to a couple who had moved from Toronto and told me house prices in Winnipeg were a huge bargain. I'd be thinking about how the curtains in the room had blown up when we'd crooned in unison: *speramus.* And then the couple asked about the chandelier and I realized it was the second time they'd asked and I pulled myself together and provide an answer, but in a moment my thoughts were lost again in the fog of voices around a dining room table and the mixed odour of incense and cat fur. I went into the kitchen and poured a glass of water. Harvey's face as he reached his hand out to me appeared before me, a waking dream. I drank more water. Vera came in and said, "I'll drop the price, you know. But I gotta get out of this stinking joint."

The couple gushed over the view of the river. They signed for the asking price. I was pleased to close the sale but also a bit disappointed. Things had moved so slowly in the previous weeks I'd been hoping to show Vera's place a handful of times over the coming weeks, just for something to do with the long, winterish hours weighing heavily on my hands.

On Saturday I spent most of the morning sitting on my cot playing slow tunes on the harmonica. I felt a deep peace coming over me; my life was going through a change. At lunch Mother did not come down, and afterward Margy and I sat with her, Margy wiping her forehead with a cool washcloth, which brought relief, and me holding her hand and telling back to her the stories she had told me as a child, about her growing up on a farm, hoeing in the garden, gathering eggs for her mother, singing in the church choir. In the afternoon I walked to the local library. Vera had put a card into my hand as I was leaving on Friday night; the name of a book was written on it: *Shambhala*. They did not have it, but the librarian directed me to a used bookstore on Osborne that did. I was struck immediately by the cover: a three-crowned, snow-covered mountain top with a bright blue sky behind it. A brief thrill of recognition ran up my spine.

I did not understand much of what I read and I don't think it was because I'd only completed grade school. Many of the sentences seemed to wind back on themselves, like a snake with its tail in its mouth. Lots of fancy words, too, that created a gauzy good feeling just in the mouthing of them but were damn difficult to follow: the sense of it. I preferred straightforward writing, which, I admit, could be seen as a failure in me. And there were paragraphs that took hold of my thoughts and gave me pause. But overall I did not understand much more about what was behind our meetings after looking into that book than I had before. I decided I'd have to go along on my intuition and give a pass to book learning. The cover, though. That arrested me.

We met one more time before Easter rolled around and most of us had to beg off for reasons of family. Vera Hahn was in a different house by then, a nice place on Scotia Street, with an equally fine view of the river and spacious dining room, where the big wood table took up occupancy. Things went much as they had the first time, except that toward the end Vera called on anyone who might have something to say. A little man with a white beard whom I had not noticed at the first meeting cleared his throat. "My mother came to me," he said quietly, "and put her hand on my shoulder and whispered *sophia et sapientia.*"

Vera nodded. "Yes," she stated, "knowledge and wisdom, or knowledge leads to wisdom." She looked from face to face around the table. "They speak to us in ancient and modern tongues and at their discretion; we must serve by standing and waiting. *Speramus*," she repeated. And a chant came from the gathering: *speramus*. The hair on my forearms stood up. A thrill ran up and down my spine.

When we stood at the entrance saying goodbye, the woman I'd noticed on the previous occasion came up to me and said, "I know. We've met before. We do not know when or why, but we feel it." She put a hand on my forearm. "Do not fight it," she added, "accept it, let it lead you to new horizons." Though a shiver ran up my spine, her smile stayed with me after she was gone. Georgie.

I had no idea what was going on and my expression must have shown it.

Vera had been watching and she said when everyone was gone, "The inner light cannot be pursued; it must come to us in its own good time."

I didn't know what to say to that, so I said nothing.

"Do not be upset," she went on. We stood for some time in silence. A winter wind was blowing outside and tree branches were rattling against the windows and roof of the house. "It's all new to you," she said, "it needs to be taken in slowly. Digested."

"It's that simple," I offered, "merely a matter of time?"

"But you're not that type, are you? Dick? You're restless, your toes are always tapping and your knees bouncing."

I was studying her, head tipped slightly sideways, quizzical.

"Oh, that. *Dick*. We know all about you, have for a long, long time." She smiled and added, "We've been watching you. You might say."

My look must have given me away.

"An officer approached you in the army. Do you remember? A captain."

She seemed pleased by the way my brow wrinkled at that. "He was not happy that you did not accept his invitation. He hoped to initiate you into our special ways."

"Captain Wiley," I stuttered out.

"Captain Wiley, yes. He invited you to a meeting."

"Which I did not go to. I meant no harm; I meant no slight."

She nodded. "He understands. He forgives you." She cleared her throat. "You met a young woman on a road one time, a long while ago. She gave you a ride."

This time I was stunned. "Ruthie?"

"Aritha, yes. An unconventional woman, an unconventional approach, as I recall. Aritha marches to the beat of a different drummer." She laughed. "But she must not be underestimated. She is wise in the Way."

I was thinking about what she'd said about her brother; I was thinking of the unbuttoned shirt and her bobbling breasts. "You mean—"

"Right from the moment you went into the carnival. We have put people in your path. Guides, you might call them. The boss man in the carnival, he gave you the calling of *Barker*; and another, too, a man who gifted you a guitar."

"No," I said. I was trying to recall the name of Early Big's brother.

"The Indians have a special gift; they comprehend the Way. They teach it to their children as part of their education. It *is* their education. Oneness, the oneness of all. They are good gate-keepers. The best."

I was breathing hard. She put her hand on my arm. Birch bark: resin overlaid with moss, a dense, masculine pungency. "Do not be afraid, Harlan, do not be frightened. You too have a special gift. But we will talk about that on another day. After you have taken this in." Her gaze on mine was steady and calming. I noticed that she was wearing an amulet on a chain around her neck: the dancing figure of the Indian god, Shiva, I'd seen it in a picture in the book, *Shambhala*.

When we parted Vera put one finger on my cheek. She winked. The pong of birch bark swirled about.

For a few days I did not sleep well. I woke often, sometimes sweating. My nights were troubled by dreams: I was climbing up a mountain trail, the stones getting bigger and bigger so I was stumbling and slipping but I had to go on, I had to get to Ernie, who was trapped on a ledge above; but just as I was within reach of him, the path turned into a rock face and I had to find foot-holds that took me up a few inches at a time, but not quickly enough because I had to get to Ernie, it was urgent. Then he was gone entirely and I was stuck at a place on the rock face from which I could go neither up nor down. The only thing I could do was fall backward. My heart raced; when I woke, blood was pounding in my throat. Others were pleasant dreams: I stood looking out toward a river. I was holding a baby in the crook of my arm and could feel his warm breath on my face. When I looked down, the baby was gone but in its place was a wolf cub, which looked at me and tried to lick my face. I stroked its head; *canis lupus* I said; the words echoed back to me from when I was a boy. I woke up feeling bewildered but at peace with myself.

Elinor was becoming tired of sneaking around. "I wish we could go out," she said one warm night in late spring when we were done putting each other's legs and lips to the test. "I want to do something. Can't we go to quiet lounge and have a drink? I want to try a Singapore Sling."

"Someone would see us. And you're too young for a lounge."

"But this is just awful. I can feel the walls closing in on me." She put her hands to her throat and made a choking sound. More theatre, I thought.

I pursed my lips and tried to look sympathetic.

"A restaurant. Somewhere hidden away, in the North End."

She put her hands on the sides of her head. They were shaking. "Oh," she continued, "I'm getting one of my headaches."

"Can I get you something? An aspirin?"

"You can get me out of this," she spat out. "It's driving me … it's." She fell back on the bed with one elbow crooked over her eyes. I put my hand on her forearm. She shook it off. "Harlan," she moaned, "do something, find me a restaurant, a quiet little place where … Singapore Slings."

I found one in Transcona, the other side of the city, *across the tracks*, as Harvey put it, but the whole time we were ordering and eating I was looking up at the sound of the door opening, terrified. I have no idea what we ate or if we went anywhere after. Maybe a walk in a park. It was hopeless; it was one agony after another. It was madness. Don't, Harlan. Do not. The sex after was bad, too. Elinor said, "This is crummy." She got up from the bed and flounced away and I lay on the coverlet, staring at the ceiling, a knot tightening my gut. What was I doing? Chasing after a schoolgirl. I was worse than the old man.

"I hate this," Elinor said time and again. She threw things around in her bedroom. She pounded on the wall with her palm. She threw herself on the bed and told me to go away. She yelled after me as I left. "I just hate this crummy life and I hate you, too!"

We argued about little things. A word I used that she didn't like. A look she gave me that I objected to. Frequently she had headaches. As often I was frustrated by her moods. I told her it was a shame to waste the little time we had together. She said to me, "You owe me, Harlan." I didn't know what to make of that but I did not object. It seemed it was in the nature of things for men to owe things to women.

I got up one Friday morning resolved to end it. I would tell Harvey and the consequences be damned. If Elinor was the woman for me, it would work out somehow, but I had had enough of sneaking around. I could not put what I was doing with her together with the Thursday meetings. They were two trains running toward each other on the same track. Doomed. Better to make a clean breast of it. I shaved and brushed my hair and went into the office and squared my shoulders, but when I saw Harvey sitting behind his desk I felt weak in the knees and decided I needed first a cup of hot coffee. I drank it slowly, flipping through real estate documents. Harvey looked up at me and smiled. Extending my education. He approved. He pushed back the cuff of his jacket and studied the face of his wristwatch. Drummed his fingers on the desktop. I poured a second cup and drank it more slowly than the first. My legs were bouncing, blood surged in my temples. Just do it, Harlan. You're a war veteran. Be a man.

Out of the blue Harvey said, "You're coming to terms with it, then." For a moment I misunderstood him, but then I realized he was talking about the Thursday night meetings.

I was so relieved I blubbed out the first thing that came into my head. "What does it mean, oneness of life, everything is me and I am everything?"

"Well," Harvey said, putting his elbows on the desk and making a steeple of his hands. "I don't understand the way Guru Hahn does, but here's how I see it. All of life is sacred. See? Your life is sacred; so is mine. That's easy; your mother, your family; mine. But so is, well, the life of a dog, say; a stalk of celery. When you cut into a stalk of celery with a knife next time, listen carefully. You will hear it cry out. It knows it was created to be eaten, that is its purpose in the great wheel of life, but still it cries out. Its life is sacred." He lifted his hands in the air and made a circle with them. "We're all a part of the great wheel of life."

"Hmm. My life is sacred. So is that of the flower of the field. Sounds like the things Mother used to read out of the Bible: the sparrow's fall and so on." I chewed on that for a while. When I looked up Harvey was consulting his watch again. He looked into my eyes and I saw they were the same green as Elinor's. I felt my stomach slide away. I felt the urge to tell him, to get the wretched business off my chest. He was such a fine man. I remembered, though, those words of his: *don't offer explanations if questions have not been asked.* But my sense of what was right and wrong was overruling it. I blamed Mother and her little sermons on honesty. It is patently not true that honesty is the best policy. That's a pile of horseshit, and you don't have to be in the carney or sell real estate to know it.

I took a couple of deep breaths and held Harvey's gaze with mine. I was a frog who couldn't decide between sitting still or jumping.

"Don't bother," he said. "I know. But I appreciate your dilemma. Your wish to be ... to be straight with me."

"Harvey," I muttered. I imagined he was getting ready to punch me in the face. I deserved it. He would punch me in the face, then throw me out into the street where I belonged.

"I'm talking about Elinor," he stated flatly. "You and my girl."

I croaked, "I don't know what to say." I braced myself for the punch. I would not attempt to defend myself; I was a low-life, a liar and a cheat, and I deserved what was coming to me.

"It's okay," he said, a pursed smile on his lips. "I'm not going to hit you."

I let out a breath. "It's deserved."

He waved one hand in the air. "There are as many ways in life as there are lives. She's a girl who lacks—who lacks a sense of direction. You can give her that."

I sank lower in my chair. I wanted to drop through its bottom and through the floor below it.

Harvey stood up. He put his hand out to me and came around the desk. It seemed he was always putting his hand out to me. I stood and took it and he repeated, "A sense of direction would be good for Elinor. She was a colicky baby and that was a sign of how her life was to proceed. Her life has been … been troubled. Do you know that she changed her name? Her mother named her Gabriella, but she was barely a teenager when she changed it. Why would a child change the name its parent had given it? I've never understood it. But that's how it goes. We each have our own life to lead. But she could use some direction. That's the way I see it. Her mother, when I tell her, may not agree. There we have some work to do."

I nodded. I'd released his hand and he glanced once at his watch. "I'm speaking of marriage," he said. "It will help Elinor settle." He left a long silence. "The rest we keep mum about, pardon the pun." He had a bottle of whisky in his desk drawer and he poured us two small shots. "Welcome to the family," he said, with a smile that could only be described as impish. The whisky burned all the way down. We spoke no more of it.

I went out for a walk. Tree branches that had been bare only a week before were covered in tiny buds. The breeze tickling the hair on my collar was from the south, the warm breath of spring. I went over everything Harvey had said. "Remarkable," I said aloud. Enlightenment had turned Harvey into a remarkable person: open and forgiving. I could not have wished for a better father-in-law. I could not do better than model my own pathetic life on his. The whisky had gone straight to my head. I stopped beneath a tree and took out my pipe and tamped in tobacco, which I lit with a wooden match. Brown nicotine surged through my veins.

An owl flew into a branch of the tree. "Hello, owl," I said aloud. And then I thought, How odd, an owl in midday. It fluttered its wings as it settled. It gazed down at me. "*Athene*," it said. I said to it, "*Sapientia et doctrina.*" It ruffled its feathers. We gazed at each other. "*Pax*," I said. It blinked its big round eyes at me and then flew off. I laughed. I felt an immense peace—and immense satisfaction at our exchange. I said aloud, "I am home."

When I told her, Elinor was not best pleased. "Marriage?" She stamped one foot and flounced out of the room. I followed her. We were at a bungalow in River Heights and I looked out the living-room window at two crows hopping about on the front lawn. I'd grown fond of crows: they were loud and bold and would consume anything that fell their way. And they were cheeky; I'd seen one do a flip on a telephone wire, a complete 360 degrees, claws gripping the wire, the sort of manoeuvre a gymnast might do on a bar. The other crows perched on the wire chirped and croaked, as if cheering.

I said to Elinor: "No more sneaking around. We can go out to the movies or to restaurants."

"Big deal."

"I thought that's what you wanted."

She stamped her foot hard. "How old are you, anyways, Harlan?"

"I just want you to be happy."

"Happy? I'm not even normal."

She said stuff of that kind when she was angry. It was best not to answer. She would come around in good time but it was best to let her have her moment. To resist meant provoking her, which meant increased displays of anger. I took the harmonica out of my jacket pocket and blew a few bars of "Don't Fence Me In." She gave me a withering look. "That's not funny," she said. I kept on playing as if I hadn't heard her. There was no sex for a week or so, and when I called her parents' place, Elinor alternated between crying and screaming into the phone, but then one day she called me at work and said, "Oh, all right, then." In the end she had a sit-down with Harvey and Myrtle, and they made the plans for a quiet affair at the end of summer. "I'll wear a white dress," she stipulated, "but not a *cake* dress, and we're not doing any of that other crap—showers and being all girly-girly. China patterns. Ugh."

When Vera found out, she said, "I know you're in love and all that, but that girl can't interfere with your work."

"No, of course not; a man has to make a living."

"Pooh," she said, waving my comment away with one hand, rings flashing the sunlight coming in the living room of her Scotia Street house. "I don't mean peddling houses. I mean your real work."

We were sitting side by side looking through an album of paintings by the man she referred to as *Guru Nick*. Pictures of mountain ranges and sunsets and sunrises, ancient warriors wearing oriental helmets and brandishing swords. I liked the mountain ranges. "Note the snow caps," she said, "and the bright blue skies, the man on the horse at the very base of the painting. We seek the inner light in outward manifestations."

"This painting here has a skull in the foreground."

"Yes. The seeker's head is bowed toward it, seeking to comprehend the oneness, even in death. The ochre mountains of the background suggest the Way lies to the inward, as the azure of the sky in the other one speaks of the Way as upward."

"Who are these two with the bear?"

"We speak to other bearers of light and wait for them to speak back in turn. Pardon the pun." She smirked. "Puns," she added, "are one of the ways we comprehend the doubleness of meaning in the unity of all that is real."

"It's all a bit murky."

"The Way is not simple or clear. It is mystic and mythical. We do not use the crude language of a how-to book. Enlightenment comes with surrender of the self, which is the opening of the self to the magic and mystery of the things that lie buried in ordinary life. Then we can pursue the greater self, the over-self, it has been called."

There were cities, too, in the paintings, cities set against a background of mountain ranges and white clouds; sometimes tiny moons on horizons. Hanging in the sky, they looked peaceful: remote and cool.

"But we must talk about you," Vera went on, "your real work, Harlan." She turned on the couch to look me in the face. "You've always known of your special power but you have been misdirected into thinking it was a matter of being able to see things at great distances. There is that. But your real gift of sight is of second sight, the power to look inward and to use what lies there for the betterment of others. Have you sensed that?"

"I have."

"You hear voices. Maybe."

"Flowers and grass seem to sing songs as I pass."

"That's a new one," she said.

"When I touch a woman, a smell comes off her immediately. The scent of apples or cinnamon or whatever. But it seems I must touch her, there has to be physical contact."

"Exactly."

"I can see inside men's heads, kinda. It's all a bit—"

"Your father, now—"

"No," I said, "I will not talk of him." I began to stand but Vera had hold of my elbow and pulled me back down. She was stronger than she looked.

"You have hated him," she said. "He is your inner demon."

"He is a demon. My brothers and I call him *Satan*."

"Well, Satan was Lucifer, who once sat on the left hand of the Lord, as Jesus sat on the right." She patted my knee. "Try to understand. You have struggled against your inner demon all your life. You have refused to accept your inner demon, refused to acknowledge a certain aspect of yourself."

"I cannot acknowledge him. The way he treated Mother."

"Now you're just being bloody-minded, Harlan."

I glared at her. It was a judgement that I myself had made of
the old man. It smarted to have it turned back on me. "I do not
accept it, I do not accept him."

"You must, Harlan. Otherwise your gift. ... your gift will be
wasted."

"Then let it be wasted."

"Again," she stated, "that bitterness. It is not your choice
only."

I bit my lip and shook my head. To even hint I resembled
him. And who, anyway, was Vera to tell me what I was and what
I should do with my life?

She patted my forearm and we sat in silence. Finally she said,
"You asked about the skull. You knew what the question is that
must be answered."

"So, what does it signify, then, the skull?" We both looked at
the book of pictures again.

"Harlan, you know better than that. To come to illumina-
tion, you must walk through the portal yourself."

I distrusted gobble-dee-dee talk but also knew it was the language of the Way, of Enlightenment. Its own special vocabulary
dealing with the mysteries and shadows of earthly life. I sighed
and nodded. Vera said, "You contemplate on that. I will make
some tea."

I didn't much go for tea, I thought it fancy and British:
"Tea?" But I was growing used to it at the meetings—raspberry
red and refreshing after the strenuous sessions we engaged in.
I fumed about the old man, and then I remembered the day I'd
witnessed him with the woman Alice and the fact that Mother
never contradicted the story about how his hand on Art's arm
stopped it bleeding. There was much I did not understand. I was
a simple prairie boy, a man with a deep grudge against his father.
I had learned in the sessions at Vera's that one key to the enlight-
ened life was letting go, letting go of bad feelings we harboured

against others, feelings that were actually poisoning our own lives. Thoughts of revenge, say, of cutting someone who had done me a wrong. These feelings ate at us from inside, made us bitter, and prevented us from wholly realizing our full potential. I'd never realized that applied to the way I felt about the old man. I had to let it go. Otherwise I would never be my own man; he would continue to live inside me, ruling my soul and corrupting my energy. It was not going to be easy. I realized that hating the old man had become part of who I was, the old self that I must die out of to be my true self. My old self had to become a skull in order for me to put on my new self.

When she came back in, Vera passed the tea to me and said, "You look at peace with yourself. That is good." We sipped tea and looked at the paintings again, and then she said quietly, "You can be a great healer, Harlan."

I looked at her, eyebrows raised.

"You have great talent—no—great resources in your being."

"I know," I said, "something about my eyes."

"Yes, but not what you think." She studied me a moment, waiting for a reaction.

I swallowed hard. "Go on," I said.

"You may not want to hear this. It's not entirely ... not entirely flattering."

"I can handle it," I said, half-laughing. "I've been in the army."

"Yes. That's a kind of brutalization that hardens you in one way. But this is—what?—about other aspects of life. Emotions. And so on."

"Go on. Out with it."

"Well, Harlan, what people see in you, what they sense in your eyes is that they can trust you." She held up one hand before I could interrupt. "They sense in you that you—like them—have been hurt by life, have been—how to put it?—*wounded* by life.

And so they are drawn to the pain inside you." She blinked. "Is this making sense?"

I sipped at the tea. I nodded.

Vera cleared her throat. She sipped tea, too. Somewhere a clock was ticking. Vera had told me she was trying to dispense with watches and clocks, but everyone seems to need at least one. Harvey was kind of obsessed with his wristwatch. Vera continued: "Wounded, Harlan. It's in your eyes. You have spent all of your life trying to get over it. Trying to get past it."

She was right. It was not easy stuff to hear about yourself. I shifted my gaze out the window. A crow flew by, carrying a chunk of bread in its beak. *Flap flap flap.* I felt myself smiling.

"Even your sexual liaisons," Vera was going on, "of which there have been many, no doubt, even your many conquests, are not really a sign of strength in you. They're a way of saying, *I am loved,* a way of proving to yourself, if not to others, that you are *worthy* of love. If you follow me."

I nodded but my tongue was thick in my mouth.

"You have to trust yourself," Vera stated, as if that summed everything up.

"You're not the first one to say that to me. What does it mean?"

She scratched the end of her nose. "It means you have to have faith that things will work out. That when you make a choice— this or that—it's the right choice. For you. Which it always will be." She could see the puzzlement in my face. "Whatever choice you make will be the right choice," she repeated softly. "Because otherwise you'll spend your whole life second-guessing your-self, caught in a web of *what ifs* and regret. You have to trust the future to bear you out. Which means trusting your own deci-sions; trusting yourself."

"But what if I make the wrong choice?"

"Even the wrong choice will be the right choice. You will

come to see it, then you will make the right choice." She raised her eyebrows and said again, "If you follow me."

I was not sure I did, but I was a growing uncomfortable, and Vera sensed it. "Enough," she said, tapping the arm of the couch with one palm. She stood and went into the kitchen, taking our mugs with her, and the sounds of water running and the kettle being put on were audible. I thought about what she had been saying. It rang true with what I'd been told since Celie shouted at me out the trailer window. Lovely Celie. I felt myself smiling again. *Trust yourself, Harlan. Stop lying to yourself.* It came down to this: I'd been lying to myself and lying to others all my life. About important things. I had to trust myself. Trust my intuitions.

Vera came back into the room and put tea mugs in front of us. She asked, "You okay?"

"A little chastened." I laughed in a grim way. "But yes, okay."

"You will be able to do your work now. Soon. Your real life's work."

I cleared my throat and said, "Helping others? To the Way?"

"Which is a kind of healing. Wouldn't you say?"

"It cannot be a scam," I said. "There can be no hint of that."

Vera nodded. "There will be nothing shabby about this. We will have you speak to a room of people. We will ask you to reach out to them, to say their names, maybe. That is all you will have to do. We will see to the rest."

"I would not go against Mother, see?"

"We understand."

After the tea, I stood and looked into my hat in a kind of daze, and then I strode to the door. When I arrived home that night, Margy greeted me at the door. "She has passed," she said.

I said, "I'm sorry. I'm sorry I was not here to hold her hand."

"Ah. She made of point of telling me to tell you that she understood. She said, 'A great peace has come to Harlan's life. I

can go now.' Do you have any idea what she was talking about?
I do not."

"I do. I will explain it to you soon."

We went upstairs and sat with her for some time. Then Margy
made some phone calls and a doctor came to the house and then
an ambulance took her body away. Over the light lunch Aunt
Helen prepared, Margy said, "She was at peace when she died.
Wasn't she, Auntie?"

"She was."

"You sat beside her and said her name, and she said, 'Helen,'
and then she stopped breathing."

"Yes," Aunt Helen said. "She recognized my voice."

Uncle Ralph blew his nose. We began to talk about details
of the funeral.

Vera was true to her word. She and other members of the
group put the word around and on a Friday night we gathered
at a community centre where there were thirty or so people sitting on folding chairs. Vera went to the front and spoke about
the Way and how enlightenment meant surrendering the self to
gain the true self through oneness. Her hands made circles in
front of her face, sending knives of light off her rings. Her voice
became soft when she called on everyone in the room to close
their eyes and breathe in and out with her as she instructed:
inhale; hold it; exhale. Good. Longer this time. When she was
satisfied everyone was at ease, she switched to talking about me.
She said I had a special gift. That if anyone came forward, they
would be touched by my special power. She motioned me to
stand at her side.

First one came up; I asked her name and asked her what
the issue was and stood with my hand on her shoulder as we
breathed quietly together. Tears formed in her eyes; she began
to tremble. Maybe five minutes passed. At the end she murmured that the pain she'd been suffering for years was gone.

She thanked me through her tears. She walked away unsteadily, murmuring, "Oh, lord, oh my good lord."

By the time I had dealt with everyone who came up, more than an hour had passed. I was exhausted. Vera had gone into a back room and she came out with tea and we sat with Harvey, drinking it. Blood surged in my temples. I was exhilarated and exhausted, both at once.

"You see," Vera said. "You're a healer."

Harvey nodded agreement. "They went away saying they would never be the same."

After that came a period of madness. The following week there were thirty-five at the gathering, and the next, fifty, and the one after that, seventy. I returned home exhausted and numb and threw myself on my cot and slept as if I'd been hit over the head with a two-by-four. Vera was right: the people came. So many needs. It seemed my life was round after round of trembling shoulders and tears on livid cheeks. One woman dropped to her knees and clasped my thighs and wept: she'd suffered from migraines since she was a teen, and just hearing me speak had cleared her head for the first time in thirty years. She wanted to pay and was digging in her purse when Vera stepped forward. "It is not our way," she said and instead gave the woman an envelope with a return address on it.

Yes, Vera had me speaking. "You have a deep bass voice," she told me, "that rumbles out of your chest like a train heard from afar on a still night: sonorous and comforting. Your voice alone mesmerizes whoever comes into its range." So, I became a pitch man again, the barker: different message; similar technique. Vera and Harvey paid for everything and drove me to meetings and bought suppers at restaurants and provided me with a smart, black suit from a fashionable shop.

I was changing people's lives, and my own life was changing. I had very little time for real estate. Harvey was taking care of listings and viewings and sales, though cheques showed up on my desk at the end of every month and I had money in the bank to make a down payment on a modest bungalow in Fort Garry that was to be our first home. I saw less of Elinor, who was often out with friends when I called on the phone. Our trysts were hurried affairs. Quick kisses at the doorway, mad dashes to the bungalow for gymnastic couplings, meals with Harvey and Myrtle. There were as well the sessions around Vera's table, which Elinor did not attend; meetings in halls that left me too tired to do anything but drive back to Aunt Helen's and collapse on my tiny cot. Things were slipping away on me and I knew I had to get in charge of my own life. But before I could get my head around what was happening, I found myself at the front of a room at another meeting: tending to the suffering with their many needs.

Vera said, "You bring magic back into people's lives."

Harvey nodded. "You show them the Way. The way to their true being."

When she heard I had a house, Vera bought a wolf cub and had a run for him built in the backyard. Stosh, I named him. I visited him twice every day. When he licked my face I was reminded of the dream I'd had, and as I stroked his fur I felt the deep peace of that dream come over me. One day Harvey showed up at the office with an owl in a cage, a fledgling. Orn, we called him. He sat on a perch in the living room. Some nights I took him outside; a lengthy piece of thick elastic attached to his foot and my wrist, which he sat on for long periods between brief flights up into nearby tree branches. He seemed uninterested in flying away.

Harvey said, "He senses the magic in you, Harlan. He wants to be part of it. Animals have these sensations. They sense the power in other creatures."

It surprised me whenever someone said things of that kind.

I was trying to take it in. One night soon after I lay on my cot at Aunt Helen's, where I went as often as possible to be close to the memory of Mother, with my heart pounding. What was happening to me? I murmured, "Mother, help me." The room echoed my voice but I fell asleep without an answer. I woke with a start from a dream, blood hammering my temples, tongue stuck to the roof of my mouth. I needed a drink of water so I stood up but my head started to swim and in a second I was on my back on the floor, looking up at the ceiling, bursts of tiny, black pinpricks weaving in and out of my field of vision. What was happening? I lay on my back for some time, until the pinpricks began to fade, then disappeared altogether. I sat up. Blood surged in my head and I felt dizzy, the way I had those times we were forced to run through the farmer's field with the twenty-seven-point-five on our backs. I had collapsed from exhaustion, I reckoned. Not good, the voice in my head said, not good at all.

I got up and tiptoed down to the bathroom on the second floor. I poured a glass of water and drank it down. Harlan, I thought, What in heaven's name is this all about?

I lay in bed Saturday morning until almost noon, covers pulled up to my chin. I'd had night sweats and my undershirt was damp. The window was open a crack and the sounds of birds in the trees competed with car motors and the chatter of voices in the street. To calm myself I thought of the cover on the book I'd tried to read, snow-capped mountains and an azure sky. It came to me that in the very foreground of the painting a figure stood gazing up toward the mountain peaks. I'd overlooked that part of the picture. I got up and took the book and studied the cover. The colours were soothing: the blues of the sky melding into the whites of the mountain peaks, the shadows at the base of the mountains indistinguishable from the valley. I understood something I'd never quite got before: the sky was part of the mountains and the mountains were part of the valley, so in

a way the sky was part of the valley: they were all one. Eureka!
I wished Vera was there to share the moment. Then seemingly
from nowhere a question popped into my reeling head: can
you have mountain peaks without valleys? Can you have rivers
without cliffs? Your self without the selfs of others? I thought of
something the old man used to intone to us when were children:
fill jomble, fill jumble, fill rumble come tumble. It was a nonsense
rhyme that suddenly made sense: everything was part of everything else and it was pointless to go around compartmentalizing
the way we did.

I sat on my cot and had a good chew on that. I took out my
pipe and lit it and watched the smoke drift away from my mouth
and break up into wisps and then threads that danced out of the
window. It was as if the dark stuff inside of me was floating out
and away. And I knew what I was going to say to people at the
next meeting and how I was going to handle things with Vera.

"I'm not going to touch them anymore," I began, "the people
with pain."

Vera's eyes widened. We were sitting on her couch drinking tea. A Persian cat was eyeing us from the top shelf of a low
bookcase. "I had the feeling," she said, "that you were wrestling
with that. So?"

"It's exhausting me. Wearing me down. I have no energy for
Elinor."

Vera screwed up her lips. "And so?"

"I am going to speak. I am going to stand at the front and
invite them to come up. Then we'll breathe together and ... and
I don't know what."

Vera smiled. "You will when the time comes."

"Yes. Remember that trust exercise you taught me?"

"Falling backward into my arms?"

"I am going to fall backward into my own arms."

Vera patted my thigh. "You have an interesting way of putting things."

"I'm the barker. It's part of the pitch."

She punched my forearm gently. "And we can collect admission?"

How she knew I was leading up to that I did not know. "Yes," I said.

She smiled again. We left it at that.

The meetings were easier then. I asked whoever came up to close their eyes and listen to my voice. We breathed together. When we were all in a rhythm, I told them to think of a peaceful place from childhood: a quiet stream in a forest or a meadow in a wood, fluffy clouds overhead. We concentrated on my voice saying: *here is the place, here is the place,* over and over. Then we said to ourselves: feel our toes relaxing, our soles, our ankles, and so on up through the body parts to the neck and finally the tops of our skulls. Our entire bodies. We repeated over and over: *here is the place.* Minutes passed: we breathed together, we said the words. I said to them, you must not let other thoughts distract your mind—concerns about the grocery list, the flat tire; you must be the gatekeeper; when one of these thoughts arises, you must look at it from a distance, welcome it but wish it on its way, let it go. Focus only on sinking into the self. We felt our bodies becoming heavier, and as we breathed out we saw a dark cloud escape our mouths, all the bad inside floating away as our limbs became heavier and we said over and over: *sinking deep and shutting down, sinking deep and shutting down.* And then we were in a kind of trance, breathing as one, feeling our bodies growing heavy, and repeating *my pain is floating away, my pain is floating away.* Some people jerked spastically, others fell to their knees, many wept, but most just let their muscles relax and felt the pain lift off of them. When I felt it right, I said, In a minute we are going to open our eyes and feel refreshed and eager to do this again and again. And we did.

I had a little more time for Elinor. We bought stuff for the bungalow and made it into *our place,* if not exactly a home. We were playing the affianced couple: going over wedding plans with Harvey and Myrtle, and the honeymoon they were paying for: a train trip to Vancouver, where Myrtle had relatives we could stay with. When we tired of that, Elinor and I went out in the car *for a drive,* a mad dash to the bungalow where we rattled the bed and each other's bones for an hour or so. Her long smooth legs wrapped around my hips. It was still very, very good, the bad things we did. She said, "You empty me, and you fill me up." And the words were exactly what the people at the meetings said. But I dared not tell her that.

One day she said, "If it wasn't for this, I'd be going bonkers."

We straightened the bed and turned off the lights. In the car on the drive back to her parents', Elinor went on, "Wedding plans, you can't imagine what a pain they are. Funeral plans would be more interesting. Ugh."

I stroked her leg. Scent of peaches in a basket. "It will be all right. Things work out."

She snorted. "I hadn't planned on my life working out this way. You know?"

"Marriage and children, you mean?"

"And the bungalow and the Chevy in the garage. Me becoming Myrtle and you becoming Mrs. Myrtle."

We both laughed.

"You wanted…?"

"Adventure? More, anyway, than what is happening now. My life was not headed in this direction."

"Me neither. I was the barker, my life was at loose ends. In a good way."

"I'm nineteen. Nineteen; and the doors that—" She was

about to go on, but she reached out and turned up the radio dial. "Ooh, listen to this, Fats Domino, 'Boogie Woogie Baby,' now this is exciting. Shaz-oww."

"He's no Frank Sinatra."

"Sinatra is okay. But not hip." She rolled her eyes. "Crooning. That is not music I can go for. Dean Martin. Frank Sinatra. That's all over."

"Things are changing, there's no doubt. After what folks went through—"

"You think it was the war changed people?"

"Wars change people. After that Great War there were riots in the streets and in Russia an entire revolution. I have the sense big changes are—"

"Ooh, listen to this part. They call it a piano roll."

We went to Vancouver, Elinor and I, after the wedding, and walked along the harbour, and up and down Robson Street, and gaped at Lion's Gate Bridge. I bought her a charm bracelet and the first amulet for it: an Indian Shiva figure. She put it around her wrist. We were staying in a hotel near Stanley Park and she stood in front of the mirror and studied the look of it against her skin. "Handcuffs," she said, finally.

"No," I protested, "an endearment."

"Everyone wants to chain me up." She was subject to these sudden mood swings. It made her exciting to be with. But also exhausting.

"It's magic," I said, trying another tack, "it will bring the magic—"

"Shush," she said, slapping at me. "Shush with your seance and magic and flimety-flamety prattle. It's all just phony-baloney talk, so much bull. You and Daddy. That horrid witchy woman with the scraggly hair."

I knew she was not enchanted by the seances and the meetings, but I had not expected such anger. I stood directly beside her. "You're making too much of this. You've become very upset. Take the bracelet off, if you don't like it."

She tore the bracelet off her wrist and flung it against the wall.

I stood with my mouth agape. I hadn't really expected she'd take me at my word.

She was trembling and she choked out: "Sometimes ... sometimes, Harlan, I wish that you and I and what is about to ... the ... sometimes."

I stroked her back and felt her crying but when I tried to take her in my arms she moved away and sat on the edge of the bed. "You're that unhappy?" She had gone from a wild school-girl sneaking away to secretly drink wine and have sex with an ex-soldier-boy—mad with lust and eager to put her life to the test—to an unhappy bride in a matter of months. It hurt my stomach to see it. My chest tightened. I sensed I was to blame, but that we could never return to the carefree days of running behind people's backs and driving each other into ecstasy with our desires. *Is that what growing up meant?* That life for a girl crazy to taste all of life's gusty juices flowing through her blood suddenly found herself looking into an empty glass?

"It's okay," she said after a few minutes. "It's probably just ... just woman stuff." She smiled wanly and lay back on the bed with one elbow crooked over her eyes. I sat beside her and stroked her arm and in a moment one of her feet jerked and then I heard her snoring lightly.

Another person's unhappiness is not an easy thing to deal with. You can share joy: dance around, hold hands, go out for a wonderful meal, whistle and sing, look into each other's eyes, go to bed for sweaty sex, smile, laugh, caper around the room, throw off clothing, howl and shout. Pain, though, is another thing altogether. The person suffering turns in on themselves, they close their eyes and ears to other voices, they shut down and they shut you out. I looked into Elinor's face, searching for the happy person she had been so little earlier, the wild, sexy girl who had shared glasses of wine with me and lain her sweet body on mine; but her eyes had glazed over; she had gone somewhere beyond my reach. My chest hurt, I wanted to wail aloud. I wished Elinor would wail aloud; wailed until she broke through the cloak of depression she was wrapping more and more tightly about herself. But I had tried that. I'd said, "Let it out, release it in a long, loud scream." She slapped me in the face. Not hard but it had stung, and not just physically. She wanted nothing to do with me. She had called the seances phony and what I did at the meetings a scam. She'd cursed and flounced out of the room. She'd muttered, *Jughead, dumb as Jughead,* a *goof*, references to a character in a comic strip, a fool.

I left and walked out into the night. A path ran beside the edge of the sea and I strolled along it for a while. I stopped and lit my pipe and looked up at the bright moon. Clouds scudded across it. A gull flew in from the water and dropped onto the path near my feet. "And who are you?" It stared at me with beady eyes. *Amor volat,* it croaked. It hopped about and then flew off. I smoked for a while and felt the chill of the air coming off the water and then I walked on. The path ran along the edge of a wood and the farther I followed it, the deeper into the wood it went. I stepped off to take a pee. Rustlings came from the bushes, and then a loud *snap*; my head jerked and I cried out, *hah!* Above me the tree branches swayed in the wind and shadows leapt from one to another, blotting out the moonlight. A shape materialized in the bushes, and a tremor of terror raced up my spine, and I ran back toward the path, and when I found it I did not stop running until I came in sight of the lights of the hotel. It took a while for my nerves to settle. I sat on a giant rock beside the path and smoked the pipe. I glanced back toward the woods and path from time to time. The whole time the words of the gull ran through my head: *amor volat, amor volat.* I had no idea what they meant. But I was terrified of what they might portend. Was Elinor right? Was my life just a con-game? Had I taken a wrong turning? I thought about Phil and the sensible down-to-earth existence he led. I felt heartsick. I wanted too much out of life.

In the morning Elinor announced that she was not going to return with me to Winnipeg. She'd spoken to her mother on the phone; she was going to stay with her aunt and her cousin, Medrie. English Bay, she said. "There are things I have to think over," she added, "things I have to work out." I offered to stay, too. "No," she said, "I have to do this alone. Trust me, Harlan." She gazed into my eyes and I saw in hers not the blankness of the night before but the slight quiver which gives away the inexperienced liar. She was not telling me something. I sighed. Anger bubbled up in my guts; she had demeaned me with ugly comments about what I did, and now, was rejecting me. My response was to withdraw, turn in on myself, as I had as a boy when the old man came after me. Stupid, Harlan, blind. The actions of a child, not a man. I knew it but I bit my tongue and thought with some spite, Okay, if that's the way you want it. I had done foolish and reckless things in my life but I had never left a desperate person alone to settle their fate on their own. I was a fool. Aren't we all.

We parted at the stairway leading to her aunt's apartment. She reached up to my face and ran one finger above my eyebrows. I stroked her cheek with the backs of my fingers. The scent of peaches was faint, snatched away by the breeze in one moment. "Harlan," she choked out, "my sad soldier-boy, my lost barker."

"We were so happy."

"Crazy in love."

"Do you understand what's happening?"

"No. Do you?"

"No."

"Life can be so sad." Her lower lip trembled. "Lately I just feel so—so discombobulated."

"I'll call every day. Once I'm back."

"That would be nice. That would be…." She turned away from me and walked up the stairs to the doors of the building. Elinor was not one for prolonged goodbyes. She did not look back.

I walked for a while along English Bay and stopped and smoked. There was a breeze coming in toward land, the waves were choppy and the gulls cried and wheeled in the cloudy sky. I felt my eyes misting over and I brushed at them with my coat sleeve. Once, a long time ago, one of the farm dogs came home missing a leg. It had limped over the fields from wherever what had happened, happened, the stump of leg bleeding, its tongue hanging out and drooling saliva. It was shivering. We wrapped it in a blanket, Mother and I, and put a bowl of water near its head. Dogs lost legs all the time. It was not uncommon to see a dog on a farm bouncing along on three appendages. I stroked its snout and lightly scratched between its eyes. "He'll recover," I said to Mother, "won't he?" She looked at me and I knew she was preparing to say something about God's ways being mysterious to man. I shook my head at her. "Don't tell me stuff about God's will," I cried out. I had never raised my voice to her. She put her hand on my head. I felt the blood pumping in her fingers and my skull. After a while she said, "Things die, some things just die." She left me to mourn the dog's death alone.

I slept through most of the train ride back to Winnipeg. I woke from fitful periods of dreaming and stared out the window and thought, Why did you leave her that way? What a fool. I sat in the dining car and ate a sandwich and drank a glass of beer. Once when I woke, the train was stopped, and in a low meadow near the tracks stood a moose. It shook its antlers and stuck its tongue out at me. I stuck my tongue out at it. It shook its antlers again but it did not move off. The train jerked, as if it was going to move backwards, but then it started to roll forward and I had to twist my neck to catch a final glimpse of the giant beast, standing quietly in the clearing, not a muscle twitching, as if it was a statue or a figure in a painting. I had a terribly foolish thought: would it be possible to tether a moose in the backyard of my house on North Drive?

I intended to call Elinor the afternoon the train arrived in Winnipeg, but Vera was waiting at the station and she whisked me off to a meeting, where I spoke to an audience of a hundred people in a school auditorium and felt their need wash toward me, an ocean wave to a shore. Heads were bowed in my direction; many wept. A few cried out, and one or two made circles in the air in front of them with their hands. They waited until I released them. Hypnosis, Harvey was calling it.

Vera said, "I have never witnessed such responses." She was smoking a pipe then, too, and she took it out and tamped in tobacco from a packet, tamped it in the bowl, and lit up, using a wooden match, as I did. She winked at me over the bowl of the pipe and blew smoke through her nostrils. "I don't inhale," she said, by way of explanation.

"Me neither," I said. I fumbled out my own makings and lit up.

Harvey said, "It's a kind of magic. They would jump off bridges, skitter about in circles, chickens with their heads off, if Harlan asked them to."

"I don't know what to do next," Vera said. "There's no precedent." She blew smoke out of her nostrils, two matching and coiling streams.

Harvey shook his arm in order to glimpse his wristwatch. "It's crass to mention money."

"It's not the money," Vera said, quickly. "But think of the power of good to be done. The people Harlan can reach."

I said, "I am not opposed to making a living."

Harvey nodded. "You're good at real estate," he said. "But it's not for you, Harlan. It's not—"

"It's not creative," Vera stated. She sucked on her pipe. She'd thought it through, it seemed. "It's commercial and only commercial." She glanced from me to Harvey. "And you're a healer, Harlan, which is creative."

"No offence," Harvey said to me, "I take no offence from her words." He fingered his upper jaw gently. He'd been having pain in his teeth, I recalled, and was waiting to have some kind of dental procedure.

In the silence we all left, Vera said, "That's right. Harvey understands."

"No offence taken," Harvey repeated. "Each finds their own way."

"The Way comes to each in its own manner," Vera said.

We stood silent for some time, Vera and I smoking, Harvey glancing at his watch. Maybe it was time to feed his mouse friends. Maybe it was just a habit. The hall we were at that night looked out over the Red River. Windows formed a bank along one wall. Moonlight danced on the water. Leaves blew down from trees. One of the paintings in Vera's album showed a scene much similar to it; she might have chosen the place for that reason: peaceful, but also haunting, mysterious.

"We could go on the road," she said finally. "Regina, Calgary, Edmonton."

"With the right advertising," Harvey said, "halls of hundreds."

Vera took a long draw on her pipe. Was she thinking a hall of a hundred each charged two dollars added up to a lot of money, if you held meetings on the three nights of every weekend? She pretended not to care about money and such things, but she was canny and she had a plan for my future, though she had never spoken of it. The mention of cities to the west of Winnipeg had called to my mind Vancouver, and Elinor. I glanced at my watch. I could never get the time difference sorted out, but it had to be past ten o'clock there, too late to call, I reckoned. Aunt Helen had said you did not call after ten, it was not polite, and I was betting Elinor's aunt felt the same. I did not want her against me.

We talked for a while longer. I watched moonlight dancing on the water as I half-listened to what was being said, and Vera noticed and said to Harvey, "More of this tomorrow. Harlan is distracted." We put our pipes away and said goodnight. But not before Vera informed me about the next night's meeting; I had been away, and she'd been busy booking in the weekend. In the morning I called Elinor again but the aunt said she was sleeping. Her voice was not what you could call encouraging, but I called at noon and the aunt said she was still sleeping. "She's having bad nights," the aunt reported. "Her eyes glaze over when we're talking to her and her mind seems miles away." There was a long pause as I thought this over. She'd been tired throughout the trip west and possibly depressed, as Myrtle claimed she was sometimes prone to be. I went out and sold a house in Fort Rouge and met with an ancient woman in the North End who was listing her house after living in it for fifty years. She was staggered by what I suggested as an opening price. I felt good about myself. I was good at the pitch; I was still the barker. Harvey and I had a celebration drink—straight whisky for him, rye and ginger for me, heavy on the ginger. I took a walk and smoked my pipe and wondered where my life was going. If I wanted, I could continue in the business of real estate; I was good at it; there was money to be made; and getting into development intrigued me: bossing a big project. Being the Man, as Harvey would have put it. But tempting as it was, there was something right about the meetings—helping people, healing, as Vera said. I was skeptical about that; I thought most of the healing was not being done by me but by the folks who came up their own selves. Or some force beyond us both. So it was not me directly, but it was me somehow, too. I was helping people: to being at peace within themselves, and at finding the Way. I thought about what Boss Man had said years ago: two roads to choose between. This was what he'd meant, then: the path of business or the path of healing. I know which Mother would have chosen. I was coming to a conclusion when a crow dropped onto the road in front of me. *Corvus brachyrhyncos,* I said to it. It turned its beady eyes on me. It hopped three times toward the middle of the road, gave me a beady stare, and then took off. I laughed. I tapped ashes out of the pipe on the heel of my shoe and went back to the office, chuckling all the way.

I phoned Vancouver at suppertime but the aunt said Elinor and Medrie had gone out for a walk. Was she trying to avoid me? The aunt also reported that Elinor had bumped into a wall that afternoon, as if she was sleepwalking. I was losing the girl I loved. And I didn't understand why. Part of me wanted to hop on a plane and go rescue her; another part acknowledged that she had told me, in effect, to stay out of her life. I sat on the couch in the house for a while, *our* house, and began to feel a great tightness in my chest, which I knew could only be relieved in one way—by weeping. So I wept for a while, as I had as a boy in that abandoned outhouse, and afterward I felt empty but much relieved. I knew then what all those folks must be feeling as they came forward and I spoke to them, and a great weight lifted off their shoulders, or a great tightness in the chest released. Yes, it was the right path for me.

At the meeting that night I was especially gentle in giving the instructions and took longer than usual to go through the steps that led to imagining light at the top of the stairway after immersion in the pool. When people began to weep I encouraged them: "Let it out," I whispered in the silent hall, "feel your chest giving way and let it all out now." Each became the child I had been that lonely night long ago, and I felt at one with them, and myself. When I scanned the front of the room, I saw tears were streaming down the faces of Harvey and Vera too. We were all children together, then, we all carried wounds.

When the meeting ended I talked to a number of folks that came forward. They brushed at tears, and so did I. It was a special moment. The hall emptied slowly and Vera made tea and we talked for a long while, Harvey, Vera, and I, sitting on stacking chairs along one wall. Harvey told me I was too good for this life and Vera did not disagree. She said I would only fulfill the destiny the fates had laid out for me if I travelled to other cities and healed people there. Harvey said maybe after that we could write a book and put in pictures and sell it in the States. Which made Vera give him a long look, but not of disapproval. It was clear that among us he had the business head. He could see where our meetings could go to on a grander scale than Vera was willing to imagine, or that I was eager to endorse. But we all understood. There was that thing in me that folks wanted to tap into.

That night I lay on the double bed in our Fort Garry house for a long while. Stars were visible out the window. I watched them twinkle and I drifted off to sleep. I woke needing to take a pee and looked at the bedside clock. Two-thirty. I climbed back into bed but could not fall asleep. I tossed and turned. Three o'clock came. Four. I was anxious about Elinor. What was she feeling? What was she doing? She was slipping away from me. I got up and drank a glass of cold water. Geese were in the air, honking loudly; they flew this way and that, then doubled back yet again. Did they know where they were going? Did any of us? Elinor and I had been so happy in the days of sneaking around and being bad; and now that was gone. Had the excitement been what sustained us? Was love just lust dressed up in the clothes of compassion? Once the thrill was gone, did love go with it? Elinor's descent into sadness seemed so sudden and so deep, but Harvey had hinted she was prone to depressions, that she needed a strong person to give her direction in life. Had I failed her there? Get on the first flight, I told myself. Fly to the woman you love, hold her, talk sense to her, love her. I determined to call first thing in the morning. I continued to toss and turn, and to lie gazing out of the window. The leaves had fallen from the trees but it was an unusually warm autumn, they said on the radio: temperatures above normal. A pale light came into the sky. Five-thirty. I got up and showered and shaved and listened to the news on the radio. The new Queen was planning a trip to Canada. An airplane had crashed in Europe. An apartment building had burnt down in the West End; arson was suspected. I made a pot of coffee and toast and chewed and sipped and listened to the weather forecast. Seven-thirty. The newspaper arrived at the door and I checked our listings in the classifieds. I had a two-storey in River Heights and a bungalow in River-view. Details were correct: my phone number, the asking price. Eight-thirty, which was early on the West Coast. I called the aunt's number. She answered on the second ring. "If you're not sitting already," she said, "sit down now." I did. My cup shook in my hand. "Elinor's been in an ... Elinor is ... Elinor is dead." Her voice cracked. I heard the ticking of electricity in the phone line, rasping sobs. Coffee sloshed onto my wrist. A second voice spoke in the background over the sobs.

Then Medrie came on the line. "I know," she began. Elinor had had a troubled night and had gone out for an early walk. She was in a neighbourhood she did not know, at an intersection where three streets came together. It was still twilight. She'd stepped off the curb. A delivery truck had hit her. She made it to the hospital in the ambulance but died in Emergency. I took it all in. I said *yes* and *I see* and *yes* again. They were words only; I was totally numb. Medrie paused. "But the baby survived," she said. "He's in prenatal. They say he'll make it."

I put the receiver back in its cradle and looked out the window for a long time. A tree in the neighbour's yard had a long, heavy branch hanging over the house; it looked as if it could fall on the roof at any time. I realized I was straddling two worlds— everyday reality and unusual perception. I was stunned into the realization that all of my life I've been unaware of certain realities while aware of others. After some time passed, I picked up the receiver and made a reservation on the next flight to Vancouver. With a trembling hand I dialled Harvey's number. He answered on the first ring; we said *no* and *it can't be* and then blubbed at each other. In the background I heard Myrtle's voice, long wails punctuated by sobs and gasps. They could not join me on the flight; Harvey was going in for root canal that morning; he'd been waiting in pain for three weeks. Myrtle would not get on a plane without him there to hold her hand. He picked me up in an hour and drove me to the airport. Every time we went over a crack in the road, he winced in pain. He had his jaws locked together and the vein in his temple stood out, squiggly blue tubing between his hairline and ear. I staggered onto the plane. It was eleven-thirty. I used the little white bag, *splork*, though it was not on the takeoff or landing. Failure, Harlan, I told myself, failed her. I took a cab to the hospital. I staggered up the sidewalk toward the entrance. Marigold, yellow and orange in a loamy bed were hanging on, a bit brown around the gills. They were singing softly as I walked past: *love and marriage, love and marriage,* a peppy popular tune. They were not in rhythm with my suffering. When I got to the entrance, I put my forehead against the concrete of the portal. Its coldness felt good to the touch. People coming up to me slowed before they passed. A man asked, "You all right there, buddy?" I raised one hand. *In a minute, just give me a minute.*

I found my way to Natal and a nurse jumped up from her desk and showed me into a room where there were three babies. She pointed at one. They had him under a glass-like half-bubble, with a heated blanket underneath. One of the nurses said they kept a constant watch and fed them a bottled mixture on the hour. I stepped over and looked down. A wrinkled red face, black tufts of hair on the scalp; little cabbage leaves for ears. I thought, Do all babies look ugly? Not to their parents. Not to their grandparents. I tapped my fingers on the top of the glass bubble. I was not trying to get his attention; I was mulling something over. Gabriel. The name Elinor had rejected as a teenager was Gabriella. Gabriel. It seemed right. A strong name. A biblical name. Gabriel had been the first among angels, a go-between for heaven and earth. I watched his little chest go up and down, his breath go in and out. I counted: one, two, ten, fifty. He was a premature birth, but he would be okay.

Elinor had been moved to a funeral home. Harvey had been busy on the phone, arranging, sorting things out. I took a cab there and the man in the black suit asked if I wanted to view the deceased. I did not, but they seemed to expect it, so I went into the room and looked down into the casket. Waxen cheeks, rouged lips, hair brushed in a manner she never wore it. "No," I said aloud, "that is not her, no, that is not my Elinor." I was clasping the edge of the casket in a fierce grip. The words croaked out of my throat. I did not mean those three items, hair and whatnot. I meant something greater: there was no spirit there any longer, no energy, no *Elinor*. She had crossed into the world of light. I felt shivers race up and down my spine and put my hands over my eyes and my whole head was burning. In a blur I signed papers that were pushed in front of me, and then I turned and strode out of there.

I walked until I found a park and sat on a wooden bench. My mind was a blank again. Not a thought. The lug-dubbing of my heart, the sound of traffic in the street. A chill breeze blew on my face. Gulls wheeled overhead, crying and dipping. None of them dropped down. Good, very good. I closed my eyes, which were burning, and the after-image of gulls in the sky—little red crosses on a black background—tracked across my eyelids. When I opened my eyes there was a mallard at my feet. A male with neck collars in two shades of shimmering green; it looked up at me. I stared back. It became interested in a brown lump near its feet and nosed at it with its beak. Dog poop. It tipped the lump over, then backed away. "Good choice, buddy," I said, chuckling. It looked up at me. *Pax*, it said. *Pax*, I said back. It waddled off.

I over-tipped the cabbie who drove me to a hotel downtown. I sat on the end of the bed. I'd lost a wife and gained a son. Not so long ago, I'd lost a mother. What would she have thought of all these goings-on? Love and death, loss and gain. It did not add up somehow. Words. I took out the pipe and lit up but the smoke I drew into my mouth tasted of rotting leaves mixed with dog dung. I put the pipe away. My chest was growing tighter and tighter and I knew what had to happen next. A familiar wretchedness lodged in my soul. I rolled back on the bed and curled up into a fetal position and began to breathe deeply. I counted: one, two, twenty-seven, forty. At fifty I began to tremble. "No," I whispered into the bed cover, "no, please, no," but what I really meant was more a *yes*. Release me. I began to shake and then the tears came between gasping sobs and I shook and blubbed "no, no, no," and wept some more, and in a few minutes the shaking began to subside and I reached up with one hand and wiped drool from my lips and moaned, "Okay now, okay." I felt empty and blank. I was back in the outhouse, a frightened boy who had found a way through. And after I was calm again, and I smoked the pipe and stared at the wall in front of me. There was a picture hanging on it, a print of a green plant with a purple flower at its top. I studied it until my heart settled. I roused myself and went downstairs and ate a hamburger, the first food I'd had and kept down in almost twenty-four hours.

But I was still blank. The loss. I would never see Elinor again, we would never touch again. Laugh together. Tell each other about our day and chuckle about who'd said what and exchange cheerful looks and feel enfolded in the warm blanket of companionship. She had died and I'd crossed into the country of grief. And grieving. I would see her everywhere in our house when I returned, a ghost. The idea made me tremble. She would be there but not there, and the loss would be great. How would I go on? Maybe I'd become one of those widowers who stumble around their house, muttering at furniture, halting before a window, unsure of where I was and what I intended to do next. Would it be worth going on? It crossed my mind that it had to be, that my going on would be her going on, too; if I did not keep memories of her, of our joyous times together alive, who would? And there was Gabriel. I determined that if I visited him, my relief would be great.

At the hospital I saw Medrie and the aunt sitting in a waiting room. They told me it was immediate family only. I sat down between them. The aunt was trembling and knitting her fingers together. Medrie leaned in toward me and put her hand on my arm. Rosemary wafted up. Maybe it grew wild on the West Coast. I looked into Medrie's eyes. Sea-blue, deep, sparkling with life. There was something in our gaze neither wanted to acknowledge. I shifted my gaze to the floor. Medrie cleared her throat. They were going to keep Gabriel in the hospital for two months; he was just into the final term. Medrie would visit every day. I would come out at the end of every month and see how he was getting on. "He'll be fine," Medrie said, patting my thigh. The rosemary scent was deeper, more potent, it ran up and down my spine. I took in several deep breaths. Her sea-blue eyes swam up at me. I could get lost in those eyes, swim down into them and never resurface. I thought. No, Harlan, no, not this time. But there's no denying life. Love asserts itself. I read it in her gaze, too. We were shameless. Aren't we all.

Medrie said, "He'll be fine."

I repeated, "He'll be fine." I didn't know if everyone was lying to me. I didn't know if I was lying to myself.

Elinor's body, Harvey told me on the phone, was on a train to Winnipeg. I fell asleep on the plane and woke with a start when its wheels touched down. Harvey was at the airport, waving at the bottom of the escalator. What had I ever done to deserve him? His tooth was fixed. He was smiling despite all he had been through. It was a lesson I could learn.

The funeral was simple. Elinor had expressed no wishes about burials and that sort of thing, so Harvey and Myrtle laid the casket to rest in the family plot in a small, quiet cemetery. Schoolgirls were there; teachers; members of the two families. Tears, handshakes, red-rimmed eyes. The rest was a blur: the words the preacher said at the graveside. It was not her, not Elinor. Elinor had passed into the world of light.

But I was stranded in the world of grief. Friends tried to help me through. *Time passes,* they said, *time heals all wounds.* I might have uttered the same words myself had I been in their position, but I was offended. What they were offering was a kind of reverse investment: hold on, a payback was in the works. They meant well. But grief overrode all that. Throw yourself into work, some said, imagining that grief could be burned off. They did comprehend the land of grief. How could they? I was a puzzle to myself. Action seemed a waste of energy, pointless filling in time; and inaction was self-indulgent pity. There was nowhere to turn; I was stumbling about in the desert of my own heart.

But life asserts itself. It won't let us curl up in a fetal ball and give over.

The weeks passed. It was an unusually mild autumn, leaves hanging on branches long after they should have fallen; flowers bravely bright in mornings after chilly nights. Houses continued to move. We were in a boom, Harvey said: following the Depression and the war, folks had tightened their belts and held on to their modest cash, but now that was over; a mood of euphoria was spreading. Folks were buying cars, appliances, smart suits, houses. The money was rolling in. The meetings were being attended by hundreds; there was a door-charge of one dollar, but you could contribute more into a glass bowl Vera placed near the front of the hall. It was often overflowing.

I visited Gabriel in Vancouver. He grew by the day, it seemed. Under the glass bubble, he burbled and rolled his dark eyes around, and studied his tiny pink fingers and pushed them into his mouth. Medrie came every day and stood with me and we trembled in each other's presence and I went away with a dry mouth and a befuddled heart. No, Harlan, no. Who was I fooling? We brought him home on the train one fine autumn day, Myrtle attending to his bottles and Harvey and I taking turns with diapers and baby powder. As the train rattled through town after town, we talked about how to handle matters once we were back in Winnipeg. Myrtle offered to take care of him, but I sensed Harvey was not keen on the idea, and I was in agreement. It would be a draining work; work requiring a young woman. I considered hiring a woman, a kind of wet-nurse sort of thing, they were around in numbers postwar: European refugees, women from the Philippines. Harvey and I would talk it over.

There were still houses to move: meetings at properties, listings to write up, showings, documents to sign in lawyers' offices, possession dates to settle, keys to deliver, cheques to be deposited. It went on well. Elinor came to me in dreams, and her ghost walked through the house and sat in corners where I did not expect her to materialize, and I started with fright. At the office, I sat blankly for hours, staring at papers the words of which I could not read. Libby made pot after pot of coffee and put mugs before me with cream added, and sugar cookies she had herself baked. I took walks. Smoked the pipe. Talked to the blackbirds and sang along with the grasses that grew down by the riverside. I carried the harmonica and sometimes sat looking at the water playing, but the tunes were all sad and made my heart heavy. There would be a day, I said to myself, when I could play again. The day would come.

Vera understood best of all. She did not try to comfort me with platitudes about time passing, or throwing myself into work. When we met, she did only one thing: she reached out and hugged me. Birch-bark resin, the scents of a fall day beside a river. She stated simply, "What is there to say?" There was nothing to say. We drank tea. She understood that I would pass through grief the way I was meant to, and that would be that. It was not one of those pools beneath a cliff you leap at and go into and then burst out of, head clear, ready to move on; when you emerged from the sea of grief, your brain had become muzzy and sluggish, a buzz of befuddlement.

But life asserts itself. Love calls us to the doings of the world.

Medrie called, asking after Gabriel. We pretended that was the sum of it. She said, "Bring him out here, come the spring. He'll love the cherry trees in bloom. So will you." We made a kind of date. Spring. The cherry blossoms would sing to our weary souls: *roll, Jordon, roll.* I recalled Medrie's teeth were quite small, but bright white; sea-blue eyes. I'd not noticed anything else, her form, her parts. But she was a woman and I was a man. It seemed inevitable. I tried very hard not think of those eyes. When she called the next time, we talked longer. Harvey was out of the office; the betrayal did not seem quite so terrible. We said things without saying things, listening to the rhythm in the other's voice, anticipating the tinkle of a laugh. I put the phone down. My chin dropped to my chest and I wept quietly. I would never recover. I would drop further and deeper into the depths of grief's sea.

Harvey burst through the door. He was holding up one wrist. Huge gobs of blood dropped onto the floor. "Slipped getting out of the car," he gasped, "there was a jagged piece of tin in the gravel." Blood streamed down his arm under his shirt cuff, which was turning dark amber.

Libby was out of her seat beside me. I grabbed Harvey's wrist. "Quick," I said, "lie down on the couch."

"No," Libby stated, "he has to sit up." She seemed to know what she was talking about. We arranged him in a sitting position.

"Grab paper towels," I shouted to her. "Wet some."

She came back immediately and I held the towels over the gash, but they were no use; the blood soaked through them immediately. "My watch," Harvey moaned, "my beautiful watch."

"Hush," Libby said.

I pulled the towels away and tried to wipe the gash clean with a wet one, but that was useless too. Blood was flowing down my wrist, then, soaking into the cuff of my jacket, falling onto my shoes. Harvey's face went from green to white. We could have bundled him into the car and rushed to the hospital, but we sensed that would be futile and fatal, at the rate he was losing blood. I took a deep breath. I placed my palm over the gash and held it down tight. I began to count: one, two, seventeen, thirty-one; when I came to forty-three I lifted my hand away. The blood had stopped; the wound had begun to scab over. Libby looked at me; her trembling mouth formed the words: *so it's true then*. I nodded. But I had been unsure of what would happen; afraid, in a way. I was exhausted. Harvey had his head resting on the back of the couch. "So much power in you, Harlan," he whispered. "So ... much ... ." He closed his eyes and in a minute he was snoring. We watched over him, a vigil. The phone rang; we did not answer. In twenty minutes he jerked awake, blinking both eyes. He fingered the wound, which had continued to scab over. "Harlan," he said, "I don't know what to ... how to ... "

I placed one hand on his wrist. It was covered in dried blood. I felt the rhythm of his pulse, regular and deep. "We hang by a thread," Harvey said. I nodded. Libby got up to make fresh coffee. Harvey gave me a wan smile. "We stand on the prairie looking into a sunset," he whispered, "golden purple hues coming in just above the treetops. We close our eyes. The light falls fast and darkness comes over us, a darkness that is not black or threatening, darkness that is not darkness, really, it's hard to describe, dusk—darkness falling fast, taking us into it."

"Absorbed."

"Enfolded. Enfolded in shadows that are not darkness."

We hung by a thread. It was true. Mother. Elinor. The old man had passed away while I was in Vancouver attending to the arrangements to move Gabriel to Winnipeg. Heart attack. Gone in a flash. Art had been named executor and was in Estevan wrapping matters up. The farm was to be sold. The money was to go to Ernie, who was taking a course in welding at a college. I was glad of that. He'd always been a kind boy: amenable, friendly, eager to learn; people took to him. Inside his head were farm dogs, mongrels cavorting in a meadow. He would get the money and make a life for himself. I was happy for him. After that, I did not pay much attention. The old man had died. Hanging by a thread. Elinor. Life was short. A sort of carney crapshoot: no knowing where the dice would fall next. Mother, the old man, Elinor. Medrie. Gabriel. The wounds would heal. But there would be scars.

The meetings became very crowded. Vera had designed a special outfit for me to wear at the mingles: a black affair without a jacket but with an open collar, a few sequins stitched into a V-neck collar: they picked up the low light in the halls, making my face sparkle. I spoke, I held my arms out, I enjoined folks to breathe along with me, throw off their old selves, enter the entranced state: *hypnosis*, Harvey called it; *mesmerism*, Vera added. I was tired every night, but exhilarated too. The plans for Chicago, Minneapolis, St. Louis had firmed up. Denver was on the list now, too; Calgary, Saskatoon, Regina. A circuit, Vera called it. Maybe as many as ten thousand tickets sold. In a good year, an ambitious real estate agent could earn five thousand dollars; a high roller, ten. This was far out of that league. It frightened me. It excited me.

One night there was a big crowd at a hall in St. Boniface. The French, I had noticed, were quite open to what I was doing, spiritually inclined, likely to become emotional. When the session had ended and I was standing at the front, mopping my brow and drinking water, a man leaning on a cane came up from the side aisle, out of the shadows. I recognized him instantly, but he said anyway, "It's me, Laurent. Larry." He'd put on some weight but his face was fleshy and red and full of Santa Claus jolliness. He'd been shot in the belly in Italy and had been bivouacked into an Italian hospital, where he'd convalesced for some months; the cane helped him get about. "I hear so much about you," he said, "you're so famous, now, a celebrity. I had to see for myself in the flesh." His eyes were red-rimmed. "My old pal, Harlan, now the healer." He trembled and took a moment to gather himself. "*Guérisseur*. You say this in English? Faith healer. Harlan, *le mystique. Merci*, my old friend."

"The healing," I protested, "it's not me so much me as it's—"

"I know," he went on. "You grant us leave to be weak."

There no better way to say it. Wounded, we wrap our arms around our hurt; clench our teeth and clam up. It's a good first reaction. We survive; we stabilize within our shell. But that cannot go on. If we go on that way, we turn to stone: shutting out feelings, hardening ourselves against them. What we need is to let go. To shake, to weep. Slacken and collapse. Larry understood this. He'd been wounded. After the shock, he'd toughened and come through the worst of his pain by forcing himself to be strong. But he had to let that go, he'd learned that our souls are puny put against life's ravages and stings, that falling to our knees and submitting to something higher is the pathway back to well-being.

I put my hand on Larry's shoulder. Inside his head were the branches of cherry trees teased by wind, pink and white blossoms breaking off and whirling into the air. I said, "Why don't you stay for a while. We'll drink tea. Talk about old times."

"*Merci, mais non.*" Larry glanced back into the room. Standing by himself along the far bank of windows was a man, similar to Larry, portly and jolly-faced. He lifted one hand up to the height of his chest and waved briefly. Larry said, "Me and my ... my friend should be going. I just wanted to see you in person, Harlan the Healer. I knew it was going to happen, you know? Even way back then when we ran through those stinking fields with the twenty-seven-point-five on our backs. You were marked out for something special, Harlan." He reached out and stroked my arm and waves of electricity surged through me; I thought I might collapse. That was it, then, touching, and being touched. That's where the release, the healing came from, that's what would save us in the end. Wordless touching. Some would call it love. It was easy as that: touching and being touched.

There seemed nothing more to say. I studied his eyes. He had reached a state of peace. Larry cleared his throat. "One thought," he said, "before we go. You should make a recording, Harlan, of what happens here; that way folks who can't get out will still be able to hear your message. And those of us who have heard it, we can hear it again. In the quiet of our rooms. Over again."

"An excellent idea."

"A thought for the future. When you are the great Harlan, healer to the world." He patted my arm once more and turned and limped away.

"*A dieu,*" I called out to him.

"*Grazie,*" he said back. He waved one hand over his shoulder without turning around. "*Buona vita.*"

There was a lightness to my step all through the following day. The coffee I perked tasted dark and mellow. When I got home from the office, I strolled out into the yard and opened Stosh's run and fed him a dog cracker. He nipped my fingers and I picked him up and rubbed his belly. Thoughts of Skipper crossed my mind; he had tried to talk to me that night long ago, and I hadn't understood and instead had blamed him. The foolishness of a befuddled boy. I had made mistakes in my life. I would make more. I put Stosh down and went back into the house.

Harvey had fixed up a room in my house for Gabriel: wicker basket that sat in a crib he would occupy one day soon; fresh paint on the walls, powder blue. A side table for baths and clean-ups. He was a placid child: he burbled and twiddled his fingers and grew beet-red in the face with the exertions of elimination. Margy had taken to coming over. Harvey too. We stood around the crib and laughed and I called him *poopy-head.* He screwed up his eyes and made snuffling noises. "Snorfer," Harvey said; "when I was a baby that's what my older brother called me: *the snorfer.*" Margy was standing beside me; she leaned her head into my shoulder: cornflowers with the overlay of honey; I felt drowsy in the aura of her kindness.

"I'm going to take care of him," she stated.

"You have a job."

"Pooh," she said, "secretary. Margy's got bigger horizons." She laughed. "I've been talking to Harvey about a position, you know, in the Harlan itinerary, arranging your schedule of appearances, kind of thing: phone calls, billboards; taking that off your hands."

"You'll be busy, with Gabriel and all."

"The devil finds work for idle hands."

"What about the birds?"

Margy had a feathered menagerie in her apartment: parrots and magpies and such in four cages: earth, air, fire, and water. "For them," she said," we find somebody. They're growing bored with me anyway."

I started to say more, about how Mother would have enjoyed seeing her children working to a common cause—and a good one. But she cut me off. "Harvey and I have arranged it," she went on. "It's a job for family, not a woman with her own kids who comes in, tired from taking care of them, or just lazy, or just not focused on what Gabriel needs. Leave it to us. To me."

I gave her a long look. "You're good," I said. "A very good person."

"*Secretum inter nos,*" she said with a smirk.

"That's two," I said, "secrets between us, then."

"Secrets make the world go round."

"I thought it was love."

"There is no love without secrets. I've been watching you all your life, big brother. You above all people know it."

It should not have surprised me. She'd been watching over me, too, as she had over the entire family. I had taken her for granted and that was about to change.

"I will take care of him," she repeated. "All will be well. Right, Harvey?"

It made sense. Gabriel fussed in his basket. Margy had a wooden spoon in one hand and she held it out to him. "Aha," she said, "see, he grabs for it with the left. Just like you, just like the ... just like Father."

"He was never left-handed," I protested.

"Oh, yes. They trained it out of him as a kid. Beat him with leather belts. Strapped his left hand down at school."

"It was a brutal time," Harvey said. "The unspoken facet of the one-room schoolhouse celebrated in story and song."

"But," Margy was going on, "you handed Father a tool, a hammer, say, or a hoe, and he always went for it with his left. Just like you, Harlan." Gabriel had the spoon in his fist and was attempting to put it in his mouth. He missed and shoved it into one nostril. He blinked and then wrinkled his forehead. We laughed. Crimson-faced, he glared at the spoon and then chucked it away; it clattered on the hardwood flooring. "Oh my," Margy said. "The family temper." We knew who she was referring to but we said no more.

I went into the bathroom to pee and heard Harvey walk down the hallway to the living room. When I was done, I looked into Gabriel's room; Margy was holding a bottle to his mouth and she put a finger up to her lips: hush. I backed away and went to sit with Harvey. There was a half-moon in the sky, visible but pale. Early evening. I offered Harvey a drink. He waved it away. He consulted his watch. "Time to be going," he said. "Myrtle. She's a bit fragile these days, she needs looking after." I nodded and when he was gone sat back in the couch with my eyes closed, thoughts drifting in and out of my brain: Gabriel, Margy, the last mingle, Laurent, how quickly life can change— and can change us.

In the photo from this time I'm holding Gabriel on one arm. He's wearing a hat and a cloth coat with a scarf around his neck. I'm in an overcoat, severe and black, double-breasted with oversized buttons, and a flat, cloth cap. My mouth is downturned, not a happy time. My hands protrude out of the middle of the picture, one crooked under Gabriel's body, the other grasping my pipe; I did not think my hands were that large.

I sat for a while and listened to the house breathing and ticking and then I took out the harmonica and after studying its reds and golds and blues in the falling light, took a few faltering puffs into its reeds. It seemed it had been a long time. I tried "Ol' Man River," but it made me sad and just as I was putting the harmonica away, Margy came into the living room, looking muzzy but with a light in her eyes. She always cheered me up, Margy, and I patted the couch seat beside me but she stood in front of me, fluffed at her bobbed hair with one hand, and asked, "You remember that night we danced?"

"We danced?" I was standing, too, and looked into her beautiful brown and green eyes.

"You held me. We held each other."

"Oh, that," I said, pretending I hadn't known at an instant what she had been referring to.

I felt again the coolness of her flesh, the way her skin had melded into mine; something sexual about that embrace, yes, the points of her nipples brushing my warm torso, but at the same time not arousing, muted. I whispered, "It was the best gift anyone has ever given me." She stood back and gazed into my eyes, the green and brown of hers twinkling moonlight.

"You are quite the romantic, Harlan." She unfastened the top buttons of my shirt.

I laughed. "No one's ever said that to me before."

"Women have been saying it to you all your life. You weren't listening."

"I suppose. I struggle with the translation." I grinned in a silly way.

She sighed. "We knew," she said. "Even then."

"*You* knew."

"Oh, Harlan," she whispered. "You do get a kick out of playing the rube."

"Here," she said, opening her arms as she had done long ago, the delicate points of her small breasts brushing my skin. My belly went warm. A weighty doziness came over me. We shuffled around the floor. I felt her warm breath on my neck. A kind of trance descended on us: shuffle and breathe; shuffle and breathe. That went on for a while, and then I noticed I was taking rapid, shallow breaths, and felt tears thickening the corners of my eyes.

"It's okay," she cooed, and she stroked my back with one hand. We stood that way for some time. "Men," she whispered finally, "you're all just wounded little boys, frightened, looking for a place to curl up and shelter and heal. Every one of you. A wounded boy needing someone to hold your hand and get you through the darkness."

"Hold our hands?"

"Yes, literally, much of the time. Needy and needing."

"Women?"

"Not always. Oddly, it can be work sometimes or throwing yourself into things without heed or care."

My breathing was coming easier and she stroked my back a few more times and then gently pulled away.

"Thanks," I muttered. "You're probably right about all that."

"I am," she said decisively.

"I'm fast coming to that opinion."

We gazed at each other calmly; we separated and she went out of the room without looking back.

I sat for a while taking in what had happened and then got up and drove over to Vera's. I enjoyed sitting quietly with her, talking about life in a general way, going over plans. A famous English writer was visiting America, a man who followed the Way, taking every opportunity to connect with his dead wife, and Vera was hoping that he would join our sessions on his stop in Winnipeg. She enjoyed entertaining fellow seekers, as she called them. She said they had a lot to teach her. Us. Sometimes I wondered if it was notoriety she was more interested in, but that was thinking unworthy of Vera—and not worthy of me, either. There was a lot I had to learn about getting along with people, trusting them, taking them at their word. My soul was burdened with a residue of carney scepticism; my hands were sticky with it.

Vera was sitting on the couch with her ankles crossed on the coffee table, blue slippers resting on a pile of papers, toes twiddling. She looked up at me and smirked: "Pink is for girls," she said, "blue for boys." We both laughed. "How is the little fart?"

"He's fine. Wonderful, actually. I'm fine."

"That's good. Have some tea."

She poured an amber-coloured drink into a mug and we sipped and then we went through the routine of lighting our pipes. I stared out the windows at the river: lawn in the foreground, elms to each side, sparkling water, pines on the far side. She had chosen well. She said, "Time heals all. It's a cliché, but it's true. Some of them are. Old folk wisdom, ancient as Seneca root."

"That's why they're clichés," I said.

"You've got the little guy to love. Shower your affection on him. He will help you find a way back to loving. To unity."

"Yes. Loving, and being loved." I was thinking of all its manifestations: Mother, Celie, Phil, Gabriel, Georgie, Elinor, Harvey, Margy.

We were sitting on the couch, side by side. She patted my thigh: whiff of birch bark through the pipe smoke. "Someone will come along."

"No. That's over."

"You're young. Someone will come along. It may not be the same. It may be more ... more subdued."

"No," I stated. But it was a lie. I just did not want to acknowledge the truth of her words.

She raised her eyebrows. "I heard someone say once that we

love more where we are loved, as compared to where we love. Do you buy that?"

"No."

"Me neither." She shifted on the couch, leaving a little more space between us. "You may not believe this, but I too am awash in desire. Yes, the old, old song: lust, passion, love." She laughed. "Just because I look the way I do—frumpy, witchy—does not mean that desire does not persist, does not rend me asunder some days. Her cheeks flushed. She touched one with an open palm and chortled. "No fear from your side," she added; "I prefer women."

I raised my eyebrows.

"They're more gentle, more giving, more accommodating. Men think that thing between their legs makes them gods or some such; stallions, masters of the universe."

I laughed aloud.

She snorted. "We encounter each other at the meetings. We know who we are, recognize how we are: we're open to each other's needs; simpatico."

"It is not only women at the sessions. Seances."

"No. But the meetings are places to find what we've been searching for in multiple ways. Love, true enough. But also companionship. Caring."

"A connection. Something beyond Self. Unity."

She chortled again. "You're a philosopher," she said, "a guide. We're odd creatures, we humans. Animals just do it, and then move on. Why do we love at all? Harlan?"

"It's what we have. It's all we have. That bit about loving where we're loved, now. There's no levels of love; no gradations; no better, no more and less: calculations, measurements. Me this much, you only that much. Sure, love grows; it gets bigger, you could say. You throw a stone in a pool and it ripples back at you. For every ripple you create, ten come back to you. That is love. And it grows deeper, too, and we walk into it and we float in it. Lie on our backs and float in an ocean of love, the little movements of our hands and feet at our sides holding us up."

Vera chortled. "You're something, Harlan. I started out the teacher," she said. "Now I'm the student."

"Just throwing out ideas."

"*Amor vincit omnia?*"

"*Conquers* is all clashing swords and war. Legionaries. Romans."

"Sustains? Fosters?"

"Nurtures."

"*Nurtures* is good, very good. Like the sea. The sea of love."

"Now who's talking fancy? But, yes, it's what we have. It's all we have."

We inhaled and exhaled and watched the smoke that came out of our nostrils curl toward the ceiling. After a while Vera said, "These papers under my feet, now." She wiggled the blue slippers about and nodded toward them. "They want you to come to Chicago. And Minneapolis. At this very moment, there are commitments for two thousand tickets in Chicago. We've got feelers out in St. Louis."

"Harvey has been busy."

"Harvey is a clever man. A good soul. A committed friend."

"All of that. Godfather to Gabriel."

Vera blew smoke upwards and we watched it curl toward the ceiling. "Do you know, Harlan, what two thousand tickets at two dollars each amounts to?"

"It's simple math."

"It amounts to a life of freedom for you. You don't have to work at the business of selling houses. It's not work of any great value, is it, an occupation of integrity?" She had spoken this way before. I let her run on. Vera had come from a River Heights family and attended a private school and afterwards gone to college.

She had opinions, she made judgements. I smoked along with her for some minutes. That clock was ticking in another room. The refrigerator hummed in the kitchen.

I leaned forward and laid the pipe carefully down on the coffee table, and then picked up the mug of tea. It had cooled; the taste of raspberry coming through was quite potent. "I don't want much," I began. "I go for the simple life. After we pay expenses and a bit for ourselves to live on, I don't want for much. Don't need a fancy house or trips to Hawaii. But if it comes to that, if it should turn into big money, my one indulgence will be the Mercedes sports car with wing doors. Crimson in colour. If it comes to that."

Vera laughed aloud. "Crimson," she hooted, "of course it would be red."

"A fantasy. Boyhood yearning."

"No harm in a few childhood fantasies."

"There would have to be money laid aside, of course, for—"

"For the education of a boy, for instance."

"Yes. But the rest," I continued, "the rest I fancy going to charity."

"Charity?"

"You put the money aside in a safe account where it earns interest and you can support good causes with it. Harvey would know the name."

"Foundation."

"Yes. Foundation. We could fund projects. I don't know, really. Design a scholarship plan and send students to Tibet or Thailand or whatever where they could study the Way with the great masters and contemplate on books like the *Shambhala*."

"Sounds as if you've got it all worked out."

"No. But you know me. Dreaming, imagining things that might happen in the future. Throwing out ideas."

"It's a good plan. Harvey and I will work it out. And you."

"And me. And Margy."

Vera cleared her throat. "You will be famous, Harlan. People will know you by your first name only. Send you letters. Someday soon we will make a recording, an LP, so folks who cannot get to hear you personally can listen to the recording of one of our—our—"

"I don't know what to call them either. One of our … I don't know how to name them. Performances?"

"Assemblies. Meetings."

"Minglings."

We stood at the door while I arranged my coat and hat. Vera put one hand on my arm. Birch bark, diluted by woodsmoke. I exulted in the headiness of it. Back when, Mother had bought a pair of moccasins for herself, made by an Indian woman, fur-lined, she wore them in the kitchen; white and red beads were stitched into the tongue. They gave off a strong scent, like this. Sometimes when she went outside and laid them aside at the door, I'd pick them up and hold them to my nostrils and drink in their dark and secret messages. The aura of Indian magic. They know stuff in their silent way.

"Wow," I said, "Chicago, Minneapolis, St. Louis. That's something."

"The recording," Vera said, blushing. "I can picture its cover photo: you in your wonderful outfit, arms outreaching, the only light in the room playing on your face and your sequins—and faces in a rapt audience. Harlan. You'll be known only by your first name. Famous. Magical."

"That would be something."

"You are something, Harlan. You are somebody."

Back at the house, I looked into Gabriel's room. He was asleep, curled up in a ball of blue blanket. Margy was slumped in an armchair, sleeping, too, her mouth open—catching flies, Mother would have said. I wished I had a camera to take a photo.

I ran a tumbler of water and drank it at the sink. I checked on Orn, blinking quietly on his perch. He turned his great eyes on me. *Pax*, I said. *Pacem*.

I walked out into the yard. When I'd opened the door to the run and picked the wolf up up, I said, "And how is Stosh this fine evening?" He whimpered and licked my fingers with his pink tongue. I rubbed his belly, then, and stroked between his eyes, which he liked. He made a little *woof*. I'd brought out a cracker and I fed it to him, feeling tiny sharp nips pricking the skin of my fingers. *Nip nip nip*. Gently, ever so gently. When the cracker was gone, I let one finger slide down across his moist teeth to the molars, where he chewed on it, as if chewing a bone, but gently, an act of endearment. It was a cool night but not chilly, a westerly breeze, not a northern. Cleansing. It felt fresh on my flushed cheeks. I crossed the lawn with Stosh in my arms to the other side of the yard, where a stand of cedars grew, four trees, side by side. I'd named them: Celie, Sheena, Georgie, Elinor. I liked to rub their leaves between my thumb and forefinger and drink in their rosemary scent. They were singing their nighttime song, a wordless murmur, a tune I'd heard a long time in the past. I could not place it, but hummed along. Stosh wiggled in my arms and made whimpering sounds. He tipped his head up to mine and we gazed into each other's eyes. His were not the eyes of the killer. I'd made a mistake about that. "I was wrong about that, Stosh," I murmured. "Forgive me." The blue and white of his eyes melded into a soft, inquisitive blend, reminiscent of one of the skies in Vera's mountain paintings. The eyes of a seeker, slightly bewildered in a glazed way, but haunting for all of that. Mystifying. Peaceful. "Forgive me," I repeated, but I was no longer talking to Stosh.

In the silence Margy had come up behind us. She was in slippers and had a green blanket wrapped around her shoulders. She put her arm in mine: faint odour of cornflowers in my nostrils. I nuzzled my head closer to hers. "He's out," she reported, "our Gabriel; he'll be out for hours."

I glanced at her. Had she overheard what I'd been saying?

"Yes," she said, answering my question. "But *wrong* is a strong word. 'Off the mark' suits better. Harlan—and Dick. You've been off the mark all your life. You've been hell-bent on being what you are not, chasing it, and wasting your energy; and equally intent on resisting what you really are. You've been off the mark there, too. You're not the Barker; you're the Warlock."